BITTERSWEET DESIRE

Unable to bear the intensity of Leah's gaze, Benjamin turned from her. "I really have to go," he said softly.

"Will you hold me first? Just for a little while?"

Drawing her into the shelter of his arms, he held her close. The crackle of the fire on the hearth and the sound of their own breathing filled the silence as they clung to each other.

He hadn't intended to kiss her, but his lips molded to hers, tasting her sweetness. She responded immediately, returning kiss for kiss.

She held him tightly to her, memorizing his scent, afraid she would never be able to let him go . . .

PASSION'S ENDLESS TIDE

RENÉ J. GARROD

ZEBRA BOOKS
KENSINGTON PUBLISHING CORP.

ZEBRA BOOKS

are published by

Kensington Publishing Corp.
475 Park Avenue South
New York NY 10016

First printing: October, 1990

Printed in the United States of America

To my children,

Gabriel, Seth,
Benjamin, and Breanna

"Bleeding bastard! Cap'n Keaton thinks he can push ol' Eddie around, does he? Well, I'll be showing him what happened to them that tangle with a good ol' sea dog likes me," Eddie slurred as he stumbled down the companionway to the hold.

Weaving a precarious path through rows of boxes and barrels, he paused to lean limply against a crate marked "Explosives." His eyes took on a feral gleam as they fell upon the word.

"A man's got a right to take a nip from the bottle now and then, and thems who interfere with a man's rights gots to be punished," he continued to grumble to his invisible audience, as he pried the lid off the crate. "Begrudging a fella a dose of liquid fortitude, after a storm like we just passed through! Why, we could 'ave got blown clean off the face of the earth.

"Well, I got a little surprise for the captain. He ain't going to 'ave no ship to throw me off of," Eddie swore, too drunk to comprehend that his method of exacting his revenge would cost him his own life, as well as the lives of a shipload of innocent men. "Be doing the world a favor getting rid of a hard man like the cap'n. Ain't a soul on earth won't thank me for it."

Striking a match on the bottom of his boot, he tossed it into the crate, and the *Sea Dragon* was no more.

The Island

Chapter 1

An endless wind swept off the Pacific Ocean over the deserted beach, to stroke the beards of lichen hanging from the branches of the thick forest of giant conifers standing guard upon craggy cliffs. Chestnut-backed chickadees and stellar jays sang their morning arias, accompanied by the staccato beat of a hairy wood-pecker. Below his winged forest companions, a white-footed mouse scampered through the bracken carpeting the forest floor.

The sound of rapidly approaching footsteps did not disturb the creatures of the northern rain forest. They recognized the sound and scent of the pale-skinned woman with the long, fawn-colored braid, and re-garded this lone human occupant of their island as one of their own.

Leah Daniels panted for breath as she sprinted through the forest, her heart beating with excitement. She refused to slacken her pace upon reaching the cliffs and lost her footing several times as she descended the steep path to the beach. Sliding on her backside, she regained her foothold as soon as she was able, giving little mind to the scrape on her hands or the abuse to her garments.

He had moved. She was sure of it. She had scarcely believed her eyes, when gazing through her spyglass she had spotted the bedraggled seaman lying upon what appeared to be a piece of a ship at the edge of the surf. The sea washed many treasures ashore, but she had waited so long for him, that she had almost given up hope.

Racing across the sand, Leah knelt beside the crude raft, gently turning the man over on his back. Her heart sank when his eyes remained closed and he did not make a sound, but when she lay her ear against his salt-encrusted lips, she could feel his breath. As Leah brushed a lock of damp hair from his brow, she uncovered a large, black and blue lump. He was alive but barely so, and she knew if she was to keep him alive she had to get him warm and dry as soon as possible.

Looping her arms around his chest, she struggled with his weight as she pulled him a sufficient distance from the lapping waves to satisfy herself; then, she laid him on the sun-warmed sand.

He was so much bigger than she, Leah knew she could not drag him up the way she had come, and she quickly resigned herself to using the long route.

"I'll be right back," she promised as she plucked a bit of seaweed from his dark beard.

Retracing the path she had just followed, she returned within the quarter hour, pushing a crude wheelbarrow laden with blankets around the bend in the cliff. Choosing a path near the surf where the sand was packed hard and wouldn't bog the wheel, she covered the remaining distance in less than a minute.

"You see, I'm back just as I promised." Leah smiled lovingly as she stroked his leathery cheek. His skin was so cold. She blinked back the tears forming in her large brown eyes. "And I want you to promise me you won't die. I need a friend. I've been so lonely since I buried Emma. You will promise to stay with me, won't you?"

Silence greeted her ears, as she had known it would, and Leah turned her full attention to the task of getting her sailor into the wheelbarrow.

A pair of spindly-legged plovers paused at the edge of the surf, cocking their heads to one side as they watched her. She fell several times, her burden mashing her into the sand. It was only by sheer dint of will that she managed to haul the man's deadweight, one limb at a time, onto the wheelbarrow. She immediately tucked the blankets snugly around him and started down the beach.

The added weight caused the wheel to mire more than once, and progress was slow, but she did not slacken her pace until she reached the base of the incline leading up from the beach. Here she was forced to pause to catch her breath.

Leah took advantage of the moment to study the man more closely. Though they were plastered to his skin and tattered, his clothing appeared similar in cut to that worn by her father, confirming her original assumption that this man made his living on the sea. The lower half of his face was covered by a thick beard and mustache the color of raven wings. Dark lashes lay against weather-ravaged cheeks. His head sported a dense mass of midnight waves.

Having seen only three other human beings during

13

her two and twenty years upon the earth, Leah had little to judge his features against. She only knew that she liked to look upon him, and so she borrowed the word handsome from the heroes peopling the fairy tales that Emma had spun for her when she was a child.

Taking a firm grip on the wooden handles of the wheelbarrow, Leah started up the hill. Of necessity she focused all her energy on getting her burden to the house.

She sighed with relief when she finally saw the face of the dark stone building peeking through the trees.

By turning her back to the door and pulling with all of her might, she was able to get the wheelbarrow up the three steps leading to the front door, and she pushed it into the entry hall. "Now, how am I going to get you upstairs?" she asked as she massaged her aching arms. "If only Papa were here to carry you for me."

After contemplating her dilemma a few moments, she knotted the corners of a blanket on one end, then spread it on the floor at the base of the stairs. Tipping the wheelbarrow up, she rolled out her seaman as gently as she was able, securing his feet within the knot; then, grasping the other two corners of the blanket, she began to pull him up the stairs on her hastily constructed litter. By the time Leah had the man stretched out on her bed, she was soaked with perspiration.

Without hesitation she stripped off his clothing and began sponging the brine from his skin.

His left ankle was bloody and swollen. Upon careful examination, she determined that it was not broken, but the damage was extensive and would require her most potent herb poultice, lest infection set in. There

14

was little she could do for his head. The only other visible sign of injury was the crisscross of scars marring his back. They were old wounds, long since healed, but she fingered them curiously, wondering how they could be made.

Small, animal sounds emanated from his throat as Leah continued to stroke his skin with her cloth, but he did not open his eyes. The texture of his flesh was so different from hers, and she paused often to let her fingertips trail over the path followed by the damp cloth. His muscled chest was thickly covered by a mat of dark curly hair, that tapered to a thin line as it descended his belly then fanned to form a soft nest about his sex. His arms and legs were long and sinewy. Leah felt a sultry stirring in the pit of her belly and she smiled. She liked the feel of him.

Satisfied that she had made him as clean as she was able without a proper bath, she tended his ankle and tucked him under the covers.

After tossing an extra log on the fire, she returned to his bedside with a fresh bowl of water and a clean cloth, to begin a painstaking process of drizzling droplets of water into his mouth and massaging his throat until he swallowed.

The hours ticked by with endless monotony. Leah acted on instinct rather than on knowledge of any medical practices. She treated him as she had the countless injured animals she had nursed back to health.

"You will get better," she spoke the words out loud again and again, believing by doing so she could make it happen. As Emma lay dying, Emma had promised her she would not be alone forever. *He'll come for you by sea.* How often had she used those words to comfort herself during the past two years? More times than there were stars in the sky. She would not let him slip away as Emma had.

Towards twilight she switched from plain water to a nourishing fish broth. She could see small signs of improvement—in the rhythm of his breathing, in the temperature and pallor of his skin—but he had yet to regain consciousness. Leah steadfastly refused to acknowledge the possibility that he might die and patiently continued her gentle ministrations.

It was late when the weight of her eyelids forced her to retire for the night. After shedding her blouse, durable brown wool skirt, and undergarments, she stood before the fire and sponged her own skin clean, then slipped under the covers.

Nestling against the man's side, she pillowed her head upon his chest. His heartbeat was strong and steady, and she sighed contentedly as she stroked his flat belly. At long last the sea had brought her a mate.

Leah awoke as the first apricot rays of the sun lit the windows. She was immediately aware that she was not alone, and her lips curled upward as her gaze caressed the man in her bed. She lingered but a moment, then eased from the mattress and into her clothes, knowing she had work to do.

After stoking the fire, she gathered up the dishes on the bedside table and hurried downstairs. A short time later she returned with a fresh pot of warm fish broth to which she had added several beaten eggs.

All that day she spooned broth into her patient's

mouth. The only time she left his side was when it was necessary to carry in more wood for the fire or return to the kitchen to replenish the soup pot.

Toward noon he began to stir more often. Blinking open his sea blue eyes, he would stare blankly at the ceiling, then close them again. Once he looked directly at her and his lips curved into a shadow of a smile before the blank look returned.

The face was that of a woman. Her loving look said she knew him, but he could not put a name to her. He could feel the press of metal against his lips and automatically opened his mouth to receive the liquid he knew would follow. It slid down his throat with little effort on his part, warming his belly. He closed his eyes, drifting back into the peace of blackness.

Leah stroked his skin, sang to him, and continued to patiently force the nourishing soup past his lips. Sometimes he fought her, sometimes he eagerly gulped at the contents of the spoon. He seemed to her to waver in a state somewhere between slumber and full consciousness. She could sense he was getting stronger, but she did not try to urge him to full wakefulness. He would come to her when he was ready.

The melody was haunting and unfamiliar, but he liked the sound. He liked the feel of the gentle hands roaming his flesh. Erotic visions floated in and out of focus. He was someplace warm. Someplace safe. He couldn't think clearly. Didn't want to think.

She changed the dressing on his ankle, examining the flesh for signs of infection. The wounds appeared clean, and there was no sign of fever when she lay her cheek against his brow. His sleep was a healing sleep, and it no longer frightened her.

17

An insistent voice warned him that he should rouse himself and take control of his situation, but he stubbornly refused to obey its command. He didn't want to wake up. His dream was far too pleasant to leave just yet. The world, with its cruel reality, could wait for him a little while longer.

Day turned to night, and Leah climbed into bed beside her seaman as she had the night before. Maybe tomorrow he would awaken from his long sleep. If not, she would content herself with his physical presence another day and go on lovingly tending, patiently waiting.

Chapter 2

Capt. Benjamin Keaton slowly blinked his eyes open, then quickly closed them again. He was in bed with a woman, and he had not the slightest idea how he had gotten there. Cloudy memories of a blinding flash, of clinging to the piece of hull blown from the *Sea Dragon*, adrift on a merciless sea, flitted in and out of his consciousness. Perhaps he was dead.

He smiled mirthlessly. Had he made it to heaven after all? He had always assumed, if there was an afterlife, he would be relegated to the depths of hell.

As he came fully awake, he began to assess his situation with a clearer mind. He was most definitely still in his temporal body. Despite his weakness and the throbbing in his head and ankle, he could feel the heat in his loins increasing in response to the naked woman lying pressed against his side.

Though she felt tiny in his arms, she was not a child. Her breasts were full, and her hips nicely rounded. He tentatively assigned her age to above twenty but below twenty-five. Her pale skin was clear, leading him to

19

conclude that if she had sold him her body—and there was no other logical explanation for her being in his bed—she was new to the profession. The face paints favored by the seaport prostitutes to enhance their beauty invariably ruined it within a few years. Or perhaps she chose not to wear the garish cosmetics common to her trade. She was barefaced now.

As he continued to study her, his ardor and confusion grew. She was plain, albeit in a pretty sort of way. Not at all the sort of woman he usually chose for this sort of recreation. For the life of him, he couldn't remember how he had gotten out of the sea and into her bed. Who the hell was she?

As if in response to his mental query, her eyes blinked open, and she stared at him with an expression akin to joy sparkling in her eyes. "Good morning."

"Good morning," he returned her greeting, though his tone was markedly less open.

Leah propped herself on her elbow as she smiled at him. He leaned closer and planted a practiced kiss on her lips. She instinctively responded, then her smile broadened.

He knew he should be up and about the business of discovering just how he had landed in this seaside brothel, but the captain decided to indulge his lusts before leaving this nubile nymph. He was not so green as to believe the morning dalliance would not cost him extra, but her smile was so inviting, he was willing to pay the price. Gathering her in his arms, he pulled her against his chest.

Leah came willingly, looping her arms around his neck. He was kissing her again, not on the cheek as Emma and Papa had done, but full on the lips. His touch evoked strange and new sensations, a pleasant kind of longing between her thighs, and she pressed closer.

She liked the feel of his hands stroking her. They made her warm. Her own hands explored the textures of his flesh, trailing over the scarred ridges lacing his back to the smooth skin of his buttock. As she massaged his muscles, she could feel his male member becoming hot and hard between their clinging bodies.

Leah was fascinated rather than alarmed, and she continued to return his kisses with unbridled enthusiasm. She revelled in the taste of him, delighted in the teasing tickle of his beard against her sensitive flesh. When his tongue slipped between her lips, she echoed his movements, stroking him boldly with her own pink tongue.

The captain moaned with carnal gratification. He had learned early in life to take his time with women, not out of a desire to give his partners pleasure, but because he had discovered an eager woman provided him with better sport. Though this particular angel of the night was definitely eager, he decided to prolong the moment of union a bit longer, to intensify the sensation of power her impassioned response yielded him.

Lowering his lips to one pink-crested breast, he pulled the nipple into his mouth, rolling the bud with his tongue until she began to cry out for him. Her thighs parted as he rolled atop her, but instead of entering her, he turned his attention to her other breast.

Leah felt frantic with need. Nature had taught her its own ways, and she wanted him to complete this mating. Though each species observed their own

21

rituals before the male mounted the female, she didn't understand why he was hesitating. She was ready to receive him. Pushing him upward, her body rose to meet his, and she encouraged him by rocking her hips invitingly against him.

Slowly, his shaft parted her woman's clough, and he plunged home. Leah stiffened as a sharp pain shot through her, her nails biting into the flesh of his back.

"You should have warned me," was the only comfort he offered before he began stroking her deep within. Almost immediately the pain was replaced by a fiery heat that left no room for thought.

The musky scent of lovemaking perfumed the air as they strained together, stoking the fire of passion as they swayed to an age-old rhythm. The creaking of the bedstraps, the rain pounding against the window pane, went unnoticed as they rushed toward fulfillment and attained ultimate satisfaction.

He immediately rolled his weight from her.

Leah sighed as she sagged limply against the mattress, cocooning herself in the aftermath of joy left by their lovemaking. How easily he had caressed away the years of loneliness. Though her eyelids felt heavy, she would not allow them to drift closed. She needed to drink in the sight of him, to assure herself he was not some imaginary being created by her mind.

Capt. Keaton lay on his back, giving himself a few moments to regain his equilibrium. His gaze wandered around the room, seeing it for the first time. Lace curtains flanked the window. The lower portions of the walls were wainscoted with richly polished alder wood; the upper sections papered with tiny lavender flowers. The room was furnished with an eclectic mix of tables, bureaus, and bric-a-brac with a discernible Chinese influence. A portrait of an uncommonly beautiful woman hung on one wall.

He rubbed at the ache in his head as he tried to assimilate the evidence provided by his eyes. The energy he had expended on lovemaking left him weaker than he had expected, but it had completely cleared the fog from his mind. There were matters that needed to be dealt with, and the first was lying next to him in this bed. He turned on his side to face her and was startled to find she was watching him.

"You were a virgin," he stated brusquely.

Leah stared at him, a perplexed expression on her face. "What's a virgin?"

"A woman who has never coupled with a man," he growled, impatient for some explanation. "I was the first."

"Yes, I know. No one else has ever come to my island." She tried to smooth the scowl from his brow with her fingertips. "Is being the first bad? The animals don't seem to care about that sort of thing at all, but if it bothers you, we can pretend there have been others."

"How very accommodating," he drawled.

"Thank you." Leah beamed at him despite the acerbity in his voice. She sensed his distrust of her. It was natural, and she knew how to deal with it. At first, all injured creatures reacted the same—the rigid set to the muscles, the wary shifting of the gaze. But once they came to know that she wished them no harm, they lost their fear of her.

"But what about last night?" he interrupted her thoughts. "Surely I wanted you or I . . ."

"You couldn't," she replied matter-of-factly.

23

The captain was about to protest the slur to his masculine prowess when something else she had said fully registered. "What do you mean I'm the only one who has come to the island? What island is this, and what is the name of this settlement?"

"My island doesn't have a name."

"The people who live here must call it something."

She shook her head negatively as she sat up, her pale hair forming a diaphanous mantle over her breasts. The captain tried to follow her to an upright position but found himself pressed back against the mattress. "No one lives here except me. Of course there used to be Emma and Mama and Papa, but they're all gone."

"You can't mean to say you live here all alone."

"Yes."

"Are you trying to tell me this isn't a brothel, and you're not a fledgling prostitute?" Even as he asked the question, he knew the answer; he just didn't want to admit it to himself.

"You use too many words I don't know. This is my house, and I'm Leah."

He studied her through hooded eyes, unwilling to believe or trust her, despite his inability to determine any good purpose behind her deceit. The fact that she had just made love to him mattered not at all. Women often used their bodies to attain their ends. She had used him, just as he had used her.

He felt an uncomfortable twinge as he gazed at her innocent face, but paid no heed. He wanted answers.

"Is this an outpost? A lighthouse? Where exactly are we?"

"I told you: on my island," Leah repeated.

"Who brings your supplies? How often do they come?"

"No one comes. I have my goats and my garden. The rest of what I need I gather from the forest or the sea," she explained patiently. Her answer didn't satisfy.

"Someone has to come. You didn't build this house by yourself."

"Papa had it built, before he brought Mama here to live."

"And where are they now?"

"Mama died three winters ago, and Papa sailed off in his ship and just never came back. I tell myself he is coming home, but I'm afraid he drowned in the sea, because he wouldn't have left me here all alone for so long if he hadn't."

He had made a crack in her relentlessly cheerful mien, but he felt little satisfaction. There was something compelling about this little wench, and his own reaction made him nervous. His questions persisted. "How long ago did he leave?"

"Right after Mama had her accident."

"What about this Emma you mentioned?"

"She died a year after Mama."

His blue eyes took on an icy sheen as he stared up at her. There were too many gaps of logic in the tale she spun, and he knew better than to be taken in by a soulful look. "I find it impossible to believe that you have been living on an island in total isolation for two whole years. What do you hope to gain by having me believe such a preposterous story?"

"I wouldn't lie to you," Leah promised earnestly, bemused he would accuse her of such a thing.

25

"Why not?" he demanded.

"You're my friend."

"I'm nothing to you," he corrected.

"You are my friend," Leah repeated adamantly. "I've been waiting for you to come to me for a very long time."

The furrows in his brow deepened with his displeasure and confusion. "What you say makes no sense. I think I'd remember if we'd met before, and as to coming for you, I don't make promises to anyone."

"You never promised to come," Leah confirmed. "I just knew you would."

"How?"

"Emma said you would, but that's really not important. You're finally here, and that's all that matters." Her own words acted as a balm to her spirits, and her sunny smile returned. Kissing his brow, she rose from the bed. "Do you have a name?"

"Benjamin Keaton, Capt. Benjamin Keaton."

"Benjamin." Leah tested the name with her tongue. "It's a very noble-sounding name, don't you think? It suits you. I'm glad your mother thought to give it to you."

"No one calls me by my Christian name."

"What do they call you?"

"Capt. Keaton."

"Well, this isn't a ship, and I like Benjamin better, so I think I'll use it." Turning from the bed she padded across the wooden floor on bare feet.

The captain watched silently as she stirred the fire back to life and began to dress without the least sign of modesty. This woman behaved and spoke in riddles. She was like no one he had met before. Though there were a thousand questions on the tip of his tongue, he did not ask them. The chances of getting a straight answer seemed slim.

As soon as she had her sturdy cotton blouse and woolen skirt in place, she started for the door.

"Where are you going?"

"To fix you something to eat. I'm sure you must be hungry and even if you aren't, you must eat to regain your strength. You've had nothing but broth for two days."

Two days? He had been here two days? He lay back against the pillows, and closed his eyes against the sight of her smiling face. She was right, he was ravenously hungry, but hunger had nothing to do with the odd feeling in the pit of his belly. She was the cause *and her words*.

He supposed he should feel grateful to her for fishing him out of the sea and nursing him back to health, but he didn't. The softer emotions were best left for the fools of the world. He told himself he would be a fool to assume anything, even that she was responsible for his rescue and recovery.

He needed her gone so he could get out of this bed and get to the window. Surely, some of his answers lay outside. Once he learned where he was, he would have a better chance of discovering who she was, and why she would want him to believe they were all alone.

Chapter 3

Benjamin lay very still, listening to her footsteps as she retreated down a short hall. Then the tread of her footfall changed. She was descending a flight of stairs. He strained his ears, countng the steps. One, two, three . . . the fifth and the ninth steps creaked. Good. They assured he would have some advance warning she was returning, and he preferred to make the trip to the window and back without her knowledge. It would give him a much desired measure of control.

While he waited, his gaze focused on the window. The pelting rain obscured the view, and without getting closer he couldn't make out a thing.

Pushing himself to an upright position, he gingerly swung his legs over the side of the bed. The sway of the room caused him to clutch the bedding while he pulled in several, long, deep breaths.

When the room had steadied, he tested the strength of the bandaged ankle by gradually applying his weight. It did not crumple beneath him, but piercing sparks of white-hot pain shot up his leg. He squeezed his eyes closed against the pain, willing himself not to cry out.

His left leg was nearly useless. He would have to depend heavily on the right, using the furniture to balance himself. Measuring the distance between the bed and the window with his eyes, he mentally mapped his route. There was only a short stretch where he would have to rely totally on his own support, and he felt confident he could make it.

It was important he find out where he was, so he would not be so vulnerable. This woman, whoever she was, sounded sincere enough, but he had found distrust a necessary tool for survival. He didn't believe she could subsist on an island all by herself for a month, let alone a span of two years. Besides, she was too small to have carried him from the sea to her bed without help. She was deceiving him, and he didn't know why. Until he did, he would not rest easy. Knowledge brought power and power brought safety—both physical and emotional.

Focusing all his energy on the goal of attaining the window, he stood on his good foot, but no sooner had he gained his full height, than great waves of dizziness began to wash over him in rapid succession. Instinctively planting his left foot on the floor to steady himself, too late he realized his mistake. His image of the room grayed, then went molasses black.

Leah started, dropping her cloak on the floor by the door when she heard the loud thud above her head. Spinning on her heels, she raced up the stairs to her bedroom. Benjamin lay sprawled on the floor, his eyes open, moaning his misery and frustration.

"What were you trying to do?" she scolded, as she surveyed him for signs of new injuries. "If you needed something, you should have asked for my help."

The instant his body hit the floor, the black cloud had begun to lift, and Benjamin was painfully aware of what had happened. Shaking his head to completely clear the mist from his mind, he glared at her as she cradled his head in her lap, too indignant with himself to bother with a lie. "I wanted to look out the window."

Leah rolled her eyes heavenward. "Maybe later. You're too weak to be out of bed just yet. I need to get some solid food into you before you try to go traipsing about. And you'll need crutches, too. The ankle isn't broken, but the tissue is badly damaged. You must stay off of it."

"Are you the one who bound it?"

"Of course. Who else is there to do it?"

That's what I was trying to find out, he mentally replied, but he said nothing to her. Using his arms to brace himself, he pushed himself to a sitting position and a more equal footing.

Leah smiled her approval of his improving pallor. "Come on. Let's get you back to bed before you freeze to death."

Benjamin sat stubbornly on the floor.

"You can help me a little," Leah coaxed.

"You got me in the bed the first time without any help. Why do you need help now?"

Leah sighed as she took in her patient's morose expression. His blue eyes appeared keen, not dull-witted, but he seemed to be having trouble comprehending the things she told him. Perhaps the injury to his

30

head interfered with his understanding. Whatever the reason for his lack of cooperation, she needed to get him back in bed where it was warm. She decided a stern approach might be what was needed to bring better results.

"I am going to put my arms around your chest, and you will use your right leg to help propel yourself upward while I lift. Now push!" she instructed as she pulled him to the bed.

Benjamin did as he was told, but he noted wryly that she had avoided answering his question. Her omission added weight to his suspicions. His lips remained firmly compressed as she tucked the blankets under his chin.

Leah returned his dour look with one of feigned severity. "I want you to promise me you will stay snug in this bed until I return with your breakfast."

"I told you before, I don't make promises."

"Then I will have to bind you for your own good. You are barely recovered from your ordeal, and I cannot allow you to do yourself harm. Now, do I have your promise, or do I have to get a rope?"

He pulled away from her hand as she tried to brush his hair from his brow. He hated to say the words, but prudence demanded he cooperate, lest he find himself in much worse circumstances. Let her fill his belly. The food would do him good. Later, when he began to feel more himself, he would try again, and this time he would succeed. "I'll stay in the bed."

"Thank you," Leah's tone softened to its natural tone as she expressed her sincere gratitude that he would not force her to do something she was loathe to do. "I'll hurry back just as fast as I can."

As soon as she left, Benjamin pulled himself up to a

sitting position. He was certain that lying prone so many days had contributed to his blackout as much as the pain of his injuries and the lack of solid nourishment. If they had been the primary cause, he would not have had the strength to make love earlier. He pushed the thought out of his mind as it formed, not wanting to contemplate the possible consequences of that imprudent action now that he was certain this Leah was not a soiled, seaside dove.

Why she had made love to him at all was another mystery he didn't care to consider, and he concentrated his thoughts on weathering the moment.

Many men would be content to lie back and accept the ministrations of a pretty woman without questioning her motivation, but he was not cut from such cloth. He would not forget that she had threatened to tie him. Her smiles made him nervous. Her acts of kindness left him wary.

Being trapped in any situation was a circumstance he could not abide, and until he regained his strength, he was most definitely trapped.

His ears pricked at the sound of a door opening and closing below stairs. He could hear Leah greeting someone; then, her voice lowered. He couldn't make out the other voice or Leah's words, but her tone was conversational. He strained his ears, but to no avail.

He might not know who was downstairs, but now he knew there was someone else on this island—if he was even on an island! The wheels of his mind turned round and round as he tried to determine into just what kind of mess he had landed.

Benjamin methodically went over each ragged piece of memory he possessed; then, he turned his attention to making sense of it all. He was reasonably certain the *Sea Dragon* was gone. He had no idea if his crew had washed ashore as he had, or if they were all drowned. He wasn't even positive he had washed ashore. He might have been saved at sea. That part of his recent past was a complete blank. He could have been adrift days, or only a matter of hours. He might never know, and he deemed such musing unimportant. What he desperately needed to know was where he was and how to get away.

If his benefactress was as innocent as she seemed, she would have no need to lie to him. He had lost his ship, his crew, and a sizable investment in cargo. He was determined not to be victimized by whatever scheme she was hatching.

Leah returned within the half-hour, bearing a tray laden with a goat cheese omelet, thick gruel made from the roasted rhizomes of bracken ferns, a bowl of salmonberries, and a pot of freshly brewed Labrador tea.

Settling the sick tray comfortably over Benjamin's legs, she fluffed the pillows that supported his back, then pulled a chair next to the bed. However, when she attempted to lift the forkful of omelet to his mouth, he clamped his hand on her wrist.

"There is nothing wrong with my arms. I can feed myself."

Leah surrendered the fork without argument. She sat silently, her hands folded in her lap, while he consumed his meal. She was used to silence, and though she would have preferred he speak to her, she did not find his muteness oppressive. Now that he was recovering, nothing could darken her mood.

33

Benjamin neither complimented nor condemned the fare. When he was finished, he dabbed his mouth with the cloth napkin provided and leaned back against the pillows. Veiling his eyes, he cast surreptitious glances in her direction.

"Where do you buy your cheese?"

"I make it myself."

"And I suppose the eggs come from the chickens you raise," he commented dryly.

"Yes. Wasn't the meal to your liking?" she asked with concern as she lifted the tray from his lap.

"It was fine. Aren't you going to eat anything?"

"I had a bowl of berries and cream in the kitchen while I was cooking."

The conversation had wandered just where he had intended, and he was ready to confront her with his knowledge and force her to end her charade of the ardent handmaiden. "I heard you talking to someone."

"Jonathan stopped by to say hello," Leah offered the information freely. "I've neglected him terribly these last few days, and he was a little angry with me, but after I explained how sick you were, he understood. I'll have to spend some time with him today though, or he might get jealous."

"I see." Benjamin digested her words with a blank expression. So, she was now willing to admit they weren't alone after all. His cool blue eyes rose to meet the warm brown ones gazing at him with a look of open affection. She didn't seem to realize she'd been caught in his snare.

The thought that she might be addlepated began to flourish within the fringe of his consciousness. It didn't make his desire to quit her presence any less compelling, but it did cast a different light on her behavior. He decided to pursue the matter a bit further.

"I'd like to meet Jonathan."

"Really?" Leah's eyes lit at the prospect of introducing her two friends. Surely, Benjamin's request could be taken as another sign of his improving health. Her already light heart quickened. "I have to do a few chores this morning, but after, I'll see if I can find him. Unless you'd prefer I find him first, so you'll have company while I'm gone."

Benjamin had no idea if this Jonathan would turn out to be friend or foe, but the sooner he met him, the sooner he would have another piece of the puzzle. Schooling his expression into a half-smile, his eyes met hers. "I am feeling rather sociable this morning. Why don't you send him up, just as soon as you fetch my clothes so I can dress."

"Jonathan won't care whether or not you're dressed, but if it will make you more comfortable, I'll get them right away."

"It will make me more comfortable," Benjamin confirmed. If he could persuade this Jonathan fellow to help him, he preferred not to have to traverse the streets stark naked.

He watched as Leah obediently exited to do his bidding, feeling more and more comfortable with his theory that she was not of sound mind. It made everything she had done and said make sense, as he could discard logic altogether.

"I'm sorry, but these will have to suffice until I can sew you some new garments." She lay a white linen shirt and pair of black trousers on the foot of the bed. "I'm afraid your own clothes are quite beyond repair, and I had to borrow these from my father's trunk."

"I'm sure they will be adequate." He reached for the clothes.

"I'll help you with those, just as soon as I change the dressing on your leg," Leah spoke over her shoulder as she busied herself with the necessary preparations. Retrieving the earthen jar from the mantel above the fireplace, she scooped a small portion of the contents into a pot and began warming it over the fire.

"What is that stuff?" Benjamin asked suspiciously, as a fetid odor began to permeate the room.

"An herb poultice. It draws out the infected matter so the leg won't putrefy."

"It smells like something straight from hell."

Leah chuckled. "Only when it's heated. As soon as it cools, the odor lessens, then disappears completely."

Benjamin was loathe to submit himself to her evil treatment despite her assurances, but in the interest of expediting his introduction to Jonathan, he bit back his protests.

He feigned disinterest as she unwrapped the bandage but was unable to constrain a grimace when he caught sight of his grisly limb.

"It will heal," Leah comforted as she skillfully went about the work of cleansing and redressing the wound. "Already it looks better than when you first came. See how well the scabs are forming, and the swelling is half what it was yesterday."

He took her at her word. There was a confidence in her voice that made him less apprehensive of her treatment. Her hands were gentle, and the leg gave him little pain when he did not try to stand upon it. Simpleminded she might be, but he no longer suspected her of some unnamed nefarious scheme.

Despite its assault upon his nose, the poultice was soothing to his leg, and as soon as she had his ankle wrapped securely, she helped him don the clothes as promised.

Standing back to survey her handiwork, Leah began to laugh. "I much prefer you naked," she announced through her giggles. "You are too long, and the clothes are too wide."

Benjamin could hardly argue with her assessment. The shirt resembled an ill-fitting sack, and the girth of the waist of the trousers was nearly double his own. Here their generosity ended, for the bottom portion of his legs stuck out like sticks below the hemline. "They'll do until I'm able to find something better," he stated ruefully.

"I couldn't find a belt, but this length of rope should keep them from falling about your ankles," she offered, still chuckling at the sight of him. "It doesn't matter much for now anyway, as you must stay in bed. I will do my best to have more convenient clothing ready for you when you can be up and about again."

"But first you will fetch Jonathan," he pressed.

"Yes. The sewing will have to wait for the evening. I am terribly behind in my work, and if I don't catch some fresh fish today, we will have naught but eggs and cheese for supper." Her expression sobered. "I do hate to leave you though."

"I will be fine," Benjamin assured her, afraid she might change her mind about going and ruin his chance to leave this place. Once he was comfortably settled elsewhere, he would send her a note. He owed her that much. But he didn't intend to stay here a moment longer than was necessary.

Leah sighed. "I suppose there is no help for it, whether I want to go or naught, but you must promise me you won't do anything foolish while I am gone. I'll be out of the house and won't be able to hear your cries for help."

"I will be fine," he repeated.

His answer seemed to satisfy her, and she gathered up the breakfast tray and started for the door.

He listened to her descend the stairs and waited to hear the opening and closing of the front door. Despite his predilection for expecting and preparing for the worst, the sense that he was in danger had lessened considerably, and he was willing to wait to meet Jonathan before he tried to quit this house on his own.

After wrapping her cloak securely about her, Leah set out in search of Jonathan. She hoped he would be able to cheer her sea captain.

Her eyes softened as she thought of the man in her bed. When he had held her in his arms, he had wanted to mate with her; yet, despite her gentle care, she sensed he did not like being here with her. He didn't smile, and his eyes were cold when they looked upon her. She sighed. His coming was not at all as she had imagined, but still it was good. Reminding herself that Benjamin was a real person and not some fanciful character she had dreamed up to ease her loneliness, she scolded herself for her lack of patience. She must give him time to come to love her.

Leah knew all Jonathan's favorite places and quickly located him sitting upon an outcropping of rock, staring out to sea.

"Come on. I have someone who wants to meet you."

His dark eyes brightened at the sound of her voice, and he hurried to her side. They covered the distance between the sea and the house in companionable silence.

A curious expression fell over Benjamin's face as he listened to the sound of Leah climbing the stairs. She was not alone, but the second set of footsteps sounded odd. The faint *thump, swish* of the gait reminded him of that of a man with a wooden leg. He glanced nervously at his own bandaged limb. He certainly hoped Jonathan was not a former patient of this bed.

Before he could ponder this gruesome thought, Leah was entering the room, a bewhiskered sea otter trailing at her heels. She heft him up in her arms and deposited him in the middle of the bed.

"Benjamin, this is Jonathan. Jonathan, this is my new friend Benjamin," she introduced the two.

Benjamin stared at the otter with a mixture of shock and disappointment. Jonathan climbed upon his new acquaintance's chest and sniffed at his beard.

"Why didn't you tell me Jonathan was an animal?" Benjamin demanded as he regarded the otter on his chest with a jaundiced eye.

"I thought you knew," Leah replied.

"How would I know that? I assumed you were talking to another person."

Her brow puckered as he nudged Jonathan from the bed. "But I've told you: we're the only people on my

39

island. You seem to understand everything else I say. Why can't you understand that?"

"Because it doesn't make sense."

"Why?"

"For one thing, you're too small to have carried me from the sea to this bed," Benjamin stated the first objection that came to mind.

"It was difficult," Leah admitted. "But I assure you, that is exactly what I did. I'm really much stronger than I look."

Recalling the firmness of the muscles beneath her flesh as he had kneaded her limbs, he could not completely refute her statement, but he remained unwilling to believe her. "It still makes no sense."

Though the creases in her brow had smoothed, her expression remained somber. Taking a deep breath, she forced herself to voice her own fear. "Perhaps you don't want to believe me, because you don't want to be on my island."

There was more truth in her statement than Benjamin was comfortable admitting to himself. If she was telling the truth about them being alone on this island (and a gnawing feeling in his gut told him it was past time he considered the possibility), it meant he was stranded. Unless . . .

"Do you have a boat?" he abruptly changed the subject.

"No. I used to have a small dinghy for fishing, but Papa burned it."

"Why would he do that?"

"I think he was afraid we might try to leave. Whenever Mama would talk about leaving the island, he got very angry. After one of their arguments, he

40

burned the boat."

Her answers were disquieting, and he continued to interrogate her. "How old were you when you came to live here?"

"Just a babe."

"And you've never left this island?"

"No."

"Help me to the window," Benjamin commanded.

He spoke with such vehemence that Leah did not dare to disobey him. Hurrying to the bedside, she slipped her shoulder under his arm and helped him rise.

It took a second for him to become steady enough to move forward; then he signaled his readiness with a nod of his head. Gritting his teeth against the pain, he tried not to burden her with too much of his weight as they slowly made their way across the room.

The moment he reached the window, he abandoned his human support and braced himself with the sill.

The rain had temporarily ceased, giving him a clear view of the terrain. Benjamin's gaze traveled a one-hundred-and-eighty-degree arc, scanning for some sign of civilization.

There was none.

Chapter 4

Capt. Benjamin Keaton turned his eyes from the unbroken landscape of forest, sea, and rock, and stared at Leah. She stood near his side, watching him expectantly, the otter nosing at her feet.

He had always had a vague notion of where he was, and the view from the window told him nothing he did not already know. He could be as far south as the Washington Territory, or as far north as southern Alaska.

He opened his mouth to speak, but no words formed on his lips or in his mind. Leah waited patiently; however, when he remained mute, she felt compelled to break the silence.

"Will you come back to bed now?" she asked softly.

"You are telling the truth," he stated brusquely.

"Yes. Of course I am. I told you before, you need never have fear that I will lie to you."

"Tell me again how you came to this island," Benjamin demanded, giving no consideration to his injuries, except the use of the wall to steady his weight.

"My parents brought me here, when I was just a babe."

"But *why* did they come here?"

"I don't know."

"Surely you must have been curious enough to ask."

Leah shook her head affirmatively. "Papa said he wanted to keep us safe, and Mama said we lived here because Papa hated her. I don't think that was true, because he always brought her lots of pretty things when he came home from his voyages."

"What about Emma?"

"Emma said I asked too many questions. No one liked to talk about it, so after a while I stopped asking."

"Who was this Emma?" he continued his interrogation.

"Papa hired her to keep the house when he married Mama, but mostly she was my friend." Leah's eyes softened at the memory. "It was she who raised me. She taught me to sew and garden and take care of myself."

"Why did your parents not have time for you?"

"Papa was often away at sea, and Mama was what Emma called . . . *distraught.*" Leah hesitated, torn between her desire to give him a complete answer, and her wish to avoid the distress that recalling her mother's unhappiness caused her. "Sometimes I don't think Mama even realized we were here with her. She didn't take to the island like I did."

"What happened to the workers who built this house?"

Leah began to gently massage the base of her skull, to ease the strain of answering his rapid-fire demands for information. "You are so full of questions. Why is it so important you know?"

43

"It is always prudent to understand the circumstances surrounding one's misfortune."

"You think of me as a misfortune?" she protested in alarm.

His face remained a frozen mask of indifference. "I think of finding myself stuck on a deserted island a misfortune. I have not settled on my opinion of you."

"I wish you would like me."

"Why?"

Her unwavering gaze met his, reflecting all the tender passions she held waiting for him in her heart. "Because I like you."

"How can you?" he petitioned angrily, turning his eyes from hers. "You don't even know me. Trust me when I tell you that once you do, you will not like me at all."

"Why would you say such an awful thing?"

"Experience, my dear Leah, something which apparently you are sadly lacking," he replied sharply. "A word of warning: don't freely give your affection to me or anyone else. It puts you at a disadvantage."

Her brows knit together as she tried to understand what he wanted her to do. "Are you saying I should pretend not to like you, even though I do?"

"I am saying you should not like me."

"Oh." Leah mulled his words over in her mind, her expression one of unhappy confusion. "I don't wish to make you angry, but I can't help liking you. I can pretend I don't. I'm very good at pretending. But I can't change my true feelings just because you wish it."

"Suit yourself, but remember you have been warned." He spoke the words in a manner designed to put an end to the subject. Leah gladly complied.

"Will you let me help you back to the bed now?"

"Yes." He nodded curtly as he accepted the offered support of her arms. Though he would have never admitted his weakness out loud, his ankle was beginning to throb with pain, and there was an unexpected lethargy in his limbs that left him feeling off balance and vulnerable.

When Leah had him settled comfortably on the bed, she took one of the pillows and elevated his ankle. Benjamin submitted to her solicitous care without comment, but his probing gaze never left her.

"Aren't you leaving now?" he pressed when she made no move to quit his bedside.

"I must, mustn't I," she spoke the words reluctantly. "I'll be back as soon as I finish my chores."

"Take the otter with you." He indicated, with a gesture of his finger, the furry creature who was now contentedly scratching at a fray in the rug.

"I thought you wanted Jonathan to keep you company."

"I *thought* he was a man. I have no use for a dumb animal."

Leah frowned at him, but she bit back the scolding on the tip of her tongue and sighed instead. "Come on, Jonathan. Let's go find some fish for our supper."

Leah exited the bedroom, the otter at her heels. Her annoyance lasted until she reached the base of the stairs, but by then she had managed to convince herself that Benjamin's rude comment might just as easily be attributed to the pain of his injuries as to bad manners.

Upon reaching the front door, she turned towards the shed housing her chickens, and Jonathan turned towards the sea. She knew she would meet up with him again when she followed later with her fishing gear, and she waved him on his way.

While Leah occupied her hands with the routine chores of keeping her garden and tending her domesticated animals, her mind busied itself with other matters. She wanted to make Benjamin happy, she just wasn't sure how to do it.

Her knowledge of the outside world was so limited, she felt at a loss to understand him. Why was he so suspicious? Why didn't he want her to like him? Why did he constantly confuse her with his words? As Leah pondered these and many other questions, she realized she knew nothing about the man in her bed except his name. She had been so busy answering his questions, she had neglected to ask enough of her own.

Her past seemed important to him, perhaps learning *his* history was the secret to understanding him. There was no doubt in her mind that this was the man for whom she had been waiting. If he was not, it meant she would be alone again, and that was a prospect her soul refused to face. She would allow no doubt to enter her heart.

Leah was accustomed to living each day without concern for the next, and she called upon that habit now. Worry was unproductive. She once again told herself that given time, she could make their relationship what she had always dreamed it would be.

The first time Leah checked back on her patient, she found him sleeping. Tiptoeing out of the room, she returned outdoors. She continued to look in on him periodically, but it was not until early evening that she found him awake. She leaned the pair of crutches she had fashioned earlier in the day against the wall near the bed, stirred the fire, lit the candles, then stood waiting by the bedside.

Benjamin pushed himself upright in the bed, shaking the languorous blanket of sleep from his brain. He hadn't intended to sleep again, and the cast of the sun disconcerted him. A glance at the face of the clock sitting on the mantel confirmed the lateness of the hour. He growled at himself.

"You're not feeling better," Leah expressed her disappointment.

"I am much improved," he informed her after a brief survey of his physical condition. He flexed the muscles in his arms to relieve the stiffness in his limbs. "I'm just not used to sleeping so much."

"It's a healing sleep and will make you stronger."

"I'm not a man who likes to lie abed."

She smiled. "I'm glad of that. I shouldn't like it if you were lazy."

The timbre of her voice made him straighten, the wary gleam in his blue eyes deepen. It was not so much what she had said, but how she said it—as though she assumed that they would be together for an extended time. He tried to dismiss her assumption as logical under the circumstances—he couldn't leave until his leg was healed—but there was more to it than that. There was a possessive quality to her mien.

"What do you want from me?" he asked abruptly.

"Your love," Leah answered without hesitation as she fluffed his pillow.

Benjamin jerked away, jarred to the bone by her unexpected answer. His eyes flashed as they rose to meet hers, but what he read in their soft brown depths was utter sincerity. He cleared his throat, unable to voice the harsh words on the tip of his tongue. What in the hell was he suppose to say to her?

As if sensing his dilemma, Leah saved him from making a reply by her next statement. "Dinner is almost ready. I'm sure you must be famished, as you slept right through your noon meal. I hope you like clam steaks."

Brushing a light kiss across his forehead, she strolled from the room.

A few minutes later she returned carrying a small table, which she set by the window. Two chairs followed, then light blue table linen, place settings of blue and white china, and intricately patterned silver. The stemware was of equal quality.

Benjamin observed her activities through hooded eyes, noting without emotion that isolation had apparently not interfered with the acquisition of creature comforts.

When the table was set to her satisfaction, Leah crossed the room to her wardrobe and withdrew a red silk wrapper of oriental design. Slipping off her work clothes and underwear, she replaced them with the delicate floral garment, brushed out her hair, allowing it to cascade in warm waves down her back; then, she turned her full attention to Benjamin.

Her rose-colored lips curved into a gratified smile as she recognized the spark of desire in his eyes. "First, we must eat and then I will bathe you . . . then we will mate again," she assured him as she assisted him with the crutches and followed him as he made his way to his seat at the table.

Benjamin accepted her words without comment, but his pulse responded to her invitation, as did his loins. In the process of helping smooth his napkin on his lap, Leah's hand inadvertently brushed his hardened manhood with her fingertips and her smile broadened. "I think you like me at least a little," she commented merrily. "I'll be back with your meal in a moment."

Leah's heart danced joyously within her chest as she hurried towards the kitchen. Her captain wanted to be close to her, even if, more often than not, his words left her with a sense of cold confusion. It wasn't all she could hope for, but it was enough for the moment.

Benjamin's scowl followed her out of the room, but she was out of earshot when he spoke a gruff warning, "I can crave your body without harboring a mote of affection for you. I'm perfectly capable of using you and walking away without a second glance."

Returning to her bedroom with a tray laden with the fried clams, a variety of fresh greens, boiled potatoes, and a bottle of elderberry wine, Leah joined Benjamin at the table.

He watched her intently, and though she could not read most of what was going on behind those fierce, sea-blue eyes, the embers of desire still glowed.

"You do very well with your limited resources," he found himself commenting as she handed him the first platter.

Leah beamed with pride. "Thank you. Emma deserves most of the credit. Of course, it was easier when Papa brought supplies from the outside. Our flour and sugar barrels have been empty for ages, and it has been so long since I have tasted chocolate, I can barely remember how good it is." The last was spoken with such wistful longing, Benjamin could not suppress a whisper of smile.

"So you have a weakness for chocolate?"

Leah sighed. "Yes. Whenever Papa would bring me a box, I would allow myself no more than a nibble each day, so I could make it last just as long as possible, but it was never long enough."

An uncharacteristic emotion stirred in Benjamin's breast and, just for a moment, he felt regret that he didn't have a box of the coveted candies to offer his dinner companion. However, he quickly recovered himself.

They lapsed into an easy silence while they applied themselves to their food. Frequent glances were stolen from both sides of the table.

Leah was intent on making sure the food was acceptable and heartily consumed so Benjamin would quickly regain his full strength.

Benjamin was not the least concerned with Leah's eating habits. His mind was too occupied with puzzling out just who she was. On the surface she appeared to be just what she said she was: a young woman raised in social isolation. This fact alone accounted for much. He had never personally experienced the kind of solitude she had endured, but he had heard stories and read accounts of shipwreck victims, and he could well believe the human mind could not help but be affected.

Her talk of liking and loving were merely manifestations of her past loneliness. It meant nothing. She had attached herself to him, because he was the only one here. It had nothing to do with him personally, and if there had been anyone else on her island, she would not have stopped to give him the time of day.

Pleased with his line of reasoning, Benjamin lowered his gaze to his fork as she looked in his direction. Unfortunately, his eyelids did not drop quickly enough to avoid a glimpse of the gentle passion in her eyes. The look belied his well-drawn conclusions, and though he did his best, he could not completely dismiss it from his mind.

When Leah had satisfied her hunger for food, she decided that now was as good as time as any to try to alleviate her thirst for knowledge. Dabbing her lips with her napkin, she smiled hesitantly.

"I would like to know about you," she began. "How you came to my island. Where in the world you have lived . . ."

Though he was disinclined to discuss his past with anyone, Benjamin saw no profit in being evasive. Reaching for the bottle of dark wine, he poured himself another glass. "We were returning from China, when my ship, the *Sea Dragon*, was destroyed at sea. We'd just weathered a violent storm and were in the process of inventorying the damage, when there was a flash, and the ship just wasn't there anymore. The next thing I remember is waking up in your bed."

"I'm sorry you lost your ship."

"You didn't have anything to do with it," he rebuked her sharply, unwilling and unable to accept her sympathy. Leah ignored his tone the best she could.

"What about when you weren't on your ship?"

"The *Sea Dragon* has been my home for the past seven years."

"What about before that?" she pressed, determined

51

to learn all she could.

"Nosey little thing, aren't you?" He continued despite his unflattering comment, "Before the *Sea Dragon,* I sailed the seas with a dirty pub-crawler by the name of Capt. Elijah Bleeny. The only thing he liked better than the bottle was the lash, and he ran his ship like a despotic tyrant. I've got the scars on my back to prove it. Met up with him at the tender age of ten, courtesy of my loving guardian."

"I don't understand."

"I was sold into service."

"They sell children where you come from?" Leah gasped, her eyes widening in horror. "How abominable! Why didn't someone stop him?"

Benjamin shrugged. "I suspect because nobody gave a damn."

"Someone must have cared what happened to you," Leah protested.

"Not a soul. My significance in the world could be measured by the tinkle of the coins the captain dropped into my uncle's palm."

Leah's complexion had paled to linen white, and her lips began to quiver.

"Sorry it's not a very pretty tale, but the world is not a very pretty place. I did all right for myself, despite the odds, and I don't need your pity."

Taking a firm grip on her emotions, she continued to question him. "How did you ever get away from that awful captain?"

"Jumped ship and headed for the Fraser River. Worked the gold fields just long enough to make enough money to buy my own ship; then, I headed back out to sea."

"Then you found happiness?" she asked, hoping for a sunny ending to his tale.

He stared at her as if she was daft. "Happiness is unenduring and easily snatched away. I can't be bothered chasing rainbows. I don't care to be happy. I've got money and independence. That's all a man like me needs."

Leah's eyes met his, and in her heart she knew that he believed he spoke the truth. She also knew he was wrong. "How sad," she spoke her thoughts out loud.

"How wise," Benjamin corrected, "and a lesson you would do well to remember, if ever you leave this island of yours. You'd be eaten alive in a minute in the real world."

"Then we'll stay here," Leah vowed.

"There is no *we*. What you do with your life is your concern. Mine is my own."

"I didn't mean to tell you what to do. If you want to go, I'll leave with you; but the world sounds like a horrible place, if people are not only selling their children, but eating each other as well. No wonder Papa brought us to the island to live."

Benjamin threw his head back and began to laugh. It was a harsh sound, his throat being unaccustomed to the act. "I didn't expect you to take my words literally, you absurd little innocent. I can assure you with reasonable certainty that unless you have a run in with the wrong tribe of Indians, you will not end up in someone's stew pot. Civilized man does not eat human flesh."

"Indians eat people," Leah repeated, wanting to be certain she understood, so she could protect herself from a heinous fate.

"Only a few select tribes. I wouldn't let it worry you."

"All right," Leah agreed somewhat ambivalently. "But what about the children?"

A lengthy explanation of the social castes of Britain, and the position of orphans therein, was not something he cared to tackle, and Benjamin gave her an answer designed to satisfy rather than inform. "I originally come from England, and that is very far from here, so you needn't worry about that either."

Leah lapsed into thoughtful silence, her brows knitting together as she tried to assimilate these new pieces of information with what Emma had told her of the outside world. Emma had painted such beautiful pictures with her words, and Leah had had no reason to doubt her. Had she been trying to protect her?

Benjamin watched the play of emotions across Leah's face with amusement and something akin to sympathy, until what she had said earlier fully registered in his mind. *"If you want to go, I'll leave with you . . ."* Despite his words, she continued to think of herself as somehow connected to him. He had no intention of taking her with him when he left the island. Still, his sense of justice would not let him forget that he owed her his life. It demanded he do something to repay her. But encumber himself with an unwanted female? No. He would leave alone, then send someone else back to rescue her. She would suffer no hardship, and he would be free of his debt to her. Satisfied with his solution, he dismissed the matter from his mind.

"What about that bath you offered?" he asked, abruptly changing the subject.

"I left the water heating on the stove. I'm sure it's ready." Grateful to be given a reason to abandon her thoughts, Leah rose to her feet and began clearing the dishes from the table to the tray. "Would you like to lie down and rest, while I prepare it for you?"

"No. I've been prone too long the way it is," Benjamin replied, more than a little disconcerted by the eagerness with which she jumped to fill his slightest request. However, he had every intention of using his present situation to his own benefit. He only took what she gave freely, and he would not be held responsible for her misguided generosity.

Leah dragged a large brass tub from an adjoining room, positioned it before the fire on the hearth, then picked up the tray and exited the room. She returned shortly, carrying two buckets of steaming water which she poured into the tub. She immediately retraced her steps, returning with more hot water.

After her third trip up and down the stairs, Benjamin's conscience nudged him to comment, "It seems a bath is more trouble than it is worth."

"It's no trouble," Leah assured him, dabbing at the beads of moisture glistening on her brow with her handkerchief to erase the evidence of her exertion. "When you are better, you can bathe in the tub off the kitchen, but for now it is easier for me to bring the water up to you, than it is for you to go down to the water. I won't be much longer."

Content he had been gentleman enough to acknowledge her efforts, he leaned back in his chair, cradling the back of his neck in his hands. "I'm in no hurry."

When the tub was filled, and soap, cloth, and towels laid out by its side, Leah smiled brightly. "See, just as I promised, no trouble at all." She crossed the room and began unbuttoning his shirt.

Benjamin brushed her hands away. He took over the task. "Though you seem to derive great pleasure from playing the role of handmaiden, I am capable of doing a few things for myself."

When he was naked, Benjamin slipped the crutches under his arms and hobbled to the edge of the bath. Using his arms, he braced his weight on the sides of the tub and lowered himself into the water. The warmth eased the ache in his dormant muscles, and he took a moment to flex and stretch each limb before reaching for the soap.

Leah stood by the edge of the bathtub, watching with hungry eyes as he drew the washcloth across his skin. All day pyretic memories of his bare flesh beneath her fingertips had teased her mind, and she was jealous of the cloth.

When Benjamin glanced up, he was both pleased and taken aback by the pleading look in her eyes. Shaking his head ruefully, he set the cloth aside and handed her the soap. "You shouldn't look at a man that way," he cautioned, leaning forward to give her easier access to his back.

"Why?"

"He will know how badly you want him, and you'll have a devil of a time keeping him from your bed."

Leah blushed with pleasure. "Thank you for telling me this. I know so little of men." She caressed the back of his neck with her lips, speaking between her adoring kisses. "May I bathe first, or do you want me in bed now?"

Benjamin turned his head so he could read her expression and rolled his eye heavenward, a sardonic smile gracing his lips. Yes, he most definitely intended to continue to take advantage of her offers of passion. He wasn't going anywhere for awhile, and Lord knew he wasn't adverse to the physical comfort she offered. If his conscience started to plague him overmuch, he could teach her a thing or two about men, so when and if she left her island, she would be better able to protect herself. It was a fair exchange.

"You may have your bath first, if you wish it," he deftly slipped her silk wrapper off her shoulders as he gave reply to her question. "I think there's room for one more."

Leah did not resist as he pulled her onto his lap. The warmth of the water felt seductive against her skin, and she shuddered with delight as he trailed a damp finger between her breasts.

"Hmmm," she sighed happily as she pillowed her head against his chest. The ends of her pale hair fanned out on the water's surface. "You feel wonderful. We shall have to take all our baths together."

"A bit crowded, don't you think?" Benjamin replied in an effort to unravel the tapestry of cozy contentment she wove about them. "I've dropped the soap, and I doubt we'll ever find it amongst this tangle of limbs."

Leah reached between their legs and after a few moments of purposeful fumbling about his lower anatomy, produced the bar of soap with a grin. Benjamin took it from her hands and worked a slow, thick lather upon her upper limbs and torso, using his labor-rough hands instead of the washcloth to scrub her blushing skin.

Leah languidly kissed the droplets of moisture from his shoulders, tasting him with her tongue as her mouth traveled to the water's surface, then up again until her lips met his in greedy embrace. Small, intimate sounds emitted from her throat as she clung to him.

Looking down into her upturned face, Benjamin made quick work of rinsing the soap from their bodies. Instinct demanded he scoop her up and carry her to the bed, but his injury forced him to allow her to cross the room on her own as he trailed awkwardly behind on his crutches.

Once they lay sprawled across the sheets, he wasted little time asserting his superior strength. Covering her body with his, he pinned her against the mattress.

Leah welcomed the weight of him, opening herself both physically and emotionally to the exaltation of his lovemaking.

Chapter 5

Leah found herself pressed against a solid wall of flesh as she blinked her eyes open. She nuzzled her nose in the dark, downy hair, offering his chest feathery kisses as she gently stretched the languor of sleep from her muscles.

Benjamin absently twisted a thin strand of her hair about his fingers as he watched her come fully awake. The experience of having another person so eager to please him was unique, and there was no doubt this Leah was eager to please. Too eager.

He knew he was taking advantage of her, but the strong always preyed upon the weak, and it was better she learn that lesson from him than a crueler source. He had never lied to her about his feelings for her. She chose the path she followed.

The nearness of her aroused his senses, besotting his mind with the remembrance of recently shared passions, and he gave himself up to the purely physical realm without regret. "Good morning," he drawled.

"Good morning," Leah returned the greeting with a

yawn. "Did you sleep well?"

"Sleep? When was I given opportunity to sleep?" he queried with mock reproach.

The apology on Leah's lips died when her eyes met his. He wore an expression of supreme male satisfaction. She laughed gaily. "You don't look any worse for the wear. In fact, you're looking better than you have since I pulled you from the sea."

"You're an excellent nurse."

The teasing light in her eyes dimmed, her brown eyes filling with concern at the reminder of his injury. "How is your ankle? I was so preoccupied, I forgot to rewrap it last night."

"It's fine."

"I should tend it at once."

"There are other parts of your patient that need tending first." He lifted the sheet, guiding her hand to his bulging nether region. "The ankle will have to wait."

Leah stroked his velvety shaft lovingly, her face taking on a dreamy expression. "You spoil me," she said as she looped her arms around his neck, pressing herself full length against him.

"I would have thought you would have had enough of me," Benjamin remarked.

"Never," she promised as she rained reverent kisses upon his face and neck. "Never."

When Leah finally arose from the bed to face the day, she did so reluctantly. The musky scent of lovemaking hung heavy on the air, and she drew in long breaths of the heady perfume.

Benjamin made to rise also, but she gently pushed him back against the mattress.

"You should rest," she admonished.

"Haven't I given you sufficient proof I'm no longer an invalid? Perhaps I should pull you back into this bed and try again."

Leah sighed wistfully as she shook her head from side to side. "I'd love to let you, but I have my chores to do."

"You're an insatiable little minx. I'm surprised you can move about without wincing," he commented dryly.

"I am a little tender," she admitted. "But I have never experienced anything so wonderful, and it's hard to stop."

Benjamin's gaze roamed from her radiant face over her well-formed breasts and hips to the pale triangle nestled between her firm thighs, then back to her face. He agreed. It was difficult to stop. He had never met a woman who gave herself with such abandon. She intoxicated his senses in a way that disturbed him. It was more than physical. Somehow she managed to touch a part of him that he did not recognize as himself . . .

His lips clamped shut, and he jerked upright in the bed. "It's time to get up!" He reached for the crutches and rose to his full height.

Leah sensed the change in him as he clomped about the room gathering his clothes, and she did not offer to help. Turning her attention to her own toilet, she dressed in her functional day clothes and twisted her hair into a single thick braid.

When he was clothed, she mutely tended his ankle,

ignoring his frequent scowls. Then she started for the door, calling over her shoulder, "I'll bring your breakfast up in a few minutes."

When she was alone, Leah allowed a frown to form on her face. The only place she seemed to fully understand her captain was in bed, where they communicated their needs with eloquent simplicity. It was there and only there that she knew how to please him. Most other times she felt like a piece of driftwood being battered about the waves. Since she was clearly incapable of comprehending his behavior, she resolved not to think at all.

When Leah returned with a plate of eggs and potato cakes, her smile was back in place. She served him cheerfully, but as soon as he was done, she cleared the dishes and left him to himself.

Benjamin stared out the window. Gray clouds obscured most of the sky, but the rays of the sun winked through a tiny patch of blue. A light drizzle was falling, bejeweling the verdant foliage with glistening pearls of moisture.

He watched the sway of Leah's skirts as she crossed the yard on her way to the cluster of sheds to the south of the house. His lips curved into a warm smile, but the moment he noticed their act of sedition, he pulled them back to a more somber set.

Too much lying abed was his problem, he told himself. He reached for the crutches. Every house was a reflection of its owner, and there were facts awaiting his discovery. He liked facts. They were solid, dependable, allowing a man to chart his course of action with detached logic.

There were many things he didn't understand about

Leah . . . the island . . . It was past time he conducted a thorough investigation of his surroundings.

There was no lethargy in his limbs nor lightness in his head as he made several trial runs back and forth across the room, and Benjamin was extremely pleased to find that, with the exception of his ankle, he was fully recovered. He pointed himself towards the door and set off.

The hall outside the bedroom was rather foreboding in contrast to the airy decor of Leah's room. Rising from floor to ceiling, the woodwork was stained a dusky brown. No portrait or landscape broke the color of the walls.

He made his way to the first door and turned the knob. Motes of dust danced on the air. A single bed, devoid of counterpane, stood against the far wall. The window was equally bare. A trail across the floor marked where Leah had dragged the brass bathtub he had enjoyed the night before. He closed the door and continued down the hall to the next.

Behind it lay another bedroom. Its disuse was equally apparent, but it seemed not to have been touched since the original occupant left it. Ashes lay on the grate in the fireplace. A silver-backed comb and bottles of perfume sat in the dust upon the dressing table. Decorated in mauves and creams, with a profusion of lace and ruffles, its owner was decidedly feminine. There was a door connecting this room to the next, but a heavy wardrobe had been placed in front of it, and he had to return to the hall to continue his explorations.

The next room he entered seemed but an extension of the hall with its dark colors and spartan furnishings.

A cavernous fireplace gaped from the wall. This room must have belonged to Leah's father, he decided, and the one before it her mother.

If taste in furnishings was any indication, they seemed an ill-suited couple. The question of why they made their home on this island again entered his mind, but he banished it, preferring to learn all he could before pondering the matter.

Two doors remained. The first led to a closet-size room, designed on an order similar to the garderobes of old. The last door at the end of the hall opened on a narrow staircase. Presuming it led to a storage area in the attic, Benjamin closed the door and began to retrace his steps. He paused when he reached the head of the stairs.

The rail was sturdy, and he quickly decided he could manage. Using the rail to brace his weight, he slid the crutches to the base of the stairs, then cautiously followed them without incident.

The first room he came upon was a parlor. The heavy damask curtains had been drawn back to let in the light, and he was faced with a hodgepodge of furnishings of every imaginable taste and description. The settee was brocade; the straight-back chair upholstered in natural leather. A battered sea chest sat next to a black-lacquered cabinet of Chinese design. Set diagonally across one corner stood a pianoforte, its ivory keys yellowed with age. As he came closer, he noticed the top was strewn with sheets of paper bearing intricate line drawings of a variety of plants and animals.

Leah's? He lifted a portrait of a blacktail deer. If the drawings belonged to her, she was a remarkable artist.

After perusing a few more of the sketches, he exited the room.

The next room he entered caught his interest more than any other. It housed a large, ornately carved mahogany desk and an impressive library. He ran his finger along several rows of books as his eyes read the titles. There were a few classic works of fiction upon the shelves, but most of the leather-bound volumes were tomes of history, geography, and the journals of noteworthy seafarers.

Though he was inclined to linger, he turned from the room, intent on seeing the rest of the house.

A quick survey of the dining room and kitchen facilities completed his tour, and he returned to the library and selected a book on world geography.

Sitting in the chair behind the desk, he opened the book, skimming the pages until he came to the section he desired. Before he attempted to return to civilization, it was imperative he pinpoint the location of the nearest settlement. Setting off in the wrong direction could cost him his life.

After reading several pages and perusing the maps of the land masses abutting the northern Pacific Ocean, he leaned back in the chair. "What I really need is my sextant," he advised himself with a sigh of frustration.

A glimmer of hope instantly sparked in his breast. Leah's father was a seafaring man. Benjamin began opening the drawers of the desk in rapid succession. The third one netted him his prize.

Lifting the sextant in his hands, he smiled broadly. He would soon know where he was. Then he could begin making his plans.

Though he was eager to calculate his exact location,

curiosity compelled him to continue his investigation of the desk. It contained several ship's logs kept by Capt. Jabob Daniels. The one he held in his hand was dated 1867. Benjamin was slightly chagrined when he realized that up to this moment he hadn't bothered to discover Leah's family name, but he did not dwell on the feeling and continued to thumb through the logs.

Jacob Daniels was a cargo captain like himself, and if the figures were to be believed, he ran an extremely profitable ship. It was also apparent, on occasion, he wasn't particularly fussy about the type of merchandise he transported. Benjamin judged him no better nor worse than the majority of men who made their living on the sea.

Though the logs painted an excellent picture of Jacob Daniels the businessman, they revealed nothing of the private family man. Benjamin was disappointed, but not surprised.

Now that he believed Leah about *how* she had come to this island, he was more than a little intrigued by the *why* of it. Was the island meant as a shelter or a prison? Or was Jacob Daniels simply a man who carried his love of privacy to the extreme? Though Benjamin chided himself that the matter was of no concern to him, a part of his mind continued to worry the mystery.

The largest drawer of the desk had yet to be touched, and when Benjamin pulled on the handle, he found it locked. He hesitated but a moment before deciding his need for knowledge was more important than the privacy of a man who hadn't been in this room for nearly three years. A quick search of the other drawers netted him nothing, but when he ran his hand under the top of the desk, he located the secreted compartment that housed the key.

Within the drawer was a trunk so large it completely filled the interior. It took several attempts to wrestle it out so he could pry the latch open.

A mountainous stack of stock certificates bulged out. Benjamin's brows rose. Captain Jacob Daniels was a rich man, indeed. As he endeavored to push the papers back into the chest, one caught his eye and he separated it from the rest.

The paper contained a rough sketch of the library, with arrows pointing to the middle of the third shelf on the east wall. He was beginning to feel a bit like a sneak thief, but he shrugged off the feeling and set off to discover what he could. Chances were the man was dead anyway.

Benjamin pulled several books from the shelf before uncovering the panel that lay behind them. It slid up into the wall, revealing a chest similar to the one he had found in the desk. It was heavy, and he abandoned the idea of carrying it back to the desk before opening it.

The height of the shelf allowed just enough room for him to open the lid. Within lay a treasure of gleaming gold coins.

Chapter 6

"There you are." Leah advanced into the library.

Benjamin spun on his good foot at the unexpected sound of her voice, almost losing his balance. "I didn't expect you back so soon."

"I wanted to make sure you didn't need anything before I left to do the fishing." Her gaze traveled from him to the gold, then back to him again.

He waited tensely for strident words of accusation to fall upon his head.

"I see you're playing with Papa's gold. It's very pretty, isn't it?" she commented in a conversational tone.

Benjamin's first thought was that he had not heard her correctly; his second was that she had taken too much sun. Cautiously he asked, "You're not going to scold me?"

"I suppose I should." Leah forced a stern expression to her face, but her mien immediately began to relax into its original, friendly state. "You should never have tried the stairs for the first time while I was out of the house. But since you seem to have managed them just fine, I can't be really angry with you."

"You're not upset about the gold?"

"Why would I be upset about that? I sometimes like to come in here and look at it myself, though it took me ages to discover it." She smiled at him "You must be very clever to have found it so quickly."

Benjamin shot one brow heavenward and shook his head slightly. "Do you have any idea how much this is worth?"

"A lot, I imagine. In Emma's stories, whenever a person found a chest of gold, it was always an occasion for great celebration. She said gold is very important in the world off the island."

"But it's not important here," Benjamin spoke his thoughts out loud as understanding dawned. Leah had no need of money, so she had no notion of wealth or poverty to judge the worth of the gold against. She had no concept of the magnitude of his transgression. He closed the lid on the gold and slipped the chest back into place.

When he turned to face her again, her gaze captured his and though she demanded none, he offered a feeble apology. "Next time I'll ask your permission before I go poking about."

"There's no need for that," she assured him. "Everything I have is yours."

"You shouldn't be so generous. I am liable to take advantage of you," he stated brusquely. Leah frowned.

"Why would you want to do that?"

"Human nature."

"I still don't understand."

"Never mind. It's not important. Why don't you be

off to do your fishing. I'll clean up the mess I've made in here."

Leah's gaze followed his to the open journals scattered on the desk top. She became very still, her eyes widening to the contour of two full moons. "Did you read those?" she asked with trembling lips.

Certain he had committed some grave trespass, he answered gruffly, "Yes."

"Will you teach me?"

"Teach you?"

"Yes." Her eyes began to flash with excitement. "Learning to read has been my lifelong dream. All these books, and I can do naught but look at the pictures! It is so frustrating."

"Were you not taught?"

"Papa said books would fill my head with foolish notions about things it was better I not know about, and he forbade me to come in here."

"And your mother and Emma?"

"Mama was not well enough to teach me, and Emma could not read herself. I suppose you think I'm wicked to go against my Papa in this, but I want to understand what all these books have to tell me. All I know of the world is my island. It makes me sad to be so ignorant."

"I am not a teacher," he informed her.

"Someone must have taught *you*. Just do as they did."

Benjamin allowed his thoughts to drift to the past. He had already known how to read when they brought him to his guardian, and until this moment he had never considered how uncommon an accomplishment that was for a lad of four. He tried to push his memory to the time before he had been forced to live with his

Uncle William, but icy fingers of brittle pain warned him away. "I don't remember how I learned to read. It is just something I seem to have always been able to do," he admitted.

"Perhaps your mother or father . . ." she suggested, hoping to stir his memory.

"I said: I don't remember," he repeated curtly. Leah was not deterred.

"But you could try to teach me."

"I wouldn't have the patience."

Her eyes clouded. "Is it because you don't want me to like you?"

Benjamin had no idea how to answer her question. He wasn't even sure why he was refusing her request. Even as a lad, instinct had urged him to strengthen his position in the world by the accumulation of knowledge, and he had taken great pains to educate himself, often risking the wrath and ridicule of those about him. He understood her need. "Go fishing. While you're gone, I'll think on the matter of becoming your teacher. Perhaps, in a day or two, I'll give you my decision," he said, preferring to put off the issue until he could think out his own motivation.

Her lips curved into a generous smile. "Thank you."

"For what?" he asked, his expression chary.

"For changing your mind. There's cheese and fruit in the pantry, if you get hungry before I return." Raising on tiptoe, Leah kissed his cheek before hurrying from the room.

Benjamin stared after her. He hadn't changed his mind. He had just said he would think about it. It annoyed him that she assumed he was going to give in to her, but what rankled him even more was the insuperable knowledge that she was right.

He was indebted to her for her care of him, for the very food on his plate, and he was not a man who liked to be beholding to anyone. He was honor-bound to teach her the skill she coveted, as payment of his debt. His acquiescence was in no way an act of kindness brought on by maudlin emotions he not only feared but despised. Just to be sure she understood that, he determined to wait several days before informing her of his decision.

Satisfied he was not committing a grave breach of his own rigid code of conduct, he began to return the contents of the desk to their proper place. The sextant remained on the top of the desk awaiting his use.

Benjamin decided now was the time to take advantage of the opportunity to determine his whereabouts. But first, he must find some point where the dense forest would not interfere with his making the necessary calculations required to determine his location with the sextant.

Once outside, he maneuvered himself a few yards so he could get a better look at the face of the house. Built of local stone, the home was an architectural monstrosity, combining a gable roof with a battlement-topped turret. The windows were square and plain; the door functional and unadorned. The plethora of mosses and vines clinging to the cold walls provided the building's only ornamentation.

To say the house was ugly was not precisely accurate; odd seemed the better word. What made it even more aberrant was the mystery of why it had been built here in the first place.

Spurred on by his goal, curiosity, and the pleasure of

being mobile again, Benjamin headed down the path leading away from the house. He passed a well-tended garden, a chicken house surrounded by cackling hens, then found his way blocked by a tiny herd of goats. Three stood on the path, eyeing him with the nonchalance characteristic of their breed, while a fourth tried to make a meal of his shirt.

"Hey, leave off!" Benjamin waved a crutch at him. "My clothes may be ill-fitting, but they're the best I've got at the moment."

The young goat *naahed* in reply, butting the crutch playfully with his horns. The mock battle lasted several minutes before the goat lost interest and meandered off.

"The rest of you go on, too," Benjamin urged them away. When they refused to move, he resigned himself to leaving the path until he had gone around them.

When he had traveled a little way further, he spied an outcropping of rock on an elevated point. Abandoning the path, he slowly picked his way across the broken terrain until he gained his destination.

The point provided a clear view of the seascape, and he immediately felt more relaxed. Gulls called to each other, swooping high in the sky, then diving for small fish unseen by him. Waves crashed with hypnotic rhythm against the distant rocks.

Below he could see Leah, standing knee deep in the surf, her thick fishing pole braced against her leg. Jonathan frolicked in the waves nearby. Benjamin watched in fascination as a gull alit upon her shoulder, with no more concern than if she were the wooden pile of a wharf. She reached into the pouch she had tied around her waist and pulled out an offering for the bird. He greedily devoured the tidbit then took to wing. Leah casually continued her fishing.

Wisps of hair had come loose from her braid and the wind whipped the tendrils about her face. She made a most enchanting picture.

He sat there watching her, allowing his mind to cloud with a pleasant fog that left no room for directed thought. He absorbed the peace of the island. No wonder Leah smiled so easily. She had never had to face the harsh lessons of the world he knew. If she did, would it change her? She would have to change or be destroyed; he accepted his own dark prediction with a certainty that was not untinged with regret.

Shaking his head to clear his thoughts, his lips thinned into a grim line. He was here to calculate his position, not moon over the lost innocence of a woman he barely knew. Raising the sextant toward the horizon, he dismissed Leah's future from his mind.

After depositing her catch in the kitchen, Leah hurried upstairs to change into dry clothes. She was not overly concerned to find Benjamin missing and took her time with her appearance. She had a wardrobe full of gowns her father had given her over the years, and most had rarely seen the light of day. Papa had liked her to dress up for him when he was on the island, but she found her loose-fitting work clothes more comfortable, and with no one to please but herself, she preferred them.

But now that Benjamin had come, the colorful satins and silks took on new appeal. She wanted him to think her attractive—not to satisfy a latent streak of vanity—

but because she hoped if he thought her pretty, he might like her better.

Choosing a coral-pink gown, she rummaged through her drawers for the constricting undergarments necessary to make the dress fit properly, and she lay them on the bed.

When she descended the stairs a short time later, she was glowing with anticipation. It took but a moment to locate Benjamin in the parlor.

"I thought you might like it if I dressed up for you tonight," she announced as she swept into the room and pirouetted before him. "Do you like it?"

Setting the book he was reading aside, Benjamin took in her appearance with a speculative gaze. The quality of the gown was undeniable, from the wide-cut vee neckline to grosgrain skirt decorated with triple flounces and overlaid with pointed lace. Ribbons wreathed the cinched waistline; fabric roses adorned the bodice. The sleeves were short and puffed. She had fashioned her hair high upon her head, adding a matching fabric rose at her right temple. Though she wore no jewelry, the flawless texture of her milk-white skin was of such excellence, jewels would have been a detraction.

The transformation from country miss to elegant lady was rather startling, but he gave no outward sign of his surprise. "I suppose you are waiting for some flowery compliment."

"No, I just want to know if you think the dress makes me pretty."

"What you wear changes nothing. Physical features are immutable. Fashion merely enhances or detracts." He picked up his book and opened it, lowering his gaze to the page.

"I see," she responded to his words in a thoughtful tone. Though she was disappointed the gown had not had the desired effect, she continued to try to draw him out of himself. "I would still like to know if you think I'm pretty."

He glanced over the top of the page he was attempting to read. "I will not lie and tell you that you are a great beauty, but you do possess a certain sort of charm."

Though he tried to concentrate on his book, he could feel Leah staring at him intently. At first he was determined to ignore her, but after a few minutes, he found he could not.

"What now?" he asked wearily.

"I am trying to determine if you are handsome, but it is difficult to tell with you hiding your face behind that beard."

"I am not hiding behind my beard."

"Would you shave it off if I asked you?"

"No," he responded through compressed lips.

"Why don't you want people to know what you look like?"

Benjamin snapped the book in his hand shut. "If the beard offends you, why don't you just come out and say it?"

"It doesn't offend me, though it does tickle when you . . ." Leah left off when he shot her a warning glance, but her smile beckoned him to remember shared delights.

He groaned at her in exasperation as his loins instantly responded to her unspoken invitation. While he defended himself on one front, she assaulted him on another. "Polite women don't speak of such things in parlors. In fact, they don't speak of them at all."

"Why not?"

"How the hell do I know? I didn't make the rules."

"Who did?"

"Isn't it time you scurry into the kitchen to make me dinner or something?" He met her question with one of his own. "Since waiting on me hand and foot seems to give you such great pleasure, I suggest you entertain yourself doing something useful."

Leah was instantly contrite. "I'm sorry. I didn't realize you were suffering from hunger."

"I'm not. I'm suffering from too many idiotic questions."

She sighed in relief.

"If you taught me to read, I would know more," Leah suggested hopefully.

"I said I would give you my answer in a few days. Nagging me will only set my mind against granting your request."

"I was not nagging. I was merely pointing out the advantages of sharing your skill with me." She met his warning with determined logic. "All I want to do is make you happy."

"And your own happiness matters not one whit to you," Benjamin taunted.

"Being with you makes me happy," Leah stated firmly. Then her soft brown eyes met his hard blue ones, and she added, "Even if I don't understand you."

Not wanting to hear his reply to either of her statements, she scurried from the room.

Benjamin growled more out of habit than heartfelt rancor. He tried to return his attention to his book, but

77

gave up after several minutes' struggle.

Grabbing his crutches, he headed in the direction of the dining room. He was not about to be outdone by a simpleminded slip of a woman.

Though he was not the most efficient domestic, he managed to set the table with the appropriate linen, china, and utensils. Several trips to the woodpile he had seen earlier in the day procured him enough wood to build an adequate fire on the hearth.

When Leah returned to find a fire crackling merrily on the hearth and the table set, her eyes widened in delight and amazement. "How did you manage all this?"

"Questions again. You are an everlasting font."

"I don't mean to be tiresome."

The sincerity reflected from her large eyes tweaked his conscience, and Benjamin started to explain his method of balancing a piece of wood in the crook of each arm and against the frame of the crutches; then, his lips clamped shut, and he stood silent, mentally chiding himself for so easily falling prey to her soulful looks.

As Leah watched the familiar blank mask slip over his face, she clenched her fist in frustration. "I'll bring our fish."

She turned from him and strode from the room.

The click of silver against china and the popping of the fire were the only sounds to fill the dining room as they consumed their meal.

Leah was too tired from her labors and the strain of struggling to do and say the right thing to try to make casual table conversation. Her only effort toward communication was the infrequent looks she cast in Benjamin's direction. After staring at him a moment or two, she would sigh, shake her head, then return her full attention to her meal.

Benjamin bore her conduct stoically.

When the meal was completed, Leah cleared the table and retired to the kitchen. Benjamin returned to the parlor and his book, but he could not concentrate on the words. After a few minutes, he threw it aside in disgust.

He was being a cad, and he knew it. More than once he had overheard a crew member or business acquaintance refer to him as a cold son of a bitch, and he had not only agreed with their assessment, but had approved of this image of himself. It kept the world at bay and his life uncomplicated.

Keeping Leah at bay was essential to his peace of mind, so why the twinges of regret? It wasn't his fault that he had washed ashore on this particular island. She made herself sad by her insistence that they were more than involuntary acquaintances, each using the other for a time to fulfill their separate needs, then moving on to become nothing more than faded memories. He had never asked for her help; nevertheless, he was a fair man, and he intended to repay her by granting her the opportunity to leave the island if she so desired. She just wouldn't be leaving with him.

The contentment he found in the logical progression of his thoughts was mitigated by the cold lump in the pit of his stomach. "Indigestion." He spoke the word out loud, but he didn't believe his own diagnosis any more than he believed that the *Sea Dragon* would rise from the sea and come sailing over the horizon. Retrieving his book, he reopened it and tried once more to concentrate on the words.

After tending the dishes, Leah joined him in the parlor. She gazed longingly at the book he held in his hand, then crossed the room to the piano and gathered her sketches into a pile. When she came to a blank sheet of paper, she set it aside, picked up her pen and ink bottle, and retired to the corner.

As she silently sketched, she tried not to think at all, but unhappy thoughts drifted in and out of her mind as she fashioned the image of the man who sat across the room. She had waited so long for him to come, and now everything she did and said seemed to annoy him. She fulfilled his needs for food and physical intimacy with enthusiasm. She provided him shelter. She knew she was ignorant of the world, but her willingness to learn should count for something. What more could she do?

"Is the drawing not progressing to your satisfaction?" Benjamin's voice broke into her thoughts.

"What? No, it's coming along just fine," she assured him as she glanced at her paper. "Why do you ask?"

"You were frowning so fiercely, I assumed something was amiss."

Her voice remained subdued. "I was only thinking."

Against his better judgment, he asked "About what?"

"About why I don't please you." The frown remained in place as she lapsed back into silence.

Benjamin covertly observed her for several more minutes before his conscience prodded him to speak again, "It's nothing personal. I don't form attachments to anyone."

"You must have loved someone *sometime*."

"No one. Never," he reaffirmed.

"How very lonely for you." She smiled sadly. "I used to think I must be the loneliest person on earth, living on my island without a soul to keep me company, but now I see I was wrong."

"I am not lonely," he protested.

"Believe what you will," Leah shrugged. Without conscious intent, she found herself asking, "Would you like to see my sketch?"

"Bring it here," Benjamin ordered gruffly, pleased to drop the subject, but rankled by her obvious dismissal of his statement.

Leah slowly crossed the room, relinquishing her drawing to his care.

His eyes moved over the dark lines depicting a man reclining on a settee, book in hand. The identity of her subject was unmistakable. "You have a remarkable talent with the pen," he commented sincerely.

"Then you don't mind that I sketched you?" Her voice evidenced both relief and surprise.

"Your skills would be put to better use on prettier subjects, but I am not offended. What is this ink you use? I noticed its unusual quality this morning, when I looked at your other drawings."

"It's made from concentrated blackberry juice. I experimented with several substances when the inkwell ran dry, and the juice proved the best."

"Do you paint as well?" he queried, in the interest of avoiding the oppression of her unhappy silence.

The animation was slowly returning to her voice, and she answered him readily, "Papa once brought me a box of paints, and I enjoyed them immensely, but my supply ran out before I developed much skill. The substitutes I concocted were poor at best."

"What about the piano? Do you play?" Benjamin asked, determined to keep the direction of the conversation on a superficial level.

"A little. Would you like to hear me play something?"

"Please," he gestured toward the instrument with a nonchalant sweep of his hand.

Leah sat upon the bench before the piano and flexed her fingers, to loosen up before she rested them lightly on the keys. Her music was pleasing to her own ears, but she wanted Benjamin's approval as well, and she had no confidence where he was concerned. Taking a deep breath, she began to move her fingers deftly across the keys.

The melody was haunting and vaguely familiar, though Benjamin could not place when he had heard the piece before. It must have been someplace agreeable, for the tune conjured a pleasant sensation of comfort and safety.

He lay his head against the back of the settee and closed his eyes, letting the music wash over him. When the last note was stroked, he opened his eyes and lifted his head slightly. "Will you play another?"

Leah smiled broadly as her gaze took in his contented expression; then, she turned back to the piano keys. She had found another way to please him.

The next selection she played was totally unfamiliar, as was the next and the next. Each time she finished a piece, she would turn to him and he would urge her to play another. The music ranged from allegro to lento, but always the same undefinable quality lay beneath the combination of chords and notes. It spoke to his soul in ways that bypassed his conscious mind, touching forsaken places.

"Another," Benjamin directed when she had played the final notes of one melody and did not begin another.

"I'm sorry, but I know nothing else to play for you," Leah admitted with true regret.

"Tomorrow you can play again."

"I'm glad my playing gives you pleasure."

He continued to lay with his head back, eyes closed, allowing himself to tarry under the spell her music had cast. His voice came from faraway and was remarkably gentle. "That it does. Tell me who taught you these melodies. They are unfamiliar to me."

"I compose them myself, when the rains keep me confined in the house for long periods. It helps to pass the time."

"Would that boredom always led to such sterling accomplishments."

Leah glowed with contentment. Rising from the piano bench, she came to sit beside him. "It is getting late, and you have been up far too long for your first day. We should go to bed."

"I'm not tired," Benjamin protested, as he reluctantly opened his eyes.

"Then we won't sleep," Leah stated, a concupiscent gleam in her eyes, despite the obvious fatigue evident in the carriage of her limbs.

He stared at her in wonder and disbelief. Her generosity seemed to have no limit. A need welled up in him to give to her in return. He leisurely trailed his finger from her temple to chin, his gaze holding hers.

"But *you* are tired." The lingering enchantment of the music guided his tongue. "Tonight you have given food to satisfy the hunger of my belly, music to satisfy the secret places of my soul. It is too much that you should now be called upon to satisfy the lusts of my flesh."

Leah leaned over him, pressing his hand to the swell of her bosom. "Then you shall satisfy mine."

Chapter 7

The passing days were pleasant enough, though Leah found it increasingly difficult to remain patient. Benjamin made no mention of when he would begin her reading lessons, and after two weeks she was beginning to fear he would never do so. Several times she started to bring up the matter herself, but his words of warning always stopped her.

She spent her days as she had always done: tending her animals, nurturing the plants in her garden, clamming, fishing . . . Sometimes Benjamin accompanied her, helping perform the day-to-day necessities of existence the best he could. Though she tried to persuade him to take his ease, she quickly discovered he could not bear to be idle. When he did not follow her about, he wandered the island on his own.

When they were together, she shared her knowledge of the forest, showing him how to find the most tender roots, the best places to dig camas bulbs, and how to make a frothy dessert from soapberries.

She introduced him to the island wildlife. Those who

had come under her loving care after some injury, she regarded as her family, and they approached her freely, allowing her to scratch their ears and stroke their brows.

Occasionally she would catch glimpses of some undefinable need in the core of her captain's blue eyes, but the look was so fleeting that she was never quite sure it was really there, and when she questioned him, he always denied its existence. If a kind word slipped past his lips, he quickly followed it with some caustic remark.

Instinct told her his abstruse behavior was in some way connected to what he had told her of his past. To grow up without love was unimaginable to her. She had known love from everyone who touched her life.

Having lacked affection in his former years, Leah was more determined than ever that he should have hers now. But she learned to give it carefully, or she was sure to spark his anger.

As yet, she had found only two things that were able to soothe the gruffness of his nature: music and lovemaking. Leah made sure they indulged in both pastimes as frequently as possible.

The sun had set, and heavy droplets of rain pattered steadily against the windowpanes of the parlor. Inside, the room glowed with warmth and light provided by the red orange flames of the fire and the flicker of candles. A blazing log on the hearth popped, causing Leah to glance up from the sketch on which she was working.

Benjamin was sitting across the room on the settee. His injured limb stretched the length of the small sofa; his other foot rested on the floor. He held an open book in his hands. Leah stared longingly at the worn leather of the book jacket, blinking away the excess moisture forming in her eyes.

"Come here," Benjamin commanded.

Startled, Leah dropped her pen and paper and leapt to her feet. However, he scowled at her so fiercely she did not move to obey him.

"Well, do you want to learn to read or don't you?"

She was across the room showering his face with kisses before his lips had stilled. Taking her place beside him on the settee, she smiled radiantly. "Where do we begin?"

"We begin by making sure you understand that I am not doing this because I like you, or because I wish to indulge you, or because I have been persuaded by the mournful looks you cast my way whenever I pick up a book. I am repaying a debt owed—nothing more. Have I made myself clear?"

"Yes," Leah nodded. "Except the part about owing a debt, but you needn't explain," she stated. "It is enough that you have agreed to be my teacher."

"The debt I owe," he expounded despite her words, "is for nursing me back to health, the crutches, the food in my belly, the clothes on my back." With a sweep of his hand, he indicated the well-fashioned linen shirt and wool trousers she had sewn for him.

She frowned at him. "But I gave those things freely, with no expectation of compensation."

He returned her frown. "I do not expect or accept

charity from you or anyone else. Do we understand each other?"

Leah did not understand at all, but she was too eager to begin her reading lesson to linger on the subject of debts, especially if futher questions might lead him to change his mind about teaching her. She answered him by smiling and taking the book from his hands. Pointing to the first word at the top of the open page, she asked, "What is that word?"

"*The*—but you are getting ahead of yourself. Words are made of letters, and you must learn them and the sounds they make, before you can begin to read a book."

"Oh," Leah voiced her disappointment as she continued to flip through the pages. "What do these words say? Do they tell you something about the odd picture?"

"The picture is a map of the western hemisphere. We are here," he pointed to a spot on the map, "somewhere off the west coast of Vancouver Island in the Crown Colony of British Columbia. To sailors the area is known as the Graveyard of the Pacific."

"What a sad name. It is so beautiful here. Why would they call it that?"

"It's a treacherous stretch of coast, and the sea bottom is littered with the wrecks of ships. Even the sailors who make it ashore rarely survive."

"But how do you know that is where we are?"

"I used your father's sextant to make the calculations. The nearest center of civilization is here." He moved his finger to the southeastern tip of the island. "A place called Victoria."

"I have never heard of it," Leah admitted, "but if we leave the island, I should very much like to visit there."

Benjamin ignored her last remark. "The alphabet," he began. "There are twenty-six letters . . ."

The wan light of predawn hovered on the horizon when Benjamin lay his forehead against his palm and closed his eyes a final time. "Enough. Enough," he mumbled sleepily. "Don't you ever tire?"

"But it is all so fascinating—like an elaborate riddle with the letters as clues," she spoke through a series of yawns. "I am far too excited to sleep."

"And I am far too exhausted to play teacher another moment." He forced his eyes open, surveying the papers scattered upon the table and floor. Leah sat at his feet, meticulously copying the letters of her name over and over again.

Though he was loathe to admit it, he had been as caught up in their lesson as she. Leah was an exceptionally adept student. He rarely had to tell her anything more than once. There was something enormously gratifying about his ability to elicit such rapt attention, and he wondered vaguely if he had missed his calling in life. The thought dissipated as quickly as it had formed, but the feeling of self-satisfaction did not. "To bed with you."

Reluctantly, Leah set her pen aside. "I suppose you're right. Do you need me to help you with the stairs?"

His dark look reminded her of his dislike of being cosseted, and she bit her lip in vexation at herself. "I'll join you upstairs as soon as I bank the fire and blow out the candles."

When Leah entered the bedroom, she was not

surprised to find Benjamin already asleep. She silently scolded herself for keeping him up so late, but her remorse was mitigated by the pleasure of the evening.

Removing her clothes, she lifted the sheets and carefully slipped beneath them so as not to disturb him. His arm snaked around her waist, pulling her against him, but his eyes remained closed and his breathing steady. Leah lay her head upon his chest, letting the lulling rhythm of his heartbeat sing her to sleep.

Despite his claim of exhaustion, Benjamin slept only a few hours before rising. His mood was strange, and he felt a need to work off his disquiet with physical labor. Slipping out of the bed, he stared down at Leah's sleeping form.

Leah Daniels was boring her way under his skin, and he was feeling suffocated by her nearness. He knew it wasn't something she did purposefully. He had never met a person so devoid of guile. But that didn't make being caught in her snare less objectionable. He wasn't used to spending so much time with another human being, *any* human being. Even on the confines of his ship, he had his captain's cabin, where no man dare intrude without invitation.

Here, no place was safe from her presence. Even his mind was beginning to turn traitor, letting her insinuate her way into his thoughts whenever he let his guard down. He knew how to fight back against skulduggery, but what weapons did a man use to defend himself against the onslaught of innocence?

He had always believed his soul made of ice, and the thought that Leah might have found a way to melt through the glacial wall that had been his armor since early youth was too disturbing to contemplate. He would not be a willing victim. Pulling on his clothes, he quietly escaped the house.

Upon reaching the back of the house, he positioned himself before the woodpile. Discarding one crutch to free his right arm, he picked up the small ax. Cautiously, he made several practice swings, each time adjusting his stance and the remaining crutch to form a more secure base. When he was satisfied, he swung the ax over his head, bringing it down on the log Leah had been chipping away at for days.

Each time the head of the ax bit the wood, he felt some of his tension diffuse. He listened to the sharp sound of metal striking wood echo off the trunks of nearby trees. It was a strong, solid sound, and for a while his task took over his thoughts.

Too soon his soothing solitude was interrupted by the appearance of his nemesis standing by the corner of the house, her soft brown eyes wide with amazement.

"What are you staring at?" he snapped at her.

"You," she replied literally. "I heard the sound of the ax and . . ."

"You hurried out to stop me before I did myself injury." He finished her sentence for her.

"No," she corrected, her muted tone contrasting his strident one. "You're a grown man, and I have learned you are wise enough not to push yourself past the limits of your physical capabilities. I just came to tell you breakfast is ready."

"Then why the shocked look?"

"Because even with your lame ankle, you have cut more wood in the space of an hour than I could have had I devoted all day."

Benjamin looked at the mound of firewood he had chopped and was rather surprised by the size of the pile himself. He hadn't realized he had been so engrossed in his endeavor, but the ache in his arm and the quantity of split wood supported her claim that he had been at his task for more than the few minutes he had assumed. Despite his discovery, he was in no mood for company.

The hungry rumblings of his stomach prevented him from regaining his solitude by a brusque "clear off," as had been his first inclination. Promising himself that after he ate he would find some excuse to be alone again, he leaned the ax against a tree.

"I'll wash up at the spring and be right in," he grumbled. "Feel free to start without me."

As Leah walked back to the kitchen, a frown pulled at the corners of her lips. She should have known he would be in a dark mood today; he had been so kind to her last night. She might not understand his pendular moods, but she was growing used to them. She had plenty to keep her busy, and she was prepared to wait out his ill-temper.

"I told you, you needn't wait," Benjamin scolded as he took his place at the head of the table. "You don't have to be so damned accommodating all the time, you know."

"And you don't have to be so *damned*," she grinned impishly as she tested the swear word, "surly. If you will try to be nicer, I will try to be less so."

"Hrmph." His head lowered into his shoulders, and

he gave the scrambled eggs upon his plate his full attention.

"I guess that means I can be as nice as I like?" Leah continued to tease him. He could be as dour as he pleased, but that didn't mean she had to join him in his mood. Since her behavior seemed to have no logical effect on his, she was determined to act just as she felt—and she felt happy.

He answered her with another guttural groan.

Leah gave herself the satisfaction of wrinkling her nose at him before leaving him be. As soon as Benjamin finished his meal, he quit the dining room.

A short time later, Leah followed in his footsteps. As she passed the library door with the tray of dirty dishes, it took all of her willpower not to stop and linger, but other responsibilities called. With a wistful sigh, she continued on to the kitchen.

The day was uneventful. Benjamin kept to himself most of the day, but after dinner it was he who suggested they continue her reading lessons. Leah scurried to his side, her face alight with eager anticipation.

His instruction lasted less than two hours, before he brought it to a halt with a request that she play the piano for him.

Knowing how much he enjoyed the music, Leah did not deny him. Later that night, when he pulled her into his arms nuzzling his face between her breasts, she smiled contentedly as she stroked the muscles of his back. She could feel his male member becoming warm and hard against her leg, and she kissed the top of his head.

I love you, Leah spoke the words in her mind so she

wouldn't vex him. As his lips claimed hers, she gave herself heart and soul to telling him with her body what he wouldn't let her say with words.

The sun rose and set in the summer sky, marking the days comprising the weeks that followed. It rained a little each afternoon, but there were always plenty of balmy hours to devote to picking berries, fishing, or strolling along the beach with no purpose except to feel the sand massage their feet and the sun upon their faces.

Benjamin discarded his crutches for a walking stick. He worked alongside Leah when he was feeling sociable, alone when he was not. He was still wary of the open affection she could not disguise, but the island had the feel of the Biblical Eden, and if not for Leah's endless questions, it would have been easy to forget the outside world existed.

Leah's ability to read improved at a startling rate, and she devoured the books in the library with the fervor of a conquering general. She seemed not to care what she read (everything fascinated her), and upon finishing one book, she took the next in the row off the shelf.

She practiced her writing by listing words she did not know or noting subjects she did not fully understand and wished to discuss.

Benjamin met her behests for knowledge with varying degrees of patience.

"What are these?" Benjamin demanded one evening

as he sifted through a stack of sketches on the piano.

Leah crossed the room at a sedate pace, by now having grown used to his brusque mode of communication and not the least alarmed by his tone. Her gaze drifted over the papers. "They're supposed to be sketches of you."

"I can see that! What I want to know is why you drew me this way?"

"I still don't know what you look like beneath your beard, so I imagined what you *might* look like. I did them the other day to amuse myself while you were sulk—while you were walking in the woods. You wouldn't care to tell me which is closest to your true face?" she queried hopefully.

"Definitely not this one." He set aside one depicting a jaw that resembled an ape's.

Leah blushed guiltily, but the giggles she failed to stifle belied her remorseful complexion. "I'm afraid I was still vexed with you when I drew that one."

In all the time he had known her, he had never heard Leah utter a harsh word, and the fact that he had finally caught her indulging in a little spite tickled him more than he could credit.

"What about one of these?" She pointed to two drawings bearing less pronounced features.

Benjamin glanced at the two sketches, then his gaze roamed over the others before he lifted one and thrust it into her hand. "This is the closest, though it's not entirely accurate. Now tell me: why the obsession with the lower portions of my face?"

"Curiosity, I suppose," she replied as she gathered the sketches into a pile and set them aside. "It was just a silly game. If you feel more comfortable hiding behind your beard, I've no objections."

"That's the second time you've intimated I wear my beard as some kind of disguise. Facial hair is considered manly."

Leah sighed. "It is only that *you* know exactly what *I* look like, and I am forced to guess. I have always been plagued by an insatiable curiosity about things seen and unseen. Maybe it comes from living on the island so long."

"A convenient excuse for making me the brunt of a joke," he scolded. "Play your music for me, and I might forgive you."

"Then you're not angry?" Leah asked, her eyes searching his as she lowered herself to the piano bench. His lips tightened into a grim smile.

"I'll think about that while you play."

When Leah awoke the next morning, the bed was empty, and she did not linger as long as she might have if Benjamin was by her side. She splashed the sleep from her eyes with the cold water she poured from the pitcher, dressed in her day clothes, and hurried to the kitchen to begin preparation of the morning meal. Benjamin was standing at the sink, his back towards her.

"I picked some huckleberries while you were sleeping. If you'll put out the bowls and cream, I'll bring them to the table as soon as they are washed."

Leah smiled at his thoughtfulness. He knew berries and cream were her favorite breakfast. Every morning she awoke not knowing what she could expect from him, and she was never quite comfortable until she did.

It was a pleasure to know from the outset the color of his mood.

When the berries were clean, Benjamin turned from the sink.

Leah dropped the pitcher of cream on the floor.

"Your beard!" she exclaimed as she stared slack-jawed at his naked chin.

"I decided I must shave or be forever plagued by your *insatiable* curiosity," he stated sedately. "Sit down and close your mouth. You look like a fish."

Leah did as she was told, but she could not take her eyes off his face as he bent to mop up the spilt cream. A dark mustache still covered his upper lip, but his jaw was completely bare. It was firm and square, with just the slightest hint of a dimple in his chin. The skin was white compared to the rest of his face, giving him a rather comical appearance. Leah raised her napkin to hide her grin, but a tiny chuckle managed to slip past her tightly compressed lips.

"What's so amusing?" Benjamin demanded as he joined her at the table.

"Nothing."

His somber eyes met her sparkling ones, and he reached across the table and yanked the napkin from her face. "Nothing, heh?"

"It's just that you look so different," she explained.

"Should I take that as an insult or a compliment?"

"I don't know. You do look awfully naked." Cocking her head to one side, Leah studied his face intently. "It will take some getting used to."

A low growl rumbled in his throat. "First you complain because I wear a beard; now, you bemoan the fact I do not. There is no pleasing you."

97

"Oh, I am very pleased," Leah was quick to assure him, "but I will be even more pleased after we get you out into the sun and get some color to your skin, so your face looks all one piece."

"Enough of your prattle," he commanded. "Fetch more cream before I grow too weak from hunger to defend myself against your barbs."

Leah started to comply, but she was stopped by the unnatural light in his eyes. If she did not know better, she would almost swear they were trying to twinkle.

Chapter 8

The day Benjamin discarded his walking stick, he also felled a cedar tree, so he might begin work on the canoe that would carry him to Victoria. He still walked with a limp and he knew the journey would be arduous, but summer would soon be coming to an end, and the weather would turn foul. If he did not leave within the next few weeks, he would be stranded for the winter.

His continued absence from the maritime world could be disastrous. The loss of the *Sea Dragon* was a heavy—though not fatal—financial blow. He had the wherewithal to purchase another ship and pick up his business where he left off. However, when he did not show up in port as scheduled, his patrons would soon begin to look elsewhere for the transport of their goods. He had worked hard to build a steady business, and he was loath to lose it.

It was settled that he was soon leaving. What he wasn't sure of was how he was going to tell Leah that he wasn't going to be taking her with him and that she must wait until he sent someone back for her. So, he didn't say anything.

He was comfortable with the way things were. She played the gentle handmaiden, seeing to all his domestic needs. He continued in his role as teacher. They made love whenever and wherever the urge struck.

He felt a sense of belonging here. Leah moved about the forest as an equal, and slowly he, too, was becoming accepted. The deer and voles did not come to him as they did her, but Jonathan often teased him when he went down to the sea, and a curious rapport had developed between himself and the little goat who had nibbled his shirt the first day he had ventured from the house.

In many ways it was an idyllic life, and in his weaker moments, he was tempted to forget the world and stay on the island forever. Then the old voices would shout warnings in his head, reminding him that to love was to make oneself vulnerable. He could now admit a mild affection for Leah, but he had no intention of letting the feeling get out of hand.

There was little danger of that, he reminded himself with grim satisfaction. In all honesty, he did not think himself capable of loving.

The thunder of the cedar striking the ground caught Leah's attention, and she picked up the bucket of clams she had just harvested and hurried towards the sound.

"What are you doing?" she asked when she came upon Benjamin standing over the felled tree, hacking away at the branches with an ax. "You know cedar doesn't make the best firewood."

"I'm carving a canoe."

Leah focused her eyes on the log destined to carry her away from her island as she absorbed the import of his words. She had always known this day would one day come, but it took her by surprise nonetheless. "Then we will be leaving the island soon?"

"The journey will be long and fraught with unknown perils. I want to leave before the season ends." He avoided a direct answer to her question; then, he swung the ax high over his head, hoping to drown out any further questions with the din of his labors.

Leah understood his purpose and retired to the freshly cut cedar stump, pulling her knees up under her chin as she perched on her seat.

The thought of leaving the island after all these years left her trembling with a mixture of excitement and anxiety. What would she find? She had only the opinions of others to judge by, and they opposed each other so often, she wasn't sure who was right. Even the books she read frequently presented diverse accounts of the same event. There was so much she didn't know—couldn't know—until she actually experienced what life was like off the island.

Realizing that there was nothing to be done but wait until she could judge for herself, she relied on the strength of her patience to calm her churning thoughts.

The sun filtered through the canopy of branches overhead, falling on the bracken fern carpeting the forest floor. She could feel the warmth of its rays on her skin. The steady thwack of the ax was accompanied by the rat-a-tat of a woodpecker, high above in a nearby tree. She drew in a deep breath of cedar-scented air.

After quietly observing Benjamin's labors for a

considerable time, another worry surfaced. Once off the island, he would no longer be compelled to stay with her. Leah started to tremble anew as a cold chill radiated up her spine.

She still didn't understand him, but she loved him more and more each day. When he held her close to his heart at night, or patiently explained a passage from a book she did not comprehend, those times made up for the others—times like now when he shut her out. She didn't want to think of a future without him.

Maybe she should try to keep him here on the island, until she was sure of his affection. Leah discarded the idea almost before it formed. Though he might not say so in words, he needed her as much as she needed him. Where they lived didn't matter. She knew Benjamin and she belonged together, and she must trust her instincts.

Despite her heartfelt belief, Leah sensed she would feel better if she occupied herself doing something useful. Picking up her clamming bucket, she started towards the spring near the house.

Over the next few days, the cedar log slowly began to be transformed into a semblance of a canoe. After stripping the trunk of its branches and bark, Benjamin split it lengthwise.

Using an ax and adze, he shaped the bottom of the craft. When it was formed to his satisfaction, he turned the canoe over and began the strenuous and tedious work of clearing away the excess wood from the interior.

Great care had to be taken during the carving process to ensure the proper thickness—one finger's width at the top, two at the bottom.

At first Leah's offerings of help met with resistance, and she was only able to observe the progress of the work, but gradually she was allowed to do more than carry a picnic lunch to the work site. It began with the request for a tool, and by the middle of the next week, her role had evolved to that of full partner.

She continued to question Benjamin about the journey, and he continued to evade her questions, though he always stopped short of an outright lie. He could see no point in upsetting her before it was absolutely necessary to tell her that she was not to be allowed to come with him.

Though he did not do so consciously, Benjamin endeavored to ease the gnawing sensation in his gut by trying to prepare Leah to face the world on her own. The wealth in her father's library assured she could buy her way into polite society, and she need not want for physical comforts, but only if she learned how to handle herself and her money properly. Leah was far too generous for her own good.

"No! You're not paying attention to what I say! My price is grossly inflated. You're supposed to haggle," Benjamin shouted in exasperation as he paced the parlor floor.

Leah's brow wrinkled. "But what about the medicine for your sick child? I would gladly give you double your asking price, if it would help restore her to good health."

"I don't have a sick child. It's a lie."

"I know that, but you said I am to act just as if this is a real market, and you are a real merchant," she reminded him of the rules of his own game. "I want to help the little girl."

"The merchant has no little girl. He's a dirty swindling lout who beats his lovers and kicks stray dogs in the street. He makes up the story about the sick child to play on your sympathies in hopes of gaining a few more coins for his pocket."

"Oh." Leah sat quietly, her hands folded in her lap as she digested this new bit of information.

"So what do you do?" he prodded.

"I call the constable and have him arrested," she stated without hesitation.

"No! You bargain with him until you get a fair price."

"But I would never do business with such a dreadful man. I would rather have him arrested."

Benjamin moaned. "If they arrested every merchant who tried to increase his profits with a woeful tale, there would hardly be a vendor on the streets. It's accepted practice."

"Then you will have to do our marketing, because I couldn't tolerate such behavior."

"You will learn to do your own marketing, and you will learn to do it right," he ordered, his blue eyes flashing with impatience. "Now, we will start over again, and I expect you to cooperate."

"But I'm tired."

"Tired is better than poor!"

So it went each night. Leah was grateful for his tutelage, but she wished he wasn't so determined that she always give the right answer. She wanted him to be proud of her, but sometimes she felt he carried her lessons past the point of the ridiculous. On the occasions that she dared tell him so, he became almost apoplectic.

When the carving of the inside of the canoe was complete, they moved it near the spring by the house and filled the interior with water. Benjamin instructed Leah to build a fire, while he gathered stones. When the rocks were heated red-hot, he used sticks to lift them from the fire and dropped them into the canoe. The stones were heated again and again, until the water in the canoe was brought to the boiling point; then, he shoved the thwarts he had prepared earlier into the body of the craft to stretch the now softened wood.

Work on the canoe progressed steadily as the bow and stern were added. In the evenings, Leah's lessons continued. She now knew how to negotiate the open-air market, rent a house, deal with bankers, interview house servants . . . In general she found the information useful, but as Benjamin became more and more obsessed with her learning to handle city life on her own, her sense of unease began to grow in proportion.

Yesterday they had positioned long strips of cedar along the upper edge of the canoe to form the gunwales, and there was now nothing left to do but the final finishing work. Benjamin stood back, admiring their handiwork, but instead of feeling a sense of pride, he was awash with a wave of guilt.

He was a coward not to have told Leah that he was leaving her behind long before now. Though he had been carefully assuring himself his long silence was for her comfort, he knew it was more for his own. He liked Leah. Too much. That was why it was important he get away from her. Too often he found himself wanting to surrender his will to hers.

"Come here," he ordered gruffly.

Leah came to stand before him and waited expectantly for him to continue.

His eyes met hers for a brief moment, but he was forced to turn away. Damn her! Why did she have to look so ingenuous? It made him feel like a villain. The matter was settled long ago. Their time together had come to an end.

Knowing the coming conversation was unavoidable, he forced himself to commence. "The canoe will be ready in a day or two, and I plan to leave. As soon as I reach Victoria, I will send a boat back to get you."

Leah stared at him for several moments—with what he viewed as unnatural calm—before speaking. "No."

He cleared his throat. "I have made my decision. The journey by canoe would be too hard for you, and—"

"I said no," she repeated, with the same lack of emotion as when she had spoken the word earlier. In truth, she was too numb to do otherwise. "I will not be left behind."

"It would only be for a short time. A ship will come to fetch you, and you can begin your new life."

"No." She turned her back on him and walked away.

It had never occurred to Leah that Benjamin would leave her behind on the island, and she found it difficult to believe he would even suggest such a thing. It was irrational to send a boat back for her when the canoe had plenty of room for them both.

He had been so attentive of late, she had thought he

was coming to care for her a little. She blinked back tears of pain. It was true they never spoke of the future, but there had never seemed a need. It was too early for him to leave her. She needed more time to prove she was worthy of his love.

The years Leah had spent on the island had nurtured in her the ability to pretend her life was as she wished it would be when reality did not suit her needs. She called upon that skill now, reinventing the truth, and was able to move through the rest of the day with remarkable composure.

Benjamin avoided Leah until it was time to meet over the last meal of the day. When he joined her at the table, she smiled at him as if nothing was amiss and began ladling the fish and potato soup into the bowls.

Having not the slightest idea how to open a conversation, or if he should open one at all, Benjamin remained mute.

All day he had been plagued by doubts, and he was no longer so pleased with his decision to leave Leah behind. A part of him was willing to accept her refusal without further argument, but to do so would be to appear weak, and he could not allow that.

They were halfway through the second course before Leah broke the silence. "I should like to begin packing tomorrow and could use your advice."

"Leah, I have given you a very good reason why you should not come with me."

"I have heard it, and I accept neither it nor your true reason, which you have yet to say."

"Which is?"

Her gaze met his. "I'm not sure, but there must be some good reason you are trying to leave me here."

"Don't give me more credit than I deserve," Benjamin advised tersely, laid low by his own deceit. "I have no *good* reason."

"Then there is no point in further argument." Leah reached for his hand and brought the palm to her lips. "When the canoe is ready, we will leave together."

"No. I am going alone."

"But why?"

"Because I am tired of your company," Benjamin shouted the words at her.

Leah stared at the remnants of her dinner, pushing a bit of carrot around on her plate. She struggled to remain calm. If he left her . . . Her mind refused to finish the thought. Why was he doing this to her? What grave offense had she committed?

She was forced to blink back the moisture forming in her eyes several times before she could raise her gaze to meet his. When she did, she spoke but a single word, "Please."

Never in his life had Benjamin heard a single syllable spoken with such anguish. He was powerless against its force. The color drained from his face.

Leah continued to stare at him, her hopes, fears, and pain reflected in her intense gaze. She did not whine or threaten or remind him that he owed her his life. She just stared in mute misery, like a dog who had been kicked by a beloved master, or a child unjustly punished for an offense she did not commit.

Benjamin knew he was defeated. He could continue to refuse absolutely, but he had not the stomach for it. "All right. You can come with me, but once we reach Victoria, we go our separate ways. Is that understood?"

She lowered her eyes as she whispered her reply, "Yes."

"Good." The legs of his chair rasped against the wooden floor as Benjamin abruptly rose. He resisted the urge to kick it.

He had bound himself to abide Leah's company a little while longer. Why? She was nothing to him. "Nothing," he spoke the word out loud. As he stared into her now upturned face, his rage at his own weakness exploded, "Damn you to hell, Leah Daniels!"

All the next day, he said not a word to her. At first, Leah feared Benjamin had changed his mind about taking her with him, but that evening as they sat in the parlor, he thrust a slip of paper in her hands.

"This is what you'll need. Don't bring anything that isn't absolutely essential. I won't tolerate sentimentality."

She nodded her willingness to comply.

"Do whatever you feel necessary to close up the house. I'll take care of everything else."

His tone was so harsh, she felt compelled to say something to soothe him. "I promise I won't get in the way."

He dropped his forehead to his hands. It had taken him all day to come to terms with her coming, and he had concluded the matter in his mind. In fairness, the decision whether to go with him or wait for a ship should have been hers from the start. He owed her that much. He was so wary of his emotions clouding his perception in her favor, he was allowing them to color his judgments in the opposite direction. He wasn't happy she was going with him, but he had decided he could live with it. His gaze instinctively sought out the comfort to be found in hers, but the moment he realized what he was doing, he quickly averted his eyes.

"I never said you would get in the way. Listen, Leah, do us both a favor and drop it. I don't want to be burdened with your gratitude, and I won't tolerate you scurrying about attempting to prove you deserve to come."

"I'll try," she promised.

"Yesterday should have never happened," he continued. "Leaving you behind was a stupid idea in the first place."

Leah wholeheartedly agreed with his last statement, and though she was curious as to what had caused his change of heart, she was prudent enough not to ask. She focused her mind on the fact that she was going and blocked out all disturbing thoughts, especially the ones conjured by Benjamin's vow to leave her once they reached Victoria.

The next three days passed quickly. While Benjamin put the finishing touches on the canoe, Leah went through the house room by room, securing windows and draping furniture.

The canoe was packed with a change of clothes, provisions, blankets, and the two chests from Jacob Daniels's study.

Though he was loath to do anything that put him any further into Leah's debt, Benjamin knew he would have to make use of the gold until his own funds could be secured. He vowed to pay back every penny with interest.

The day of their departure arrived. Leah stood on the beach, her eyes drinking in every detail of her island.

"Are you ready?"

"Yes," she replied, but her feet felt leaden and she could not move.

After waiting several minutes for her to walk towards the canoe, Benjamin gruffly asked, "What's wrong?"

Leah had no idea, so she latched on to the first logical thought she could sift from the anarchy of emotions broiling in her mind. "I'm afraid for my animals."

"We can't take them with us, and you've done all you could. They are used to fending for themselves for the most part anyway."

"Are you certain they'll be all right?"

"Yes," Benjamin assured with confidence. "Now get in the boat. We don't want to miss the tide."

Still Leah hesitated. She understood life on her island. She felt safe here. The unknown, which she had always viewed as fascinating, suddenly seemed terrifying. However her terror of being left behind was even greater.

"Well, are you coming or aren't you?" he urged.

Her gaze moved from him back to her island. Taking a deep breath, she bent down, scooped a handful of sand from the beach, and slipped it into her pocket. She faced Benjamin squarely. "Now, I'm ready."

Together they slid the heavy laden canoe into the surf. The steady slap of their wooden paddles joined the rhythmic roar of the ocean as they headed southeast, away from the island and into the open sea.

Chapter 9

Leah feared she would be overcome by her racing heart as she forced herself to dip her oar into the surf again and again. She could taste the salt spray on her trembling lips, feel the sting of the sea breeze as it blew across her skin. The roar of the ocean seemed unnaturally harsh, and when she glanced over her shoulder at her island, she had to fight a crest of panic.

For days she had thought of nothing but her need to be in the canoe when Benjamin left the island. Now she was flooded with thoughts of all that she must face, and all she had left behind.

Jonathan followed them a little way out to sea, but instinct urged him to return to the shelter of the cove where he made his home. As she watched his familiar, sleek body vanish from sight, she prayed he would soon find a mate, so he would not miss her overmuch.

Leah tried to blink back her tears, but they spilled over her eyelashes. She was glad Benjamin had his back to her and could not see her crying. She did not want him to think her ungrateful.

Letting the rhythm of the sea envelop her senses, her arms continued to ply the paddle. She lifted her face to the morning sun, soaking in its warmth as a man lost in the desert might drink at a spring. The sky was bright blue and cloudless. She watched as a gull soared overhead, with wings outstretched to catch the breeze; then, it turned and headed away from them. His distant cries marked his path as he disappeared into a dot on the horizon.

The bob of the boat had a lulling effect, and slowly her tension began to ebb.

The course Benjamin charted quickly brought them to the coast of Vancouver Island. They traveled parallel to the irregular coastline, keeping a cautious distance between themselves and the dark rocks extending from the shore into the sea. In places the cedar, spruce, and hemlock blanketing the hills grew down to the tidemark. In others, sheer rock walls towered above narrow beaches.

Once they were navigating down the coastline, Benjamin allowed his mind to drift to the woman sharing his canoe. He knew she was strong, but he had no idea how she would hold up during the journey. Today would be a test.

He was still battling conflicting emotions concerning his decision to let her come. A part of him was pleased she was here to ease the loneliness of the journey. He could use the extra time to review his lessons on the dangers of city life. However, an equally earnest part of his mind warned that each day he stayed with her gave *her* opportunity to further enmesh him in her silken web of artless devotion. An unnamed fear caused his gut to knot.

Morning turned to afternoon, and the strain of their unremitting labors began to dull Leah's senses. Benjamin had hardly spoken a word since they shoved off, but she was too tired to care. More and more frequently, she was compelled to pull her paddle from the water and allow her aching arms a brief respite.

When he finally gave the signal to put ashore, she was past the point of conscious effort. They made camp under the shelter of a stand of spruce trees, but Leah was sound asleep long before the meal of dried fish and boiled sea milkwort that Benjamin had prepared was ready.

The next morning they rose at dawn to resume their journey. Leah stood absently massaging her aching arms as she waited for the fire to heat the water for their morning tea.

"I told you it wouldn't be easy," Benjamin admonished, but there was more sympathy than rancor in his voice.

Leah smiled wanly. "I'm sure I'll get used to it. How are you feeling? I know you worked harder than I did."

"I'm bigger than you are," he replied gruffly, unwilling to admit his own arms felt like lead. They had days of paddling ahead of them, and moaning over his aches and pains would not put them any closer to their destination. "The water is ready. Why don't you make the tea, while I finish reloading the canoe?"

As soon as the ground fog lifted, they shoved off. At first Leah endeavored to make small talk, and though Benjamin responded genially to her attempts, at length she concluded it took more effort than it was worth to be heard above the thunder of the ocean.

The hours glided by in endless monotony as they

dipped their paddles into the sea. Even the majestic scenery could not bestir her senses.

Leah did not regret her decision to come, but she was disheartened by what she viewed as her own lack of endurance. If Benjamin intended to desert her in Victoria, she should be using this time to convince him otherwise. She should nurture him at the end of the day, not collapse on her pallet. Allowing her worries to distract her from the throbbing of her arms, she tried to formulate a plan of action, but nothing original came to mind.

As she sat contemplating the virtues of putting into shore early for the night, a movement on the horizon caught her attention. At first she thought it was a herd of sea lions, but as the objects came closer, they began to take on human form.

Benjamin's back stiffened.

"What is it?" Leah asked in alarm.

"Indians."

Her eyes widened. "The kind that eat people?"

"It's hard to say," he replied, then immediately regretted his honesty when his ears caught Leah's sharp intake of breath. "Let's not jump to conclusions until we find out what they're about."

She sat tensely, watching the Indians approach. With nothing but the broad expanse of Benjamin's back to guide her, she had no way of determining if he was as frightened as she.

Four canoes approached, each bearing eight men. In one stood a man holding a spear and sounding a single note which all joined, swelling it in the middle, then slowly letting it die out. Their hair was dark and worn loose and their skin pale. Though devoid of all raiment, their persons were lavishly adorned with tattooing on the back of their arms and forelegs, and an assortment of bone, feather, and copper ornaments dangling from their earlobes or piercing their hawk-shaped noses. Upon reaching them, the Indians began to paddle rapidly around and around their canoe.

"Stay calm," Benjamin ordered in a low voice, as he cautiously shifted his position to allow greater ease in communication. He managed a tight smile and nodded silent greetings at the men in the circling canoes. Leah followed suit.

Feeling thoroughly intimidated by her first contact with the larger human community, she instinctively reached for Benjamin's hand and held tight. He spared her a glance, but no more.

After what seemed an eternity, the Indians' paddles were raised from the sea, and the singing stopped.

The man holding the spear addressed foreign words to Benjamin. He replied in kind. Leah understood nothing, and her wide-eyed gaze darted between the two men. Benjamin caught the look.

"We're speaking *Chinook*. It's a pidgin language developed by the traders using words from the languages of the local tribes and a little French and English," he explained under his breath.

"What did he say?"

"He wants us to come with them to their village."

"Why?"

"I don't know the language well enough to ask," he admitted, silently cursing himself for his lack. His business dealings rarely brought him into contact with the Indian population, and there were wide chasms in his knowledge of their language and culture. He had

116

made the effort to study the the available literature, but he was not all that confident of the reliability of his sources. Trappers and missionaries alike brought their own brand of bias to their accounts of their encounters with the Indians.

He wasn't even sure with which tribe he was dealing, though the style of the canoes and their location on the coast led him to believe them to be Nootka.

He was feeling as wary as Leah, but he knew enough to cultivate an aura of calm confidence. A display of fear always put one at a disadvantage, whether dealing with naked savages or tailor-dressed nobility.

He squeezed Leah's fingers tightly in warning. "Try to look relaxed and friendly," he whispered. "We have no choice but to follow them to shore, and I don't want to borrow trouble. Just follow my lead, and try not to make any sudden moves."

Leah nodded her assent.

Benjamin said something to the leader of the group; then, he dipped his paddle into the water and began rowing towards the shoreline. The Indians kept close.

As they approached the beach, the first thing to come into view was a fifteen-foot-high pair of male and female greeting figures. Carved of wood and huge in proportion, they stood like waiting parents with outstretched arms.

Even before they put to shore, Leah's attention was caught up by the profusion of new sights and sounds, and for a few minutes she was too absorbed to remember to feel frightened.

The Indians' summer camp was bustling with activity. Women stood over fires tending pots with unknown contents. Others sat on mats weaving conical

117

hats from strips of cedar bark. Still others tended row upon row of candlefish, drying them under the late summer sun. The women wore aprons of shredded cedar bark that reached to their knees and decorative bands about their wrists and ankles. Long earrings dangled from their earlobes, and many were tattooed similarly to the men.

Youngsters ran to and fro, bare and carefree. She could hear their laughter. Leah was intrigued by her first glimpse of children. They moved so fast, and they were so tiny. She wanted to touch them and hold them in her arms, but instead she stood obediently by Benjamin's side.

Her eyes drifted to the row of houses. Framed with cedar posts, the wooden siding was tied on. The roof boards were loose and inclined slightly. Near the doorway, heavy support posts were carved with a variety of human and animal faces. Painted in red, black, and blue green, their features were simplified and violently dramatic. As she gazed at them, the fingers of fear crept back up her spine.

Many of the villagers had ceased their labors and come for a closer look at the two strangers. Though the village was comprised of less than two hundred, Leah felt overwhelmed by the sea of humanity. She focused her gaze on a small boy standing near the edge of the crowd, in hopes of steadying her nerves, but when their eyes met, he made a fierce face and shook a stick at her. Her gaze quickly moved past him, alighting upon a tall, blank-faced man. In his hand he held a staff. Dangling from the gnarled tip was a human skull. A tiny squeal escaped her lips.

The villagers were staring at them with an intensity of unreadable intent. She raised her eyes to Benjamin for direction. He stood ramrod straight, staring back at the Indians with equal concentration. Try as she might, she could not muster an expression of like potency. It was all she could do not to take to her heels and make a dash for the cover of the forest.

The tension was unbearable. The man with the staff moved a step closer, and Leah fought the scream of terror rising in her throat. Then their collective regard shifted in mass to the sky. Leah's gaze followed theirs to a raven soaring overhead. It circled once, twice, spiraling downward until it fluttered to a halt upon her shoulder.

A reverent murmur passed through the crowd, and their cold stares became expressions of awe.

Leah glanced at the raven from the corner of her eye. She did not recognize him, but she sensed his presence had somehow eliminated the danger, and she accepted his assistance with a whispered word of thanks.

He remained on her shoulder a moment longer, then took to wing.

The murmur of the crowd grew to an excited roar as the villagers shouted *huacas!* again and again. They swept Leah and Benjamin towards the largest of the cedar houses, ushering them inside, amid much animated chatter. The owner of the house made a long speech; then, suddenly they were left alone.

"They're not going to hurt us," Leah stated as she turned her attention to Benjamin. He was watching her with the same veneration she had seen in the eyes of the Indians.

"Why do you look at me that way?"

"Because you may very well have saved our lives."

"But I did nothing."

"These Indians regard the raven as sacred. They believe it was he who created man. How one of the birds from the island found you here, I don't know, but I'm glad he chose this moment to repay whatever favor you have done him."

"But he's not from the island. At least, I didn't recognize him," she reflected.

Benjamin's expression remained reverent. "Then you must have earned the devotion of a guardian angel."

His willingness to credit her with more sway than she felt she possessed made Leah uneasy, and she purposefully turned her attention to more earthborn matters, while she thought about what he had said.

Her gaze drifted about the dwelling. The center of the house held a large sunken room with a fire pit. An adjustable space in the roofing planks allowed for the smoke to escape. Surrounding this central area on three sides was a wide wooden ledge, divided into sections by cedar bark mats. Ornately carved storage boxes lined many of the walls.

"Do you really think they would have hurt us?" she mused out loud.

"I don't know," Benjamin answered truthfully. "Generally the local Indians war among themselves and leave the white man alone, but we are a long way from a settlement, and we are only two. They might have been tempted to avenge some of the wrong done them, or we may merely have been objects of curiosity. It doesn't really matter now. The raven has shown his approval of you. There is no longer any need to fear for our safety."

"What do we do now?"

"We stay here and wait. That much of that speech I understood. I believe they are planning some kind of celebration. Tonight we will accept whatever hospitality they have to offer, but in the morning, we will have to find a way to make them understand that we must leave."

It was dark by the time their Indian host came to fetch them. Leah had fallen into exhausted slumber listening to Benjamin explain what he knew of the social structure of the tribe. The nap had done wonders, and she felt refreshed and eager to enjoy the hospitality of these strange yet fascinating people.

They were escorted to a bonfire where the residents of the village were already gathered. The moment they were seated, great quantities of food began to be served. Leah was always offered the wooden trencher first, then Benjamin, before the others were served. They were served whale blubber, salmon, smoked herring roe, and dried fish. Bowls of wild berries followed. Eulachon oil was drunk like wine.

There was an air of friendly festivity among the crowd. Leah willingly ate the food she recognized and nibbled at the unfamiliar. She noticed Benjamin did likewise. She was soon sated, but more food kept being pressed upon them.

She tried to politely decline, but her efforts only earned her a collective scowl.

"You're insulting them," Benjamin offered an explanation for their hosts' reactions. "To refuse an offer of food or a gift shames your host. They gain prestige in

121

the eyes of their tribesmen by displays of generosity."

Leah had no desire to insult or shame anyone, and she forced herself to pinch another finger full of fish from the trough. The feasting continued for what seemed hours, Leah politely accepting whatever was put before her, until she began to fear she would be ill. Already a few of the guests had made hasty exits to the bushes to purge the contents of their stomachs. No one seemed the least concerned, and always the afflicted returned a few moments later to rejoin the meal.

She turned to Benjamin for guidance. He was looking a bit peaked himself. "Do we really have to keep eating?" she asked in a plaintive tone. He nodded morosely to her, then quickly smiled at their hosts.

Much to Leah's relief the trenchers were finally cleared away. The music of a pea whistle joined the babble of the crowd.

Leah started as a loud cry rent the night air. Three men jumped into the center circle, shaking bird-shaped rattles and strewing the air with white down as they crouched and sprang into the air, turning tight circles as they danced around the fire.

Their faces and bodies were painted white, black, and red, with designs imitative of the carved house poles. A hush fell over the crowd.

The dancers were shortly joined by a fourth. Dressed in a costume of shredded bark, with a wooden mask depicting a dark bird with a huge beak, he crouched low to the ground, turning his head with sudden jerks to the left and right. He swooped and spun, pulling the strings hidden under his mantle of bark to open and close the beak, producing a loud clattering. Leah recognized the face within as belonging to the man whose home they shared.

A group of men and women began to sing, their voices harmonizing as they told the tale of the raven in words neither Leah nor Benjamin understood.

The bright colors, the flicker of the fire, the chanting, Leah found herself captured by the pulse of the ceremony, and she smiled broadly when the raven dancer *flew* in her direction.

She hesitated but a moment before accepting the raven's invitation to join him in his dance. The singers voiced their approval by escalating the volume of their song.

Her heart pounding with excitement, Leah did her utmost to mimic the steps of the dance. Her wool skirt swirled about her ankles as she and the raven danced around and around each other and the fire.

Benjamin watched Leah and the Indian dancer with a mixture of envy and pride. Envy for the free spirit that allowed her to accept a foreign culture without judgement. Pride that he could call her his friend.

Though he was entertained by the spectacle, he could not dismiss a lingering ill-ease. They were clearly the guests of honor, but he knew too little of the culture to predict with any accuracy what would happen next. Did the dance have some significance beyond entertainment? He certainly hoped not, as he had not a sufficient grasp on the language to explain Leah's ignorance or his own.

He also had more material concerns. Their canoe held the treasure from Leah's father's study, and theft was an everpresent danger; however, he didn't know how to return to check the contents of the canoe without arousing the suspicion of their hosts. Besides, if the money was going to be stolen, there was little they could do about it. Two against two hundred were suicidal odds.

Trusting in fate to provide a benign outcome to this encounter was not within his power to do, but after inventorying his other options, Benjamin accepted that he had no other choice. The muscles of his face hardened, but he kept his sociable smile firmly in place.

Much to his relief, Leah was returned to his side when the dance ended. She was breathless and flushed from exertion, but no harm had befallen her.

Other masked dancers took center stage, and the tribe's people who shared their crest provided a vocal backdrop for their stylized movements.

"This is all very exciting, don't you think?" Leah commented when she had caught her breath. "I don't think we ever had any reason to fear them. Indians are very nice people."

"I prefer to remain cautious, and you would do well to do likewise," Benjamin advised. "The evening isn't over yet."

She frowned at his words. Raising her hand to his cheek, she attempted to stroke away the tension in his jaw. He endured her attentions with ill-concealed annoyance.

"I think you worry unduly," Leah said. "Perhaps if you were invited to join in a dance, you would feel better."

Shackling her wrist in his hand, he pushed it to her lap. "I have no desire to prance about the beach like a crazed chicken. Now watch the dancers and stop chattering at me."

The evening's festivities lasted late into the night.

Several groups performed, each dance pivoting around a specific animal. Only certain tribe members were allowed to participate, depending on the animal being honored.

When the last dance was performed, and the rattles and pea whistles grew silent, Leah and Benjamin were escorted back to the house of the raven dancer. There they were shown into one of the sleeping cubicles partitioned from the main room with mats. The owner, his wife, and children retired to another cubicle, and the remaining compartments were soon filled by various other family members.

Leah lay awake in Benjamin's arms, listening to the shuffling of feet and the sound of the surf. The hoot of an owl was presently joined by a nasal snore. A child whimpered softly.

Though she could not see his face in the darkness, she knew Benjamin was still awake also. She snuggled closer, pillowing her head upon his chest. Long before he closed his eyes, she had drifted into a peaceful sleep.

The next morning Benjamin and Leah were showered with gifts of food and blankets and allowed to depart without incident.

A pair of canoes escorted them a short distance from the village before turning back.

The sky was a brilliant blue, but by noon it had begun to fill with ominous black clouds, blotting out the sun. The waves took on the color of the sky.

"We best put to shore," Benjamin called over his shoulder as the first droplets of rain pelted the canoe. A gust of wind snatched away her words of reply, and after donning the oilskins they had scavenged from her father's sea chest, they both put their full energies into paddling the canoe to land.

Before they had gone more than a few yards, the storm was upon them full force. The canoe bounced and bobbed rolling from side to side along the crests of the ever-rising waves. Leah tried to focus her eyes on the tree-lined shore ahead of her, but the rolling of the horizon made her nauseous. She could hear Benjamin shouting instructions at her, but she could not make out the meaning of the words over the roar of the sea.

As they neared the shore, jagged black rocks rose to the surface of the water, hungry to taste the bottom of their craft. A loud thwack vibrated the air as the side of the canoe hit something solid, and the craft rolled wildly.

Leah didn't have time to be frightened. It took every ounce of her strength and determination to keep the canoe upright and headed toward the beach. Time lost meaning as they fought the waves.

As they pitched about in the foam, the only thing that anchored Leah's world was the sight of Benjamin's broad back before her. The muscles of his arms strained to pull the paddle through the water. His perspiration mixed freely with the rain.

Finally, their ears were greeted by the blessed sound of the hull scraping against the sand of the beach. Hauling the canoe beyond the reach of the waves, they expelled a mutual sigh of relief.

"Rest here while I search out a shelter," Benjamin shouted above the wind.

Leah nodded her reply, too spent to do otherwise. She closed her eyes against the sting of the rain as he started off down the beach.

A short time later he returned. "There's a cavern up ahead in those rocks."

Without further instructions, Leah untied the rope that held the tarp protecting their belongings, lifted an armload of provisions from the canoe, and started in the direction he had just come from. Benjamin followed, carrying the chest of gold.

The cave had been beaten out of the rock by waves of a long-ago age. It was wide and shallow, but deep enough to provide protection from the wind and rain, and high enough to allow ample room to stand upright. The walls sloped at odd angles, but the floor was relatively level. Leah voiced her approval before returning to the canoe for a second load.

It took several trips to empty the canoe of their belongings. They dragged the craft further inland to be sure it wouldn't be endangered by the high tide, then flipped it over.

Benjamin ran his hand over the hull, checking for damage. The collision with the rock had left a deep scar, but the integrity of the canoe had not been compromised.

Returning to the cave, their first order of business was starting a fire. While Leah shredded bits of cloth from a dry petticoat, Benjamin gathered armloads of driftwood. The wood steamed as it took to flame, but the core was sufficiently dry to sustain a fire.

The bulk of their belongings had miraculously escaped the crashing waves, but the clothes on Leah's back clung to her skin, abetting the chill in her bones. After spreading blankets by the fire, Leah began stripping off her dank garments, laying them out on the rocks to dry.

The sight of her naked, moist flesh glowing in the firelight wet Benjamin's appetite. He told himself it would be cruel to put upon her after the physical strain of outrunning the storm, but despite his good intentions, when he removed his own damp clothing, his desires were obvious.

Leah laughed.

"We don't have to just because I want to," he mumbled in embarrassment.

"I know." She smiled as she stepped into his arms. "But it has been days, and we really don't have anything better to do while we wait out the storm. Do we?"

He needed no further urging.

"Why are you always so willing to please me?" he mused out loud as he lowered her to the blankets.

A thoughtful expression passed over Leah's face. "I don't know," she replied between impassioned kisses. "Does there have to be a reason?"

Benjamin trailed his lips from the base of her throat to the swell of one ripe breast. Her skin was like silk, and as she wrapped herself around him, he couldn't muster the strength to answer.

Outside the storm raged. The sound of the wind harmonized with the sea in a symphony of savagery.

Within the cave, a tempest of another sort reflected the mood of nature. Having been almost engulfed by the pounding waves, their lovemaking became a celebration of life. Each kiss sweeter than any that had gone before, each caress warmer because it had almost been lost to them.

When they had sated their hunger, they slept.

For two days the storm imprisoned them in the cavern, but for both it was a welcome respite. There was nothing to do but eat and sleep and love each other.

Benjamin refused to recognize his need for the comfort to be found in Leah's embrace as anything but lust, but as he held her in his arms, it was with great tenderness, and when he slept, he allowed himself to dream idyllic dreams of the future. Always Leah was there by his side, smiling up at him with her heart in her eyes. He never remembered his dreams when he woke, only the feeling of warmth and contentment.

Leah was ever-cognizant of Benjamin's vow to leave her once they reached Victoria, but it was easy to believe it was an idle threat when they clung together in feverish embrace. Try as she might, she could not convince herself that he felt nothing for her, as he was wont to claim. He had changed his mind about leaving her on the island; he would change his mind again.

The morning the sun broke through the clouds dawned foggy and cold, but by the time they had put away the breakfast dishes, the sky had turned azure blue and not a cloud was in sight.

Loading the canoe, they set off.

The rest had done her tired muscles good, and Leah found herself able to concentrate on the scenery. In the distance, to the south, they could see a huge, spired rock pillar rising one hundred and fifty-seven feet into the air. Benjamin explained that they were entering the Straits of Juan de Fuca, but they shared little other conversation.

Leah idly wondered what they would encounter today. Judging by the first leg of their journey, she fully expected to be called to face some sort of challenge.

The day passed without adventure, as did the next and the next. The only thing to distinguish one day from another was that each morning they started a little later, and each afternoon they put into shore a little earlier. Benjamin was compulsive with his explanations of tidal currents, wind factors, and weather conditions, as if daring her to oppose his will.

Leah accepted his decisions without question. Though she longed for a proper bath and a fresh change of clothing, extending their journey assured them more time together. She found herself constantly wavering between the fear that he would abandon her once they reached Victoria, and faith that he would stay with her. His frequent mention of his plans to leave did little to bolster her confidence.

Benjamin excused his lack of enthusiasm for ending their journey as concern for Leah's health, telling himself it would be unwise to have her arrive in Victoria too spent to deal effectively with the demands of city life.

In his more honest moments, he admitted to himself that though he was truly concerned he not push her too hard, his real worry was that the innocent Leah he had come to know would soon become jaded and lost to him. In a way, he felt like an executioner, bringing her into the world. Though he knew she must if she was to survive, he didn't want her to change. It was a unpalatable dilemma, and one he had no hope of resolving. So, he drew out their journey to postpone the inevitable.

It had been over two weeks since they had left the

island, and as Benjamin banked the fire for the evening, he knew this would be their last night alone together. His hungry gaze roamed over Leah as she bent to spread their bedding. As if sensing his look, she straightened and walked into his arms.

It suddenly occurred to him how rarely he had had to ask Leah to make love to him. She always seemed to know when he needed her. His need of her now was intense, spurred by the knowledge that after tonight, he could never have her again. Not unless he was willing to commit himself to her for life, *and he was not.* The married state was not something to which he aspired. Besides, once Leah had a chance to meet other men, her affection for him would evaporate like a cloud of steam. She would realize she deserved better than him. His thoughts induced a wave of pain.

Cradling her face in his hands, he lowered his lips to hers, intent on making this one last time together worthy of memory.

Their lips met, tongues caressing as they slowly lowered to the bed of blankets, shedding their clothes as they descended. Above, the stars twinkled through the branches of the trees. Below, the musty scent of earth filled their nostrils. The light of the fire reflected off their bare skin, painting them golden.

Leah, if I could love any woman, it would be you. Fearing he had spoken the words out loud, Benjamin started.

"What is it?" she asked, rotating her head from side to side as her eyes scanned the tree line.

Benjamin immediately relaxed when he realized he had not betrayed himself. "It's nothing." He smoothed the hair from her cheek. "Nothing at all." Before she could form any further questions, he covered her lips with his, devouring them with a hunger that distracted her from thought.

He caressed her skin with infinite tenderness, trailing his fingers down the inside of her arm to the curve of her hip. His lips followed his hand, tasting the salt of her skin as his nose drew in heady whiffs of her scent.

His teeth found the arch of her foot, sending chills from the tips of her toes to the top of her head. Leah pulled him up, rolling until she sat atop him. Lowering herself, she teased his chest with her breasts as she massaged the muscles of his shoulders.

Their lips met again and again as their bodies molded to each other. He suckled at her breast while she rained reverent kisses upon his head. The heat of their bodies matched that of the fire as they stroked every inch of each other's flesh.

Parting her thighs, Leah urged him to enter her. She arched against his body, pulling him deeply within her. They moved as one with slow, fluid movements to the beat of a primitive dance, evoking all that was earthly to join in exaltation with the divine, making love in its purest form.

They did not cease until they were both physically and spiritually exhausted. They slept entwined in each other's arms.

It was still dark when Benjamin awoke. He felt restless and cautiously rose to add more fuel to the fire. Despite his care, when he returned to the bed, he could see the flames reflected in Leah's eyes. She opened her arms to welcome him back to their pallet.

He nestled in her embrace, but when she parted her lips, he pulled away. His eyes met hers as he was assaulted by a jarring thought. Every time they made love, there was the possibility he could get her with child. At first he hadn't cared, but he was no longer completely indifferent to her fate.

He'd been lucky so far. He didn't want to leave her with any unnecessary encumbrances. Why he'd ignored the issue this long was a mystery to him, but with Victoria looming on the horizon, he could no longer block it from his mind. It was past time they had a serious discussion.

Sitting up on the bed of blankets, he took her hand in his. "Leah, you shouldn't let me make love to you."

Her brows knit together in surprise and confusion. "Why not?"

"Because what we do might lead to the creation of a child. You wouldn't want that."

Her eyes began to twinkle in delight at the thought. "I would be greatly honored to have your child."

"No, you wouldn't," he gently rebuked. "If my calculations are correct, we will arrive in Victoria tomorrow, and it is very important that you understand about men. If you let them, they will take advantage of you, and your reputation will be ruined."

She nestled against his legs. "I'm not sure I understand."

"Ladies do not make love to men unless they are married to them. Society is not tolerant of indiscretions." He cleared his throat. "If you make love to me or any other man, people will not like you."

"Would you still like me?"

"That is neither here nor there."

"Your opinion matters very much to me," Leah argued.

Resorting to his teacher's voice, he stated, "You're getting off the subject. If you like me, you will find the men of Victoria far more tempting. They are practiced in the art of wooing, whereas I rarely make the effort to be nice to you. You must restrain yourself and keep them at bay."

She yawned. "I don't mind in the least denying other men, but I don't think I could be happy without your physical affections. Even if I could, I shouldn't like to try."

Benjamin frowned at her. Maybe he should take up the matter one point at a time. His eyes ran over her supple flesh, draped only by the diaphanous mantle of her hair, and he swallowed hard. He was reasonably sure he could depend on his own restraint, so he would concentrate on protecting Leah from the *gentlemen* of Victoria first. They were the real threat, as he would not be there more than a day or two. "I don't think I am making myself clear," he began. "Society relegates women to two categories—good women and bad women. Those who are judged as good have nice houses, fancy clothes, and the respect of society. They don't make love. Those who are judged bad are free with their favors. Men pretend to like them, but they only want to use them. They leave them to die in the streets."

Leah sat up in alarm, instinctively clutching his hand. "Are you going to leave me to die in the streets?"

He averted his eyes. "No. I will see you are well situated before I go."

His words and actions gave little comfort; nevertheless, she did not retreat from the topic. "But you're a man."

134

"Our situation is different. We were thrown together on your island. If we had met somewhere else, I would never have taken you to bed."

"Then I'm glad we met on my island," Leah stated vehemently.

"You aren't even trying to understand, are you?" He groaned as he faced her once more. "If I was a gentleman, I wouldn't have made love to you on the island either. But I'm not a gentleman. I used you."

Capturing his other hand, Leah cradled them both against her breasts. Her eyes met his, willing him to listen to her words, not only with his ears and mind, but with his heart. "No. I want you just as badly as you want me. There is nothing wrong in what we do."

"You're making this very difficult."

"I'm sorry, but I am not going to agree with you when I know you are mistaken."

"I have been in the world. You have not," he argued.

"That doesn't make you right about everything."

He could feel himself being pulled under her spell, and his voice became harsh. "So you will make your debut in Victoria by falling into the bed of every bloke who asks you to spread your legs for him. The women will shun you, the men will laugh behind your back, and all your money won't do you a whit of good. I applaud your stupidity."

"I already told you, I won't let any man but *you* touch me," Leah reminded, her intense gaze never wavering. "And please don't yell at me."

"I want to yell at you."

"Why?"

"I don't know and I don't care. I just don't want you getting hurt!"

135

"Is that what this is all about?" she asked in bemusement.

"Yes," Benjamin admitted morosely.

Leah smiled, looping her arms around his neck as she pillowed her head against his chest. "How very lovely. I knew you were mistaken when you said you didn't care for me."

Victoria

Chapter 10

The midday sun shone brightly on the waters as Benjamin and Leah paddled past the plastered brick tower of Race Rocks Lighthouse and turned into Victoria Harbor. Dense stands of oak and willow mixed with fern and hazel thickets on either side, but Leah was oblivious to the local flora.

All around them boats of every size and description plied the waters. Sleek sailboats glided alongside canoes, barges, and rowboats. A weather-ravaged schooner headed past them toward the open waters. Another large ship rocked calmly in its berth, belching white clouds of steam at irregular intervals.

Leah's gaze moved past the docks and riveted on the buildings ringing the Inner Harbor. Stone and brick warehouses squatted near the water's edge.

The business district began near the wharves and was mostly built of weather-beaten wood with an occasional brick structure. Painted signs advertising the services and merchandise available rose above the roof lines or hung from second-story balconies. Plank sidewalks provided protection for the pedestrians traveling the dirt and gravel-paved streets.

Radiating from the business district, the two-story wooden homes of the residents filled the landscape. Some were plain; others were decorated with barge-board and topped with finials. Many were surrounded by tidy flower and vegetable gardens.

The streets were alive with activity. Men and women bustled this way and that. Children played in the streets. Heavily muscled horses pulled wagonloads of goods, creating clouds of dust in their wake.

The population was composed of humans of every conceivable size, shape, and color. A man as black as night strode the ridge of one roof, a chimney brush in his hand. On the sidewalk below stood a cherub-faced fellow with fat ruddy cheeks, and a belly that strained to equate his girth with his height. An appropriately round hat topped his head. A group of three, tiny, dark-pigtailed men with amber complexions and almond eyes scurried down another avenue.

The women were dressed in ankle-length gowns of gray, blue, lilac . . . every color of the rainbow. Their bodices were fitted; their skirts full and bustled. Most wore modest bonnets, which they secured to their heads with soft scarves tied under the chin.

The dress of the children reflected that of the adults, except the hemlines of their skirts and trousers were shorter.

What impressed Leah most was the sheer volume of people. So many in one place boggled the mind.

She glanced at Benjamin. She no longer feared he would leave her the moment they docked. He had spent the better part of the morning repeating his warnings about the wiles of men, and explaining their personal sleeping arrangements once they reached Victoria. Separate beds and separate rooms. She was not at all fond of the idea, but his words did confirm her faith that they would remain together, at least a little while longer, allowing her to completely surrender herself to the excitement of the day.

They had reached the dock, and a word from Benjamin elicited the help of a tall, blond man in securing their craft. His sturdy blouse and breeches named him a common laborer. When he offered his work-roughened hand to assist Leah from the boat, she readily accepted. "Thank you." She met his gaze and smiled warmly.

"You're very welcome." He winked, returning her smile. His face registered pleasant surprise when she echoed his wink. "Where do you come from? I don't recognize you from these parts."

"The lady has been residing on an island west of here, and she doesn't talk to strangers," Benjamin supplied the answer. "Off with you."

"No need to be surly, mate. I was just trying to make polite conversation."

"Well, make it elsewhere."

"Benjamin, there is no need to be angry with him," Leah interjected. "He said nothing about wanting me in his bed. And even if he did, I would have remembered to say no thank you."

The dockhand's eyes widened, and his smile stretched into a capacious grin.

"Leah," Benjamin growled at her.

"Did I say something wrong?"

"Don't talk to strangers. In fact, don't talk at all," he

instructed through clenched teeth. His expression was lethal as he turned it on the other man. He pressed a gold coin into his palm.

"I didn't hear the lady say a thing," the fellow assured him as he pocketed the coin, his once merry mien suitably somber.

"I'm glad we understand each other."

Benjamin grabbed Leah by the arm and pulled her in his wake. "We are going to hire a coach to take us to the hotel. Come along."

A conveyance was secured almost immediately, and she stood, lips compressed, while Benjamin and the driver loaded their belongings.

When she glanced over her shoulder, she noticed the man on the dock was gone and she dismissed him from her mind, turning her attention to the horse within arms' reach. She had seen drawings of the animals in her father's books, but they had ill-prepared her for the size and majesty of the beast. Leah stroked the sleek, black coat, murmuring words of praise to the horse.

"You like old Blackie, do you?" the driver commented, with obvious pleasure in her interest. "Best city horse I've had. Takes a regular riot to spook him."

Leah nodded and smiled her reply, her eyes meeting his directly. She didn't want to disobey Benjamin's directive to keep silent, especially if this kind, old gentleman would bear the brunt of his ire. The exchange with the dockhand had left her thoroughly bemused, but it was clear to her that Benjamin was in another one of his churlish moods, and she felt obligated to protect the citizenry of Victoria from it.

Benjamin frowned at her as he helped her up into the

carriage. Didn't she realize her open, friendly manner put her in danger of being accosted by riffraff? . . . Of course she didn't, he chided himself. Last night's lesson and this morning's lecture on the evils of men had been too little too late. He had been remiss in his duties.

A disgruntled groan accompanied the realization that he would probably be forced to stay by her side a little longer than he had planned. He had to teach her how to protect herself in *all* situations before he could feel comfortable leaving her. He groaned again, wondering—not for the first time—why he couldn't have washed up on any other island besides hers.

Leah was too busy absorbing the cornucopia of new sights and sounds to pay more than cursory attention to his grumbling. Craning her neck this way then that, she strained to glimpse the merchandise displayed in the shop windows. Every sign was read; every street lamp noted. She smiled at everyone they passed.

The crunch of gravel greeted her ears as they turned on to Fort Street; then, they were again on a dirt roadway. A few minutes more and they came to a halt before an imposing building on the corner of Broad and View streets.

The Driad Hotel rose three stories into the sky and was topped with a mansard roof. Long, arched windows on the street level twinkled in the sunlight. A porte cochere extended from one brick wall, allowing patrons to alight from their vehicles unsullied in foul weather. The driver pulled their carriage beneath the overhang.

Benjamin stepped down, turning to help Leah to the ground. He fished in his pocket for another coin, grimacing at his forced extravagance. As soon as he had Leah safely closeted in her hotel room, his first order of business would be to visit a bank to deposit her funds, and exchange some of the gold coins for pocket money.

"Thank you for the pleasant ride." Leah's compliment to their driver intruded upon his thoughts.

The man doffed his top hat and grinned broadly, but before he gave voice to a reply, Benjamin pressed his payment into his palm and his attention was diverted. "Sir?" He stared, dumbfounded, at the ten-dollar gold piece.

"I expect you to be available to drive the lady and myself when we need transport. I assume *that*," he indicated the coin with a tilt of his head, "will be sufficient to retain your services."

"Yes, sir, more than sufficient. Just send out word you need William Barnes, and I'll be here lickety-split." His curious expression plainly showed he thought the gold coin in his hand at odds with the couple's weather-ravaged dress.

"Is there something you have to say, man?" Benjamin's tone and visage made it clear questions would not be welcome.

"No, sir."

"Good. Now, help me carry in our baggage, and you may be on your way. Be back here in thirty minutes."

Leah followed behind the two men, her eyes never still. Her gaze darted from this sight to that as she tried to drink in everything at once.

The interior of the hotel was as elegant as the exterior. Chandeliers hung from the ceiling. Wainscoting and paper covered the walls. A knee-high,

144

brass spitton gleamed in the corner next to a potted plant.

The idea of bringing the forest indoors tickled her, and she started to giggle.

"What's so funny?" Benjamin asked.

"I was just thinking how very odd it is that city people cut down the trees on the outside, then try to grow new ones inside."

Having never stopped to contemplate such matters, Benjamin let a noncommittal *uh* service for a reply. He dismissed her and addressed the man standing behind the large counter. "I would like two rooms. One for the lady and one for myself."

Leah quelled her disapproval, reminding herself that she should be grateful Benjamin was staying at all.

The desk clerk ran his skeptical gaze over the pair, but his dubious perusal was halted by the clink of golden coins on the counter. He straightened to attention.

"Yes, sir. And how long would you like to stay with us?"

"The lady will be leaving as soon as she can secure private accommodation. I am undecided how long I will stay."

"We are here to serve your convenience," the clerk assured him.

Leah listened to the exchange in fascination, noting for the third time in the space of their arrival how the appearance of gold molded men's attitudes. It seemed to be the accepted way of getting a person to do what you wanted him to do. Benjamin had told her she was rich, but until now she hadn't been quite sure what that meant. Now that she did, she was happy to find herself so well situated.

A porter approached to take charge of their belongings. Benjamin relinquished all but the two trunks housing the gold and stock certificates.

Leah held back the thousand questions on the tip of her tongue as she was ushered toward the staircase. When they were alone, she was determined to satisfy her questions, but she knew from experience that Benjamin would not cooperate if she annoyed him by ignoring his advice to be silent now.

Their rooms were located on the second floor. The porter opened the door to Leah's first. It boasted a double bed, mirrored dresser, and armoire. A gold brocade, upholstered chair sat near the fireplace.

"It's very lovely," Leah commented as she stepped over the threshold.

"Thank you—"

"Miss Daniels," Benjamin supplied the missing name as he indicated which bundles should be left with Leah. He then turned his attention to her. "I'm going out as soon as I'm settled in my own room. Stay here, and don't open the door to anyone but me."

"But what am I to do with myself?" she protested.

"Take a nap."

"I'm too excited to sleep. Can't I go with you?"

His brow furled at her eager expression. "No. It will be easier to conduct business without you tagging along. There will be plenty of time to see the sights . . . *later.*"

"I could have a bath sent up," the porter offered his condolences. "I know my missus thinks there's no better way to while away the time than soaking in a

146

good hot bath."

"Miss Daniels thinks that is an excellent idea," Benjamin answered for her.

Although Leah was not adverse to washing away the grime of their journey, she was fast becoming impatient with Benjamin's habit of answering questions directed at her. She might be a little inexperienced with dealing with the outside world, but she was capable of more than standing mutely in the corner. "A bath would be very nice and," she turned her head so only Benjamin could see her wrinkle her nose at him, "a box of chocolates, please."

"Yes, Miss. I'll have both sent up, as soon as I have the gentleman settled."

William Barnes was waiting under the porte cochere when Benjamin stepped out of the hotel, a trunk under each arm. "Take me to the Bank of British Columbia," he directed as he settled himself into the carriage.

Less than an hour in the city had Benjamin thoroughly convinced his services as a mentor would be needed more than for a day or two. It would probably take a good month before he could trust Leah on her own. That would delight her to no end, he was sure, but he wasn't certain he was going to tell her of his change of plans. He didn't want her becoming any more dependent on him than she was already.

A few minutes later he was entering the bank. He accompanied his request to see the manager with the information he would like to make a large deposit. Not only did it assure he would receive prompt service, but it would grease the gossip wheels. Older societies might

147

require noble birth as an entrance into polite circles, but Victoria was still young enough that money spoke louder than blood. Though he personally had no use for the upper crust, he wanted Leah to associate with the right people. It afforded a woman a certain safety. He plotted his strategy out in his mind. Let the town know she had money, be seen in the right places, and it wouldn't be long before the invitations started arriving at her doorstep.

At this point, his thoughts of Leah's future brought a scowl to his face. A suitable marriage was the next logical step. He didn't plan to be around to witness the nuptials, but he would make it clear to any fortune-hunting beaus that he was not adverse to cracking their heads should they try to offer Leah false affections.

"Captain Keaton." The sound of his name being called brought his musings to a halt. "This way, please."

"I would like to open an account in the name of Leah Daniels." He set the two chests on the desk and unlocked the lids. "The gold should present no problem, but the stocks are a different matter. They are in her father's name. The man has not been seen in over three years and is presumed dead, but I'm sure there are certain legalities that must be met."

It was over two hours before Benjamin left the bank a satisfied man. In addition to tending Leah's financial future, he had arranged for some of his own funds to be transferred from his bank in San Francisco, and obtained the name of a reputable real estate agent.

He had three more stops he wanted to make before returning to the hotel. The first was at a tailor shop to obtain a suit of clothes capable of cultivating a

148

gentlemanly image. The second was at the bathhouse, and the third was at a dress shop. Necessity had demanded Leah leave her wardrobe behind, and he didn't want her roaming the streets until she was properly attired.

For now, one dress would do. Tomorrow he would take her to be fitted for a more complete wardrobe.

He set about the tasks he had set for himself with businesslike efficiency; however, dusk cloaked the city by the time he stepped back through the doors of the Driad Hotel. Dressed in a new suit of black wool with matching bowler perched upon his head, he held a large package under his arm. He went directly to Leah's room and knocked softly on the door.

It opened before his knuckles had a chance to rap the wood a second time.

"Finally," Leah exclaimed as she tried to usher him into the room. He stood firm in the doorway.

"I told you not to open the door for anyone but me, and here you are flinging open the door without question," he scolded.

"But it's you."

"You didn't know that."

"Yes, I did."

"And how is that possible?"

"I was watching for you out the window; then, I recognized the sound of your footsteps in the hall. I like the new clothes. They make you look very elegant. Can we go out now?"

"Not until you change." He thrust the package into her hands.

"A dress?" she guessed at the contents and received a nod in reply. "Come in while I change, and tell me all

149

about everything you have seen and done."

"I can't come in."

"Why not?"

"It wouldn't look proper. I've explained this all before."

Leah sighed in exasperation. "You said we couldn't sleep in the same room, and I've tried to accept that, but you said nothing about visiting each other. You have seen me change a hundred times. I don't see what all the fuss is about."

After covertly checking the hall to be sure no one was about, Benjamin stepped into the room and closed the door firmly behind him. He noted the empty chocolate box laying on the bed with wry amusement.

Leah slipped her arms around his neck, molding her lips passionately to his as she pressed her body enthusiastically against him. "I missed you."

Ignoring the surge of heat afflicting his loins, he firmly set her away, a determined expression on his face. "That's not why I came in, and I am only going to stay a minute. I just don't want the whole world listening into our conversation," he rebuked in low tones. "You have to stop talking about our relationship as openly as other people speak of the weather."

"Why?"

"Because you embarrass yourself with your free tongue."

"I don't feel embarrassed."

"The point is: you should." He began to pace. "I know this is partly my fault. I should have spent less time teaching you how to negotiate in the marketplace and more time on social amenities, but dammit, I didn't know you were going to be so thick-skulled."

Leah shook her head at him. "I'm only being honest."

"You don't always have to say what you think."

"Then how will my friends know my opinions?"

"You don't have any friends," he reminded.

"Yes, I do. There is Mr. Barnes, the man at the dock, the porter, the man at the desk downstairs, a full score of people I waved at from my window this afternoon, and, of course, you."

"I am the only one on the list who even comes close to qualifying, and that is all the more reason you should listen to me. I'm saying this for your benefit, not mine."

She smiled wanly. "You really are upset, aren't you?"

"Hell, yes. The first time in my life I care a whit about protecting a woman's reputation, and she fights me every step of the way. If you were any other woman, I wouldn't bother to care what happens to you."

"If it's so important to you, I will learn to be more reticent." She reached up to smooth the lines from his brow, but he pushed her hand away. "I promise."

The sincerity in her eyes gave no quarter to doubt, and his expression became a little less grim. "Change your clothes, and meet me in the lobby in fifteen minutes. I'll take you to dinner."

Leah stared at the blank door where Benjamin had stood but a moment before and sighed loudly. Life on her island was definitely less complicated. This thing called reputation seemed to hold as much sway as gold. No, if Benjamin was to be believed, it held even more power. She couldn't see how anyone could be offended by honesty, but he seemed so sure of himself. However, she was determined to judge for herself if it was so.

Imprisoned in this room, the afternoon had dragged endlessly, and it had taken every ounce of her will-power to resist the urge to ignore his orders and go exploring on her own. She liked Victoria. Every direction she turned there was something new to catch the eye.

Leah eagerly unwrapped the package Benjamin had tossed on the bed. The dress he had selected for her was of blue poplin and belted with a sash of the same material, fringed with darker blue silk. The neck was high and round; the sleeves long and fitted. Accompanying the gown was a new muslin petticoat, stockings, and a pair of dyed leather slippers.

After donning the gown, Leah struggled a few moments to fashion her hair in an intricate coiffure she had spied on a lady passing her window earlier in the day. She soon gave up and settled for a less elaborate chignon.

There was no clock in the room to mark the passage of time, and she headed down to the lobby as soon as she was ready.

Benjamin was stationed at the base of the stairs like a sentry. He mutely offered his arm when she came abreast him.

"Where are we going to eat?" she asked in hopes of initiating a conversation.

"The hotel dining room."

Nothing else was said until they were seated at their table. Leah sat perusing the patrons while Benjamin did likewise to the menu. After a few minutes, he lay the menu aside and gave his dinner companion his full attention. "Are you ready to order?"

152

"Yes, I'm quite hungry," she replied.

"What would you like?"

"Whatever everyone else is having is fine with me. I don't want to be a bother."

"This is a restaurant," he explained. "Everyone is having something different. Just pick something off the menu." He tapped the booklet before her with his forefinger.

Leah picked up the menu and began reading the list of entrees. She couldn't believe her eyes. There were so many choices. It seemed a great inconvenience to her for the poor soul who was in the kitchen to try to prepare so many different meals at once. She wrinkled her brow thoughtfully. "I'll have whatever is easiest for the cook."

Benjamin sighed. "Never mind. I'll order for you."

Leah nodded her agreement and went back to observing the other dinner guests. Her attention returned to her own table when the waiter came to take their order, but it soon wandered again.

Benjamin endured her curiosity stoically, until she began to smile and wave her fingers at everyone who met her gaze. "Stop that," he hissed under his breath. "You're making a spectacle of yourself."

"I'm only being friendly." She continued unabated.

"You're being rude. It's not polite to stare. You'll make the other guests uncomfortable."

"Oh, I don't think so." She gestured to an elderly couple seated at a corner table and another younger pair across the room from them. "See how they return my smiles."

There was no denying the pleasant expressions on

153

the faces turned their way, and Benjamin lapsed into morose silence. Anyone else would have been met with a host of censorious glares, but Leah seemed to have the ability to charm everyone who crossed her path.

It might be easier to understand if she was a great beauty, but she was not. He had come to like to look upon her, but a cold analytical assessment could not rate her individual features above average. Besides, men and women returned her smiles with equal enthusiasm.

The arrival of their soup called Leah's regard back to their table. One sip was enough to set her interest in another direction as she tried to identify flavors and textures foreign to her palate. A plethora of questions poured forth. Relieved they were no longer the center of attention, Benjamin answered them the best he could and continued to do so throughout the meal.

During dessert he discussed the arrangements he had made with the bank. ". . . As soon as my funds arrive from San Francisco, I will reimburse you for the money I have taken from you," he continued.

"Don't be silly. The money is yours to use freely as you may need or want."

"No, it is not!" Benjamin glared at her. "That is exactly the sort of attitude that will end you in the poorhouse. Haven't you understood anything I have tried to teach you about the importance of guarding your money?"

"Of course I have, but I didn't think your statements applied to you. You would never try to cheat me."

"You don't know that. I could be the greediest bastard who ever roamed the earth. For all you know, I deposited a few dollars in your account and have kept the rest for myself."

"Did you?" she asked, her expression complacent.

"No," he admitted.

"Then you are not a greedy bastard, are you? Your own actions argue my position."

Benjamin growled, but Leah continued to smile serenely. She lightly stroked his hand with her own.

"My dear captain, I have trusted you with my life as you have trusted me with yours. Everything I have I will always share willingly with you."

Chapter 11

"Are you ready?" Leah called through the closed door when Benjamin did not instantaneously answer her knock the next morning.

He peered through the window at the sun peeking over the horizon and pulled the covers over his head. He had mitigated the disappointment caused by his refusal to take her out of the hotel last night after dinner by agreeing he would do so first thing in the morning. It was obvious she had taken him literally.

She knocked again.

Wrapping a quilt around himself, he padded across the floor on bare feet, opening the door no more than a crack. "No, I'm not ready. Go back to your room and wait for me there," he whispered.

"But it's morning," she protested.

"Do you have any idea what time it is?"

"No. There isn't a clock in my room."

He wasn't expecting a reply, especially such a sensible one, and he stared at her dumbly a moment before he spoke again. "Listen, Leah. I know you're anxious to get started, but nothing of interest is open at this hour. Why don't you go back to bed and—"

She turned her back on him and started down the hall; however, before Benjamin could congratulate himself on his easy victory, she had walked right on past her own door.

"Where are you going?" he rasped, torn between the need to have his voice reach her and not be overheard by the other guests.

"Out," she replied succinctly.

A door opened near Leah and a matronly woman wearing a ruffled nightcap poked her head out. She stared at them.

Benjamin groaned.

"Good morning," Leah greeted. "I am going on my very first shopping expedition today. I think the weather is going to be perfectly lovely, don't you?"

The older woman's eyes began to twinkle as recollections of her own youthful exuberance, long since dulled by the years and experience, teased her mind. "Well, you have fun, dear. But mind you don't spend all your money in one spot. There's lots of fine places to tempt a girl to loosen her purse strings."

"Thank you for your advice. I shall be very careful. Benjamin is well versed in the ways of tricksters and charlatans and their like, and he shall be right by my side, so you needn't worry on my account."

"Oh, he is, is he?" The woman ran a critical eye over the dark head poking out of the door down the hall. "And how did he come by this knowledge?"

"He's a sea captain and has been almost everywhere in the world." Leah smiled radiantly.

"Is he a relative?" the matron probed.

"No. He—"

"I am acting as Miss Daniels's guardian," Benjamin interrupted.

"I see." Her withered lips twitched as she speculated on the true nature of the couple's relationship. As her measuring gaze took in Leah's ingenuous expression and the hard planes of Benjamin's face, her faded blue eyes remained affixed on Benjamin. "Well, let me tell you, Captain, I can plainly see Miss Daniels is a sweet young woman. I suggest you take care to *guard* her diligently. I can be a vindictive old woman when I put my mind to it. If you don't believe me, just ask anyone what happened to Mr. Schnell when he tried to poison his neighbor's cat."

On that parting comment, she withdrew her head and closed her door.

Cursing under his breath, Benjamin glanced up and down the hall. No other doors had opened, but in his mind's eye he saw a crowd of ears pressed to the walls and curious eyes glued to the keyholes. His gaze returned to Leah, standing in the hall wearing her new blue dress and an amused expression.

"Would you please wait for me in your room," he hissed. "I'll fetch you as soon as I'm dressed."

"I would rather wait in the lobby."

"Leah!" Her name was a feral growl rumbling from his throat.

"You haven't already forgotten about poor Mr. Schnell, have you?" She clamped her hand over her lips to stifle her giggles and turned to continue her original direction. However, after three steps, she reconsidered her course and returned to her room.

Though Benjamin's first and second inclination was to punish Leah by canceling their plans for the day, he was a man of his word. Besides, he held no illusions that she would remain in her room for long if he did not come for her. As soon as he had prepared to meet the day, he presented himself at her door.

Feigning resignation to his fate, he listened to her animated chatter with uncharacteristic quiescence as he escorted her to the hotel dining room. When it came time to order, he purposefully ordered a huge breakfast for them both.

Before the waiter left their table, Benjamin exchanged whispered words with him, slipping a few coins into his palm.

"I'm really too excited to eat so much," Leah protested, but he merely smiled at her.

The service was maddeningly slow, but each time Leah brought the absence of their meal to Benjamin's attention he either refuted her concept of time or chided her for her impatience.

Despite her lack of hunger, when the meal finally arrived, she wolfed down her portions in the interest of being on their way. But Benjamin had other plans. He further tested her patience by meticulously chewing each bite of sausage, drawing out the meal well past its natural conclusion.

Benjamin grinned wickedly as Leah struggled to maintain a cheerful mien. No one, man or woman, wangled with him without paying the price. It shouldn't be much longer before she realized their matronly acquaintance was not the only one capable of a little vengeance.

159

"You're finished," Leah announced with obvious relief when he lay his knife and fork across his empty plate.

"I think another cup of coffee before we go," he said, dashing her hopes with a signal to their waiter. "Would you like another?"

"No, thank you," she declined as graciously as she was able. She had never been particularly fond of the coffee her father had brought to their island, and her reacquaintance with the brew after its long unavailability had done little to alter her opinion. Now she glared at the umber liquid in Benjamin's cup with something akin to malice.

Benjamin ignored her dark look and leisurely sipped his beverage. When he ordered another cup, she could bear no more.

"You are doing this willfully, aren't you?"

"Yes."

Her eyes darkened. "Why?"

"Because you need a lesson in obedience." He lifted the cup to his lips once more, covertly watching her over the rim. Leah's gaze locked with his.

"I waited in my room, just as you asked," she protested.

"*After* you created a scene," he reminded. "If you expect me to help you get settled in Victoria, you are going to have to follow my directives better than you have been willing to thus far."

His assessment of her behavior seemed unfair to Leah, as she considered the hours he had spent alone in her room the day before and the patience she had exhibited during breakfast this morning, but she kept

160

her opinion to herself. She doubted it would be understood, and she was sure it would not be appreciated.

"Well . . . I am waiting for an apology," he prodded.

Gnawing on her bottom lip, she considered begging his pardon to soothe his temper, but rejected such action as insincere. "I cannot truthfully say I feel sorry for anything I have done."

Instead of the acerbic reply she expected, his expression suddenly mellowed. "I may not appreciate your obstinacy, but I applaud your honesty. It is nice to see you have resisted corruption thus far. Come along. A few of the shops should be opening by now."

Leah was unsure how she should interpret his words. Becoming corrupt was the furthest thing from her mind and certainly posed no temptation. Shrugging her slim shoulders, she decided to concentrate on what she did understand. She was finally to be allowed to explore Victoria.

Stepping out into the sunshine, they strolled down View Street toward Douglas, a main business thoroughfare. They progressed at a snail's pace as Leah insisted on stopping to investigate everything she saw.

Trying to divine the workings of the gas street lamps held her fascination for quite some time. Then a boy pedalled by on a two-wheeler, and Benjamin was forced to capture her hand to prevent her from loping down the street after him so she might question him about the device.

The shops lining Douglas Street were as diverse as they were numerous. The strolling couple stopped to sniff the aroma of a tobacco shop. Perusing the shelves of a general store took a full two hours. There were butcher shops, bakeries, hardware stores, and millineries.

Leah looked at everything, but she bought nothing but a newspaper, several ladies' magazines, and a dime novel. As she pulled Benjamin from one shop to the next, he bore her enthusiasm with resigned amusement, answering her questions the best he could.

"What do they sell here?" Leah asked, as she tried to step through the doors of the Adelphi Saloon. Benjamin put a restraining hand on her arm.

"You can't go in there."

"Why not?"

"It's for men only. They sell spirits," he explained.

"Like the wine I make from elderberries?"

"Nothing so tame. Some of the stuff in there could burn a hole in your socks."

"Those men put spirits on their socks?" Leah stood on tiptoe peering through the window, her expression one of utter amazement.

"I keep forgetting how literal you can be," Benjamin mumbled more to himself than to her. "Suffice it to say, the stuff is not good for you. Now move away from the window, before someone sees you gawking like the goose you are."

Their next stop was an apothecary, then a cobbler shop. Here Benjamin insisted they both order a pair of fashionable, leather walking shoes. At noon they stopped at a small café for a sandwich and tea, but Leah was impatient to be on their way.

"Haven't you seen enough yet?" Benjamin complained good-naturedly. In truth, it had been a pleasant morning, and he was not resentful of the squander of his time.

"I don't think I shall ever have enough," she replied. "There are so many things to see and people to talk to. I was a little worried before, but it is easy to feel happy here." Reaching across the table, she captured his hand and brought the palm to her lips. He snatched it away, shaking his head in warning.

"You find reason to be happy wherever you are," he commented. "You blind yourself to dusty streets and overzealous merchants, and see only gas lamps and friendly smiles."

Leah grinned. "Perhaps that is why Providence washed you ashore on my island. He knew you needed me."

Benjamin was unsettled by the abrupt shift in the course of their conversation. Why was she soliciting his gratitude? She should know she already had it. Why else would he still be with her? "I believe I have already thanked you for saving my life."

"I don't mean that," she stated, her eyes warming as they continued to gaze at him. "Anyone could have nursed you back to physical health. I was referring to the way you look at the world, always expecting the worst from everyone. It's not good for you."

"Off your island barely a fortnight, and already you think yourself an expert on the ways of the world?" he chided, pushing his chair back.

"I have already seen enough to know you are wrong to be so suspicious of everyone. I like people."

He tossed his napkin on the table as he rose to his feet. "You also like me, which is more than enough evidence to impeach your judgment of mankind. But enough of this conversation. It is pointless and inane,

163

which most conversations with you tend to be, but we are no longer on your island where I can indulge you at my leisure. We both have appointments to meet."

"We do?" Leah followed him to her feet.

"Yes," he continued, his tone businesslike. "There is a dress shop not more than a block from here. I stopped there yesterday to arrange a fitting for you, and I am going to see a Mr. Sullivan about leasing a house. If you get done before I come back for you, hire a coach to take you back to the hotel."

"Can't I walk?"

"No. I don't want you traipsing about the streets alone." As an afterthought, he added, "And try to remember not to talk about things you shouldn't while you are there. Our business is nobody's but our own."

Leah suppressed a sigh as she studied him out of the corner of her eye. Benjamin had become a regular tyrant since they had arrived in the city. She was glad for his concern, but she found the fetters upon her freedom hard to bear. However, now was not the time to discuss his odd behavior.

When they had reached the dress shop, Benjamin ushered her inside. "Good afternoon, Mrs. Whiting. This is Miss Daniels, who I spoke to you about yesterday."

"Ah, Miss Daniels, I see you are wearing one of my dresses," the proprietress greeted. "It looks lovely on you, does it not?"

"I like it very much," Leah agreed.

"I knew you would. We use only the finest materials and my stitches are the straightest in town. Of course all that quality takes extra time and effort and—"

"And you won't get an extra penny above what we

agreed yesterday by flattering yourself, so you may as well get on with it. Miss Daniels," Benjamin bobbed his head, in Leah's direction and left the shop.

Leah stared after him. She wasn't sure what she was supposed to do next. Besides, she wanted to ask him why he always referred to her as Miss Daniels when they were in the company of others. She preferred Leah.

"If you will step into the back of the shop, we can get started, Miss Daniels," Mrs. Whiting called her attention, her tone now far more formal than friendly. Leah turned from the window.

"You mustn't mind him," she soothed as she followed the dressmaker into the back room. "It is just his way, and he doesn't mean anything by it."

Reading sincere sympathy in Leah's eyes, the woman's tight expression relaxed perceptibly. "I'm sure you're right," she agreed as she draped her tape measure over her neck. "We will make you gowns so pretty, they will coax him right out of his ill humor. Now, let's get your dress off so we may begin."

After every part of her body was measured and noted on a slip of paper, Leah was allowed to dress again. The dressmaker brought over a book of the latest patterns, instructing Leah to peruse it while she gathered the fabrics she thought most suitable. "Here is the list your guardian left with me yesterday." She handed her a slip of paper from the counter. "You might want to use it as a guide."

Leah skimmed the list and was rather startled by its length. There were day dresses, evening gowns, a riding habit, two tea dresses, and on and on. It seemed a lady was suppose to have a special dress for every activity.

165

She thought it rather ridiculous, but decided to bow to Benjamin's superior knowledge of such things.

Leah allowed Mrs. Whiting's expertise to guide her in the selection of patterns and fabrics, though she did not hesitate to say so if she was uncomfortable with a particular suggestion. They had almost finished fulfilling the requirements of the list, when the bell above the door of the shop began to tinkle.

Into the shop swept a tall, flaxen-haired woman of striking beauty. Her trim figure was draped most elegantly in a gown of spotted foulard, with hat and ribbons that matched the bloom in her cheeks. "Oh, you're busy. I can come back later," she sighed in disappointment, addressing her words to Mrs. Whiting.

"There's no need. We are just about finished," Mrs. Whiting assured her. "Miss Daniels, I would like you to meet Miss Hastings, one of my best customers."

"You make me sound vain," Miss Hastings chided, her rose-colored lips curving into the impish grin. "And you know there is only a little truth in that . . . just enough to condemn me to perdition."

"But you are so beautiful. I only think it proper you are a little vain," Leah voiced her opinion in the matter.

Miss Hastings laughed gaily as she extended her hand in greeting. "I believe I have found myself a new friend. And since we are going to be friends, you must call me Louisa."

"And you will please call me Leah." Leah clasped her hand warmly. "I like it so much better than Miss Daniels."

"Leah it is." Her expert eyes ran over the large number of fabric bolts stacked in disarray about the

166

usually neat shop. "Tell me, Leah, what good fortune has led to this buying spree?"

"I don't think one would call it good fortune really. The canoe wasn't large enough to bring my clothes from home."

Louisa nodded. "I thought you were newly arrived in our fair city. Where are you staying?"

"At the Driad Hotel."

"And where did you come from?"

"My island. It is many days' travel west of here."

"But there is nothing but savage Indians out there," Louisa protested. "Weren't you terrified?"

"I had never met any Indians until a few days ago, and they are very nice people," Leah corrected. "They invited us to a party with singing and dancing and more food than I care to think about."

"Really!" Louisa digested this startling bit of information before resuming her interrogation. "So you are here with your parents."

"No. They're both dead. Benjamin brought me to Victoria."

"Who is he?" Before Leah could answer, Louisa interrupted herself. "Oh dear, I'm being far too inquisitive, aren't I? You must tell me if you think I'm rude."

"I really don't mind," Leah assured her. "I ask far too many questions myself. Benjamin is a sea captain. Capt. Benjamin Keaton. He washed ashore on my island when his ship wrecked. He was hurt when I found him, but when he was better, we carved a canoe and he brought me here."

Louisa gasped. "You can't mean to say you were living on that island all alone?"

"Yes. At least since my parents and Emma died."

"Merciful heavens! You are a true adventuress. We must go somewhere where we can talk more."

"But I haven't finished with Mrs. Whiting, and you have yet to begin," Leah reminded her new friend.

"We can have your business settled in a trice, and I can come back tomorrow."

True to her word, Louisa helped Leah complete her selections in short order, and the two strolled out of the shop arm in arm. Once out on the street, Leah hesitated.

"What's wrong?"

"I'm suppose to take a coach back to the hotel," she confessed ruefully.

"Nonsense, the weather is perfect for a leisurely stroll." Louisa gestured to the cloudless blue sky.

Since Benjamin's objection to her walking was based on his desire she not do so alone, Leah decided he would not object to her accepting Louisa's invitation. She had never had a friend her own age, and she liked Louisa's forthright manner. "All right let's walk, but I think we should go directly to the hotel, just in case I have made a wrong decision. We can go to my room or sit in the lobby and talk."

"Is this Capt. Keaton the one who is giving the orders?" Louisa queried as they started down the street.

"Yes."

"And do you always obey him?"

"Not always, but most times," Leah admitted.

"Why?"

"Because I love him," she stated matter-of-factly.

"Oh my dear, you are a perfect backwoods miss." Louisa rolled her eyes heavenward. "I can see I shall

168

have my hands full setting you straight. Just because you love a man doesn't mean you have to do what he says. It's past time we women ban together and show men we have minds of our own." She paused, lowering her voice. "I am willing to hazard a guess you have become lovers."

Leah swallowed hard. She couldn't lie to her friend; yet, she didn't want to earn Benjamin's ire. She swallowed again. "I'm not suppose to talk of such things. Benjamin says it will make people dislike me."

"He's right, of course," Louisa agreed.

"Then you don't want to be my friend anymore?" Leah asked in dismay.

"Once you are a friend of Louisa Hastings, you are always a friend." Louisa gave her a reassuring squeeze. "I am a progressive woman, and I cannot bring myself to condemn my sisters for indulging in activities that men freely engage in without censure. However, I must caution you, my kind are few in number. With all but me, keep silent. I will have a word with your sea captain about his duty to you."

"Oh, don't do that," Leah pleaded. "You will only make him angry at me."

"It sounds to me as if he has you thoroughly cowed." Louisa snorted. "My advice is to rid yourself of his encumbrance at once."

Leah's eyes widened in alarm. "I can't do that."

"If money is a problem, I can advance you a sum until you get on your feet. Father gives me a generous allowance."

"It has nothing to do with money. I am quite rich. The reason I can't leave him is love," Leah tried again to explain her feelings.

Louisa shook her head pityingly. "I sink to my knees daily and thank God I have never fallen under love's wicked spell. It warps the mind. I would guess us to be of the same age, but I can plainly see I am the far wiser."

Benjamin covered the distance between the real estate office and the dress shop with long strides. Mr. Sullivan had shown him two houses he deemed suitable for Leah's needs, and he hoped to take her to see them so they could settle the matter before the day was out. When he reached the dress shop, he was informed she had just recently departed. He started toward the hotel.

Nodding to a passerby, he returned the man's smile and tipped his hat to a lady he met a few yards further down the sidewalk. As he settled his bowler back on his head, he realized what he was doing. *Leah.* There was no doubt he had changed since he had met her. Whether for the good or bad, he would reserve judgment.

Turning the next corner, he stopped dead in his tracks. Up ahead *walking* down the street—in direct defiance of his orders—was the object of his musings. She was arm in arm with some woman he had never seen in his life. With malice aforethought, he closed the distance.

"Benjamin!" Leah exclaimed in delight. "I would like to introduce you to my new friend, Louisa. She has just invited us to a dinner party she is giving next week."

"I strictly forbade you to walk," he ignored her greeting.

Louisa quickly stepped between them. "Miss Hastings to you, sir."

"What?" He stared at the blonde-haired woman in confusion.

"I said I prefer you call me Miss Hastings over Louisa. Louisa is a name I reserve for my friends, and if you insist on abusing this poor innocent, we shall never be that!"

Benjamin blinked at her, then turned his gaze on Leah. "Leah, where did you find this harridan?"

"In the dress shop," she replied with a sinking heart. She had hoped that upon meeting Benjamin and Louisa would take an immediate liking to each other, but it was clear just the opposite was true.

"And you told her I abuse you?" he asked in disbelief.

"No. Of course not," Leah protested. "You know I always tell the truth, and that would be a lie."

"Then tell me what is going on," he demanded.

"We were walking back to the hotel," Leah stated the obvious, then quickly added, "I thought you wouldn't mind since I wasn't walking alone."

"Is she staying there, too?"

"No," Louisa informed him with cool disdain. "I am the daughter of a very prominent—and I might add—popular member of the Canadian Provincial Legislature. We reside near Beacon Hill Park."

Benjamin met her leveling glare with one of his own. "Would you like me to call you a coach to take you home, *Miss Hastings?*" He pulled Leah to his side. "Miss Daniels and I have business to attend."

"I am perfectly capable of calling my own carriage, should I deem to do so desirable. I will tell you plainly, sir, my dislike of you is as strong as my liking for Leah.

171

Good day."

Mute with frustration, Leah frowned.

"The woman must have been given sour pickles to suck as an infant," Benjamin commented as they watched her march down the street.

Leah moved her scowling gaze from Louisa's back to him. "Then the two of you have much in common."

Chapter 12

"Which do you like best?" Leah pressed as they stood in the yard in front of a whitewashed, clapboard house. They had toured both homes in strained silence, and she was tired of the chilly atmosphere. Both homes were lovely, and seeing no reason she could not be happy living in either of them, she deemed it politic to defer to his judgment in this matter. Much to her relief, Benjamin seemed equally eager to be more friendly.

"The final decision is up to you."

"Then I shall choose this one," she said.

"Why?"

"Because the rent is a little lower, it is closer to the water, and with a little rearranging of the furniture, there is a place in the parlor that would be perfect for a piano. I miss playing for you."

He nodded his head in approval. "I will see the real estate agent in the morning about securing the house for you."

"You'll be living here too, won't you?"

Benjamin stiffened at her question. "Certainly not. ɪ have already explained why that is not possible."

"You said we couldn't share the same room. This house is plenty big enough for the two of us."

"Size has nothing to do with it, appearances do. Men and women do not live under the same roof unless they are blood relations."

"I don't see how a house is any different than a hotel, and we share the same roof *there*," Leah argued.

"There are many things you do not see. Why can't you just accept my word for it?"

"Because I don't like living apart. I was lonely last night in my bed. I needed you."

Benjamin had suffered the same loss of comfort, but he vowed he'd be damned before he admitted as much to Leah. She would only use it against him. He turned so she couldn't glimpse the look of lustful longing he feared might be in his eyes. "You'll get used to it."

"But where will you stay?"

"At the hotel."

Leah sighed. She wanted Benjamin by her side, and she was loath to accept his dictates; yet, she knew arguing would net her nothing. When he believed himself right, he was intractable. She didn't want to risk angering him to the point that he would desert her altogether. "I suppose it is not a very long walk between here and there, and we can visit each other often."

"I don't think it wise you visit me at the hotel. In fact, the sooner we get you out of there the better. We can only hope that old biddy we disturbed this morning doesn't have a hinged tongue." He consciously avoided any mention of Louisa Hastings and the damage she might do. She had expressed a liking for Leah, and if that were so, her social position could prove useful. But they barely knew the woman, and he would not judge her above claiming false affection to gain titillating tidbits of gossip to contribute at afternoon teas. They would have to wait to see if her actions supported her words.

"Why are you so concerned with what people might say about us?" Leah asked as they started back to the hotel.

"I don't care a whit what they say about *me*. It's *your* reputation I am trying to protect."

"But I don't care a whit about what they say about *me*."

Benjamin frowned at her. "That's because you don't know any better. If you are going to have any kind of a future here in Victoria, you are going to have to learn to observe the social amenities. Which reminds me, in the presence of others, you must remember to call me Capt. Keaton, just as I must call you Miss Daniels."

"I was going to talk to you about that. I don't really like being called Miss Daniels. It sounds strange."

"Well, accustom yourself to it, because it is what I and everyone else will call you. The use of first names implies intimacy."

"Then we should use first names," Leah contended.

Benjamin stopped in mid-stride, turning to face her. He glanced up and down the plank sidewalk to be sure no one was within earshot. "You're missing the point again. Whatever we shared in the past is done and best forgotten. No one must know how it has been between us. I am your temporary guardian, nothing more," he lectured her in a low voice. "I am sure you are capable of calling me Capt. Keaton as I ask."

She smiled wanly. "I know you don't believe so, but I really am trying to understand. It is just very hard to pretend I think one way, when I feel another."

"Well, you must learn to do so if you are to survive in the world."

Leah's natural inclination was to refute his claim, however Louisa had expressed the same sentiments. Considering their mutual antipathy, she felt if they agreed on anything, it must be so. Still, she did not like it one bit. "It seems to me that the people you think would cause us trouble would do better to tend to their own business. I have no desire to tell them what they should do, and I don't see why they should have any say over what I do."

Taking her by the elbow, he guided her down the street. His tone remained tight. "I agree, but yours is a fairy-tale notion of the world, and we must deal with reality. Now about the matter of hiring a maid."

"A maid?"

"Yes, I think she should be an older woman, someone who could easily do double duty as a chaperone. A widow who is down on her luck would be ideal."

Leah's memories of Emma were nothing but fond, and the idea of having someone else to live in her house held much appeal. Her expression became thoughtful. "If I can't have you, I will settle for a maid. But what is a chaperone?"

"Someone who watches over you when men are about, to make sure they don't try to take indecent liberties . . . and, in your case, to make sure you don't throw yourself into the arms of every Tom, Dick, and Harry."

This time it was Leah who stopped. She stared at him with a mixture of bemusement and exasperation shining from her dark eyes. "I have already told you, I am interested in no one but you."

"That is because you have yet to meet any eligible young men." Benjamin led her out of the path of a passing pedestrian. "This dinner party, if the invitation still stands, will be a good opportunity to see what is available locally."

"You are going to let me go?" Leah voiced her amazement. After his reaction to Louisa, she had feared to even mention the possibility.

"Yes," he affirmed somewhat reluctantly. "I have no faith whatsoever in your judgment of men. I will narrow the field for you, separating the chaff from the grain much as I did with the houses; then, you will be free to choose among the remaining contenders."

His words left her even more dumbfounded. What about all his warnings? It didn't make sense. In her mind, she reversed their roles in hopes of gaining some insight. It left her even more confused. The idea of sharing *him* with another woman was totally repugnant and, until this moment, had never crossed her mind. "You wish to share me with another man?" she squeaked, her expression jaundiced.

Benjamin ignored her tone and proceeded, using a businesslike timbre to disguise his own discomfort with his plan. "I said nothing of sharing. I have told you time and time again, I will not be staying in Victoria. You need someone to watch over you. A husband is the logical choice. Now, why don't you describe your idea of a desirable beau to me, to help guide me in my search."

"A beau?"

"What you would call a mate?"

Leah smiled lovingly. "That's easy. You."

A low growl rumbled in his throat, and he started back down the street, Leah in tow. "The joke is not appreciated. I have told you before, you only like me because you have experienced nothing else. Once you do, you will consider me the dregs of the barrel." He paused to rein in his ire and gather his thoughts. She certainly wasn't making this easy for him, but he knew her well enough to realize she wasn't trying to thwart him out of obstinacy. It was her damned inexperience that guided her tongue.

Taking a deep breath, he assumed the mien of a long suffering teacher. "Perhaps I should list some of my requirements, to help guide your thoughts in the right direction. A man in his late twenties, twenty-seven would be ideal, from good family, with a fortune of his own making. He must be even-tempered, honest, sober, and faithful. It matters not to me if he is handsome, but he must be in good health and reasonably fair of face. Is there anything else you feel is important that I have missed?"

"I should like him to be tall, with raven black hair, a mustache, and blue eyes," Leah spoke the words softly.

Benjamin ignored her remark. He wasn't particularly fond of the idea of turning her over to another man's care either, but the alternative was to marry her himself, and that was a far less appealing prospect.

He had always been a loner, and he preferred to return to that way of life as soon as possible. He wasn't comfortable with his feelings for Leah, and the notion they might grow stronger the longer he stayed with her

178

was truly terrifying, though he was not sure why. He slammed the door on his fear.

They had reached the lobby of the Driad. Leah interrupted his thoughts with a plaintive question. "May I go up to my room?"

Benjamin was startled to see his own fear reflected in her soft brown eyes, but his mien remained business-like. "Yes, of course. It has been a long day, and you are probably exhausted."

"Yes." Leah admitted to fatigue, but her exhaustion was not caused by the activities of the day. Though he did not say it, she was not so naive that she didn't realize Benjamin intended to hire this maid/chaperone person to keep *them* apart as well. In fact, she sensed that was his main purpose. She didn't want him to push her away. It made his threats to leave her alone in Victoria all the more daunting.

Reminding herself that she had survived the long years alone on the island by living one day at a time, she vowed not to think of the future. Benjamin was still here with her, and in her heart she felt he cared more than he was willing to admit. Perhaps if she cooperated with his plan to introduce her to other men, he would see the futility in his scheme to redirect her affections. Or perhaps he would prove her wrong. In either case, there would be time enough to be miserable when and if he abandoned her.

Leah spent a restless night, tossing and turning on her lonely bed.

A formal invitation to Louisa's dinner party arrived the next day while Benjamin was out finalizing the lease of the house on Simcoe Street. It was addressed to Leah but, much to her relief, the invitation was extended to Benjamin as well.

She dashed off a quick note accepting Louisa's offer of hospitality, and urging her friend to come to visit at her earliest convenience.

During the night she had settled on a plan, but she needed someone like Louisa to tell her how to go about executing it. She might be willing to allow Benjamin to introduce her to other men—if for no other reason than to prove to herself and him that she would still value him above all others—but she was not willing to meekly allow him to install some stranger in her home to keep them apart.

Louisa arrived within the half hour. The two women closeted themselves in Leah's room.

"I sensed an urgency in your message to meet you," Louisa announced as she pulled the gloves from her fingers and tossed them across the back of a chair. "Is he abusing you again?"

Leah pursed her lips in vexation. "No, and you must stop saying such things, Louisa. You are both my friends, and I won't have either of you speaking unkindly of the other."

Louisa had the decency to look shamefaced before she dismissed the matter from her mind. "Then how can I be of assistance?"

Rubbing the palms of her hands together in nervous agitation, Leah paced the length of the room. "I hesitated to call on you for help on such short acquaintance, but you did say you were my friend, and I thought you would be the one to best advise me in this matter."

"There is nothing I like better in this world than voicing my opinion." Louisa laughed at her own admission. "Now what earthshaking matter have I come to settle?"

"I need to hire a maid, before Benjamin hires someone horrible for me," Leah blurted out.

"You really must learn to call him Capt. Keaton, or everyone in town will guess at what your relationship has been with him. I can only do so much to protect you. But never mind that just now." She drummed her fingers on the arm of the chair as she thought, delighted to be given the opportunity to thwart the captain with Leah's approval. "Let me see, a maid. Who should we get for you?"

"Someone who is warm and gentle . . . and *progressive* like you," Leah listed her requirements.

"Ah, someone who will turn a blind eye on your little tête-à-tête with Capt. Keaton. That should please him plenty." Louisa's smile faded.

"No. It will not please him at all," Leah corrected the misconception. "He wants to hire someone to keep us apart."

Louisa quirked a fine blonde brow. "He does, does he?"

"Yes, and I can't allow it."

"Does he give you a reason?"

"He thinks he must protect my reputation, but what good is a reputation, if I can't have him?" she protested.

Leah's words forced Louisa to begrudgingly allow the captain to move up a few notches in her esteem. She listened thoughtfully as Leah continued.

"If the people of Victoria look down on me because I don't wish to hide my love for him, I can't say as I have much admiration for their character."

"You will find people the same the world over, dear

181

Leah. There are certain rules of conduct that must be observed, or you can find yourself in a perfect stew. Regardless, the matter of a maid should be settled to your advantage as an issue of principle, even if I don't concur with your motives." Louisa continued to tap her forefinger against the arm of the chair while she pondered the options. Abruptly, she rose to her feet. "I think it best we retire to my home. Your Capt. Keaton will surely try to interfere if given the opportunity, so we must guard against an encounter with him until the matter is settled. Besides, my own staff may know of one or two ladies eligible for the post."

"I don't think Benjamin . . . I mean Capt. Keaton," Leah corrected herself after receiving a warning scowl from her friend, "would like me to go out."

"Don't be such a mouse. He has no authority to order you about." Louisa retrieved her gloves and began easing them on as she started for the door.

Leah hesitated. "But I do so hate to go against his wishes."

"Then why have you called me here? Isn't the point of all this to foil him?"

Leah agreed with a reluctant nod of her head. "I suppose you're right; only, I know what I am doing is for his good as well as my own."

"Hrmph! I don't know why you take his feelings into account at all." Louisa's eyes flashed with righteous indignation.

"That's because you have never been in love."

"Father says the same thing. He dreams of the day some man will sweep me off my feet and rid his household of his pretty little nuisance." She flourished her arms, then pointed to herself. "That's his nickname for me: Nuisance. Not very flattering, but I fear mostly accurate from his point of view, which is unfortunately male."

"I am sorry you and your father don't get along," Leah offered her sincere sympathy.

Louisa laughed. "Don't be silly. We are the best of friends."

Leah looked confused. "But you just said—"

"Father and I argue for the sheer joy of it. It's a game with us. But you have caused me to digress again. Are you coming or not?"

"Coming," Leah confirmed. "Just let me jot a note to leave at the desk in the lobby, so Capt. Keaton," she pronounced his formal name carefully, "won't worry, should he get back before I do."

Worry was exactly what Benjamin did when he returned to the hotel and received Leah's note. On one hand he wanted to nurture the friendship of Leah and this Louisa person, but on the other he resented the woman. Leah had not mentioned why she had gone to Miss Hastings's home, and he was instinctively wary.

"God, man, you're turning into a mother hen," he scolded himself out loud as he paced the perimeter of his hotel room. Before going to see the house agent this morning, he had made it a point to investigate Miss Hastings's story. She was everything she claimed to be. She had the reputation of being a bit outspoken, but that certainly was not news to him, and though she was not universally liked, she was universally respected.

All this boded well for Leah's future, but still he was not comfortable to have her alone in the company of someone he barely knew.

Wearing a hole in the carpet over some woman was not his habit, and the fact that he was doing so now made him even more testy. When Leah returned shortly after noon, she was greeted by a snarling bear of a man.

Upon answering her knock, Benjamin grabbed her by the arm and ushered her down the stairs and out of the lobby without speaking a word of greeting.

With a firm hand on her elbow, he guided her to the park at a pace so brisk she had not sufficient breath to voice more than a token complaint. Once they were in a suitably secluded location, he released her arm, turning to face her.

"What have you been doing all day? I need your signature on these papers." He pulled a document from his pocket and thrust it at her.

"I've been hiring a maid," she replied calmly, just as Louisa had instructed her to do.

Benjamin was startled out of his foul mood. The fact that she had taken the initiative in such a practical matter was heartening. "Did you find one?"

"Yes."

"What are her qualifications?" he demanded, though his tone was markedly less harsh.

"She is sixty years old and a widow," Leah began with the information she thought would please him most.

"A bit ancient for a maid, don't you think? I hope she isn't doddering."

"She is in fine health," Leah assured him. "The family she had been working for recently moved back to England. She's an American and didn't think she

184

would be happy living there, so she stayed behind. She has an excellent letter of reference from them. Louisa said she is more than qualified for the position and her salary requirements are fair."

Amazed, Benjamin lowered himself to a nearby rock. "I can't believe you have been so sensible," he complimented. Leah blushed guiltily.

"Those aren't the real reasons I hired her," she confessed. "They are just the ones I thought you would approve. I hired her because I liked her smile, and she needed the work."

"I should have known," he commented dryly. "When do I meet her?"

"You already have," Leah admitted with some reluctance. Leah bit her bottom lip, hoping she had not made a grave error in judgment. She had made her decision with her heart, not her head. In fact, now that she thought about it, her new maid might be more willing to serve Benjamin's purposes than her own.

Clearing her throat, she continued, "Remember the woman we met yesterday morning at the hotel?"

"The busybody who stuck her head out into the hall?" Benjamin asked.

"Yes, that's Mrs. Findley. She said the Driad is the best place to stay when a person is looking for 'the right kind of people.' I'm not sure what that means, but it has something to do with paying to rub shoulders with the privileged."

"It means she is a savvy business woman." He paused, thoughtful. Recalling Mrs. Findley's terse words to him gave him more pleasure than pain. He didn't imagine he could have chosen a more ferocious watchdog. "I will save my final opinion until I have read her letter of recommendation, but I think you may have chosen well."

His approval of her decision—no matter if it was tentative—somewhat mitigated Leah's vexation with her own lack of foresight. In truth, no other candidate she had interviewed could be said to be better suited to her purpose. She smiled broadly. "I'm glad you approve. I was afraid you might be angry, but the moment I recognized her, I knew I wanted her. She reminds me a little of Emma—all soft and round."

The remainder of the day and all of the next was spent moving Leah into her house, stocking the larder, and seeing to the myriad of details establishing a new residence requires. By nightfall both Leah and Mrs. Findley were comfortably settled in the house on Simcoe Street, and Benjamin felt he was one step closer to extracting himself from Leah's life.

The next step was making sure Mrs. Findley understood her duty. Cornering the housekeeper in the kitchen while Leah was upstairs seeing to the bed linens, he proceeded to do just that.

"Mrs. Findley, though your letter of reference is in order, this particular position involves duties of a nature not usually encountered by domestics. I would have a word with you.

Mrs. Findley dried her hands on her apron and turned to face him, her expression chary. "And what might they be?"

As Benjamin met her gaze, he was suddenly uncertain how to begin. "I'm sure you've noticed that Miss Daniels is . . . different. How much has she told you of her past?"

"Only that she has been living on an island to the west of here. I gather it was quite remote, and she had little opportunity to meet other people."

"Very good." He nodded his head in approval of Leah's reserve. He had been half-afraid she had already told the housekeeper more than she should know. "It is important that you understand that until recently she has never been off that island. Her acquaintance with mankind was limited to her parents and a housekeeper. She is extremely naive about city life. I have tried to teach her, but it is critical you watch over her. I don't want her hurt. Unless I give permission, she is not to be let out of the house without escort."

"What does Miss Daniels have to say about that?" Mrs. Findley asked.

"She has no say in the matter."

"Unless I am mistaken, she is of legal age," the housekeeper countered, in an effort not only to clarify her position but ascertain Capt. Keaton's intentions.

"The age of consent is measured in years. Miss Daniels's ability to manage her own life must be judged by another measure. Her lack of experience makes her as vulnerable as someone half her age."

"I see."

"I'm not sure you do." Benjamin paused to clear his throat, weighing how much he could safely tell without compromising Leah. He had been carefully watching the woman all day. Her words and actions evinced he could trust her, but he couldn't bring himself to do so completely. Finally, he resumed his speech, choosing his words warily. "My concern is not just for matters of domestic commerce. There are some who would take advantage of Miss Daniels's affectionate nature."

Mrs. Findley ran her gaze up and down his frame, openly assessing him in a manner that gave no hint of her hired position in the household. "Are you among them?" she demanded.

Benjamin's countenance darkened with anger. Whatever he had been to Leah, it was over. He lowered his voice to an ominous growl, intent on crushing the housekeeper's impertinence. "My relationship with Miss Daniels is none of your concern. I can handle myself. It is the other gentlemen of Victoria you must guard against."

"Guarding against *them* will do little good, if *you* compromise her," Mrs. Findley stated, refusing to cower before him.

He took a step closer. "Do you think me a fool? I have no intention of compromising her."

"So you harbor nothing but brotherly concern?"

"Exactly. I am acting as her guardian, nothing more. It is not a chore I relish, but there is no one else to do it, and I would be a villain to abandon her to her own devices so soon."

"Then you plan to leave Victoria?"

"Yes, just as soon as I can assure myself that Miss Daniels can handle her own affairs."

"Does she know?"

"She has been told," he confirmed. "But as I said, you needn't concern yourself with me. It is Miss Daniels's welfare I charge you with. She has not yet learned to guard her tongue as well as she should, and needs someone trustworthy by her side to gloss over her frequent faux pas. It is of the utmost importance she be accepted by good society."

"And if I must choose between your interests and hers?" she pressed.

"Miss Daniels comes first," he answered without hesitation.

Mrs. Findley's tight lips relaxed into a satisfied smile. She held out her hand, offering tentative friendship. "I had my doubts about you, Captain, but you have put them somewhat to rest. Whether you had asked it or not, I would have looked out for Miss Daniels. Together we shall see she comes to no harm."

The next few days progressed smoothly. The first of Leah's dresses were completed, Mrs. Findley proved genial and efficient, and—much to Leah's relief—Benjamin and her maid got along just fine.

As long as she had Mrs. Findley by her side, Benjamin did not complain about her going out without his escort. He was becoming more tolerant of her friendship with Louisa. He was attentive. Best of all, he made no mention of leaving Victoria any time soon.

Except for the issue of separate beds, which Benjamin seemed determined to enforce despite her frequent invitations, Leah judged herself content.

He visited several times a day on the auspices of continuing her lessons in life, but though he managed to fool himself, he did not fool her. Her intuition let her believe he missed her almost as much as she missed him. Her heart told her it was only a matter of time before he came to his senses and moved into the house.

Leah's days were filled with so many new sights and activities, she was usually too busy to think too much on her future. It was only at night, when she lay in her lonely bed that she could not ignore the empty ache in her arms. They had been separated less than a week, but she found it hard to be patient.

The day of the dinner party arrived. Though Leah had met many of the citizens of Victoria on the streets, both Benjamin and Louisa stressed the importance of making a good impression at her first formal introduction into society.

Much of her friend's time was taken up with preparations for her party, but when they were together, Louisa constantly drilled her on the art of proper deportment. Mrs. Findley took over in her absence, and Leah found herself the frequent recipient of a gentle scolding as they went about their day-to-day activities. She was too friendly. She was too forward. She mustn't talk to painted women.

Leah thought all the formalities a hindrance to honest communication, but she postponed voicing her opinion until she had had a chance to see what this all-important "good society" was about.

Mrs. Findley dressed her hair in a chignon *à marteaux,* and helped her select a gown of apricot faille with an underskirt of ceil blue. The lace-edged, square neck flattered the line of her shoulders, and she felt quite elegant as she perused her reflection in the mirror.

Promptly at eight Benjamin, garbed in a silk-lined dress coat and top hat, arrived in a fashionable carriage, complete with Mr. Barnes as driver.

"Leah," he greeted as she opened the door to him. His blue eyes darkened a shade as he took in her radiant visage.

"Do you approve?" she asked as she curtsied, then

190

slowly turned to model the new gown and coiffure for him.

It was not the gown, but rather the joyful enthusiasm for life dancing in her eyes that was his undoing. He swallowed hard, fighting the spasm of desire that racked his body. "Yes," he replied hoarsely.

Smiling, Leah captured his hand and brought it to her lips. Their eyes met.

"I thought I heard the door." Mrs. Findley swept into the hall, carrying two cloaks.

Benjamin snatched his hand away.

Leah frowned.

Letting her scolding of Leah for answering the door herself die on her lips, Mrs. Findley pretended to be oblivious to the undercurrents in the hall. "I think we're ready. Let's go." She settled one cloak about Leah's shoulders, then allowed the captain to help her with her own before bustling them out the door.

After exchanging greetings, Mr. Barnes helped Leah into the carriage, then handed Mrs. Findley up. She took the seat beside Leah, adjusting the fabric of Leah's skirt so it would not wrinkle. Benjamin sat on the opposite seat.

The housekeeper covertly watched them both. It was impossible to live in the same house with someone like Leah and not be aware of the strength of her feelings for the captain, and the scene she had just witnessed in the hall had Mrs. Findley more than a little worried. Captain Keaton had done nothing even bordering on the improper in their brief acquaintance, but he had never really said what had gone on between him and her mistress before they came to Victoria.

"I think this evening is going to be fun, don't you?"

Leah solicited Benjamin's opinion when the strain of silence became more than she was willing to bear.

"It could prove enjoyable," he agreed without emotion.

"I'm sure you'll have a lovely time." Mrs. Findley joined the conversation, patting her hand. Leah faced her housekeeper.

"I'm still concerned about you though. I think it ridiculous that you will not be allowed to eat at the same table," she complained. "It's worse than ridiculous. It is rude."

"Now dear, Miss Hastings has explained why it is so. The evening will be just as enjoyable for me below stairs as it is for you above. I'm rather looking forward to the opportunity to catch up on the gossip."

"Just mind you don't start any rumors of your own," Benjamin warned.

"What would I say?" Mrs. Findley's withered lips pursed at the implied insult to her loyalty. "Only that I work for the sweetest mistress in the world, and what a lady she is. I would never do or say anything to harm Miss Daniels."

Benjamin let the subject drop. Leah did have a knack for inspiring the protective instincts of those who came to know her. Even he was willing to vouch Mrs. Findley's devotion was genuine. If anyone was in danger of sullying her reputation, it was himself. He was finding it increasingly difficult to resist her romantic overtures, and she was wont to launch an attack if they were alone even an instant. He shifted uncomfortably in his seat as his body responded to his thoughts.

To his chagrin, Leah instantly noticed his discomfort, and she raised her eyes to his, expelling a long, mournful sigh.

"What's wrong, dear?" Mrs. Findley queried with motherly concern.

At a warning glance from Benjamin, she bit back a frank reply, but as she spoke her intent gaze held his. "It's nothing, really. I'm just missing my island."

Mrs. Findley cleared her throat. "It's to be expected. You were there so long, and everything here is so new. It must be a little intimidating."

"Confusing is a better word," Leah replied softly as she continued to stare openly at the captain. "I am not used to so many fetters on my freedom, and everyone I meet seems wont to tell me of some new rule of dress or conduct I must follow."

"You'll become accustomed in no time," Mrs. Findley reassured her, as she prayed it would be so.

"Perhaps you're right." Leah sighed again, giving neither of her carriage companions confidence in her belief of her own statement.

Chapter 13

The moment the carriage came to a halt before the Hastings' residence, Leah temporarily forgot her longing to lie naked in Benjamin's arms. The yard was ablaze with torches lighting the pathway leading to the porch.

The doorman took their wraps and announced their arrival. She and Benjamin were ushered into a crowded room, while Mrs. Findley retired below stairs.

Though she had been openly impressed when she had visited Louisa's home on other occasions, Leah was taken aback by the splendor before her. The Hastings' home's moderate-sized ballroom had been transformed into a kaleidoscope of color. Joined by generous bows of carmine, blue and gold ribbons festooned the walls. Flowers were everywhere. Overhead, ornate gas chandeliers illuminated the frescoed ceiling, the light dancing off the lustrous gowns of the ladies.

"Ah, Miss Hastings's new little friend." A dapper gentleman stepped forward. "The name is Thaddeus

Blake, if I may be so bold as to introduce myself."

"Pleased to meet you, sir." Leah offered her hand as she recited the words, just as she had been instructed.

Benjamin stood at her side, ramrod stiff. His blue eyes measured the fellow from head to toe. He appeared prosperous enough, but looks could be deceiving. Besides, he was far too forward to be trusted. Thaddeus Blake was definitely not good enough for Leah.

"Leah, I'm so glad you've finally arrived. I have so many people who want to meet you." Louisa swept forward in a rustle of sapphire silk, displacing Mr. Blake. "Captain." She nodded her head curtly in Benjamin's direction.

"Are we late?" Leah asked in concern. "Just this morning Capt. Keaton was lecturing me on the importance of punctuality and—"

"Don't be silly," Louisa interrupted. "You're perfectly on time. Besides, it's fashionable to be a little late to social functions. I was just impatient for your arrival." She cupped the side of her face with her hand and said in a whisper, "Some of these people are deadly dull, you know."

"Oh," Leah smiled, pretending to understand.

Louisa continued, barely pausing for breath, "Father, this is Miss Daniels, who I have told you so much about. Leah, this is my father. It is a pity you two must meet for the first time in such public circumstances, but Father's schedule is so impossible, what with his duties in the Legislature. Of late, I rarely see him myself."

"Pleased to meet you, Miss Daniels." Mr. Hastings allowed Leah to extend her hand before bowing slightly. Leah curtsied. Mr. Hastings waited for his daughter to proceed with the introductions. When she did not, he cast a censorious glance her direction and extended his hand to Benjamin. "My daughter appears to be remiss in her manners."

"Capt. Benjamin Keaton," Benjamin supplied the missing name.

As the two men exchanged greetings, Louisa looped her arm in Leah's. "Come along, Leah. Captain, I'm sure you can find something to do to entertain yourself." She shooed him away with a wave of her hand and pulled Leah into the crowd.

"Of course," he replied curtly. Retiring to a corner where he would be inconspicuous, his watchful gaze never left Leah.

"Mr. and Mrs. Sterling, I would like you to meet my dear friend, Miss Leah Daniels. She is newly arrived in our fair city, and I have taken her under wing."

"Pleased to meet you, Miss Daniels," they spoke in turn.

"Pleased to meet you," Leah answered in kind. Before the conversation could progress any further, she found herself being whisked off in another direction.

"Mr. and Mrs. Johnson . . ." Louisa began. And so they continued around the crowded room, until Leah had been formally introduced to every guest. Less than a quarter way through the introductions, she began to lose track of which name belonged to whom, but she continued to smile through her confusion. There was little else she could do. Louisa was even more animated than usual, and Leah doubted she could have squeezed in a question if she had tried.

"There. I believe we have observed the formalities

with everyone, even the late arrivals," Louisa announced, as her eyes scanned the room for anyone she might have missed. "I fear I must relinquish you and tend to my other guests. Who would you like to talk to while I am occupied? No, wait! I know just who would be suitable. John Carlyle. He seemed rather taken with you, don't you think?"

"Which one is he?" Leah asked.

"The handsome one standing over by the window." She gestured in that direction. "I can't believe you didn't notice the way he looked at you."

Before Leah could reply to that comment, she found herself being bustled across the room.

"Mr. Carlyle, would you be a dear and entertain my friend Leah for a few moments?" Louisa queried.

"My pleasure." He smiled broadly. "My pleasure, indeed."

When they were alone, comparatively speaking, John Carlyle gave Leah his full attention. "I wonder why she chose me for the honor of your company," he mused.

"Because she thinks you're handsome," Leah replied.

He choked on his breath. "Say what?"

"Louisa said you are handsome," Leah repeated. "At least, that is the only reason she gave me for bringing me to you."

"Indeed." His lips twitched with amusement. "I was under the impression Miss Hastings wasn't particularly fond of men."

"She doesn't have very much good to say about your sex in general," Leah concurred. "But she does give credit where credit is due."

His chest puffed and he stood a bit taller. "And what about you, Miss Daniels? Do you think that I am handsome?"

Tilting her head back, Leah studied him carefully before replying, "I like darker hair on a man and blue eyes as opposed to brown, but otherwise I see no reason to disagree with Louisa."

John laughed merrily. "An honest woman. What a delight! Wherever did Louisa find you?"

"In Mrs. Whiting's dress shop," she replied.

Standing sentinel in the corner, Benjamin's gaze followed Leah about the room, assessing each and every person she met. He was not generous with his opinions. Though the ladies did not escape his biting cynicism, it was the gentlemen who bore the brunt of his jaundiced regard for humanity. If they smiled at Leah, he judged them too forward. If they appeared reticent, he named them snobbish. Not one measured up to standard. When Louisa deserted her by the window, Benjamin stiffened.

He could not hear the conversation, but the sound of riant male laughter carried to his ears again and again. What on earth could Leah be saying to tickle the fellow so? He shuddered as several possibilities came to mind.

He was about to stride across the room and rescue her, if necessary, when an elderly gentleman stepped into his path. "Capt. Keaton. There you are." He held out his hand. "I've been wanting to meet you. I've just been talking to Miss Hastings, and I hear you are quite a hero."

Benjamin spent the next fifteen minutes trying to

disabuse the man of the notion. It quickly became apparent that, despite her dislike of him, Louisa had painted the tale of Leah's escape from the island in terms most complimentary to him. The purpose, he could only guess, was to protect Leah's reputation, and he was careful to say nothing that would thwart that purpose.

Sociable discourse was not one of his strong suits, but his business dealings had taught him how to play the game. He forced a genial smile to his lips and pretended interest in carrying on the conversation. Leah would not be well served if he acquired the reputation of a churl.

When he was finally able to extract himself, Benjamin made a beeline to Leah's side.

"Capt. Keaton." Leah smiled in delight when he joined them. "I was wondering where you had gone. This is my new friend, Mr. Carlyle."

The two men exchanged greetings.

"We were just discussing the possibility of a picnic before the weather turns," John filled him in on the conversation. "What do you think?"

"Who would be going?" Benjamin queried.

"We thought Mr. Carlyle, Louisa, you, and me . . . and maybe another one or two couples. Please say we can go," Leah pleaded.

"And who would pair with you?" Benjamin demanded.

"You, of course," Leah replied, exchanging a conspiratorial grin with John Carlyle. "Mr. Carlyle wants to be with Louisa."

"I see." Benjamin successfully hid his relief. He wasn't particularly fond of this Carlyle fellow. He laughed too much. But as long as he wasn't sniffing after Leah, he supposed he could tolerate his company.

"Well, is the picnic on?" John pressed.

"I have no objections."

"Thank you." Leah would have expressed her pleasure in more effusive terms had the dinner bell not rung at just that moment.

As the guests gathered around the table, Louisa and her father helped direct them to their assigned place setting. Mr. Hastings sat at the head of the table with Louisa to his right. Next to her sat a Col. Archibald Kramer from the British Royal Navy, then Leah, Benjamin, and an elderly lady (whose name Leah could not recall) and her husband. The other side filled in like fashion, alternating men and women whenever possible, until all forty guests had taken their place. John Carlyle was relegated to a chair near the foot of the table.

The matron on Benjamin's right immediately solicited his full attention, and it soon became apparent she had no intention of relinquishing it. Louisa was too busy playing hostess to give more homage to one guest over any other. Having no one she knew to talk to, Leah had no alternative but to be drawn into dialogue with Col. Kramer. His fascination with the sound of his own voice left little opening for her to contribute to the conversation.

And then the food came. There were soups, fish and poultry terrines, a variety of vegetables and breads, and that was only the beginning. Remembering her experience with the Indians, Leah heaped her plate high and began to eat.

She watched in growing dismay as the servants

continued to bring in platters of food. After a while, Leah noticed some of the other guests were beginning to cast surreptitious glances her way, but she remained undaunted.

At length, the colonel was moved to comment, "I say, you are a hungry little thing."

Benjamin caught his words and turned towards Leah, who was nodding her reply as she chewed another bite. His jaw dropped when his gaze fell upon her heaping plate.

"What do you think you're doing?" he hissed in her ear.

"I don't want to insult Louisa and her father," she whispered back.

Completely confused, he demanded, "Explain yourself."

"I have not forgotten our feast with the Indians, nor what you said about refusing food being an insult. I don't want to hurt Louisa's feelings," she said softly.

Understanding dawned. "You don't have to do that *here.*"

Leah looked bewildered. "I don't? Are you sure?"

"Look around the table," he directed. "Didn't you notice no one else is overfilling their plate?"

"Yes, I did. I just thought they were being rude, so I took even more."

Benjamin rolled his eyes heavenward. "Lord, there is a lot you don't know. At this rate, I shall never be free of you."

"What are you two whispering about," Louisa interrupted.

"A small lesson in etiquette," Benjamin informed her, his tone still hushed. "It appears we were remiss."

His eyes lowered to Leah's plate.

"Oh, dear," Louisa exclaimed as her gaze followed his. "Excuse me, Colonel, would you mind changing places with me?"

The befuddled colonel willingly gave up his place.

As soon as she was seated in his seat, Louisa leaned close to her friend. "A lady doesn't pile her plate to the ceiling, no matter how hungry she is."

"But I'm not hungry," Leah disclaimed.

"Then why this?" Louisa indicated the plate with a discreet turn of her hand.

"It's a long story," Benjamin explained through a tight smile. "Everyone is starting to stare. Call the maid and have her remove the plate."

Louisa concurred with his advice and carried it out at once, directing the maid to bring back a clean plate.

Leah sat in between, wondering what new offense she had unwittingly committed. She had only been trying to be polite.

"Will one of you two please explain what I have done wrong," she begged.

"Later," they answered in unison.

Louisa continued, "Just follow my lead."

The rest of the meal progressed without incident. Leah carefully mimicked Louisa, painstakingly filling her plate with no more and no less than her friend.

After dinner, the men retired to one parlor to drink and smoke while the ladies gathered in another.

Several of the women kept staring at her oddly, and after a few minutes, Leah could stand it no more. "Excuse me, but will someone here please tell me what I have done?" she demanded plaintively.

"Leah, darling, we can discuss it later," Louisa tried

to hush her.

"No. I would like to know now."

Her gaze moved from one member of the group to the next as she waited expectantly. Finally, it settled on a thin, middle-aged matron dressed in a powder blue gown, whose lips fairly quivered with her eagerness to speak up.

"Well, dear, you really were making a pig of yourself at the table, weren't you?" she blurted out. The other women present cringed, discreetly withdrawing to various corners of the parlor. Their ears, however, remained riveted to the conversation.

"I know, but not because I wanted to," Leah informed her. "When I was with the Indians—"

"Indians!"

"Yes, we spent the evening with some, and they had a feast for us with singing and dancing. It was really quite exciting."

"My stars!" The lady brought her hand to her bosom. "Fetch a chair. I fear I may faint."

Louisa sniffed. "Now, Mrs. Johnson, you know you shall do no such thing. We have all endured your threats for years, and you've yet a decent swoon to your credit."

"Louisa, she might be truly ill," Leah protested, moving a chair beneath the woman.

Mrs. Johnson stiffly settled herself on the chair, raising her chin to such a lofty angle her hatchet-shaped nose pointed toward the ceiling. "Now there, Miss Louisa Hastings. You could learn a few manners from your friend."

"You mean the one who was eating like a pig?" Louisa taunted.

"I'm sure there is some reasonable explanation," Mrs. Johnson sputtered.

"Of course, there is," Louisa assured her with false confidence. "Leah, why don't you tell us what it is."

The rest of the ladies had slowly drifted back to surround the three women. Leah's explanation of the Indian feast was interrupted by frequent questions and occasional gasps. When she had finished, she had earned the admiration of some and the curiosity of all.

Her life on the island was retold, though when she came to the part about Benjamin washing ashore, Louisa took over the tale and presented an edited version. Louisa painted a rather sterile picture of her relationship with Benjamin, but Leah noted the ladies seemed well pleased with it, and she did not protest her friend's blatant omissions of fact.

It was late when the gentlemen came to collect their ladies to take them home. The evening was interesting if it was anything, and despite a few uncomfortable moments, Leah had thoroughly enjoyed herself.

Mrs. Findley was already in the carriage when Benjamin handed Leah up. The housekeeper smiled sleepily as she settled herself beside her. "Did you have a nice time, dear?"

"Very pleasant."

"I'm glad. You can tell me all about it in the morning." She closed her eyes and snuggled into the corner. Leah tucked the carriage blanket about her lap as she dozed.

"Did you really enjoy yourself?" Benjamin queried, truly interested in her opinion of high society.

Her eyes met his. "Yes."

"No more problems?" he pressed.

."Not really." She shrugged off the encounter with Mrs. Johnson. "Did you enjoy talking to the gentlemen?"

"I didn't go to enjoy myself," he disabused her of the misconception. "I accomplished what I set out to do."

"Which was?"

Benjamin turned his gaze from her, focusing on the leather seat. Watching Leah laughing with other men had been damned hard on him, and he hadn't found one he liked well enough to replace him in her arms. *He* wanted to be there. He just didn't want the strings attached. He answered her brusquely, "I narrowed the field."

His words brought to mind feelings she had experienced when last they sat in this carriage, and her desire returned full force. She had made a sincere effort to foster feelings for the gentlemen she met, and she liked quite a few of them, but not in the same way she cared for Benjamin. There was no stirring of passion in her breast, no intense feelings of belonging together. Her eyes misted as she gazed at him. She didn't want some other man; she wanted *him,* and she wanted him tonight.

If he required it, she would keep up a facade of vapid friendship while in the presence of others, but privately she would not be constrained.

She ran her tongue over her lips to moisten them.

Lapsing into silence, she tried to think how she might accomplish her ends.

When the carriage came to a halt before Leah's house, Benjamin helped the ladies out. Mrs. Findley hurried ahead to light the lamps in the house, leaving him to escort Leah to the door in relative privacy. Leah

205

saw her chance.

"There is something I need to show you," she announced.

He tapped his heel impatiently. "Can't it wait till morning?"

"It is important to me that you see it now. Why don't you send Mr. Barnes on his way," she suggested, determined to have her own way.

"How long is this going to take?"

Leah shrugged. "I'm not sure. It's entirely up to you."

Despite his wish to retire to his own company, the eagerness lighting her eyes persuaded him to give her a few more minutes of his time. "I suppose I can walk back to the hotel."

While Benjamin returned to the carriage to give their driver permission to leave, Leah slipped into the house and dismissed her maid for the night. Mrs. Findley was too tired to put up more than a token protest.

Leah waited until she was sure her housekeeper would not see her and stepped back into the yard. "Lovely evening, isn't it." She gestured to the ceiling of stars. "Not a cloud in the sky. Remember how we used to sit under the stars on the island."

Benjamin glanced skyward, but said nothing.

"You should have a very pleasant walk, don't you think?"

"I hope you didn't keep me here to show me the night sky," he warned.

"No, of course not," Leah soothed. "I noticed it just now. Don't you think it's beautiful?"

"I suppose it is."

They stood, side by side, in companionable silence,

enjoying the quiet of the night. She delayed going in until she was certain her maid would be safely in bed upstairs.

When they entered the house, Leah took Benjamin by the hand and led him into the parlor.

"Well, what do you think?" she asked.

"About what?"

"The piano. It was just delivered this afternoon."

He shook his head in exasperation. This was the all-important something that couldn't wait until morning? Even for Leah it hardly made sense. Feigning interest, he ran his hand over the wood grain and tested a random key. "It's very nice. Now, I must be going."

"You've already sent Mr. Barnes home. Can't you sit while I play one song for you?" she pleaded prettily.

"What about Mrs. Findley?"

"I sent her up to bed."

"Won't the music disturb her?"

"Once she's asleep, nothing on earth can wake her till morning. Listen. If you're very quiet, you can hear her snoring. One song?" she continued to cajole.

He sighed. "I suppose one song wouldn't hurt, though I don't know why this couldn't have waited until tomorrow."

"Because I need you tonight." Leah sat down at the piano bench and began to play before he could respond to her last statement.

Benjamin retired to the settee. It had been a long and hectic night, fraught with dangers new to him. He could handle physical danger without fear, but protecting a lady's reputation had left him drained.

He had guarded his every word and action, purposefully protraying Leah as a woman above reproach. In the morning, he would have to check with their hostess to make sure Leah had not unwittingly undone any of his careful groundwork. He might not like Louisa Hastings, but he was convinced she had Leah's best interests at heart. They were reluctant allies, but allies nonetheless.

As the haunting music filled the room, he slowly began to relax.

Leah glanced in his direction and smiled, deftly moving from one song to the next without a break in the notes. This is what he needed. It had always worked so well on the island.

Letting the music weave its spell, Leah continued to play until she was satisfied she had attained her end. Benjamin lay sprawled, eyes closed, on the settee as she crossed the room on silent feet, discarding her clothing as she covered the distance between them.

When she reached him, she wore only a thin chemise. Straddling his hips, she joined him on the settee, holding him close as her passion hungry lips sought his again and again.

Benjamin moaned with pleasure, stroking her tongue with his. He loved the taste of her. His hands moved up and down her spine, massaging her back. His loins were on fire for her. Sweet Leah.

As she artfully unfastened the buttons of his vest and shirt, running her fingers through the fur of his chest, he abandoned himself to her gentle touch. He wanted her. He needed her. It felt so good to lie wrapped in her arms. No one would ever know he had succumbed to her.

"No!" He abruptly pushed her away. "Leah, what are you doing?"

"I'm loving you," she stated, undeterred. Clinging to him, she grabbed his earlobe between her teeth and nipped it softly.

Chills ran up and down his spine. "Stop that!" he ordered, fighting his own passions as well as hers. Sliding himself from the settee in an effort to extract himself from her embrace, he landed on his knees on the floor. "How many times do I have to tell you we can't do this anymore?"

"You can tell me as many times as suits you. It will make no difference. I want you." She continued to pursue him.

He managed to struggle to his feet as he fought off the encroachment of her silken limbs. "Leah, I want you to stop it this instant!"

"No."

"Yes! Get control of yourself now, woman." He held her at arms' length. "Your behavior is unseemly."

Leah's eyes welled with tears of frustration. "Don't you want me?"

"Of course, I do." He spoke between ragged breaths. "If I followed my instincts, I would bed you on the floor here and now."

Leah smiled, pressing her breasts against his chest. "Your instincts are good."

"My instincts could get us both in a helluva lot of trouble. Now back off." He set her away.

Buttoning his shirt as he strode towards the door, he retrieved his hat.

"Good night, Miss Daniels."

He was gone in an instant.

Leah stared at the door. She needed him so badly she felt she would scream. Why was he complicating their lives? He wanted her. She wanted him. It was simple, straightforward. Even the dumbest animal in the forest understood and acted on its needs.

She didn't care if people did not approve. It was certainly none of their affair. She would never presume to tell them what to do. And it wasn't like they were peeking at the windows watching their every move. As long as they refrained from coupling in the streets, who was to know what they were doing anyway?

Leah spent a full hour mumbling and grumbling to herself before she was calm enough to go to bed. Climbing under the covers, she hugged her pillow to her. It was a poor substitute.

In a room on the second floor of the Driad Hotel, a similar scene was taking place. Benjamin punched his pillow, rolled this way then that, did everything he could think of to get comfortable, but to no avail. Leah had lit a fire in his loins that refused to be quenched.

No wonder he had never gotten involved in the life of any other woman. It was pure torture. Never before had he let his lust override his reason. He should escape now. Book passage on the first ship out. He punched his pillow again.

No. He couldn't do that. He had set himself up in the role of Leah's guardian, and by God he was going to fulfill his self-decreed mission. The physical costs to himself were unimportant. He couldn't bring himself to throw her to the wolves.

He knew what he had to do. It was clear that Leah was a woman whose passionate nature demanded she have a man by her side. She was still naive enough to think she wanted him, but that would soon change; then, he would be free. No matter how distasteful the task, he would have to put more effort into redirecting her affections.

Despite having found fault with every man present at Louisa Hastings's dinner party, he began to reassess them as possible husbands. Finally, he reluctantly settled on three candidates. They weren't perfect, but they were worthy of further investigation. He would begin checking their backgrounds in the morning.

Having settled on a plan of action, Benjamin fell into fitful slumber. He woke frequently, and when he did sleep, his rest was tormented by disturbing dreams. Leah was there. Standing by her side was a faceless man. A swarm of children clung to their legs. If he walked toward her, she and the children smiled. But every time he turned to leave, the children disappeared into mist, and Leah slowly faded with them.

Chapter 14

A knock on the front door sent Leah to her feet, and she was halfway across the parlor floor before Mrs. Findley's words stopped her.

"Leah, dear, how many times must I tell you, it's not proper for the lady of the house to answer the door?"

"But I like answering the door," Leah demurred.

"I can't see why. More times than not it's a traveling salesman or beggar or some other charlatan bothering a body."

"I'm not bothered. I think it's rather exciting to see who I might find. Besides, if I can help out someone less fortunate, I'm glad to do so."

Mrs. Findley tried a different tactic. "Capt. Keaton would not approve."

Leah's brow crinkled. She was still feeling the sting of last night's rejection, and at the moment, she was not inclined to bow to Benjamin's wishes in any matter. "I know, but if he will not make this his house, he can't help make the rules here," she stated brusquely. While she was speaking, the knock came again. "I'll be right back." She exited the room, leaving Mrs. Findley to contemplate her words.

Returning a few minutes later, Leah took her chair by the fire. "There are fresh eggs in the pantry," she informed her housekeeper.

Mrs. Findley looked up from her knitting, her gaze searching, but her comment pertained to the matter at hand. "Well, at least it's something useful you bought this time. Not like that contraption you purchased day before yesterday."

"How was I to know we didn't need a curtain crimper? The salesman said every house must have one."

"Of course, he did," Mrs. Findley patiently schooled her. "That's how he makes his money. He would hardly waste his time knocking on doors to tell you his product is useless. I am accustomed to dealing with his sort. You should let me do it."

"I'll learn," Leah promised; then, she grinned impishly, "if I am given the opportunity to practice. You worry too much about me."

"I just feel I should be serving you better than I am. You hardly let me do a thing around here."

"You do more than your share," she assured her. "Besides, I don't want you for a servant. I want you for a friend. That's why I hired you instead of letting Capt. Keaton choose someone for me."

"You seem a little miffed with him this morning," Mrs. Findley adroitly changed the subject to the one that truly interested her. "Did you exchange words?"

Leah scowled, her shoulders sagging as she sighed loudly. "No, he is just being stubborn. And he is obsessed with this thing called reputation."

Mrs. Findley was much relieved to discover the source of the problem. Capt. Keaton might profess brotherly concern, but she was too old and too experienced to be taken for a fool. However, his behavior had been exemplary towards her mistress in the time she had known him. "A few days ago, I had my doubts about his character, but no more. He is a good man, and he has your best interests at heart."

Leah sighed again, a wan smile replacing her scowl. "I know he is good, and I know he thinks he is doing what is best for me, but he is wrong. The whole world is wrong."

"Wrong about what?"

"If a man and a woman love each other, they should be together."

"No one would argue with that," Mrs. Findley agreed.

"Then why wouldn't he stay with me last night? I needed him."

"Oh dear," Mrs. Findley gasped. Apparently, she hadn't been diligent in her duty. Leah spoke openly of her affection for the captain, but she had no idea she would go so far as to invite him to share her bed. "You mustn't talk that way," she admonished. "He did the right thing by leaving. You should be proud of him."

"I don't feel proud. I feel lonely," Leah complained, folding her arms across her chest.

"A lady does not invite a gentleman to share her bed."

"When I was on my island, I did."

"And did he accept your invitation?" Mrs. Findley pressed, despite her reluctance to hear the answer.

"Of course," Leah announced, deciding it was past time for her to be plainspoken with her housekeeper. "It was the natural thing to do, and he had the good sense to do it. Unfortunately, since we have come to Victoria, he seems to have lost all the good sense I admired in him."

"Oh dear," Mrs. Findley exclaimed for the second time, her knitting needles picking up speed. So that was the way it was. Though she wished he hadn't succumbed to temptation, she really couldn't condemn the captain as a heartless villain. After all, he was a man, and men were weak. She knew not a one who had the intestinal fortitude to turn away a willing woman. That the captain had done so last night spoke well in his favor, despite his earlier breach. Nevertheless, she determined to have a word with him at first opportunity. Summoning a parental voice, she stated, "Your relationship with the captain was not all it should have been while on your island."

Leah pursed her lips in vexation.

"Don't fret. I shan't judge you poorly for it. I'm sure you didn't know better," she soothed, pausing to catch her breath. "But what you have done in the past must be your secret and his. Here in Victoria, your behavior must be beyond reproach."

"In other words, I must live a lie," Leah condensed her housekeeper's discourse into five, crisp syllables.

"No. You just keep the truth to yourself," Mrs. Findley attempted to explain the delicacy of the situation.

"That is what I have been doing," Leah protested. "I wouldn't have told anyone he spent the night with me.

He knows that, and he still wouldn't stay."

"I'm glad to hear it."

"Why?" Leah demanded with a mournful mien.

"Because it proves he cares for you."

"It does?" Her face registered surprise, but the change did not completely erase the lines in her brow. "It seems just the opposite to me."

"That's because you are inexperienced in the ways of men." Mrs. Findley lay her knitting aside and patted her hand. "I have lived a good many more years than you, and I know of what I speak. The only thing guaranteed to turn a man from his beastly nature is sincere affection. I don't know why I failed to see that was the way it was between the two of you from the start."

Leah mulled Mrs. Findley's words over and over in her mind as she joined her in the routine chores of tending house. Mrs. Findley put forth her usual protest, but more from habit than any belief she could convince Leah to leave the menial tasks to her.

Louisa arrived in the early afternoon to discuss Leah's impressions of the dinner party, and invite her to join her and a few friends in a game of croquet on the grounds of Government House.

Having seen no sign of Benjamin all day, she readily accepted.

It took little time for her to catch on to the rules of the game, and much to the delight of all, she had a natural knack for the sport.

Louisa's friends were all female, and as they strolled around the field, they discussed the upcoming visit of Susan B. Anthony with much animation. Louisa was a most ardent supporter of Miss Anthony, and a promise was secured from Leah to attend the lecture with them.

Capt. Benjamin Keaton spent his day searching out new lodgings and moving his belongings from the Driad Hotel to a boardinghouse. The accommodations were considerably less expensive, something he deemed most desirable since he was committed to an extended stay. The home was also conveniently close to Leah's.

His business, he knew, would suffer because of his decision to stay, but he could send letters to his business associates in various ports. He had no intention of telling them his continued absence from the maritime world was caused by a woman, but he would apprise them he was still alive and eager for their business . . . just as soon as he attended a few bothersome details created by the shipwreck.

When he was settled, he stopped by Leah's house to give her his new address. He was both relieved and distressed to find she was not at home, but he kept his emotions well guarded as Mrs. Findley gave him the information.

"You didn't let her go alone?" he queried.

"She is with Miss Hastings and a full half-dozen other ladies. She is in good hands . . . for the moment."

"What does that mean?"

"It means I know about last night."

"Oh," Benjamin groaned, his cheeks becoming perceptibly ruddy, his high coloring caused by a mixture of anger and embarrassment.

Mrs. Findley ignored his discomfort. "Miss Daniels's absence affords us a perfect opportunity for a frank discussion. Come into the parlor, and tell me your intentions towards your ward."

"I believe I have already made my intentions clear," Benjamin stated as he followed her into the parlor.

Mrs. Findley automatically lifted her knitting basket to her lap as she took the seat nearest the fire, indicating for him to pull up another with a nod of her gray head. She looked him squarely in the eye. "I don't believe you were completely honest with me. There were a few details you failed to mention."

"Such as?" Benjamin asked warily.

"Such as: the fact you compromised Miss Daniels while the two of you were alone on that island of hers."

His lips tightened. "I suppose she felt compelled to tell you every detail of our private life.

'No. I doubt she would have told me at all, if I hadn't pressed her."

"Rightly so. It is none of your affair."

"Maybe not. I cannot affect the past. But you yourself have charged me with her future here. Though I give you credit for leaving last night when she would have had you stay, I cannot excuse your behavior on the island. There are consequences to such ill-advised indulgence. I think you should marry her."

Benjamin stared at her. Having no idea how much Leah had told her put him at a disadvantage. Enough to compel Mrs. Findley to suggest marriage, but not so much that she was unwilling to give him credit for his behavior last night. He doubted she would be so generous if she had witnessed what happened. He had been mentally flagellating himself all day for his lack of control.

If the possibility of marriage had crossed his mind, it was not surprising the housekeeper's thoughts had traveled the same path. Regardless of her opinion and his own culpability, he was not going to be coerced into anything, especially so permanent an alliance as marriage. "No."

"Why not?" she demanded.

"I'm not the marrying kind."

"Should have thought of that before you trespassed upon her person."

"I repeat, I am not the marrying kind."

"Are you sure?"

Benjamin growled. "Yes, I'm sure. You are putting your nose where it is not welcome."

Mrs. Findley remained undeterred. She was not the least bit intimidated by Capt. Keaton's dark looks or his ominous tone. She might be a mere housekeeper, with few if any rights, and she might not be able to dictate his actions, but she could give him something to think about. "As I said before, I cannot change the past, but I can try to affect Miss Daniels's future. Do you deny you took advantage of her?"

Benjamin's expression evinced his continued annoyance; nevertheless, he answered her. "Have you ever known Leah . . . Miss Daniels," he corrected himself, "to lie?" He countered her question with one of his own.

"No."

"Then you have your answer. I regret my actions on the island, but I, like you, cannot change the past. I will only be held responsible for the present."

Mrs. Findley measured him with her gaze. "Which brings me back to my first point. What are your intentions towards Miss Daniels?"

"I intend to find her a husband," he stated without emotion.

Mrs. Findley hid her surprise. "Why not yourself? You do seem the most likely candidate, and I'm sure Miss Daniels would be agreeable," she continued to press him.

He hesitated a few moments before replying, "I don't want to marry her."

"You could do a whole lot worse," she reprimanded.

He nodded his head in agreement. Benjamin recognized Mrs. Findley—like himself—had only Leah's best interests at heart. It was enough of a reason to excuse her impertinence and try to help her understand. If he was ever to eliminate himself from Leah's life, he needed the housekeeper as an ally.

He was rather startled when he realized he seemed to be collecting confederates at an alarming rate. For a man who had never trusted his fellow creatures in the past, his change of attitude was more than a little disconcerting.

He frowned at the housekeeper as she sat staring at him expectantly, trying to conjure some genuine feeling of distrust of the woman, but to no avail. He believed in her sincerity. At length, he forced himself to speak.

"Trust me when I say it would never work. Despite what you may think, I am not totally cold to her feelings. In the end, she wouldn't be any happier about a marriage between us than me. In a few weeks, I will be leaving Victoria, as I have planned from the start. Just as soon as I can secure her future. You can help me or thwart me, but it will make no difference in what I do."

220

"And her love for you makes no difference?"

"No."

"You are a hard man, Capt. Keaton," the housekeeper pronounced judgment upon him.

Rising to his feet, he started for the door. "I most wholeheartedly agree. Which is exactly why I am not suitable for Miss Daniels. Good day, Mrs. Findley."

"Good day, Capt. Keaton."

His discussion with Mrs. Findley spurred Benjamin to action, and he spent the remainder of the afternoon making discreet inquiries into the character of the three men he was investigating as possible husbands for Leah.

It was a laborious task, as he could not prevent his thoughts from moving beyond the marriage vows to the conjugal bed. It made him angry to think of another man lying in Leah's arms when *he* needed her so badly. *No!* He didn't need her. He wanted her. There was a world of difference inferred by the use of those two words. One could deny a want. A need demanded satisfaction.

Regardless of the source of his pain, he moved through the day an unhappy man. Thoughts of Leah heated his blood to the boiling point, causing him to squirm within the confines of his clothing. Though he could find no damning evidence against them—in each case the facts weighed heavily in their favor—not one of the men he investigated pleased him.

When he arrived back at the boardinghouse, there was a note waiting for him from the object of his labors. He alternately growled and sighed as he strolled down the street towards her house.

Though a part of him was anxious to see her, his wiser self warned caution. He had barely resisted her advances of the night before, and he didn't want to find himself in such a situation again. A man only had so much fortitude, and despite his good intentions, his had been stretched to the limit.

Thinking about Leah all day had only intensified his hunger for her. Lovemaking had become a habit while on the island, a habit he was finding hard to break. There were plenty of places in town to buy physical release, but that wasn't what he was craving. It was something undefinable that only Leah could give.

Even as he scolded himself for coming, his knuckles knocked eagerly at her door.

Leah sensed the strength of his need the moment her eyes met his, and she instantly forgave him for shunning her the night before.

"I'm so glad you came." She greeted him with a passionate kiss before he could disengage himself from her embrace.

She frowned, disappointed and confused. Had she misread his intentions? Her instincts told her no; yet, he had pushed her away. Was she the only one who felt the physical pull between them? Did his actions mean he cared for her as Mrs. Findley promised, or had he simply grown tired of her? Her frown deepened with each unanswered question.

"Where is Mrs. Findley?" he asked, searching for the housekeeper and the safety her presence would offer, as he valiantly struggled to rein in his lust.

"She's out back using the privy," Leah replied.

Cursing his timing, Benjamin crossed the hall with

rapid strides to put a defensible distance between them, until he could attain the aid of a chaperone.

Leah followed him into the parlor. "Is something wrong? You're acting strange."

He swallowed the hard lump in his throat. "I'm fine. Why did you send for me?"

"No reason in particular. Since I missed your visit this afternoon, I thought this evening would do as well."

Benjamin stared at her ingenuous expression. Why did she have to look so damn soft and inviting tonight? His voice was husky when he spoke, "What have you been doing with yourself all day?"

As Leah started to recount the events of the afternoon, he heard the back door open and close, and he let out a sigh of relief.

Her eyes clouded with concern. "Benjamin?"

"I'm fine," he repeated gruffly.

"Are you sure?"

He ignored her question as he turned to greet Mrs. Findley. "Do come in and join us," he invited eagerly as he led the older woman to a chair. "Miss Daniels was just telling me about her day."

Mrs. Findley's eyes narrowed as she nodded a greeting and picked up her knitting basket. The click of her needles joined the crackle of the fire.

Leah was distressed—but not overly so—by the intrusion. If Benjamin's resistance was a sign of affection, she should welcome it, even if it was hard to bear. As yet she wasn't willing to embrace Mrs. Findley's opinion, but there was enough doubt in her mind so that she was willing to test the theory. Smiling warmly, she resumed her account where she left off.

Besides the lecture, Leah had received two invitations to tea, and she and Louisa had solidified plans for a picnic in Beacon Hill Park the next Saturday. Benjamin listened with feigned interest, but he found after spending a good part of his day engaged in the distasteful task of trying to find a man to take his place in Leah's bed, he could not take his mind off what it was like to lie in her arms.

Her hands danced as she spoke, and he imagined them kneading his flesh. Her laughter tickled his senses. He could not pull his gaze from her moist, rosy lips as they formed themselves around each word.

At length, the tightness in his loins became so painful, Mrs. Findley's exhortation that he marry Leah himself started to look more and more appealing. He damned logic. Damned all other men. Damned himself. Before he burst out with some regrettable declaration, he seized a lame reason to excuse himself and bolted out the door.

Leah and Mrs. Findley exchanged bewildered glances, but said nothing.

The next morning Leah received a note from the captain, informing her that he expected to be fully occupied the entire day and would not be by to see her. Several days passed, with pressing business always given as the reason for his continued absence. To give truth to what would have been a lie, he looked into some local investment possibilities.

Leah stretched her arms high over her head as she stepped into the early morning sunshine. Surveying her yard, she mentally mapped where she would plant her flowers and vegetables the coming spring. She liked this time of day, when the streets were still quiet.

Absently plucking at a weed or two as she moved around the perimeter of the yard, she straightened when she heard the rattle of the paper boy's bicycle.

"Good morning, Cory," she called, reaching into her pocket for a coin.

"Morning, ma'am." He braked to a halt and handed her a copy of the *Colonist*.

"How's your mother? Is she feeling better?"

"Good as new. She said to thank you for those herbs you sent over. Whatever they was, that tea they made cleared her cough right up."

Leah smiled. "I'm glad I could help."

"Anything my family can do for you, just holler."

She nodded.

Propping his foot on the pedal, Cory adjusted himself on his seat. "Well, I best be going. Can't have my papers being late."

"No. Of course not. See you tomorrow." Leah started to wave him on his way, when she was struck by a delightful idea. "Cory, after you deliver your papers, do you think you could stop back here? I have nothing at all planned for today and . . . Would you teach me to ride that?" She pointed to the two-wheeler. "It looks like ever so much fun."

He grinned a toothy grin. "Sure, why not. Trouble is: you're going to have a problem with your skirts." He waggled an ink-stained finger at her blue woolen day dress. "Saw a lady the other day trying to ride, and her skirts got all tangled up in the chain. She flipped clean over on her head."

"Oh, dear, I wouldn't want that to happen." Leah

paused to think. "Wait. You don't have any trouble riding in those." She indicated his knickers with one hand, while she fished in her pocket for more coins with the other. She poured them into his hand. "On your way back here, you can stop at the general store and pick me up a pair. If it's not too much trouble."

"No trouble but . . ." He eyed her curiously. "Are you sure? I mean . . ."

"Oh, I know it's not the latest fashion, but it does seem more sensible than landing on my head."

"Yes, ma'am," he agreed, but made no move to be on his way.

"Didn't I give you enough to pay for the knickers?" Leah asked in concern.

"It's plenty of money," he assured her. "It's just, well, I like the way you're out here most every morning to send me on my way with a smile, and I don't want to do anything to cause you mischief. Are you sure you know what you're doing?" he repeated.

"Oh probably not, but it won't be the first time," she replied gaily. "You really best be on your way. I don't want you getting a scolding at the newspaper office on my account."

Cory Jones nodded his carrot-topped head and resumed pedaling down the street. Leah returned into the house.

"You're looking rosy-cheeked this morning," Mrs. Findley commented when Leah joined her in the kitchen. "Sit down and read your paper while I finish getting your breakfast."

Leah slid into a chair and opened the paper. Her eyes scanned the headlines, but she found she was too excited to really concentrate on the morning news. She

226

rose to her feet, set the salt and pepper on the table, sat again, popped up to fetch the cream pitcher . . . About the fourth time she sat and rose again, Mrs. Findley could stand no more.

"What is wrong with you? You're acting as if you swallowed a jackrabbit."

"I'm just excited, that's all," Leah replied.

"Capt. Keaton coming by today?" the housekeeper queried with a knowing expression. Her opinion of the captain suffered hourly revision, but she knew Leah remained steadfast in her affection.

"No. I am going to learn to ride a bicycle," Leah announced. "Cory Jones is going to teach me."

Mrs. Findley was momentarily startled to silence, but she quickly recovered herself. "You are, are you?"

Her tone caused Leah to cringe. "You're not going to tell me it's improper?" she asked mournfully.

As far as Mrs. Findley was concerned, bicycles were an invention she could live without, but if she were a younger woman, she knew she would have been one of the first to try them out. Bicycling was not yet common for young ladies, but it was not unheard of, and when the contraptions became more readily available they were predicted to become all the rage. Leah had been trying so hard to please everyone. She deserved a little fun.

"Just mind you don't break your neck," she admonished, turning back to the stove.

"Oh thank you, Mrs. Findley." Leah gave her a heartfelt hug. "I'll be careful. I promise."

Waiting for Cory Jones's return proved a difficult task for Leah. She was bursting with energetic anticipation. She did the dishes, swept the floor, and was halfway through polishing the furniture before she heard a knock at the door.

"Cory," she greeted the boy with relief, taking the package from his hands. "Come in. Mrs. Findley just stepped out to pick up the laundry, but there are cookies on the kitchen table. Eat as many as you like, while I run upstairs and change."

Her invitation was eagerly accepted, and she dashed upstairs.

Discarding her day dress and petticoats, she pulled a cotton blouse from her wardrobe. Donning the blouse and knickers with lightning speed, she paused only a second to glance at her reflection before hurrying downstairs.

"Ready," she called.

"Yes, ma'am." Cory tried not to stare as he joined her in the hall, but was only moderately successful. He swallowed hard. "Guess we better get at it."

Leah's first attempts to master the bicycle ended in failure, but she remained undeterred, even when she tore out the knees of her new knickers on one particularly nasty fall.

Cory helped her to her feet again and again, running alongside her, shouting instructions when she managed to maintain her balance for a few yards.

They were both too intent on their task to pay attention to the small crowd that was beginning to gather on the sides of the street.

Picking herself up from the dust yet another time, Leah gritted her teeth in determination and put her foot on the pedal once more. This time she traveled one yard, then two, then three, continuing on to the end of the block.

"You've got it!" Cory shouted in triumph.

A few sympathetic bystanders joined his cheers, but most of the citizenry were too busy shaking their head in disapproval.

"Outlandish, don't you think?"

"Shocking," another said.

"Knickers on a lady! Why, it is too rude to be believed! I feel a swoon coming on," commented Mrs. Almira Johnson. "And to think I invited her to tea. How shall I ever live down the scandal?"

Her companion patted her hand sympathetically.

Elated by her hard-won success, Leah continued down the next block, around the corner, then traveled down the next street. The wind whistled in her ears as she sailed down a hill. She panted with exertion as she pumped up an incline.

She had long since left a gasping Cory behind, and at length, she reluctantly turned towards home. Mrs. Findley would not be pleased if she found out how far she had gone on her own.

As she pedaled up Simcoe Street, Leah was rather confused by the number of pedestrians gathered near her house. She smiled and nodded a greeting as she rode past, but dare not lift her hand from the handlebars to wave.

As she pedaled past her house to the corner, a shriek pierced the air, causing her to brake to a sudden stop. Rolling end over end, Leah landed cross-legged in the dust.

"Oh my stars! Miss Leah Daniels, what has possessed you? Are you hurt? No, I can see you aren't." Mrs. Findley scurried towards her. Removing her apron, she wrapped it around Leah's waist to form a

229

makeshift skirt as she bustled her towards their house. "Young man, I left my laundry lying in the street. Fetch it," she spoke over her shoulder as she pushed Leah through the front door. Slamming the door behind her, the housekeeper stood on the porch. "All of you. Shoo!" She waved at the crowd. "I mean it! Shoo!"

As she stood, determined to see they carried out her will, an enterprising young newspaper reporter was already making his way towards the house from the rear. He slipped in the back door and quickly located Leah.

"Good morning, Miss," he neglected to introduce himself as he held out his hand. "I was wondering if you could answer a few questions for me?"

Though she was a bit startled to see a stranger standing in her hallway, Leah replied, "I would be glad to help you, if I can."

He pulled out a pad and pen. "First your name . . ."

Having seen to her duty regarding the crowd and regained enough of her composure she felt able to face her wayward mistress, Mrs. Findley stepped through the front door. She immediately recognized the reporter and his purpose.

"Out, you scoundrel," she ordered, shoving the laundry into Leah's arms so she could grab an umbrella from the stand. She waved it menacingly, and when he did not retreat fast enough for her liking, she thwacked him over the head. "Say one unkind word about my mistress in that paper of yours, and you'll live to regret it," she threatened as she beat him out the door. When he was gone, she threw the bolt behind him. Returning to the front door, she locked it also. Slowly, she turned to face Leah.

"Now, Miss Leah Daniels, what do you have to say for yourself?"

Having watched the whole scene in stunned silence, Leah simply stared. She was not in the mood to have her success spoiled by a scolding. "I like riding bicycles," she offered unrepentantly.

"It's not the bicycle I'm complaining about, and you know it." Mrs. Findley shook the umbrella at her. "Look at yourself! There's no telling how many people saw you dressed like that. I don't know how I am going to repair the damage you've done."

"The knickers will mend."

"Don't get cheeky with me, young lady. It's your reputation I'm worried about, not those beastly pants."

"It seemed more sensible to wear these than a cumbersome skirt. You did say you wanted me to have a care for my safety," Leah reminded, adding, "I really don't see what all the fuss is about."

"It's indecent for a lady to show her limbs. Lordy, in sixty-eight a woman had the temerity to wear a pair of bloomers, and you would have thought she had assassinated the queen for all the furor it caused in this town. And look at you! Knickers! Capt. Keaton will have both our hides, and rightly so."

Mrs. Findley's complexion had gone from pink to red to scarlet, and Leah began to fear for her health. All desire to rebel fled. Taking one withered hand in her own, she apologized contritely, "I'm sorry. If I had known it would cause you this much distress, I wouldn't have worn them."

Mrs. Findley paused to catch her breath, her eyes

softening as they gazed at her mistress. "I know that. There's not a mean bone in your body. But sometimes . . . Well, never mind. Just promise me you won't ever wear them again."

"If it mean's that much to you."

"Believe me, it does," she assured her. "If I wasn't already gray-haired, you would have turned me so today. Let's just hope we can survive the storm when Capt. Keaton finds out."

Mrs. Johnson could not resist going directly from the scene of the scandal to the home of Louisa Hastings to inform her of her new friend's shocking behavior.

Louisa smiled sweetly, said little, and bustled the woman out the door at first opportunity. Though rebellious of the strictures of society, Louisa understood its foibles better than most, and she immediately set to work to remedy the situation.

Calling on five of her most intimate friends, she soon had them coerced into cooperation. A visit to the general store procured the knickers. Her groom obtained bicycles for those who did not have their own. By three o'clock, all was ready.

Louisa and her band of valiant ladies stopped by Leah's house to assure her all would be well before challenging the streets of downtown Victoria.

"Good afternoon, Mrs. Findley. I would like a word with Leah," she requested.

Mrs. Findley's gaze moved over the six knickers-clad ladies and she nodded numbly. "She's in the parlor. I'll

232

get her."

When Leah stepped out onto the porch, she was as surprised as Mrs. Findley. Louisa stood at the front of the group, her head held high. Her friends stood chins to their chests, looking thoroughly miserable.

"We just came to tell you not to worry." Louisa's blue eyes danced with fiery zeal. "The best way I know to silence wagging tongues is for someone else to do something even more outrageous."

"Oh, Louisa, you don't need to do this for me," Leah protested. Having listened to Mrs. Findley lecture her on the folly of wearing men's clothing for well over two hours, she was well aware of the sacrifice being made on her behalf.

"Nevertheless, we will make our stand," Louisa announced.

"I should come with you," Leah argued.

"No, that would never do. We seek to rectify, not compound your misery. All of our positions in society are secure. If anyone is singled out, I will make sure it is I. Rest assured, no one will even remember your little indiscretion when we get through." Louisa turned to her reluctant troops. "Come, ladies. Our sister is in need of our services. To Fort Street."

Capt. Keaton stepped out the offices of the *Colonist*, having just placed an ad to try to determine if any of his crew from the *Sea Dragon* had survived the wreck as he had, and stopped dead in his tracks.

Pedaling up and down the street was a bevy of females dressed as young men. At their head was

233

Louisa Hastings. Panicking, he scanned the other women and was relieved to find Leah was not among them.

He turned from the scene. If Miss Hastings engaged in such antics, her social position notwithstanding, she was an unsuitable friend for Leah. He could not risk the association foiling his plans.

His lips set in a grim line, he strode to Leah's house.

"Capt. Keaton," she greeted him with uncharacteristic reluctance when he was shown into the parlor. She and Mrs. Findley exchanged worried glances behind his back. They waited with bated breath for his diatribe to commence.

"I know you are not going to like to hear this," he began, surprising them both with the gentleness of his tone, "but you must cease all contact with Louisa Hastings at once."

"What!" Leah cried in alarm.

Mrs. Findley remained tight-lipped and withdrew to the corner of the room.

"I know you like her, but I should have trusted my first instincts," Benjamin continued. "She is a hoyden who will only lead you into trouble. You ladies will never guess what she is doing this very moment."

"Riding a bicycle in knickers with five of her friends?" Leah offered wanly.

"I should have known she would try to pull you into it," he stated in clipped tones. "Well, at least you had the good sense to tell her nay."

"She wouldn't let me come," Leah defended her friend.

"She wouldn't . . ." he started to repeat her words. "Well, I guess I am forced to give her a little credit."

"You should give her more than a little credit," Leah admonished. "She deserves it all. It is very brave of her and her friends to do this for me."

Benjamin stared at her slack-jawed. "I don't follow you."

"Maybe I should explain," Mrs. Findley interrupted. "You see, Miss Daniels asked the paper boy, Cory Jones, to teach her to ride a bicycle. I gave my permission, not thinking any harm would come of it." Her lips clamped shut, and she tried to think of a diplomatic way to tell him the rest.

"And . . ." he prodded.

"It really is more my fault than her's," she assured him, well aware of her own deficiency in the matter.

"No, it isn't," Leah protested before Mrs. Findley could say more. "I'm the one who wore the knickers."

"You *what?*" Benjamin bellowed.

"I didn't want to get my skirts caught, so I wore knickers. Only I didn't know I shouldn't. Or at least I didn't know it would cause such a furor. A crowd gathered. And then there was that reporter. Mrs. Findley explained what a muddle I made of things. She had gone to fetch the laundry before Cory arrived and deserves no blame whatsoever. Anyway, Louisa, I'm not sure how she heard about it because she wasn't here, took it upon herself to come to my aid," Leah explained in one breath.

"Diversionary tactic," Benjamin mumbled to himself as he dropped his head in his hands. "It might work. Then again, it might not. Dammit! I ought to throttle you. No. Don't say it. You didn't know any better." He continued caustically, "Just because you have seen no other woman in the entire city wearing

235

knickers is no reason for you to assume it isn't done."

"I am sorry," Leah protested his tirade. "And I have already promised Mrs. Findley I won't do it again. Personally, I don't see why my wearing knickers should cause such an uproar, but in the interest of peace, I will learn to ride in a skirt."

He stared at her, his eyes alternately flashing with his desire for mercy and need for revenge. "Leah Daniels, you are the most exasperating woman I know. I'm leaving now. I'm going to shut myself in my room and pretend I never met you. Don't go out. Don't do anything. In the morning, *after* I read the papers, I'll be back."

The *Colonist*'s account of Leah's little adventure was guarded and set on the last page. The *Gazette* was not so kind, but both papers gave far more space to Louisa and her merry band. Nevertheless, there had been plenty of eyewitnesses, and the town was small enough that Leah did not escape notice.

Those who knew her were forgiving, and more amused than outraged, and after a day or two, she could no longer prevent herself from chuckling at all the predictions of dire consequences. Only Mrs. Johnson was moved to revoke her invitation to tea, but two other invitations arrived the same day, and Leah was not the least distressed.

When she did not have engagements that specifically excluded male companionship, Benjamin was constantly by her side. This was a consequence of her folly she judged most wonderful indeed. She took advantage of every opportunity to demonstrate, in ways subtle and not so subtle, that he was a welcome part of her life, and the invitation to share her bed was always open.

Benjamin regarded this change of circumstance in an entirely different light. Leah's overtures kept him in a constant state of rut. He alternately cursed her and himself, relying more and more on Mrs. Findley's presence to keep him on course, and steadfastly refusing to acknowledge that his attraction to Leah went beyond the physical.

To make matters worse, the housekeeper was not insensible of his problem. He often caught her studying him out of the corner of his eye. It was demoralizing.

If he could leave in good conscience, he would do so in an instant. He was playing a dangerous game—with his peace of mind at stake. He had to find a way to stop Leah from tempting him. He fingered the list of names in his pocket. One of the men named there would surely be his salvation.

Chapter 15

Foul weather had forced the cancellation of the picnic. The party had rescheduled the outing for the next weekend.

The morning of the picnic dawned cloudy, threatening to again ruin their plans, but by ten o'clock the sky began to clear.

Though Benjamin was on Leah's doorstep at the appointed hour, he looked less than happy to be there. Mrs. Findley handed the basket she had packed over to his care, and Leah and the captain walked to Louisa's home.

There they were joined by John Carlyle, two other gentlemen, and two ladies. One of the men, Frank Moss, was top on Benjamin's list of prospects. Gritting his teeth, he thanked Providence for the unexpected opportunity. Before anyone could protest, Benjamin took Louisa by the arm. "Get that Moss fellow to escort Leah," he whispered in her ear.

"What?" she replied in an equally low voice as she tried to disengage herself from him without drawing notice to her efforts.

"Leah is too attached to me. She needs to get to know other people. Get Frank Moss to act as her escort this afternoon," he repeated.

She nodded in understanding, in complete agreement with his motives and his methods. If she could persuade her friend to form an affection for some other man, she could break the hold the captain held on her. That done, she could work towards her ultimate goal of molding Leah into an independent woman like herself.

"Let me see, how shall we pair off?" Louisa asked, pursing her lips thoughtfully. Before anyone could answer, she continued, "I know. Mr. James and Carolyn, Mr. Carlyle and Beatrice, Mr. Moss and Leah, and the captain can escort me."

Picnic baskets traded hands, and with the exception of Leah and John Carlyle, everyone seemed happy with the arrangement. The eight of them set out on foot to the park.

As Leah's gaze moved between Louisa and Benjamin, she felt the stirrings of an uncomfortable emotion she could not quite identify. Benjamin didn't even like Louisa; yet, he was smiling in satisfaction. Louisa was so beautiful, perhaps . . . But Louisa was her friend. She would never . . . Besides, she didn't like Benjamin anymore than he professed to like her.

"I say, I almost thought we would have to give it up, what with the weather," Frank Moss commented, interrupting her chaotic flow of thought. Leah forced herself to give him her full attention, gifting him with a cordial smile.

"I was a little worried, too, but it looks to be another lovely day. I still haven't gotten used to all the sunshine you get here."

"We are rather ideally situated. Not many places this far north can boast weather fair enough for a picnic in October."

Mr. Moss's fascination with the weather continued to dominate their conversation. Leah responded politely and tried to appear more interested than she was. Her gaze often drifted to Benjamin and Louisa. They too were conversing, but their voices were low, and she could not make out enough words to even guess at the topic.

She tried to ignore the odd feeling in her breast but was less than successful, and frequent fleeting frowns stole across her fair face.

When the party settled on a suitable spot for the picnic, the men spread the blankets. Benjamin positioned himself near Louisa, leaving Leah feeling even more disgruntled. Smiling tightly, she determined to have a pleasant afternoon, despite his lack of chivalry.

Throughout the meal Frank Moss was solicitous of her every need. Despite Benjamin's warnings of the evil designs of men, or perhaps because of them, Leah did nothing to discourage his attentions. If the captain was going to neglect her, she saw no reason she should bow to his will. Besides, Frank was acting the perfect gentleman.

Gay conversation, punctuated with the latest local gossip, provided the afternoon's entertainment. Leah's frequent and forthright questions peppered the exchange, eliciting occasional rounds of good-natured laughter.

The incident with the knickers was mentioned and discussed—the newspaper articles having elevated both Leah and Louisa to the status of celebrities, complete with supporters and detractors. The issue of the propriety of a lady wearing knickers inevitably led to Louisa's favorite topic of late, Miss Anthony's upcoming lecture, and a lively debate of women's rights ensued.

Mr. Moss, Mr. James, and Carolyn sided with the traditionalists. Louisa and Beatrice were for progress. John Carlyle joined the two ladies, but the devilish twinkle in his eye led Leah to doubt his conviction.

Though Benjamin said little, when he did voice his opinion it was for the independence of both man and woman. He had no objection to women being given the vote, stating he doubted their choices would be any more stupid than the majority of men.

Leah listened intently, but said nothing. Politics were too new to her to feel comfortable arguing either side.

When it came time to go, no one seemed eager to end the afternoon. Even Benjamin seemed to have enjoyed himself. Plans were made to go yachting in the bay the next week, if the weather continued to hold fair.

"You're unusually quiet," Benjamin commented after they had said their good-byes and were walking towards home. "Didn't you have a good time?"

"Did you have a good time?" Leah countered his question with one of her own.

"Was I miserable?" He paused, shrugging his shoulders. "No. But you know how I feel about your friend Louisa."

"I thought I did," she stated plaintively.

"What's that suppose to mean?"

"I don't know." Leah echoed his shrug. "I want the

241

two of you to be friends, but . . . Louisa is so beautiful and I am plain. I don't want you to like her better than me."

"I don't like her at all," he assured her. "She's an opinionated, managing terror of a woman."

"But she *is* very beautiful," Leah argued.

Benjamin's cool blue eyes warmed as he surveyed Leah from head to toe—soft brown hair, eyes that glowed with a love of life, a firm chin, pillowy breasts, a trim waist, inviting hips, tiny, boot-clad feet. His heart quickened, sending hot blood surging through his veins. "I like your looks far better than hers."

"Then why were you so . . . cozy . . . with her?" Leah asked softly, making no attempt to hide her hurt.

Despite himself, he was flattered by her jealousy. However, he could ill afford the luxury of indulging his masculine ego. Stiffening, he answered her plainly, "So you would have the opportunity to get to know Frank Moss. I am considering him as a husband."

"I don't want a husband."

"You've been listening to Louisa too much. I agree independence is better, but considering your affectionate nature, I would feel more secure if you were comfortably married," he recited the line of reasoning he had been following with less than wholehearted enthusiasm.

"What about my feelings?"

"I just asked you if you liked Mr. Moss," he reminded.

"For a friend, yes." Leah drew in a long breath and let it out slowly. "As a mate, no. You are the only man I love that way."

"You don't love me."

"I know you don't like me to say it, but you have left me no other avenue of expression. I am forced to use words."

Benjamin was not deaf to her meaning. He clenched and relaxed his fists over and over, as he tried to fight off the unwelcome feelings caused by her reminder of passions denied. "You don't love me," he repeated sternly.

"Yes, I do."

"Well, I'm not on the list. I have told you before, I am leaving as soon as I have you settled."

"I know you have." Her eyes glistened with unbidden tears. "I just don't understand why."

Benjamin turned his head from her. He had no ready reply. He only knew he felt compelled to leave. It was a gut feeling. One he could no more explain to her than he could to himself.

As usual, when he started contemplating the merits of abandoning his life as a loner and staying with Leah, he was awash by a wave of dread. Unable to divine its source, his muscles tensed.

They reached her house. Benjamin stopped outside the white picket fence.

"Aren't you coming in?"

"No." He turned abruptly. "I'll see you in a day or two."

For the first time in his adult life, Capt. Benjamin Keaton did not know what he wanted. Every time he had himself convinced he could handle the situation, Leah did or said something to disturb his equilibrium. He didn't want her to love him. He had hoped she would have discarded the foolish notion that she did long before now.

When he was thinking rationally, he knew he should wash his hands of her and leave Victoria. He had done what he could for her. There was no reason he should feel responsible for her fate. The trouble was, where Leah was concerned, more often than not, logic deserted him. Every time he ordered his feet to carry him to the docks to book passage to his home port, they became leaden. No matter how hard he tried, as yet he had been unable to leave. There had to be a solution to his dilemma. He just wished someone would tell him what it was.

A sleepless night afforded him more than dark shadows under his eyes. Sometime between three and four in the morning, he had settled on a new plan of action.

Since he was clearly incapable of making a clean break, he would do the next best thing. He would make himself physically absent, but still be near enough to come to her assistance should Leah be in real need.

Mrs. Findley and Louisa would be his eyes and ears. If the incident with the bicycle had proved nothing else, it had proved the devotion of the two ladies. Both had done everything in their power to mitigate the damages caused by Leah's foolish behavior.

He already trusted her in their care. He would simply be asking them to cover for his strategic scarcity. He would regain his comfort. Leah would grow used to his absence. Everyone would benefit.

Benjamin found asking for help of any kind a distasteful task, but he realized he must for Leah's sake. He was determined not to compomise her reputation, and he knew if he continued by her side, he was in grave danger of doing just that. He cursed himself for his weakness as he covered the ground between the boardinghouse and Louisa Hastings's door.

"I would like a word with Miss Hastings," he stiffly informed the butler.

"Yes, sir. I will see if she is receiving callers this morning."

"Tell her it concerns Miss Daniels," he instructed, certain the information would gain him a more positive and prompt response.

"Yes, sir."

Benjamin twirled his hat in his hands as he waited in the hall, glancing at his pocket watch every few seconds. He wanted the interview over and done with before he came to his senses.

"Capt. Keaton, to what do I owe this honor?" Louisa gibed as she wafted into the hall, her hand extended. She withdrew it as the captain attempted to perform the formalities.

"Miss Hastings." He nodded curtly. "I would like a private word with you concerning out mutual acquaintance."

"She hasn't done something dreadful again?" Louisa asked, her distress evident in her voice. "Father threatened to lock me in my room for a week after I wore those knickers. Of course I informed him I would never tolerate such brutish behavior, but I don't think his heart is up to another incident so soon."

"As far as I know, Miss Daniels is not in need of heroic actions," he assured her. "I have come to discuss the matter I touched on yesterday."

"Ah," Louisa nodded her head sagely. "We can

speak freely in the parlor. I have been thinking on the matter myself."

Despite the foul taste in his mouth, upon leaving the Hastings's residence, Benjamin was confident Louisa Hastings would cooperate with his plan. In fact, she made no attempt to disguise her delight that he would be distancing himself from Leah's affairs.

She had even offered to join Leah on her daily stroll in the park, so he would have an opportunity to speak to Mrs. Findley, apprise her of the change in situation and solicit the housekeeper's help without fear of interruption.

Benjamin retired to a coffeehouse to impatiently wait out Leah's departure.

"Capt. Keaton, I'm afraid you just missed Miss Daniels, but I'm sure you can catch up with her if you hurry," Mrs. Findley greeted as she opened the door to him.

"I came to see you."

"Well, come in then, and state your business." She ushered him in, closing the door behind him. She followed him into the parlor.

Turning to face her, he began, "I have come to ask a favor of you."

"Yes."

"I have come to the conclusion that I am entirely too involved in Miss Daniels's life, and that involvement is a detriment to her future."

Mrs. Findley responded to his words with a frown. Apparently, the captain was having a little trouble noticing what was crystal clear to her. Despite their

246

polar personalities, he and Miss Daniels belonged together. In part the housekeeper's opinion was swayed by what had gone on between them on the island, but there was something else, less tangible, that compelled her to do what she could to keep them together. "I see. Go on," she urged with no further display of emotion.

"I believe I can trust you to watch over her, guide her progress, and report to me should there be any problems that need my attention. Miss Hastings has already agreed to do the same. I, of course, will still watch over her from afar."

"You want me to act as your spy," Mrs. Findley stated to confirm his intent.

Benjamin nodded. "It is not a very delicate way to put it, but essentially yes."

"May I ask why?"

"Miss Daniels's attachment to me is . . . not in her best interests. I think it would be better for her if she did not see me so often."

"Having a bit of trouble controlling your passions, are you?" Mrs. Findley queried.

He went pale, then reddened under her knowing gaze. Damn! Was he that obvious?

"Seems to me—now I'm going to speak plainly, Captain, so I hope you won't hold it against me—you are making matters more complicated than they need be," she continued. "I've been watching you, and despite your brusque ways, you're a decent man. I don't approve of long courtships. Why don't you just marry the girl and be done with it?"

His look blackened. "I believe I have already made my views on marriage perfectly clear."

"I believe you have, but that doesn't mean you can't

be changing your mind. Think about it. She loves you. You love her . . ."

"Now wait a minute!" He bore down on the housekeeper. "I don't love Leah Daniels. I don't love anyone but myself."

Mrs. Findley stood her ground. "Then what are you doing hanging around here?"

"I am fulfilling an obligation. Miss Daniels saved my life. Naturally, I feel some responsibility to see she makes a good start here."

"Oh yes, that brotherly affection we talked about. My vision may not be what it used to be, but I'm still far from blind. You'll have to come up with a better excuse."

"I do not have to justify my actions to you or anyone else. Will you help me, or won't you?" Benjamin demanded.

"I'm not sure I should," she stated honestly.

"Then I'll find someone else to do it." He started for the door.

"Where?"

Her question caused him to stop and turn towards her once more. There wasn't a soul he could get on such short notice, especially one as ideally situated to the task as Mrs. Findley. His tone remained harsh. "I don't know. I had counted on your cooperation."

"I know you can't see it, but we really are on the same side. We only want what's best for Miss Daniels," she soothed, fearing she might have already pressed him too far. He was such a strange man. She wasn't sure how to effectively deal with him.

"It is not in her best interests to nurture the hope that I will stay forever," Benjamin rebuked. "I have

248

made it clear from the start, my presence is only temporary. I thought you were a sensible woman, and would make sure Miss Daniels understood. My life is the sea. I will never marry her. The best she could hope for would be to be my mistress, a woman I might visit should I happen to be in port. Is that what you want for her?"

"No," Mrs. Findley admitted. "But she will be so unhappy if you stop coming to see her. I thought—"

"Well, you thought wrong. Don't deceive yourself or Leah with romantic delusions. I know my own mind. Now, I will repeat my question once more: Will you or will you not help me?"

Reluctantly, her frown deepening the age lines on her face, the housekeeper replied, "I'll do it."

As the day or two stretched into a week, Leah knew Benjamin was purposefully avoiding her, and she was not sure why. She shouldn't have told him she loved him. She knew he didn't like to hear it. But she needed to make him understand, and he wouldn't let her love him without words like she had on the island.

He said he didn't like Louisa, but Leah knew he had visited her more than once since the picnic. Louisa readily offered this information. He came to see Mrs. Findley frequently, but always while Leah was out. He answered her notes with excuses why he could not come. If she caught a glimpse of him in the streets, it was always of his back hurrying in the opposite direction. Her only consolation was the fact that he was still in Victoria at all.

The yachting was cancelled due to rough weather,

but Frank Moss arranged for the two of them to drive to the seaside. He did not object to Mrs. Findley's escort or her insistence that they never move beyond the range of her ever-watchful eye.

John Carlyle was a frequent and welcome visitor. He was funny and professed to be no more enamored with the strictures of good society than she. When they were together, he solicited her advice on how best to advance his suit of Louisa, and she asked him how she might capture the heart of the captain. Neither was of much help to the other, but they enjoyed a comfortable friendship.

Another gentleman, an Elijah Bennet, took her to dinner one evening.

Though she was never allowed out without Mrs. Findley or Louisa by her side, Leah kept herself busy attending teas, taking long walks in the park, and helping her housekeeper with the shopping and household tasks. Louisa introduced her to charity work. Mrs. Findley took her to church. The gentlemen of Victoria were most attentive, and she found she ate dinner out more than she ate at home.

Leah found pleasure in all these things, but her pleasure was always mitigated by a sense of loneliness. Though everyone around her treated her with nothing but kindness, she still missed Benjamin's daily presence.

The day of Miss Anthony's long-awaited lecture arrived. Louisa was almost beside herself with joy. She could not sit still in the carriage as they rode to the lecture hall.

Leah found the lecture inspiring, and she agreed with many of Miss Anthony's points. It surprised her so many injustices toward women existed in the world.

When the topic turned to marriage, she listened intently. The custom of marriage was often on her mind. She liked the idea of knowing your mate would always be with you and no other. Still, she was not convinced that vows and documents signed and spoken before witnesses could bind a heart. Only love could do that.

While Miss Anthony was not particularly complimentary of marriage in general, she was adamant that it should be founded on mutual love. Her speech confirmed Leah's own belief that she should not compromise her feelings on the matter. If she could not have Benjamin, she would have no one.

Having no one held little appeal; nevertheless, that night, as Leah lay in her lonely bed, she tried to imagine her life without Benjamin. To be happy was her nature, and if he proved truly intent on abandoning her, she would have to learn to stop loving him. Unfortunately, she had no more idea how to do that than she did about why she loved him in the first place.

The intense attraction she felt for him was inexplicable. She could make a list of his virtues, but she could do that for most of the other men she had met, and she didn't love them. She recognized his faults, but they didn't seem to matter. Deep in her heart, she believed they belonged together, and no amount of logical analysis could dislodge the feeling.

Sighing heavily, she fluffed her pillow and pulled it over her head.

If Miss Anthony's lecture did little to resolve her impasse with Benjamin concerning their future, it did inspire in Leah a desire to move out and about in the world more on her own.

She was tired of being treated like a child, or worse, some china doll with a hollow head, by everyone who was close to her. Benjamin, Mrs. Findley, Louisa, they were all guilty of trying to manage her life for her.

She had a mind of her own, and that mind told her all the rules and regulations that had been governing her every waking moment, since the day she first set foot in Victoria, were a burden she was no longer willing to bear. If other Victorians wanted to stay up nights worrying about the proper way to hold a teacup, or who they should or should not greet when walking upon the streets, it was their right. She, however, would forge her own trail.

There were still a few sections of the city she had not explored, and she was determined to remedy that this very day. Circumventing Benjamin was no problem. She hadn't seen him in weeks. He appeared to have completely lost interest in her. Mrs. Findley was a more difficult problem. She had too much respect for the older woman to wish to argue with her. Leah decided it would be best to send her housekeeper on some errand before she attempted to venture out on her own.

Having yet to meet a soul who meant her harm, she felt not a whit of trepidation. Danger was not lurking on every corner. She felt ridiculous for letting things go on as they had for so long, and she was through having her freedom stifled by others' unfounded fears on her behalf.

Shortly after noon, Leah managed to provide the conditions necessary for her escape. The sky was overcast, but she had a new wool cloak to keep her warm, and she was oblivious to the weather.

She wandered the streets without much thought to her direction, stopping here and there to explore a shop. She was friendly to everyone, and they in turn were friendly to her, supporting her belief that getting along with other people was a straightforward matter of honest communication. All the silly rules of conduct she had been subjected to these past weeks were an impediment to congenial living.

At length she found herself in the Chinese district. Many of the households she had visited employed Chinese immigrants, but she had never had the opportunity to talk with any one of them. She was sure they would be a most interesting people.

Leah approached a girl of twelve and greeted her, but the child looked startled, shook her head, and scurried down the street.

Though she continued to smile at those she passed, no one seemed eager to strike up a conversation, so she contented herself with poking about the shops.

There was an odd odor, similar to the smell of boiling potatoes, in the air. At first Leah ignored it, but at length her curiosity demanded satisfaction.

Through a window, she could see a man standing behind the counter. He was smiling at her, and she stepped into his shop.

Returning his smile, she asked, "Excuse me, but could you please tell me what that odd odor is?"

He spoke a rapid string of syllables in a foreign tongue; then, his lips again formed a serene smile.

She shook her head to signify she did not understand him any better than he had understood her; in a rush of inspiration she mimed her message by bringing her hand to her nose and sniffing the air.

"Ah." He held out his hand and pointed to her reticule.

Leah cooperated by counting out coins, until he nodded his head that she had paid enough. She followed him down a long hall. As he opened the door for her, she was immediately assailed by a cloud of pungent smoke.

Before she could retreat, the door closed behind her.

She had paid her money, so she might as well see what lay below, she told herself, despite a distinct feeling of foreboding.

The staircase was lit by a row of candles on the wall, and she cautiously descended.

The room below was filled with an assortment of adults: men, women, Chinese, white, young, old. They lounged on pillows while they drew in smoke from strange-looking pipes. Many stared glassy-eyed into the distance. All had the look of ill health.

"Come here, honey. I'll share with you." A grizzled man with a missing tooth motioned her to his side with his skeletal arm.

"No thank you," she replied timorously.

"What? Jack not good enough for you?" His words slurred into a snarl.

Leah blinked at him. There truly was nothing she could say in his behalf. She found it impossible to hide her revulsion. His filthy hair lay plastered to his head, his skin was dark with grime. Bits of dried food flecked his beard. "I just don't think I want to smoke that stuff," she offered what she hoped would be an acceptable answer.

"Then what you doing here?" he demanded.

"I don't know," she squeaked.

"First time? A little shy?" he queried, turning sympathetic. He struggled to his feet. "All the more reason you should let old Jack show you how it's done. Tell you what, you can just lay in my arms, and me and my pleasure pipe will take you where you want to go. It's a little piece of heaven they sell here."

Leah stood rooted to the spot. She didn't know exactly where she was, but she knew it wasn't heaven, and she didn't want to be here. The smoke stung her eyes. It made her feel sick. And these people. There was something not right about them. It was eerie the way they stared.

Turning on her heels, she started up the stairs, but the man who had offered to share his pipe with her grabbed her arm before she had traveled more than two steps. Terror welled in her breast, causing her to react instinctively.

Balling her fist, she swung hard, her knuckles popping as they made contact with the side of his head.

Chapter 16

"Captain, you got to come. I think she might have got herself in real trouble this time. Mrs. Findley ain't home, and well, I thought someone ought to know." Cory Jones tugged on the captain's arm, urging him out the door of the boardinghouse.

"Know what?" Benjamin queried.

"About Miss Daniels."

Benjamin pursed his lips, wondering into what kind of mischief Leah had gotten herself. He might have chosen to be physically absent, but he had been closely following her activities through both Mrs. Findley and Louisa. His surrogates allowed him to watch over her without subjecting himself to the physical torture of rebuffing her amorous advances.

He knew from his information that Leah still insisted on nurturing friendships with everyone she met, and recognizing this freckle-faced boy as the one who delivered her paper, it didn't surprise the captain that he was no exception. "Where is she?" he pressed, trying to appear unconcerned.

"I just saw her stepping into one of those Chinatown places."

Benjamin well knew that Leah was devoid of prejudice and would frequent a Chinese merchant as readily as any other. Not yet particularly alarmed, he asked, "Who was she with?"

"No one that I could see."

"She was alone?" Benjamin asked in disbelief.

"Sure was," the paper boy confirmed as he continued to tug at the captain's arm.

The planes of Benjamin's face hardened. He had given Mrs. Findley strict orders that Leah was never to be allowed out without an escort. His own observation of *her* had led him to believe she agreed with his precautions, but apparently he had been deceived. He should have never entrusted Leah's care to another. "Tell me the name of the store you saw her go into."

"Wasn't a store at all. That's what's got me worried. She didn't seem the sort, being a lady and all."

"Where did you see her?" Benjamin repeated, his impatience growing in proportion to his alarm.

"An opium den. Can't tell you the name, 'cause I can't read Chinese. I would have gone in after her myself, but my Ma would skin me alive if she ever heard I went into one of them places."

"Take me to her," Benjamin commanded, his feet swiftly carrying him in the direction of Chinatown.

The tone in the captain's voice was such that the boy did not even think to do otherwise. Together they dashed down the streets. As he ran, Benjamin cursed himself for a fool. If anything happened to Leah, because he had not been there to protect her . . . He couldn't finish the thought. Cory came to a halt before

257

a brightly painted shop front.

"Stay out here," Benjamin issued the order as he continued without pause through the door.

The proprietor was startled by his abrupt entry, but could do naught but scold him in rapid Chinese as he pushed past him to the door at the end of the hall. Benjamin slammed the door open, just in time to see Leah landing a second frantic blow on the head of the dissipated reprobate.

This time her efforts gained her release, and he sunk to his knees. "Damn, I hate a reluctant wench," he spat the words at her.

As he made to rise, his glassy gaze fell upon Benjamin, and his clawlike hand stopped in mid-reach.

"Touch her again, and you're a dead man," Benjamin warned with lethal earnest.

Babbling complaints about Leah's unfriendly behavior, the fellow crawled back to his cushion and sucked dejectedly on his pipe. No one else in the room gave a moment's notice to the drama.

Leah wasted no time turning to make good her escape, running headlong into Benjamin's chest.

"Thank you!" she cried in joyful relief, throwing her arms around him and at the same time urging him up the stairs. "We have to get out of here. This is a bad place."

He mutely aided her escape, holding her tightly to him, but the moment they reached the street, he set her away, shaking her hard as he released his fear and fury. "What in the hell do you think you were doing in there? I've a good mind to beat you here in the streets! Can't trust you for a moment, can I! Even you should have more sense than to frequent an opium den! I don't care

258

how curious you are. Stay away from that stuff! It'll kill you!"

Having the captain, flesh and blood, standing beside her again was as wonderful as having escaped the smoky pit, and she was more hurt than angered by his abuse. He was frightened. She could read it in his eyes, and she also knew she was the cause of his fear.

"I'm sorry," Leah answered contritely, the moment her teeth stopped rattling.

As he stared into her moisture-filled eyes, Benjamin's tirade came to an abrupt halt, and he released his grip on her shoulders. Damn! He was shaking like a leaf. He didn't like to feel this way—filled with concern, fear, lust, and guilt at his neglect, all at the same time. "Don't look at me that way. This is all your fault."

"I know it is."

"What on earth possessed you to go there?" he demanded.

"I didn't know it was a bad place. I just asked that man in there about the funny smell. He asked for some money and took me to that room. What are they doing down there?" she asked tremulously.

"It's an opium den. People go there to numb their brains and forget their troubles."

Her eyes widened. "They don't look happy. They look sick."

"They are. What they're doing doesn't work," he assured her.

"Then why do they do it?"

"They're addicts. The stuff gets a hold of them, and they get so they think they can't do without it. I don't understand how it works, but I know enough to avoid the stuff. It's poison."

259

"You all right, ma'am?" The paper boy tugged at Leah's sleeve, calling attention to his presence. "I would have pulled you out myself, but I couldn't on account of my Ma."

"Cory." Leah smiled at him. "What are you doing here?"

"I'm the one that told the captain you were down here. Guess it was a lucky thing I did."

"Yes. I'm very glad you did. You are the hero of the day. Thank you." She hugged him.

He blushed, stepping out of her embrace. "Well, I guess I'll be going. See you tomorrow, when I bring by a paper."

Benjamin turned her toward him after she had waved the boy on his way. "And now I am going to take you home where you belong; then, I'm going to fire Mrs. Findley."

"You'll do no such thing!" Leah protested as he escorted her down the street. "I'm the one who made a mistake. You may punish me if you feel a need, but you will not do so by sending Mrs. Findley away."

"I am not firing her to punish you. Mrs. Findley has been remiss in her duties," he stated.

"She had not. In fact, if anything she works too hard," Leah argued.

"She knows better than to let you out of the house on your own. We had an agreement, and she has not held up her end."

"What sort of agreement?" Leah asked, her steps slowing.

"She promised to look after you for me. She knows you are not to be let out of the house without Miss Hastings or herself watching over you. I forgave her the knickers. This is a breach I cannot overlook."

"Mrs. Findley did not let me out. I sent her on an errand so I could leave without her knowing it," Leah informed him.

"Which only proves my point. She has fallen for that trick before. She is not up to the task. I can see I'll have to watch over you myself, if I want it done right."

Leah greeted his words with a mixture of frustration and elation. Despite her recent experience, she did not feel she needed *watching*. No real harm had been done, and she would not repeat her mistake. But she had missed Benjamin terribly, and she could not help but welcome the prospect of once again enjoying his company whatever the cause. "I was beginning to think you didn't care what happened to me," she said softly.

"Of course I . . ." He interrupted himself. "I am merely doing my duty by you. Don't read anything else into my concern."

"If it means you will spend more time with me, I will try," she said without conviction.

"And don't get attached to me." His pace began to reflect his growing agitation, and Leah was forced to scramble to keep up.

"I'm already attached to you. I know you won't like to hear it, but I still love you."

"What about all the gentleman Louisa has arranged for you to meet?" he petitioned. "She has assured me she is providing the cream of the crop."

"Are you behind that, too?" she panted.

"Yes," he replied tersely. "Now stay on the subject. Who among them do you like?"

"I like them all."

"Surely you can be a little more discriminating than

261

that with your affection. What about Carlyle? He hangs about your place a lot."

"He is a friend, nothing more."

"You must prefer one or two above the others," he continued to pressure her.

"There is one."

Benjamin tried to ignore the twinge of jealousy her admission provoked. He had done his best to be pleased with the situation he had created, but distancing himself from Leah had not helped nearly as much as he had hoped. He thought about her day and night. She was like a disease with him. Why wasn't he eager to hear the name of the cure? "Who is he?" he asked more gruffly than he intended.

"You."

"Dammit, Leah! This is not a game we're playing." He slammed his fist against his thigh. "I am trying to settle your future."

"Then stay with me and let me love you," she implored.

"You do not love me. How many times must I tell you that?"

"You can tell me as many times as you like. It won't change the way I feel."

His voice had risen, causing more than one curious glance to be cast in their direction. Benjamin paused, taking a calming breath before he continued in a more muted voice. "All right, if you're going to be stubborn about this, you will have to defend your position. What unique quality do I possess that makes you prefer me above all other men?"

"I have spent many nights lying awake asking myself that very question."

"And," he prodded.

"I don't have an answer to it," she admitted. "I can list many things I admire about you, but I can do the same for a half-dozen other men."

"Ah, hah!"

Leah met his gaze directly and continued, "I believe the reason I love you is I know in my heart it is the right thing to do. It's very hard to explain, but I am certain loving you is what I am supposed to do."

"You can't explain it, because your feelings are irrational, and they are wrong," he stated with conviction.

"No, they are rational, and they are right. Every morning the sun rises in the east, and in the evening it sets in the west. Each spring vibrant flowers burst forth from tiny seeds in seemingly barren ground. The tide ebbs and flows without any effort on our part. Just because I don't completely understand why something is so, doesn't make it any less real."

They had reached Leah's yard, and Benjamin opened the gate for her. As he stood staring down at her upturned face, he decided to try a different tack. "I don't want you to love me."

"I know." She nodded her head sadly. "That is why I have tried to stop. But I can't any more than I can dictate the movements of the sun."

"In the end your feelings can only hurt you," Benjamin warned.

Her gaze held his. "Because you will leave me."

"Yes."

"You don't have to go."

"Yes, I do."

"Why?"

Benjamin had no more rational reason to offer for his need to leave than Leah did for her love, but he couldn't bring himself to admit that out loud. "I have my reasons."

"Is it because you don't love me?"

"Yes," he seized onto her explanation with gusto.

It was hard to hear him say it, but Leah did not flinch. She was willing to give enough love for them both. Her love was strong enough to sustain them for a time. Until he was ready . . . Until he . . . "I don't mind. We can be as we were on the island."

"That's not good enough for you."

"What do you have to offer in its stead?" she countered.

"Someone else. Some man who can love you as you deserve to be loved. Someone you will love better than me."

In one breath he said he did not love her. In the next he voiced heartfelt concern for her future. Was that not love? She quirked a brow and smiled at him. "When you find such a man, bring him to me. But in the meantime, do not tell me how I should feel."

"I am trying to do what is right for you."

"Then follow the dictates of your heart instead of your head."

"Ah, here comes Mrs. Findley," Benjamin stated, grateful for an excuse to abandon their conversation. "She is someone with whom I know how to deal."

"If you fire her, I shall hire her back immediately," Leah warned, concern for her own future replaced by her need to protect Mrs. Findley's. "She is my housekeeper, and unless you are willing to share my home, I will allow you no say in its keeping."

264

"Capt. Keaton," Mrs. Findley greeted him, a perplexed expression on her face. "I thought you were staying away . . ." The rest of what she was going to say trailed off as she realized she might have already said more than she should.

"It appears I overestimated your ability to supervise Miss Daniels." He came right to the point. "I found her engaging in fisticuffs in an opium den."

Mrs. Findley's eyes popped to the size of saucers, and she brought her hand to her bosom to still the pounding of her heart. "Merciful heavens! I left her by the fireside with a book."

Leah's cheeks colored slightly under her housekeeper's perturbed gaze. "I felt like exploring on my own," she stated softly.

"In an opium den," Benjamin reminded.

She had taken all the browbeating she intended to take, and Leah faced him squarely, her hands on her hips. "Well, I didn't know any better, but now I do. It was an honest mistake."

"All your mistakes are honest. You're worse than an infant." He advanced on her. "Do you have any idea what might have happened to you, if I hadn't come along when I did?"

Leah stood her ground. "I imagine I would have had to hit that man again."

"Well, I can imagine a lot worse," he growled. "However, I have learned my lesson. I am taking over."

"If that means you will be with me again, I am only too glad to see you come to your senses. *However* I, too, have been learning a few things," she stated, despite her pleasure at having him by her side, unwilling to meekly submit to his plans to continue to make her a prisoner in her own home. "I went to a lecture given by a Miss Anthony, and she was quite informative. You might not find me so easy to bully."

His gaze turned cold. "So you have become a radical."

"No," Leah admitted with rueful honesty. "I only agreed with some of what she said. Independence is well and good, but I have known true independence, and it is a lonely way to live." Her lips curled into a puckish grin. "I would rather have you, with all your faults."

"I'm honored," he scoffed.

As Mrs Findley listened to the exchange, she struggled to suppress a smile of satisfaction. She agreed with Leah; it would be good to have the captain back where he belonged. She was too old to be playing nursemaid. Though her initial distress had been alleviated by the fact that Leah had clearly escaped unharmed, her heart was still pounding at the thought of her sweet mistress being lured into one of those evil places. Besides, no man worried after a woman the way Capt. Keaton did unless his heart was no longer his own. She had been careful to say nothing these past weeks, but she was firmly of the opinion this separation did no one good. "If you two must argue, do it indoors where the neighbors can't hear you," she chided, ushering them both towards the door.

Leah immediately fell silent, but she was not subdued. It felt so good to have Benjamin home again, even if they were locking horns. She had missed him sorely. Clasping his hand in hers, she pulled him towards the door, bestowing radiant smiles upon his reluctant person.

"Leah, stop flirting with the captain," Mrs. Findley admonished as she shooed them into the house. "I swear I shall have aged a full year before this day is out. Try to remember what you have been taught, and act like a lady."

Leah did not release her hold on him, "I don't want to act like a lady. I want to act like myself."

Benjamin felt the laughter rumbling up from his belly long before it reached his lips. She was doing it to him again—making him forget he didn't want to be with her. How did she manage to ruin his carefully laid plans again and again, and still remain in his good graces? He should be struggling to suppress curses not laughter. The first of a long series of guffaws rent the air.

"Don't encourage her. You have no idea what a difficult task you have set for me, civilizing this young lady," Mrs. Findley scolded, battling to contain her own good humor.

"Oh, I do. Believe me, I do," Benjamin commiserated. However, he continued to smile warmly at the object of his frustration and affection. *A fairy child. That's what she was.* He wasn't going to admit how much he had missed Leah's silly little smiles, but as long as he was here, he might as well enjoy them. She never was any good at staying angry for long. He liked that about her. There were a lot of things he liked about her.

His thoughts heated his blood, and his defenses lowered yet another notch. What good had his self-imposed exile done him?

He wasn't any happier having others watch over her than when he had set the task for himself. It was disheartening, but he pushed his latest failure to the back of his mind. He felt compelled to protect her, so he might as well make the best of his fate. He was tired of fighting her. His fervid gaze warmed Leah.

"Will you stay for supper?" she invited.

"Yes," he replied, before giving conscious thought to the decision.

Mrs. Findley, watching the exchange of feverish looks, knew it was time to intercede. "If we are going to have a guest, I'm going to need help in the kitchen," she informed Leah as she pried her hand from Benjamin's.

"Are you sure?" Leah queried, her disappointment clearly written on her face. "You never needed my help before. In fact, whenever I offer to help, you put up a protest."

"That was then, this is now. Come into the kitchen. I'm an old woman. I need you by my side. The captain can entertain himself in the parlor."

Leah did not comment further on Mrs. Findley's abrupt change of heart, but she remained disbelieving of her motives as she followed her into the kitchen.

"Now, you sit there out of the way," the housekeeper ordered.

Leah remained on her feet. "I thought you needed my help."

"I'm sure you're bright enough to have seen through that feeble lie. Your captain is not at his best tonight. I'm protecting him from his own weakness."

"You mean because he smiled at me?"

"It's the way he smiled. I've seen that look in a man's eyes before. He's wanting you, and I can plainly see you haven't got the sense to tell him nay."

"Why should I?" Leah's tone evinced her delight in

Mrs. Findley's assessment of the situation, and she turned to hurry out of the kitchen and into Benjamin's arms. The housekeeper blocked her path.

"Because he's not your husband, and he has no intention of becoming so. He's made that perfectly clear to me," Mrs. Findley stated, despite her belief that the captain was blind to his own true feelings. He was here with her mistress again and that was good, but she didn't want to give false hopes, or allow him to make Leah his dockside doxy as he had threatened. "If he's not willing to pay the price, I'll not have him shopping in this candy store."

"Louisa says ladies who accept money for love-mak—"

Mrs. Findley clamped her hand over Leah's mouth. "We don't speak of such women in a proper house. I don't want him giving you money for your favors. I want him to make an honest woman of you."

"But I'm already honest, too honest, if you and Louisa are to be believed."

"You mistake boldness for honesty. A man doesn't respect that kind of woman."

Leah remained unconvinced. "But if he wants me . . ."

"You're missing the point, young lady. If I didn't know you better, I'd swear you were doing it on purpose, too. While I'm living in this house, I am going to do my best to keep you and the captain on the straight and narrow. No ifs, ands, or buts about it. I suspect I'm overstepping my bounds by doing so, but I can't help myself. I've come to love you like a daughter in spite of your queer little ways . . . or maybe it's because of them. Doesn't much matter why, but I am

269

determined to do right by you."

If there had been any doubt as to her housekeeper's motives for meddling, Leah was forced to discard them. Her annoyance at being kept away from Benjamin—especially if Mrs. Findley was right and he would willingly succumb to an invitation to her bed— was not lessened, but she gave the older woman a hug of affection.

"I am very fond of you, too, Mrs. Findley, and I know you are doing what you think is right. The trouble is you're wrong."

"Me and everyone else on earth?"

"If they think I should deny Benjamin my love, and it seems they do: yes. You are all wrong."

"It is you who is wrong, my dear. You cannot stand against the masses."

"Why not?" Leah argued passionately. "I read a novel where the hero did just that, *and* the masses learned from his conviction, and everyone was the better for it."

"That was fiction. You must live in the real world," Mrs. Findley admonished. "Why make life harder on yourself than it must be? You must learn to listen to the advice of your friends."

Leah sighed. "It seems all I do is listen to advice. There are rules for everything. Why, they devote whole magazines to the proper way to dress. There are articles on the proper way to eat, the proper way to sleep, the proper way to say hello. It's riduculous. Doesn't anyone like to think for themselves?"

"Rules make society run smoothly."

"Well, the rules they make to keep Benjamin and me apart are wreaking havoc, not peace. I love him. I want

270

to be with him."

"I know you do, and I am trying to help you. What has your frankness gained you?" She did not give pause for Leah to answer, but continued, intent on making her point. "His absence. Now he is back, but it might not last. Don't be so open with your feelings. Let him wonder. Let him pursue you."

"And you think that will make him want to stay with me?"

Mrs. Findley nodded her head affirmatively, but her words were less reassuring. "I can't say for certain. We can only pray."

Leah lapsed into thoughtful silence. At length she asked, "Do you think we belong together?"

"Yes, dear, I do, and I've told the captain as much, but he's a stubborn man. Don't get your hopes up too high, but I'll do what I can to help him see the light. Give him time to prove his feelings for you one way or the other. It's the only way." Mrs. Findley squeezed her hand. "It may not seem so now, but when you have been around men a little while longer, you will come to understand."

Leah sincerely doubted she would ever understand, but knowing she would get nowhere, she let the subject drop. She would continue to do what she felt was right where Benjamin was concerned, even if that meant bucking the tide of popular opinion, but she would not close her mind to Mrs. Findley's counsel. Only time would prove which of them was right.

The evening passed pleasantly, despite the fact Mrs. Findley never gave Benjamin and her a chance to be alone, even for a moment. After being neglected for so long, Leah was happy enough just to have him near again, and though she cast frequent pleading glances in her housekeeper's direction, she did not voice complaint.

For his part, Benjamin appeared in a genial mood. He had not said a word to Mrs. Findley about terminating her position in the household. In fact, whereas Leah met her housekeeper's hovering presence with exasperation, he seemed to greet it with heartfelt relief.

His reaction caused Leah to muse on Mrs. Findley's words. Had it been her frankness that had kept him away for so long? On the island, he seemed to delight in her boldness, but she was only too aware how much things had changed between them since they left her island. She resolved to be a little less forward, to test the theory. If subtle seduction would keep him at her side, she was willing to give it a try.

They spent the better part of the evening catching up on the details of each other's lives during the past weeks. Leah was surprised how little of what she said was new to Benjamin. Through the notes they exchanged she had kept him apprised of most of her activities, but he knew far more than she had ever told him. She wondered at his source of knowledge, her suspicious gaze falling on her housekeeper again and again, but she did not question him about it.

When it came time for him to go, Leah walked him to the door. Under Mrs. Findley's watchful eye, she raised on tiptoe and chastely kissed him on the cheek.

"Will you be back tomorrow?" she asked.

"Yes."

"When?" Mrs. Findley quizzed.

"Eleven o'clock." He turned his gaze back to Leah and commanded, "Don't go anywhere without me."

It was the first time all evening he had alluded to the incident in Chinatown, and Leah nodded her compliance. "I prefer your company wherever I go."

His expression evidenced he was less than pleased with her statement, as did his tone when he said, "Good night."

The Christmas season was upon them, and with it the usual round of social activity took on a frantic pace.

Leah found her time occupied with holiday preparations from dawn until dusk. There were presents to be bought and others to be made. She insisted the house be decorated from top to bottom. Extra care went into the baking of the cookies to be served with tea.

The holiday had been acknowledged on the island, but there was no celebration. Here life took on the aura of a prolonged party, and Leah threw herself into the festivities with unmitigated enthusiasm.

She was celebrating more than the birth of the Savior she was learning about in the church Mrs. Findley took her to every Sunday. She was celebrating Benjamin's return to her side.

Reluctantly, she had embraced Mrs. Findley's advice to be less frank with her feelings, and since the day he had rescued her from the opium den, he had been in attendance. He helped with the heavier household chores. Smiled often. Most evenings found them sitting before the fire, reading together. They discussed various passages from the popular novels of the day, newspaper articles of mutual appeal, local and world politics.

Mrs. Findley encouraged his presence, pampering him, inviting him to dinner almost every night. More often than not he accepted. There was an air of contentment about him. His care was solicitous, reminding her of the better times on the island.

He always accompanied her on her daily walk in the park. Leah loved this time to talk together. It afforded them a measure of privacy, as the only time Mrs. Findley did not insist on hovering over them was when they were in the public eye. The natural beauty of the park lent Leah its serenity, and even the most foul weather could not deter her from this daily indulgence.

Benjamin still could not resist voicing his distrust of her ability to discern the less than noble motives of her fellowman, and he complained loud and long whenever she left the house without Louisa, Mrs. Findley, or himself by her side, but she was always careful to stay out of trouble, and grudgingly, he was coming to accept that she would no longer allow him to impose such restrictions on her freedom.

She and Benjamin never spoke of the future, and Leah was careful to keep her need for more than the exchange of an occasional platonic kiss to herself. He was with her. He had ceased to talk about leaving Victoria. It seemed Mrs. Findley was right, and she schooled herself to patience. Though ofttimes she thought she read desire in his eyes, she did and said nothing lest she was mistaken. She didn't want to take the risk of offending him. They were friends again, and for now that was enough.

Central to all the holiday activity was a gala ball to be given at Government House. Louisa helped Leah select a gown of festive green moiré silk, with triple-puffed sleeves and yards and yards of cloud white lace.

They had gone for a fitting, and her friend's coachman had just dropped her off at her door. After brushing a light dusting of snow from her cloak, Leah hung it to dry on the peg by the door, and stepped into the parlor to warm her hands by the fire. To her delight, she discovered Benjamin sitting there.

"Did you have a nice afternoon at the dressmakers?" he greeted, laying his newspaper aside.

"Yes. I think my gown will be beautiful. Have you given any thought to what you will wear?"

"I'm not going," he stated without emotion.

"What!" Leah cried in dismay. Everything had been going so well between them. He had not balked at accompanying her to any other social function. "You have to go. I have been looking forward to dancing with you."

Benjamin shifted uncomfortably in his seat. "There will be plenty of other men with whom you can dance."

"But it's *you* with whom I've been looking forward to dancing," Leah protested, fearing he had renewed his interest in foisting her off on some other man. "You must come."

There was a long, pregnant pause.

"I can't dance," he finally admitted.

Leah laughed with relief. "Neither can I. That's why I'm taking dance lessons. *You* are the one who arranged them for me. I can't believe you were so foolish not to have said something before now. I'm sure Monsieur Perrault will be able to squeeze in a few extra lessons so you will be ready in time."

"You don't expect me to dance with a man?" he argued, hoping to put an end to the matter.

Leah's expression became thoughtful. She was not yet confident enough of her abilities to offer her own services, so she offered another's. "I'll ask Louisa to come be your partner."

"I don't like Louisa," he demurred, his expression obstinate.

"Then Mrs. Findley can do it," Leah countered cheerily.

"I thought I heard voices." Mrs. Findley stepped into the parlor at just that moment. She had been listening in the hallway and had timed her entrance with the skill of a seasoned matchmaker. "What is it you want me to do?"

"Benjamin doesn't want to go to the ball, because he doesn't know how to dance. I told him you would act as his partner while he learns," Leah informed her.

"I'm sure Mrs. Findley has better things to do with her time."

"No, I don't," Mrs. Findley thwarted his attempt to escape. "Fact is, I used to be quite light on my feet in my younger years. I'll be glad to be your partner."

"I don't want to learn to dance," he protested.

Her withered lips twitched as she struggled not to smile. "Everyone needs to know how to dance, Capt. Keaton. Besides, who will watch over Miss Daniels, if you don't go?"

"Miss Hastings," he promptly offered.

"Miss Hastings will be too busy tending her own dance partners to properly watch over our Leah. All that prancing about gets the young men's blood up, and it takes all a lady's concentration to keep them at bay. No," she paused dramatically, "I can see no help for it. You'll have to go to that ball."

Chapter 17

M. Perrault's delight at having his hourly fee doubled by the addition of a new student quickly faded to resignation, then ill-concealed vexation.

"No amount of money is worth putting up with ze cantankerous Capt. Keaton and his disparaging remarks about ze art of dance," he informed Leah and her housekeeper when he arrived early one afternoon.

"You can't give up on him," Leah pleaded.

"But his attitude, *Mademoiselle!* He is not fond of ze dancing. I think he would be as happy as I, if he did not come."

"Dancing is new to him, and he feels awkward. It is true, he was most reluctant to have your lessons in the first place." She continued to explain, "He always gets bearish when he agrees to do something of this sort. It will pass. It's just he gets a little uncomfortable when he has to be close to other people."

"I care not why he is a boar."

"His bluster is more for me than you. I'm certain he doesn't mean half of what he says," Leah assured him.

277

"Half is bad enough. I cannot teach under such conditions." He folded his arms over his chest.

"You just leave the captain to me," Mrs. Findley advised him. "He's a fast learner, and a few more lessons should do the trick. Miss Daniels has her heart set on him taking her to the ball. You will break it if you abandon the captain."

Where money could not have persuaded him, M. Perrault's regard for his Leah could. She was the perfect student—attentive, graceful, ever-complimentary of her teacher's superior skill. She was quick to laugh at her own mistakes and never criticized.

"Your smiles will be my compensation for enduring your troublesome friend," he relented, bowing low over Leah's hand. His pleasant mien transformed to one of long suffering at the sound of footsteps on the porch. "He is here. I shall say a prayer for patience, while you ladies let ze dragon in."

"Good afternoon, Capt. Keaton," the dance instructor greeted with forced cheer when Mrs. Findley ushered his male student into the parlor.

"M. Perrault," Benjamin nodded his head. "What new torture have you devised for us today?"

"Ze waltz," Perrault replied through tight lips.

"Well, let's get it over."

Leah took her place before M. Perrault, and Mrs. Findley positioned herself before the captain.

"Bite your tongue, Capt. Keaton," Mrs. Findley advised in a low voice. "There are only a few more lessons to tolerate."

Before Benjamin could reply, Perrault's instructions intruded.

"Now, we move our feet like so." Monsieur traced

out the pattern on the floor. "One two three, one two three, one two three . . . Ready. Take your partner in your arms and one two three . . ." He slowly eased from counting the beats to singing the rhythm in a nasal voice.

Benjamin opened his mouth, but before a syllable slipped past his lips, Mrs. Findley deftly brought her foot down on his instep. He ignored her clumsiness, but a few moments later, he found her foot on his toes. Then it happened again.

For a woman of sixty and such ample girth, Mrs. Findley had proved light on her feet on every other occasion. Something was amiss.

"Are you feeling quite well?" he queried in a whisper, hoping the woman wasn't falling ill. He was growing rather fond of the old biddy.

"Fit as a fiddle," she assured him.

"Good! Good! Now let's try some turns," the instructor's voice forced Benjamin to abandon the conversation.

He gave his full attention to the placement of his feet, until he got the hang of twirling the housekeeper around the room. He glanced at Leah. She seemed to be enjoying herself as usual. He didn't mind her pleasure so much as he minded the instructor's response. He showered her with effusive compliments, grinning like a fool.

Despite his desire that Leah fall out of love with him, it would never do to have her infatuated with her dance instructor. The man was a toad, and he was probably a fortune hunter to boot.

He opened his mouth to speak. Mrs. Findley stepped on him again.

"Ouch!" he exclaimed.

She smiled sweetly. "Sorry."

He started to ask her what was wrong with her, when she stepped on him again.

Benjamin was beginning to discern a pattern. Every time his lips so much as twitched, he found the woman tromping on his feet.

"What is going on here?" he demanded in a low voice, executing a bit of fast footwork to prevent further assault upon his person.

"I'm preserving the peace," Mrs. Findley replied without missing a beat. "Your caustic tongue has our instructor threatening to quit."

"I pay the man well enough," he argued.

"It wouldn't hurt you to be a little nicer to him."

"I don't like the way he fawns over Miss Daniels. He is here to teach her to dance, not fill her head with flattery."

Mrs. Findley's lips curled upward. "He is only being charming."

"He's a popinjay."

"He's a gentleman."

"If you'll recall, I didn't want to learn to dance in the first place," Benjamin reminded, his expression taut.

"You would do well to learn more than dancing from him," Mrs. Findley counseled.

"Hrmph."

"Capt. Keaton, Mrs. Findley," M. Perrault scolded. "You must pay attention to me. Whatever you are whispering about can be discussed at a later time. Learning to dance demands full concentration." He stomped his left foot on the floor three times in rapid succession. "Have I made myself clear?"

280

Mrs. Findley sent the captain a warning glance, causing him to amend the remark on the tip of his tongue.

"Perfectly," he replied, meeting the smaller man's gaze as he flourished a bow. "We do apologize."

M. Perrault was startled by the civility of his reply, but he remained composed. "Apology accepted. Now, let us begin once again."

"Popinjay," Benjamin muttered under his breath.

Mrs. Findley nodded sympathetically. "I'll concede he is a bit of a twit, but he is also the only dance instructor in town. Buck up, Captain, you can survive a few more lessons."

The night of the ball arrived and was greeted with joy from all corners.

Leah was filled with anticipation.

Benjamin was filled with relief at being released from the clutches of M. Perrault.

And Mrs. Findley nurtured hopes a festive evening might put the captain more in a mood to offer for her mistress's hand. There was no doubt in her mind the captain's harsh nature was losing its razor edge. Why the other afternoon she had caught him slipping a bowl of milk and bread out the back door, for the strays Leah was wont to collect. Day by day, he was growing more comfortable in the domestic environment Leah provided. Yes, there was no doubt about it. He was softening. It warmed her heart to think her gentle mistress might soon attain her heart's desire.

In every household, preparations had begun early in the day. Ladies soaked in scented baths. Gentlemen visited the barbers' for a trim and shave. Hair was crimped and twisted. Neck cloths starched.

"Hold still," Mrs. Findley admonished, as she tried to fasten a sprig of false flowers at the crown of Leah's chignon. "You'll never be ready in time, if you don't stop bouncing about."

Leah ceased her wiggling, but her heart continued to beat with excitement.

"That's better." Mrs. Findley put the final touches on Leah's hairdo, then tied her dance card onto her wrist with a ribbon. "Now, don't forget. Whichever gentleman has signed your card is the one you must dance with, and don't let anyone sign your card more than twice. It will set tongues to wagging."

"What about Capt. Keaton?" Leah asked as she studied her reflection in the mirror. "I should like to dance with him more than twice."

Mrs. Findley pursed her lips. The captain was certainly aware what message excessive attention to his "ward" would send to the populace. But his inexperience and ignorance of dance floor etiquette might be used to further her cause. When he danced with Leah, that look would creep into his eyes. Others were bound to notice his regard was of a romantic nature. If he publicly proclaimed his interest by standing for more than the usual number of dances, assumptions would be made about his intentions.

Perhaps the resulting gossip would be just the little push that was needed to convince him to marry the girl. Her eyes lit at the prospect. Leah would be held blameless if a proposal of matrimony was not the result. The captain would suffer all the censure. Mrs. Findley would not stand in the way of fate. "You may dance with the captain as many times as he asks you," she stated cheerfully.

"How wonderful," Leah exclaimed.

"Now, don't get your heart set on dancing the night away with him. He may not ask you more than twice."

Leah nodded her head in compliance, but the rose in her cheeks and fire in her eyes could not be muted. "I hope he does, just the same."

"So do I, but as you well know, the captain has a mind of his own." Mrs. Findley cocked her head at the sound of a rap on the door. "That must be him now. Let's not keep him waiting. We want him in a good mood."

Leah answered the door while Mrs. Findley fetched their wraps. Her eyes sparkled as they took in Benjamin's top hat and tails. "You are quite the most handsome sight I have ever seen," she announced as she ushered him into the hall.

"I feel a fool," he mumbled morosely.

Leah's expression became more sober. "I know how you feel about socializing, and that you are doing all this for my sake. I fear I have neglected to thank you often enough for your sacrifice."

For once in his life, Benjamin felt culpable for his lack of social grace. He was here. He was committed. He had absolutely no right to spoil Leah's evening. "My sacrifice is small enough. Who knows? It might be good for me," he offered with false conviction.

Leah smiled broadly. "Exactly my thinking."

Mrs. Findley arrived with the cloaks, and they were soon on their way up the hill to Government House.

Government House's former name was Cary Castle, called so because of the crenels and merlons topping the tower that was part of the original structure. Over the years additions had been made by the royal governors who made their home there, and it sprawled atop the hill like a gangly adolescent.

The yard of the old stone residence was already filled with carriages when they arrived, and they were forced to wait their turn to alight.

The Honorable Sir Joseph William Trutch, the premier, the mayor, and their families stood in line in the drawing room to receive their guests. Hundreds were invited. The press of humanity was overwhelming, and Leah clutched Benjamin's hand. Sensing her distress, he gave her hand a reassuring squeeze, knowing the crowd was such that no one could possibly be aware of the intimacy.

No one did notice except Mrs. Findley, whose sharp eyes were always on the lookout for some sign that she was not mistaken in her faith in the strength of the captain's affection for Leah.

"Take some deep breaths, dear. It might help," she advised.

Leah did as she was told, and soon began to feel a little less suffocated.

It wasn't long before the single gentlemen milling through the crowd made their way, one by one, to Leah's side to request a spot on her dance card.

As the card rapidly filled, Leah began to fear she would be left no opportunity to dance with the captain. This was a circumstance she refused to allow, and she quickly scribbled his name in several of the remaining blank spaces.

When she had a few moments, she was able to spy a few of her female friends here and there across the room, but could do no more than wave from afar. Louisa was surrounded by a flock of gentlemen and did not see her. She was beautiful as always in a gossamer gown of icy pink, and she presided over the gentlemen like a queen. Leah thought it amusing that her friend was not adverse to the attentions of the men for whom she claimed she had no use. In fact, ofttimes she feared Louisa encouraged them, so she might have the pleasure of scalding their ears with a sound setdown.

Her gaze continued to search the crowd for more familiar faces.

At nine o'clock the doors to the ballroom were opened. Fearing they would be separated by the force of the crowd, Leah grabbed Benjamin with one hand and Mrs. Findley with the other.

Outside the night might be gray and cold, but inside the ballroom everything was lightness and warmth. Fir boughs tied with bright red velvet ribbons decorated the walls. The musicians stood at the ready on a raised platform decorated in like manner. Great bowls of red Christmas punch were available to quench the dancers' thirst. Candles and gas lamps lit the room.

Mrs. Findley retired to a quiet corner to join the other unattached ladies serving as chaperones, leaving Leah and Benjamin on their own.

Benjamin, realizing he still held Leah's hand in his, peeled her fingers from him with whispered words of encouragement. "Don't worry, it won't be as crowded in here."

Glancing about the colorful sea of humanity, Leah was little comforted by his words. The improvement was minimal, but she had to admit that she was growing more used to the crush. Before she could comment to this effect, the sound of her name being called caught her attention.

John Carlyle pushed his way through the crowd to their side. "I hope all your dances aren't already promised," he greeted.

"There are still a few spaces left," she assured him.

He beamed. "May I have them all?" he begged with courtly aplomb.

Leah laughed. "Mrs. Findley said I should only allow you two."

"Fie on her. I shall steal three." He reached for the card.

"The lady said two," Benjamin admonished with a warning growl.

"Two," he conceded graciously, signing his name twice on her dance card. "What's this?" he demanded, his smile never slipping from place. "I see you are playing favorites with the captain."

"Yes," she replied gaily.

Benjamin's eyes narrowed. "I have not signed your card at all."

Leah blushed but smiled unrepentantly. "I took the liberty of doing it for you," she admitted holding up the card for his inspection. His name had been entered no less than six times.

"It seems you have succeeded in capturing the lady's heart," John offered his congratulations. "My loss is your gain. Best fill in your program, so you don't end up with two ladies for the same set. Ruffles their feathers, you know." He turned his head, scanning the crowd. "Speaking of ruffled feathers, I must find Miss Hastings before her card is filled."

"Haven't you seen Louisa yet?" Leah queried.

"No. I was hoping you might tell me where to find her."

Leah shook her head. "I saw her in the drawing room, but I've since lost track of her. I have never seen so many people in such a small space."

Mr. Carlyle would have continued the conversation, if Benjamin had not called it to a halt. "Miss Daniels, I would like a word with you in private."

"Good luck." John gestured to the crowd for the captain's benefit, but his words were really meant for Leah. He threw her a wink before disappearing into the crowd.

Benjamin's efforts to guide Leah to a quiet corner were frustrated time and time again by some acquaintance or another stepping into their path. A conversation inevitably ensued, and at length he was forced to abandon his course.

He had resigned himself to one or two dances, but six? Surely that was beyond the call of duty. He had no interest in making a spectacle of himself. He would have to find a way to . . .

"I'm sure the captain would love to dance with you." It was not Leah's words, but the dance card dangling in front of his nose that penetrated his musings.

"What's this?"

"A dance card, silly. You will dance with Carolyn, won't you?"

There was no way he could politely refuse. "Of course," he replied as he put his name to the card. Another quickly replaced it, and his heart sank. Counting Leah's six, he was now committed to eight dances. The evening was rapidly getting out of hand. His hope had been to satisfy Leah with a dance or two, then escape to some corner to wait out the evening. What had he gotten himself into?

As they left the ladies, Leah whispered in his ear. "I think you should go over and offer to dance with Kathleen."

"I don't know a Kathleen," he protested.

"You've yet to meet," Leah confirmed his claim, "but I'm sure you'll like her."

"I don't want to dance with Kathleen. I don't *want* to dance with anyone," he informed her.

"Oh, don't be stubborn. As long as you're here, you might as well enjoy yourself. Please ask Kathleen to dance with you." Her sunny smile tugged at his heart.

"Why is whether or not I dance with this woman so important to you?"

"She's very shy, and Carolyn said hardly anyone has signed her card. She is a wonderful person, but few realize it because she is so hard to get to know. It would give her confidence a much-needed boost, if her dance card were to fill."

"You can't resist coming to the aid of every unfortunate creature you meet, can you? Who is she?" he asked wearily.

"The one in the blue dress standing by the wall."

Benjamin's gaze followed her to the pale young woman with her back pressed against the wall. She was painfully thin and plain, with dark brown hair and large dark eyes. She looked as miserable as a mouse caught in the jaws of a ship's cat. Well, at least they had something in common. He didn't want to be here either.

"I'll ask her to dance," he heard himself surrender, before he could bite his tongue. "But this is the last favor I am doing for you this evening." At this rate he wouldn't have a moment's peace. How was he suppose to watch over Leah if he was busy watching his own feet? It was a moot question, as the size of the crowd made the task impossible in any case. What could Mrs. Findley have been thinking when she insisted he come to this affair?

"Thank you." Leah smiled her gratitude and ignored his last remark. "I knew you'd understand."

The music was beginning, and Leah glanced at her card to see to whom she had promised the first dance of the evening. It was Frank Moss, and much to her surprise, he miraculously materialized at her side.

"I believe this dance is mine." He eagerly offered his arm.

She nodded, allowing him to lead her out onto the dance floor. A few moments later, Benjamin followed in their footsteps, Kathleen on his arm, and took the place behind them for the first quadrille. Leah cast her loving gaze upon him before turning to face her partner.

After the first dance she lost track of him, as one dance led to another. She conversed gaily with her string of partners, delighting in the festive atmosphere. She found dancing a joy, and her pleasure radiated in the bloom of her cheeks.

It was not until the fourth dance that she caught a glimpse of Louisa. The light shimmered off her gown, and she sparkled from head to toe as she danced with her father. When John Carlyle claimed her friend for the next dance, he and Leah exchanged smiles from across the room.

John was scheduled to partner her next, and at last

she and Louisa were able to trade a quick greeting before they were whisked away by their respective partners.

"Your friend the captain is full of surprises this evening," John commented when the steps of the dance brought them close enough for conversation.

Leah moved up and back in the line before she was able to ask, "What do you mean?"

Their conversation continued in snatches as they moved through the steps of the dance.

"He has taken it upon himself to strong-arm me into signing up to dance with that little mouse, Kathleen Drummond. Was headed towards another gentleman once he had me convinced. He had me fooled. I would have never guessed he was a decent fellow."

"I have been telling you so all along," Leah admonished, but even she was surprised to hear Benjamin had taken Kathleen's welfare to heart.

"So you have. I keep forgetting you are as smart as you are sweet. At least now that I have witnessed the better side of the irascible Capt. Keaton with my own eyes, I will not feel so put out that you prefer him over me. There is hope my shattered soul may mend with time. My poor heart will survive to beat for another."

"You are incorrigible," Leah scolded. "You don't love me; you love Louisa. Or so you say. With you I'm never sure."

John grinned. "Keep them guessing, that's my motto. I love Louisa because she will not have me. Who knows, if she should ever change her tune, what I would do?"

"Well, there is little danger of that. Louisa loves

nothing better than she loves the cause of women's rights."

"And you?"

Leah's eyes softened. "I love nothing so well as my captain."

"Speaking of the devil, here he comes now. I think I'll find my next partner." John was gone in an instant.

"Capt. Keaton." She curtsied after a quick glance at her dance card confirmed he was indeed her next partner. To her delight the dance was a waltz.

She eagerly took her place within the circle of his arms. It felt like heaven to be there again, and she sighed in contentment.

As he moved her about the crowded dance floor, with an ease at odds with his oft-claimed dislike of dancing, she was moved to comment. "Thank you for what you did for Kathleen."

Benjamin voiced his disapproval that his act of altruism had reached her ears with a primitive groan. "She looked so pathetic when I left her standing against the wall, it was either that or dance every dance with her myself. It was the lesser of two evils."

She should have known better than to expect him to take credit for his noble deed, and Leah regretted mentioning it at all. She wanted nothing to spoil their waltz.

M. Perrault had always partnered her during their lessons, and this was the first time in what seemed to her an eternity that Benjamin had willingly held her in his arms. The feel of his sinewy muscles beneath her fingertips delighted her senses. She abandoned all thought, letting the rhythm of the music and the pleasure of his nearness enchant away all concerns.

Benjamin gazed down at the woman he held in his arms. She said not a word, but the movements of her body were like a siren song. Each day he felt a new thread of her silken web bind him to her. He wanted her beneath him to ease the hunger in his loins. Though she no longer begged him to take her to his bed, not doing so was a constant battle with him. But he wanted her for more than that. She amused him. He liked her company.

Somehow she had changed him. The very fact he was at this Christmas ball was proof enough of that. Lately, he was finding himself doing so many things he deemed out of character, he barely recognized himself. Before long he would be as utopian as she. His sea-blue eyes met her sparkling brown ones, and he smiled. Tonight that prospect didn't seem so terrible a fate as it once had.

The dance ended. Leah was immediately whisked away by her new partner. Benjamin was free for the next dance; then, he must perform his gentlemanly duty with Carolyn.

Many dances later, Benjamin and Leah were again paired together, this time for a lively jig. There was little opportunity to engage in conversation, but they communicated much with a look and the touch of the hand.

When Benjamin once again left her side, Leah's disappointment was mitigated by the realization that he had begun to truly enjoy himself. His smiles were genuine, not forced for the sake of politeness. The stiffness was gone from his carriage. The gleam in his eyes less grim. Despite having lived in the world all his life, in many ways he was as much a novice as she when it came to experiencing its pleasures. It was wonderful to see him let down his rigid guard.

At midnight the doors to the supper room were opened, and the guests offered an abundance to sate their appetites.

Leah was escorted into the room by her latest dance partner, a Mr. Ephraim Elliot. The table was loaded with pies and pastries, apples, oranges, cold meats, and breads of every description.

Her eyes searched for Benjamin, but she could not find him in the crowd. However, in the course of her search, her gaze did light upon several persons she knew including John Carlyle. Their eyes met, and he smiled roguishly as he helped Kathleen Drummond fill her plate.

Toasts were proposed. They drank and cheered the health of the queen, the colony's recent union with the Dominion of Canada, and a host of other lesser personages and events. Mayor Robertson made a speech.

Upon returning to the ballroom, they were entertained by several musical pieces performed on the piano by the wives and daughters of their hosts and hostesses. Then the dancing began anew.

This portion of the program included twenty-one dances. There was not a blank spot on her dance card as Leah looked over the list of names, and she smiled and sighed at the same time. Despite the respite provided by the late night supper, her feet were beginning to hurt. She noticed quite a few guests drifted towards the door, but she was determined not to miss a moment of the fun.

Though her eyes constantly scanned the crowd fo. him, she did not see Benjamin until it was time for him to dance with her again. Her eyes lit with joy when she spied him making his way toward her.

"Miss Daniels." He bowed his head as he cradled her hand and took his position in the line of men opposite the ladies. The music began, and the head couple—a beaming John Carlyle and Kathleen Drummond—stepped out to sashay under the arch provided by the other dancers' outstretched arms.

"Are you ready to go home yet?" Benjamin queried, keeping his voice low as the dance proceeded.

"I can't. I've promised every dance on the program. I hope you don't mind too much."

Benjamin shrugged. "Dancing isn't half bad without that irritating little Frenchman breathing down my neck," he admitted. "I'll survive."

It was their turn to dance to the center and Leah was prevented from commenting, but she smiled her approval.

Though she enjoyed dancing with all her partners, Leah impatiently looked forward to every dance she could share with Benjamin. Each touch sent a trill of excitement through her veins, and the waltzes they shared were nothing short of euphoric. No one would guess at the captain's inexperience as he moved with graceful ease through the steps of the dance, unhindered by the slight limp remaining from his injury.

The ball was better than she had imagined it would be, and despite her exhaustion, Leah could not help but be a little disappointed when it drew to an end at half-past three.

The crowd had lessened considerably, but still they

had to wait in line to retrieve their hats and cloaks. In all the excitement, Leah had completely forgotten about her housekeeper's presence, and she was relieved to find Mrs. Findley looking as if she had weathered the evening well.

The ride home was chilly despite lap blankets, but the brisk air was welcome after the stifling conditions of the crowded ballroom. In the few minutes it took to reach her house, Leah chattered gaily about the various sights and scenes of the evening. Benjamin responded with uncharacteristic charm.

Upon reaching the house, he escorted the ladies to their door. Good-byes were said. Leah thanked him for the evening with a genteel kiss on the cheek.

As he walked back to the waiting coach, Benjamin glanced over his shoulder at the house. It seemed to be smiling at him.

Chapter 18

It was December twenty-fourth, and much of the day Leah and Mrs. Findley had been tying ribbons around brightly papered packages. Towards mid-afternoon Benjamin arrived to see that the wagonload of wood he had ordered to replenish their stockpile had been delivered.

After carrying in enough kindling to fill the wood box by the kitchen stove, he joined the ladies in the parlor. His eyes surveyed the growing pile of packages in dismay. "What did you do? Buy a gift for every person in Victoria?" He turned to the housekeeper, knowing by Leah's serene expression he would make little impression on her. "And where were you when she was buying all this? You are suppose to make sure she doesn't squander her money."

"Now, Captain, it's Christmas, and it only comes once a year," Mrs. Findley argued.

"That may be so, but poverty lasts all year long."

"I did my best to convince her such generosity wasn't necessary, but you know how Miss Daniels is when she takes a liking to someone."

"I haven't done anything foolish," Leah asserted. "If you need more proof than my word, you can look at the household accounts."

"Believe me, I intend to do just that." He picked up a package and weighed it in his hand. "What are in all these anyway?"

Leah took the package from his hands, rattled it, then brought it close to her face so she could sniff it. "Ginger cookies," she announced. "The others are jars of apple butter, mincemeat, and the like. That one over there is a set of toy soldiers for Cory Jones. This is a hat I saw Louisa admiring in the window of the millinery, and the one in the corner is a wool scarf for Mr. Barnes . . ."

"Enough. The damage to your pocketbook is already done. Have the decency to spare me a few of the gruesome details," Benjamin admonished, but his tone did not match the acrimony of his words.

"Why don't you go with her to deliver them, Captain?" Mrs. Findley suggested. "I still have to bake pies for tomorrow's dinner, and I've not the time. There'll be a hot supper waiting for you when you return."

"I can already have a hot supper at the boardinghouse," he protested the housekeeper's blatant attempt to manipulate him.

"Not as good as mine. Besides, we're going to need your help around here this evening. No use walking all the way back to that boardinghouse, when you have to come back here again."

"You're awfully free with my time," he complained.

"It's hard for two women alone to get on in the

world. Some tasks require the strength of a man." Mrs. Findley sighed. "I wouldn't ask for your help if we could get along without it."

"All right. You've convinced me," he capitulated with a token grumble.

Mrs. Findley's lip curved into a crooked smile. "Don't look so glum. It'll be good for you."

Leah listened to the exchange, but said nothing. Over the weeks she had watched Mrs. Findley deal with Benjamin. These little arguments were commonplace. Though subtlety was not her housekeeper's strong point, she usually got her way. Leah didn't know if Benjamin yielded out of respect for an elder, or because at heart he wanted the same end, but he didn't seem to be suffering from his defeats.

The day before, Leah had arranged for Mr. Barnes to arrive at three to help her deliver the packages. His arrival brought a halt to her musings, and the gifts were loaded into large baskets, a crate, anything that could be found to make their transport more convenient.

Mr. Barnes received his gift with surprise and much pleasure, immediately exchanging his old scarf for the new one and pronouncing it worthy of the finest coachman in London. Benjamin stood back, watching the scene with a skeptical eye.

Their first destination was the business district, where Leah saw fit to visit every merchant with whom she had ever chanced to do business. No one was overlooked, not the butcher nor baker nor cobbler.

Try as he might, Benjamin could not help but be moved when he witnessed the true delight with which Leah's small tokens were received. She gave for the sheer joy of giving, with no anticipation of reward, not even a smile in return for her efforts.

He did not understand how she could be so, but it was becoming harder and harder to deny that he admired her ability to face life with her special brand of affectionate enthusiasm.

The world had not spoiled her as he had feared it would. Though she was not so naive as she had once been, she maintained her noble view of humanity, and more often than not, those she met lived up to her expectations. It was as if they felt compelled not to disappoint her.

The affluent were given small tokens of affection; the poor gifted with baskets of food, a blanket, a pair of boots to replace ones with ragged soles. Every child received a toy.

By the end of the afternoon, Benjamin was so thoroughly befuddled by the effusion of good will, he had not the sense to protest when he discovered the task Mrs. Findley required of him that evening was decorating a Christmas tree.

An aura of family reigned in the room as they tied ribbons to the branches of the tree. They all felt it, but Benjamin felt something else.

His only memory of Christmas was that of being locked in his room while his uncle and his family celebrated without him. There were no presents for him, and the only part of the Christmas goose he was allowed to share was the mouth-watering aroma that drifted up the stairs and seeped into his cold room.

He compressed his lips. He would not let those dark memories intrude upon this Christmas. It belonged to Leah. The realization that he had neglected to buy her a single present struck him like a blow.

"I have to be going," he announced as he strode rapidly to the door. "Thank you for the dinner and good company."

Dropping the ribbon she held in her hand, Leah followed him into the hall. "Benjamin, what's wrong?" she asked in dismay.

"I just realized there is something important I forgot to do." He shoved on his hat as he stepped through the door.

"You won't forget Christmas dinner is at three," she called after him.

"I'll be there," he assured her. "You can count on it."

Benjamin shoved his hands in his pockets as he covered the distance between Leah's house and the business district with long strides.

There was more than one merchant who complained about being dragged from the family hearth on Christmas Eve, but every one of them complied with his request that they open their store for him.

He made his selections with the efficiency of a man who was used to trusting his decisions. When he returned to the boardinghouse, he was a satisfied man.

Christmas Day dawned bright and cold. After a breakfast of tea and scones with jam, Leah and Mrs. Findley exchanged their gifts to each other. Neither woman mentioned the captain's abrupt departure the evening before, or their private fears he might not come today.

They attended church, then set about the task of preparing dinner.

At two o'clock there was a knock at the door. Upon

opening it, Leah found Benjamin standing on the porch, his arms laden with gifts.

"Merry Christmas," he greeted as he stepped over the threshold and headed for the tree.

"Merry Christmas," she returned with a broad smile as she followed him into the parlor. "Mrs. Findley, it appears we have more gifts to deliver before the day is out."

"They're for you," Benjamin said as he placed the packages beneath the tree.

"All of them?" Leah queried in disbelief.

"All of them," he confirmed.

"Well, I best be getting back to my dinner," Mrs. Findley excused herself before she was betrayed by a grin. "You two enjoy yourselves."

"I'm overwhelmed," Leah commented as he handed her her first gift. "You needn't have been so generous."

"It's nothing," he dismissed her protest. "You probably won't like half of it anyway."

Rather than risk spoiling the day by insisting he take credit for his generosity, Leah let the subject drop. Eagerly, she unwrapped the paper from the first package. It contained a copy of Charles Dickens's *The Old Curiosity Shop*.

After thanking him, Leah handed him the first of her gifts to him. It was a hand-embroidered dress shirt.

Gift followed gift with the appropriate expressions of gratitude. Leah unwrapped three more novels, a history of England, silk gloves, a shawl, an amethyst brooch, a chess set, a silver comb and brush set on a mirrored tray, and the biggest box of chocolate truffles she had ever seen in her life. His thoughtfulness moved her near tears.

Though her gifts to him were less numerous, Benjamin was no less touched. In addition to the shirt, he received a spyglass he had been admiring in a shop window and an oak-framed sketch of his favorite place to sit and think on the island.

"I thought you might like to hang it on your wall in your room at the boardinghouse . . . to help you remember," Leah stated, a note of wistfulness in her voice.

"Do you still miss your island?" he asked gently.

"I love it here. But sometimes, yes, I miss it." Her gaze met his. "Do you?"

Mrs. Findley entered to announce dinner, saving him the discomfort of answering.

Benjamin purposefully steered the topic of conversation to less uncomfortable subjects as they supped on roast duck stuffed with giblet dressing, mash potatoes, peas, carrots, and freshly baked bread. For dessert Mrs. Findley served a chocolate custard pie, smothered in whipped cream, which she proudly proclaimed was responsible for convincing her late husband to propose to her.

"My tongue has tasted heaven," Leah exclaimed, closing her eyes as she savored her first bite. Benjamin was inclined to agree with her assessment, but he was less effusive with his praise.

With the passing of the holiday season, life settled into a pleasantly domestic routine. The winter weather brought some activities to a halt, but there were plenty to replace them.

Though Leah continued to attend afternoon teas and soirees, much of her time was devoted to doing charity work. It gave her purpose and pleasure to lighten the load of the less fortunate, and because she did not view herself as superior to those she helped, and was pragmatic rather than visionary in her solutions, to see her walking down their streets was a favorite sight among the poor.

Benjamin was a constant presence. He chopped wood, carried water, and ran the occasional errand for Mrs. Findley. Often he escorted Leah around town as she went about her daily activities. Though he did not approve of her venturing to the less savory sections of town to deliver a basket of food or a bottle of medicine, he had accustomed himself to the fact that she would allow him only so much say over her activities. His initial fear for her physical safety was soon mitigated by the witness of his own eyes. Her rapport with the people was such that if anyone ever so much as thought to lay a hand on her, an army of defenders would rush to the rescue.

A sense of permanency prevailed. Benjamin continued making cautious investments in local firms, and was becoming a respected member of the business community. Leah was his wife in every way but one. They neither spoke of the future nor the past, though Leah often thought of both.

Both Louisa and Benjamin had ceased to parade men before her like a marching band, and she deemed this a good sign that they were coming to realize her heart and mind were her own to rule. Despite his physical neglect, Benjamin was attentive in every other way. The harsher edges of his personality surfaced less frequently. She supposed things could go on as they were indefinitely, but she wanted more from life. She wanted him for more than a friend. She wanted Capt. Benjamin Keaton body, heart, and soul.

The trouble was: she was afraid to do or say anything to remind Benjamin of her profound love for him, for fear of driving him away again. There were many times she sensed his need of her was as great as hers for him, but she said nothing. Time had proved Mrs. Findley right. She must allow him to come to terms with his own feelings. Patience was a virtue that had served her well on many occasions. She could only pray it would do so in her present situation.

As January came to a close, Leah was forced to confront a new complication in her relationship.

Benjamin had stopped by early in the day to say good-bye before leaving on an overnight business trip to Nanaimo. After pouring them both a cup of tea, Mrs. Findley sat down with Leah at the kitchen table. Twisting the handkerchief she held in her hand, she captured Leah's gaze with her own.

"Leah, dear, is there something you would like to tell me?" she asked gently.

Leah looked perplexed. "No."

"Being a woman and your housekeeper, I could not help but notice, and I have been worried for you for quite some time. With the captain gone, I figured this would be a good time to talk. At first I brushed my thoughts aside, but it has been too long. I feel I can no longer ignore the matter."

"Mrs. Findley, you will have to speak more plainly,

if you want me to have some idea what your talking about," Leah admonished as she sipped her tea.

The older woman cleared her throat. "How long has it been since you had your last monthly flow?"

"It last came the week before I left my island to come to Victoria."

"And its absence doesn't alarm you?"

"I really hadn't given it much thought. It's been late before."

"This late?" Mrs. Findley prodded.

Leah thought back and shook her head. "No, I guess not. Is that cause for concern?"

"You really are an innocent, child. I suppose it is only natural that you would have no idea what is happening to you, and I must admit you have showed no sign of the sickness that afflicts so many women."

Something terrible must be happening to her or Mrs. Findley would not be so evasive. Leah's eyes widened in alarm, and when she clasped her companion's hand, her own was the temperature of ice. "Would you please stop talking in circles? If I have contracted some dreaded disease, I should like to know!"

"Calm down. It is neither good for you nor your baby."

"Baby?" Leah repeated, shaking her head in hopes of ordering her thoughts.

"Yes, I think you are carrying the captain's child," Mrs. Findley stated reluctantly.

Leah's eyes lit with wonderment and joy as she placed her hands on her belly. A child of her own, created from the love she and Benjamin had once shared. It was almost too good to be true, but somehow she knew what Mrs. Findley said was true. She had been so busy adjusting to her new life, she had ignored the subtle changes in her figure—the fullness in her bosoms, the slight spreading of her hips. She nodded her head, a knowing smile gracing her lips.

"Of course, you realize this means the captain must marry you. I will speak to him at once, threatening force if necessary."

"No!" Leah protested, her joyous expression evaporating and being replaced by one of utter dismay. "I don't want you to force him to do anything he does not want to do."

"Don't you want him for a husband?"

"I want him to be with me always. Whether we are married or not matters little to me."

"Well, it will matter to a lot of other folks. This baby will ruin you if you don't have a husband," Mrs. Findley chided.

"You yourself have said we must give the captain time to prove his feelings," Leah argued.

"We no longer have that luxury."

"My baby will be a joy not a burden," Leah stated with conviction, as she rose from the table and began to pace.

"I wish it was so, child, but even if he marries you this very afternoon, tongues will wag, and many you thought your friends will desert you. It takes nine months to make a baby. There is no way we can pass it off as an early child. I could flog the man for what he has done to you."

"If you are angry with him, then include me in your wrath also. We share equal responsibility for the creation of our child."

"I cannot be angry with you," Mrs. Findley objected.

"Then don't be angry with anyone," Leah advised.

"If he does his duty by you, without kicking up a fuss, I will forgive him," she avowed.

Leah continued to frown at her. "He has done nothing wrong."

"Robbing a lady of her good name is one of the most reprehensible crimes a man can commit. In your case, he should feel doubly culpable. But, never fear, though he is a strange man, in my heart I believe when I tell him of the baby, he will understand what he must do and pay the penalty like a gentleman."

"I will not allow my child and myself to be relegated to the status of penalty in his eyes. I would rather face a lifetime of censure from others than be a millstone about Benjamin's neck! I love him."

"Think about yourself for a change," Mrs. Findley exhorted.

"I am," Leah assured her, then fell silent. Never had she wanted Benjamin to stay with her because he was made to feel guilty. He must *choose* to love her! The emotion couldn't be forced. Their happiness was irrevocably entwined. One's could not be had at the expense of the other's. Though she believed he loved her, he had yet to believe it himself. Until he did, until he convenanted to stay with her of his own free will, the existence of the baby would remain her secret. It was the only way she would ever be sure of his love. She turned to face her housekeeper. "You must promise me that you will let me handle this in my own way."

Mrs. Findley met her gaze. "I cannot give you such a

promise. The matter is out of your hands."

"No, it is not! It is my life, my child, and my decision. I will handle this in my own way. If you breathe a word of this to him, I swear, I shall never forgive you!" Leah spoke the words with deadly earnest, then turned on her heels and exited the room, leaving her stunned housekeeper to stare into her untouched cup of tea.

If there was any doubt in Mrs. Findley's mind, by nightfall she was convinced she had gone too far. She had felt a member of the family in this household, but now she was treated like the servant she was.

Leah did not speak to her unless it was to give an order. She would not eat at the same table. She refused to meet her gaze. If it had been anyone else, she might have been able to convince herself her mistress's behavior was nothing but a temporary display of temper, but malice was so foreign to Leah's nature, Mrs. Findley knew such was not the case.

If she confronted Captain Keaton with the results of his misdeed, she would lose something far more important to her than her employment. She would lose Leah's good opinion. The loss of Leah's affection and respect would be like the death of a beloved family member. It would be hard to bear.

But silence had a price, too. Leah would hold her head high, but the cruel barbs and social condemnation would hurt her nonetheless, and there would be nothing Mrs. Findley could do to shield her.

Leah loved with such intensity, and that was the crux of the problem. She was no more capable of putting her own interest above that of her captain than she was of shooting a dog in the streets for barking. It was rare, that kind of love. Perhaps she had no right to interfere.

After much soul-searching, Mrs. Findley finally came to a decision. Early the next morning she knocked on Leah's door.

"Come in," Leah answered stoically, sitting up in bed.

Mrs. Findley stood at the foot of the bed. It was clear that Leah had not been sleeping any better than she had. "You can have your promise," she stated. "Though it goes against all I have been taught, I will say nothing to Capt. Keaton without your permission. But I think *you* should tell him about the baby at once. Do it in your own way, but tell him."

"Thank you." Tears of relief filled Leah's eyes as she scrambled to her knees and opened her arms to embrace her housekeeper. "You will see I am right. I have to follow my heart, and it tells me he needs my love as I need his. But it also tells me I must treat him gently. I want him to love me for myself, and I think he does, but if I tell him about the baby, and he stays, I will never know for sure."

"He will find out about the baby soon enough, whether you or I say a thing," Mrs. Findley reminded, settling herself on the edge of the bed.

"I have thought about that," Leah assured her.

"And what do you intend to do?"

"I'm not sure. I have been up all night worrying about you, me, and the baby."

"And the captain?" Mrs. Findley queried.

"I have worried about him most of all."

"I wish you would let me do something to help you." The older woman sniffed.

"There is nothing you can do. This is between Benjamin and myself." Leah smiled wanly. "Perhaps when he comes home, the sight of him will inspire me, and I will know what I should do."

She did not expect Benjamin until late afternoon, and Leah hoped a visit to Louisa might help her clarify the extent of her dilemma, in relation to her position here in Victoria. Mrs. Findley tended to be an alarmist where such matters were concerned. Perhaps things were not as bad as they seemed.

Knowing Louisa would not be pleased whatever the circumstances, Leah did not feel ready to tell her friend about her condition, but Louisa was well versed in the conventions of society and did not mind discussing any topic. Too, she was so used to her frank questions on other matters she was not likely to become suspicious. As soon as the hour was respectable, Leah set out on foot to the Hastings' home.

The butler opened the door to her, then left her waiting in one of the smaller parlors while he announced her presence to his mistress. Louisa did not keep her waiting long.

They exchanged greetings and engaged in conversation for well over a half hour before Leah brought up the matter that was foremost in her mind.

"Louisa, I know you think the single state is the ideal, but is there ever a time when people should get married, even if they don't want to?"

"I can't think of one."

"What about if there is a baby involved?" Leah pressed.

310

"Oh, so you have heard the gossip about Kathleen Drummond and John Carlyle, too." Louisa set her teacup down on her saucer with a hard clank, her eyes igniting as she drew herself up. "I can assure you, there is not a word of truth in it, and when I find out who started that vicious rumor, I am going to give them a piece of my mind. Poor Kathleen. Of course time will prove the gossips wrong, and she will have her small revenge, but in the meantime, it must be hard to bear. I hope she takes some solace in the fact that her true friends know John is marrying her because he loves her. I have never seen a man so smitten."

"John Carlyle is marrying Kathleen?" Leah asked, her tone one of disbelief.

"Yes, didn't you see the announcement in the Tuesday morning paper? Anyway, I must admit they make an odd couple, which is probably what is rallying the small-minded in our midst to speculate on so nefarious a cause for their engagement."

"I knew nothing of their romance," Leah professed. "Of course, I noticed he was unusually attentive at the Christmas ball, but I really haven't seen much of either of them of late."

"That is because they have been keeping each other's company. Besides, with Capt. Keaton always hanging about you, there are few who have the nerve to cross your threshold."

Leah ignored her last remark. "I will have to stop by Kathleen's on my way home from here, and offer my congratulations. You aren't too disappointed about Mr. Carlyle wanting to marry her instead of you?"

"Not in the least. It saves me the trouble of turning him down, and then convincing Father not to have an

311

apoplectic fit." Her eyes met Leah's. "I could ask the same question of you. Are you disappointed he did not ask *you* to be his wife?"

"You know full well John Carlyle and I are only good friends, never anything more. If he had asked me to marry him, I, too, would have turned him down."

Louisa grinned. "Then it is a lucky thing he fell in love with Kathleen, isn't it? Though I hate to say it, Kathleen is not a strong enough woman to stand on her own, and if she must marry some man, John Carlyle is not a bad choice. But if you didn't read the announcement or hear the rumors, why the question in the first place?"

"It was just something Mrs. Findley said to me yesterday." Leah fussed with the fabric on her skirt, choosing her words carefully. "If Kathleen was going to have a baby, and Mr. Carlyle wouldn't marry her, what would happen to her?"

"There is a good chance that her family would throw her out, so the scandal would not attach to her sisters. In any case, no good family would ever allow her in their home again. Her chances for any kind of decent future here in Victoria would be utterly ruined," Louisa explained without mincing words.

Inwardly Leah cringed, but outwardly she did not display her distress. "What about her friends?"

"Sometimes close friendships survive, but it is a rare thing. Parents don't want their daughters to be seen in the company of a fallen woman, and would discourage any association. She would move in different circles, have to find work. The best thing in such a case is usually to move away."

"Wouldn't she have the same problem in a new town?"

"Yes, but if she bought herself a ring, she could pretend she was a destitute widow. A lie might be easier to live with than the truth."

Leah hesitated before asking her next question. "If she stayed, would you still be her friend?"

"Kathleen and I are not close, but I would do what I could to lighten her load," Louisa assured her.

"And what about Mr. Carlyle? What would happen to him?" Leah queried.

"Absolutely nothing of consequence." Louisa pounded the table with her fist, the volume of her voice rising along with her ire, as she continued to explain the injustices of such a situation. "He might be frowned upon, but little more. If he refused to marry her, most likely he would also deny the child was his."

"He wouldn't be so cold?" Leah protested.

Louisa's fiery gaze met Leah's, and she began to laugh. "No, he wouldn't. Look what you've done with your questions. Poor Mr. Carlyle is innocent as a lamb, and you have me ready to go after him and beat him with my father's cane. We best discuss something else, or I might get so riled I will do something rash against the first man I see, just on general principle."

"I have one last question," Leah interjected.

Louisa nodded blithely, having long since grown used to Leah's relentless quests for knowledge on subjects of social congress.

"Mrs. Findley said a man can be forced to marry against his will. Is it true, and if it is, how is it done?"

"Usually by an irate father and a shotgun." Louisa

continued to chuckle. "He gives the guilty fellow the choice of death or his daughter."

"And if he chooses the daughter, nobody cares that the baby was conceived before the marriage?" Leah pressed, willing it to be so.

"If he chooses the daughter? Come now, Leah, you don't really think even the most committed bachelor is going to agree to be shot. But to answer your question: When the baby comes early, fingers will be counted and a few brows will raise, but in time all will be forgiven and forgotten by most."

Despite Louisa's answer, Leah could not feel much satisfaction. "I can't see how a union with such an inauspicious start has much hope for happiness."

"I quite agree. Likely, the husband will stray, the wife will wither from lack of affection, and the children born to their union will grow up miserable brats."

Well, she had come here for forthright answers and she had gotten them. It seemed her situation was every bit as bad as Mrs. Findley believed it to be. "You were right when you said we should speak of something else." Leah rubbed her brow. "This whole conversation is starting to give me a headache."

"I've never known you to have a headache, or any other bodily complaint to speak of," Louisa voiced her concern, testing the temperature of Leah's forehead with the back of her hand. "I hope you aren't coming down with something."

"It's nothing, really," Leah reassured her friend.

"Just the same, I think you should go home and lie down."

"I think you're right." Leah seized upon a reason to

quit her friend's company. She had a lot to think about, and she thought best when she was alone.

When Benjamin returned to Victoria and the house on Simcoe Street, he was immediately aware that something was amiss. Mrs. Findley showed him in, but instead of staying in the parlor while he visited Leah as was her habit, she quickly excused herself, and he did not see her the rest of the evening.

Leah, though she welcomed him, was unusually subdued. She sat by the fire, her hands folded in her lap, looking thoroughly uncomfortable.

"How was your trip?" she asked.

"It went well enough. I think the mine may be worth a small risk of capital." When she did not respond to his statement, he charily asked, "What have you been doing with yourself?"

She shrugged. "Nothing special."

He had expected to be confronted with some tale of misadventure, and her answer caught him off guard. "Nothing out of the ordinary happened while I was gone?"

"No." Leah shook her head. Nothing had happened while he was gone. What had *happened* had happened when she had been wrapped in his arms, but still her answer felt like a lie.

They lapsed into silence. After a few minutes of exchanging forced smiles, Benjamin rose to retrieve a book from the shelf.

Leah did likewise. She opened her book to the marker, and settled herself in her favorite chair.

They often spent the evening reading together, but tonight she could not concentrate on the words on the page. She knew she had to talk to Benjamin; yet, she was loath to do so.

Everything had been going along so well between them. Well, that wasn't exactly true. She still missed the passion they had once shared, and Benjamin showed no sign of compromising where that was concerned, but in every other way, she judged their relationship satisfying.

She had been taking great care to do nothing that might push him away, but now her situation required her to risk upsetting the well-ordered world they had fashioned. Leah chewed her bottom lip.

On more than one occasion, Benjamin had clearly stated that he wasn't fond of ties, and she was afraid he would view a marriage between them as a bond of the very worse sort. Inescapable. No matter what Mrs. Findley or Louisa said, she had no desire to force him to marry her against his will. He had never wanted to create a baby with her. He had said as much the night before they arrived in Victoria. She would not steal his freedom to buy her own comfort.

Her thoughts drifted down another path. She did love him. If he married her, she would do everything in her power to make him happy. And he was fond of her. Perhaps she was worrying overmuch. He hadn't threatened to leave her for a long time now. He was so much gentler, more at peace with himself and the world than he used to be. Perhaps she was judging him by old standards, and he would welcome the idea of a commitment.

On the other hand, the baby might make him feel he

had to marry her. He might grit his teeth and do the *proper* thing. Where she was concerned, the opinions of others held undue sway with him. Leah knew a marriage of duty was a very real possibility, and it was an end she could not accept. She remained determined to discover his true feelings before she told him of the child.

Whatever the outcome, she owed it to herself, the baby, and Benjamin to let him make his own decision concerning their future. Laying her book aside, she raised her eyes. For several minutes she sat mute, staring at him.

He looked so comfortable sitting on the settee, book in hand. She hated to disturb him. Leah opened her mouth to speak, lost courage, and retreated to the pages of her book.

Three nights later found them in a similar position before the fire, and Leah still had not mustered the nerve to broach the subject that was uppermost in her mind. Thus far inspiration had eluded her, and it looked likely to continue to do so. Mrs. Findley's obvious absences were beginning to elicit questions, and she was running out of excuses to explain them.

Of its own volition, one hand lowered to her belly. As she covertly watched Benjamin, she tried to assure herself she could put aside their discussion for another time. But for how long? A few more days? A week? A month? Nothing would change between them in so short a time, and she ran the risk of losing her chance altogether.

There was nothing to be gained, and much to be lost, by postponing the conversation. She could skirt around the issue, but Leah could see little to be gained by such an approach. Taking a deep breath, she came right to the point.

"Benjamin, would you like to marry me?"

He bolted upright on his seat and stared at her as if he was sure he hadn't heard her right. "What?"

She held his gaze. "I asked you if you would like to marry me."

He lowered his eyes to the floor but continued to observe her beneath his hooded lids as he mumbled, "I was afraid I heard you correctly."

Benjamin told himself he shouldn't be surprised. He hadn't left, as he had said he would. He all but lived at the house. He had walked into this trap with his eyes open.

He shifted tensely on his seat. She had every right to ask her question. The firelight reflected in her hair as she sat by the hearth, her hands folded in her lap, patiently awaiting his answer. She had grown beautiful in his eyes. He wanted to tell her yes, but he couldn't seem to make his lips form the word.

He realized, of late, he had made a habit of refusing to think beyond the moment. It let him be more comfortable with his own actions. He stayed because it felt good to be with Leah, but the knowledge he could walk out the door at a moment's notice should his feelings become too intense felt equally good. Now his day of reckoning had come.

"Did you know that John Carlyle is going to marry Kathleen Drummond?" Leah queried, to end the agony of his protracted silence.

"No. Is that what brought this on?" he asked, closely guarding himself lest he betray his own emotions.

Leah shook her head negatively. "When a man and

318

woman love each other, it is customary to marry and have a family. I love you and . . . I was hoping you might have come to love me."

"Marriage is out of the question." Benjamin cursed himself as the words sprung from his lips. He had not meant to be so abrupt.

Leah's shoulders sagged under the weight of his words, but the thought of their baby growing within her womb gave her the courage necessary to press on. "Why?"

"I'm a sea captain."

"My father was a sea captain, and he married my mother."

"You yourself said their marriage was not a happy one," Benjamin countered.

"We would be different," Leah vowed.

"Don't wheedle," he reproved.

"I'm not wheedling. I just think it would be nice if you married me. We could live in this house or on your ship. I could take care of you, and you could do whatever you like. Nothing really matters to me, except that I have your love and we are together."

Benjamin said nothing. The picture she painted did sound idyllic. It would be tempting, if he didn't know himself so well. He was meant to be alone. It was how he liked to live. It was his nature. He played the old arguments over and over in his head, grasping at some logical reason why he could not give her what she wanted.

She had really never asked anything of him except the one thing he didn't know how to give—love. His face darkened in anger, not at her, but at himself.

"If you prefer to go on as we have, I'll understand,"

Leah stated softly, misreading herself as the object of his ire.

She had given him a choice, and he had made his feelings clear. Her logical mind had accepted the possibility that he might say no, but her heart had not. Leah told herself she should be grateful she knew the truth, but the truth was hard to bear. What was she going to do now?

Eventually he would learn of the existence of the baby. Would it make him even more angry? Everything was suddenly so complicated. She didn't want to lose Benjamin, and she didn't want to lose her friends. Clutching her book to her bosom, she gently rocked herself to and fro as she stared into the fire.

Benjamin wanted to say something; he just didn't know what to say. He wanted to comfort her, but he feared he would only give false hopes.

Marriage, family, those things were for other men. A wife and children would make him vulnerable. He didn't want to be responsible for anyone but himself. He didn't want to love. He didn't know how.

Discordant emotions tangled about his heart like seaweed tangled about a man's legs, dragging him down to dark depths, and he was assailed by a sudden sensation of drowning. Grabbing his hat and coat, he bolted out the door.

"I was very fond of Mrs. ... main
protested, as he tried to assimilate th... ... of ...

Chapter 19

He had listed every reason he should go, and
countered every one of them with an excuse why he
should stay. Benjamin sat on the edge of his bed, his
head in his hands, a thoroughly miserable man.

He knew what he wanted, *needed* to survive in his
world, and a wife did not figure into those plans. He
was a sea captain, a loner, a man who needed no one
but himself.

Then why the hell was he still in Victoria? He had
said he would go, and he should have done so long ago.
Leah did not need his guardianship. She had proved
she could get along just fine without him.

What about that opium den? his alter ego demanded.
If you hadn't been there . . . But that had happened
before Leah had managed to make friends with half the
citizenry of Victoria. And she was wiser now. The
chances of a like incident occurring were slim.

He continued to rub his brow as he argued with
himself. Business took precedence over pleasure, and
however comfortable and complaisant he had become

with life here in Victoria, he had a living to earn. The investments he had been making of late could not sustain him forever. *Why not?* the quiet voice within asked. *Already you've turned a tidy profit.*

"Because I don't want to stay!" he shouted out loud, pounding his palm with his fist. "If I stay, I'll have to marry her as she asks. It's the only decent thing to do."

What would be so bad about that? he asked himself. No man could wish for a more beautiful or loving wife than Leah. It would end the daily battle he fought with his loins. It would . . . be a lie.

How could he stand before witnesses and swear to love Leah for eternity, when he was incapable of that tender emotion? Where once he had been proud of the fact, deeming himself superior to those who wallowed in their emotions, he now felt himself less than a whole man. Leah deserved better than him. He must leave for her sake, as well as his own. He must leave without delay.

Benjamin stroked the ends of his mustache, trying to conjure some feeling of pleasure with his decision—without success. Why couldn't he be like other men? Why did his heart constrict every time Leah spoke words of love? He had no answers to comfort himself. No hope. A cold sense of dread was his only companion.

He knew what he must do, had known from the very beginning, he scolded himself for his lack of fortitude. Slamming his hat on his head, he shoved his arms into his overcoat and headed for the docks.

"Benjamin," Leah greeted as she opened the door. "I

didn't expect you so early. Come in and join us. We were just about to sit down to our breakfast."

"I've already eaten," he stated gruffly.

Her expression sobered. "Is something wrong?"

"No," he replied, a bit too abruptly to be believed. "I came to talk to you about something, but it can wait until after your meal. I'll just make myself comfortable in the parlor, until you're through."

"Are you sure? she asked, hesitating.

Welcoming the brief reprieve, he dismissed her with a wave of his hand. "Absolutely. Now run along and eat. You're looking a little pale."

When Leah returned to the kitchen, Mrs. Findley looked up from her bowl of porridge.

"Who was it, dear?"

"Capt. Keaton. He's waiting in the parlor."

"I see." Mrs. Findley pursed her withered lips, but said nothing more as she stirred a spoonful of sugar into the contents of her bowl.

Leah was not blind to the look of disapproval in her eyes. She had told Mrs. Findley about the conversation she had had with Benjamin last night, and her housekeeper had not one good thing to say where the captain was concerned.

She herself felt more sadness and confusion than anger.

She shifted nervously on her seat. She had little energy to spare worrying about Mrs. Findley's feelings on the matter. Concern for Benjamin consumed her. Something was terribly wrong. She could feel it in the marrow of her bones.

After taking a few tasteless bites, Leah rose from the table. "I'll be in the parlor, if you should need me."

"You should eat more," the housekeeper called afer her.

"Later."

As Leah approached the parlor, she could not dispel the cloud of impending doom enveloping her. She had said all the wrong things last night. This morning he looked so serious. She was more than a little afraid to hear what he had to say.

Benjamin did not comment on her brief absence as he mutely offered her a chair by the fire.

"Leah," he began, then clamped his mouth shut.

"Yes?" she prompted, forcing herself to smile despite her trepidation.

He stared at her expectant face, cursing himself for what he was about to say, but knowing he must say it nonetheless. "Leah," he began again. "I am leaving for San Francisco tomorrow. I must see about buying a new ship and getting my life back in order."

She rose to her feet, meeting him on a more equal level. Taking a deep breath, she asked, "How long will you be gone?"

"I'm not sure."

"But you are coming back," she stated, a note of desperation tainting her voice.

"I'm not making any promises."

"You never make promises," she echoed his words of long ago as she fought for calm. Accepting that she could not have him for a husband was one thing, but to have him gone from her life altogether . . . She should never have asked him to marry her. It was too soon. But the baby . . . The baby had forced her to take a stand. She could use it now to make him stay.

Leah clenched the fabric of her skirt as her eyes

searched his. No! She must be strong. She must let him go, if that was what he wanted.

Benjamin swallowed hard. "You'll be fine without me. You have your friends, a fine house. Your banker is a good man. He will watch over your funds and prevent you from being overgenerous. You'll be fine without me," he repeated.

She blinked back the tears forming in her eyes, and forced a brave smile to her lips. "Of course, I'll be fine. After all, I've had more practice taking care of myself than most people."

"You're not going to beg me to stay, are you?" Benjamin asked with a mixture of relief and disbelief.

"Would it do me any good?"

"No."

"Then begging would be foolish. You know my feelings for you. You know how strongly I believe we should be together. I can't make you love me, no matter how much I might want to."

"The fault is not yours, but mine." Unable to bear the intensity of her gaze a moment longer, he turned from her. "I'm sorry I can't be the man you want me to be."

Leah stroked his back with a trembling hand. "I know. And I am sorry you cannot see in yourself the man I see in you."

"Well, I should be leaving," he stated dully.

"Will you hold me first? Just for a little while," she whispered, laying her head against him.

Benjamin felt his resolve weakening. "I don't think that would be wise."

His refusal broke the last thread of her hard-earned composure. "Oh God, Benjamin, please! It is so little to ask."

Drawing her into the shelter of his arms, he held her there. The crackle of the fire on the hearth and the sonance of their own breathing were the only sounds to be heard in the room as they stood locked in embrace.

Minutes ticked by. For Leah, it felt as if they flew on frantic wings; for Benjamin, they plodded, torturously. His desire to stay warred with his fear of forming a permanent attachment. He had gone over and over the matter in his mind. He was better off alone.

Once he was gone, Leah would seek affection elsewhere. She would find the happiness in which she put so much stock. The thought of her lying in another man's arms, loving him with abandon, caused his gut to constrict with jealously, but he accepted his discomfort as the price he must pay for the privilege of being alone. She would soon fade from memory, and he would go on as before.

As he drew in a whiff of her fresh, feminine fragrance, he began to tremble.

He hadn't intended to kiss her, but his lips molded to hers, tasting her sweetness. She responded immediately, returning kiss for kiss, opening her mouth to the exploration of his warm, moist tongue, as his hands roamed over her.

She held him tightly to her, kneading his tense muscles, memorizing his scent. The fire of their passion was bittersweet, but for a time neither of them had the will to quench it.

Hungry kiss followed hungry kiss, until they were both ragged for breath.

He set her away from him. "I really have to go."

"When does your ship sail?" she asked softly.

"Six o'clock tomorrow morning."

326

"I won't see you again before then, will I?"

He could not meet her eyes. "No."

Leah's hands moved to cradle her womb. It's rounding was imperceptible to any eye but hers, but knowing she carried his child comforted her. Though he was walking out the door, Benjamin would always be with her. Her eyes caressed his stony visage. "I hope you find what you are looking for, and if you should ever discover it is me, I want you to know I will always love you. Don't be afraid to come back, if you discover you were wrong to leave."

"Leah, I won't be . . ."

"Shh." She put her fingers to his lips. "Don't say it. Just say good-bye like you will be back tomorrow."

Tilting her head back with a gentle finger under her chin, Benjamin brushed his lips against hers one last time. "Good-bye, Leah."

The door quickly opened and closed, and Leah was alone in the hall. She stood staring at the empty space before her, before sinking to her knees and dissolving into a storm of suppressed tears.

"Leah, what's wrong?" Mrs. Findley came running from the back of the house at the sound of her heart-wrenching sobs.

"He's leaving Victoria. When he holds me, I feel his love for me. We belong together. I know we do. But he doesn't understand," Leah spoke between sobs.

"The cad! Finds out he's got a girl in trouble, then skips out of port. I'd have never thought him capable of such cruelty." Mrs. Findley dabbed at her own tears of disappointment. "I have a mind to go after him and tell him a thing or two. And if I had a pistol, I'd shoot him where it counts."

Leah clutched her housekeeper's arm. "Mrs. Findley! Don't even think such a thing! He doesn't know I carry his baby."

"You didn't tell him?" the housekeeper asked in disbelief.

"No."

"But it might make him stay."

"I know." Leah shook her head in agreement.

"Well, if you won't tell him, I will."

"You are sworn to secrecy," Leah reminded her tersely, as she wiped at the tears streaming down her cheeks. "I will not tolerate your interference!"

"Leah, my dear, I am only trying to help you," Mrs. Findley soothed. "You love him so much. A man should pay the piper if he's inclined to dance."

"He'll feel trapped."

"He set the snare himself when he lifted your skirts," Mrs. Findley countered.

Leah buried her head in her hands. "It wasn't that way at all between us. It was warm and beautiful and special. I will not have him held accountable for something in which we share equal blame, if blame must be assigned. I am glad I have his child, especially now that I know I shan't have him. I will give our baby all the love I would have given him." She was again overcome with wracking sobs.

The housekeeper lowered her portly frame to the floor and gathered her in her arms, rocking her like she would a small child. She stroked her head, whispering words of comfort, steadfastly avoiding voicing any opinion that might cause her more pain.

At length, Leah's tears washed away the bitter edge of grief, and she was left with the dull ache of loneliness. Rising from the floor, she helped Mrs. Findley to her feet.

"I think I'll stay in today," she announced despondently. "It looks like we might have a storm, and the silver could use polishing."

Mrs. Findley forewent mentioning there was not a cloud in the sky, or that she had polished the silver not two days past. She patted Leah's hand sympathetically. "I'll set the polish out before I do the marketing ... unless you'd prefer I stay here with you."

"No. You go on." Leah smiled affectionately. "I need to be alone for a little while."

The day was an exercise in misery. Leah kept praying Benjamin would knock on the door and greet her with the news that he had changed his mind, but she knew it wasn't going to happen.

There was a wall around him. She had succeeded in boring chinks between the stones, but it still stood firm. She could feel his love, but he could not, and her love wasn't enough to free him from his self-imposed prison. Had he been there so long he was afraid to leave? Remembering her own feelings when it had come time to leave her island, she could sympathize, but she was also angry. She had pressed on despite her fears. He was running away.

Leah sighed heavily. Maybe she was wrong about everything. He might not return her affection at all. She was a burden, an encumbrance, a duty to be discharged. She had saved his life and must be repaid. Hadn't he said as much on numerous occasions? Perhaps it was time she started believing him.

*　　　*　　　*

Mrs. Findley knew she must break her promise to Leah. To remain silent while there was still hope her mistress could work the matter out in her own way was one thing, but the captain's impending departure forced her to take action now. Leah had not said when he was going, but she sensed she had only two or three days at best.

She would not allow Leah to have this baby by herself. She needed the captain by her side. Eventually he would come to love her. How could any man not love a wife as sweet as Leah?

Mrs. Findley knew the cost to herself would not be small, but she prayed that in time Leah would forgive her.

When the marketing was finished, she stopped by the boardinghouse. The captain was not in, and she left a note stressing the urgency of her need to see him.

The afternoon came and went, and she had not received a reply to her message. Giving Leah the excuse that she needed to visit a friend, Mrs. Findley set out for the boardinghouse directly after supper. He was still not at home. Hour after hour of waiting netted no captain, and she was forced to leave another note and return home.

Capt. Benjamin Keaton was willfully playing the coward. Upon receiving Mrs. Findley's first note, he had concluded the lady's urgent need was to convince him he should stay in Victoria, and he was in no mood to be harangued. He had made his decision. He had said good-bye. He could think of nothing she could say to persuade him to abandon his plans.

The latter was not wholly true. It was his fear that she *might* convince him to delay his departure that made him avoid her. His resolve was so precarious he dare not risk a confrontation.

It was well after midnight before he returned to the boardinghouse to settle his bill and gather his belongings.

Early the next morning, Leah rose and dressed in the blue gown Benjamin had purchased for her the day they had arrived in Victoria. Despite his wish to the contrary, she needed to see him one last time.

Mrs. Findley had come in late, and in any case Leah had no desire to disturb her. She sensed she would fare this parting far better if she relied on her own strength, rather than another's sympathy. Tiptoeing from the house, Leah eased the front door closed.

A light fog filtered the rays of the sun as it peaked over the horizon, and she pulled her cloak more tightly about her as she hurried down the street.

She was informed that Benjamin was already gone when she reached the boardinghouse, and she hastened toward the waterfront.

Upon arriving at the harbor, Leah inquired at the shipping offices. The only ship departing for San Francisco that morning was a steamer. Hurrying to the appropriate dock, she scanned the deck for some sign of Benjamin. It took several minutes to locate him, and she waved frantically to catch his attention

Benjamin's eyes surveyed Victoria's skyline. The

early morning sun painted the whitewashed buildings pink and inviting. It was a good place for Leah. Her many friends would see that she came to no harm.

As he stood basking in this pleasant thought, a movement on the dock below caught his attention. He immediately recognized Leah, and he cast his gaze in a different direction, pretending not to see her.

Damn! Why had she come to see him off? Probably to make this as hard on him as possible. He dismissed the thought as unworthy the moment it had formed. Leah was above such subterfuge. Still, he couldn't help wishing she hadn't come.

He was doing the right thing, he told himself for the thousandth time that morning. At first, it would be hard on them both, but in the long run, they would each be better off for his decision.

The steamer belched clouds of hot vapor into the air as it prepared to leave, and he fought the urge to jump ship. It was not until the steamer had slid from its berth that he trusted himself to glance in Leah's direction. She was still waving, and he felt his own hand rising in response. Though he was too faraway to see her expression, he could feel her smile.

For the first three weeks of Benjamin's absence, Leah nurtured the hope he would return. From the moment she had first laid eyes on him, she had known she and Benjamin were meant to be together. Even though he was gone, the feeling remained strong.

The trip to San Francisco would take three to four days. Allowing time for him to conduct his business and make the return trip, she told herself she really couldn't expect him back yet; nevertheless, she found herself making excuses to be near the harbor whenever a ship from San Francisco was scheduled to arrive. One week faded into the next, and hope turned to resignation.

Boredom was not a problem. Charity work occupied much of her time. Mrs. Findley and Louisa saw that her days and nights were filled to overflowing. There were invitations to teas, dinners, and the theater, and she often accompanied her friend while Louisa indulged in her first love: shopping.

They rarely spoke of Benjamin, but when they did, Louisa earnestly expressed the opinion that she thought his leaving was for the best. Leah bore her sentiment stoically, maintaining a blank mien, but when she was alone, she allowed her shoulders to slump and her tears to fall.

The afternoon sky was as gray as Leah's mood, as she sat at the piano playing what had been conceived as a lively tune to the tempo of a funeral dirge.

Mrs. Findley was gone for the day, tending a sick friend, and she had the house to herself. She didn't mind being alone. In fact, she preferred it. She felt compelled to put forth a facade of strength for Mrs. Findley's sake, but she felt tired—so very, very tired.

A strident knock at the door brought her fingers to a halt, and she rose from her seat to answer it. Before she reached the hall the knocking began anew.

"Your maid's had an accident, Miss," a man she did not know informed her. "The doctor sent me to fetch you to his place."

"Mrs. Findley?" Leah numbly expressed her disbelief as she grabbed her cloak and hurried out the door. "Is she badly hurt?"

"I best let the doctor tell you."

A coach was waiting in the street. Though the journey took but a few minutes, it was plenty of time for Leah's imagination to conjure all manner of injury, from a twisted ankle to a broken bone.

She comforted herself with the knowledge that the injuries could not be too severe or she would be taken to the hospital, not a private physician's home. Regardless, Leah vowed she would not let Mrs. Findley lift a finger until she was completely healed.

She was ushered through the front door, into what served as a reception area for the doctor's examination room. The physician stood waiting, his expression grim. Leah's heart began to pound rapidly within her breast.

"Are you Miss Daniels?" he asked.

"Yes. May I see her, please?"

"In a moment." He took her hands in his. "Sometimes these things just happen. It's nobody's fault, really. She never saw the horse coming. I doubt she suffered much."

"You're talking as if she was dead," Leah forced the words from her lips as her eyes searched his for some sign of denial.

"I'm afraid she is. As her employer, I thought you might know how to notify her relatives."

Leah paled. "No, she can't be dead. There must be some mistake."

"There's no mistake. Her body was recognized by several who witnessed the accident, and they knew her well enough to direct me to you. I am sorry, Miss. It is clear you were fond of your servant."

"She was more than a servant, she was a friend," Leah whispered.

He nodded sympathetically. "I'll take you in to see her now, if you wish."

The physician had done his best to disguise the worst of Mrs. Findley's injuries, but to little effect. Leah held her limp hand in hers, as her tears flowed freely.

The doctor put an arm around her shoulder. "Comfort yourself with the knowledge that she lived a long life. She is at peace now."

Mrs. Findley was laid to rest on a hill facing the sea. The sermon Rev. Donnally preached was uplifting, and there were many who came to say good-bye.

Leah performed her duty with a serenity that belied her churning emotions. Her mind could accept what had happened, but her heart screamed in protest. It wasn't fair. Everyone she loved died or went away.

Feburary blew into March. The house felt empty without Mrs. Findley. Leah stopped nurturing the thread of hope that Benjamin would return to Victoria and be a part of her life. Though Louisa devoted every spare minute to her friend, a life of endless parties and shopping expeditions held little appeal. Leah knew it was time she started to seriously consider her options.

It was becoming increasingly difficult to disguise her expanding figure, and she was growing tired of biting her tongue every time she thought of the child she carried, which was almost constantly now that he had begun to move. The flutter in her womb was ever so faint, but it always brought a smile to her lips.

She loved the tiny being who grew within her without reservation. Through him she would always have a small part of Benjamin. They would be together, as she had believed from the start. It was different than she had thought it would be, but despite the price she would pay, she wouldn't wish her baby away, even if she had the power to do so.

She found her thoughts returning to her island again and again. It was a safe place, a place she belonged, a place she wouldn't have to paste a false smile on her face to spare others from her glum mood. Though she knew she would never be content to live out her life there, she found herself longing for the peace and serenity to be found on its shores. Each day the urge to return became stronger.

By mid-March, Leah knew she could no longer avoid coming to some sort of decision, and once she accepted her own conclusion, she knew exactly what she was going to do.

"Louisa, I didn't ask you to come to tea today just because I wanted your company. I need to say good-bye," Leah began.

"What?" Louisa exclaimed.

"I am leaving Victoria. At least for a little while," she repeated for her friend's benefit.

"But why? I know Mrs. Findley's death was hard on you, but that is all the more reason you should stay here with your friends."

"I need some time alone . . . to sort out my thoughts." Leah busied her hands pouring their tea. "I can't do that here, not with so many people around me."

"Where would you go?"

"Back to my island."

Louisa's eyes widened. "You can't be serious."

"Yes, I am," she stated firmly. "I don't expect you to understand. I just need to go back. It's hard to explain."

"It's because of *him,* isn't it?"

Leah nodded. "I know you don't approve of my loving him, and that is part of the problem." Her gaze was direct, with no hint of apology, when it met her friend's. "You see, I'm going to have his baby, and I can't share my joy with anyone. In the eyes of society, I have committed some grave sin, but in my own eyes I have only followed the inclination of my nature."

"A baby? When?" Louisa asked numbly.

"June, I think."

"I should have guessed it was more than your love of chocolates putting weight on your hips. My dear sweet Leah, I am so sorry."

"I don't want pity," Leah protested. "Why do you think I have avoided telling you before now? I knew you wouldn't share my happiness. I want this baby. I need this baby."

"You need Capt. Keaton," Louisa amended.

"Yes," Leah replied. "But I shall never have him, and I can't waste my life mooning over something I cannot change. He has given me a child to love, and for that I will always be grateful. I have thought long and hard on the matter. A few days ago, I found a cargo captain who is willing to accept my money to make a small detour to drop me on my island. We sail the day after next."

"So soon?"

"Yes."

"For all my poor opinion of him, I can't believe Capt. Keaton would do this to you," Louisa spoke her thoughts out loud. "I should have thought he would offer to marry you, when you told him you were with child."

"I never told him," Leah admitted.

"Why not?"

"Because I agree with you. He would have asked me to marry him *but for the wrong reason.*"

"But he has left you to deal with the consequences of his lust all alone."

"The consequences of our love," Leah corrected. "When he held me in his arms, I know he loved me. He wouldn't say so, but I know."

"Then why isn't he here?"

"That is something I don't know. It is as if he is afraid of his feelings. Once, a long time ago, he told me he had never loved anyone. It was the saddest thing I had ever heard. When I cry myself to sleep at night, I cry for him as well as myself."

Louisa cradled Leah's hands in hers. "I still think he should be told. I will demand Father send a telegram to San Francisco at once. A private detective can be hired to find him. If your captain will not do the honorable thing, there are ways to persuade him."

"Louisa, if you value our friendship at all, you won't interfere," Leah admonished.

"But you can't have a baby all alone."

"I will manage. I know what I'm doing. There is a certain serenity in solitude I doubt those raised in a city

338

will ever come to truly understand. I desperately need that serenity. I must learn to be happy again, for the sake of my baby as well as myself."

"What about your house?" Louisa tried a more practical approach.

"I have arranged for the bank to keep up the payments on the lease. Cory has agreed to weed the garden and put food out for the strays. I won't be gone forever, just a few months. My reception when I return with the baby will determine if I will stay."

"Then it is all planned? There is nothing I can say to dissuade you?"

"Nothing," Leah assured her.

Louisa sat silent as she tried to determine the right thing to do. If Leah stayed in Victoria, there was no question she would stand by her, but it would do little good. Leah could only look forward to social censure. Louisa didn't want to put her through that, but she didn't want her to leave either. The thought of her all alone on an island frightened her. However, the fact of the matter was that Leah was not as malleable as she had once been. She had not asked her opinion. She had made her own plans. Informing her of them was merely a courtesy.

Louisa looked into Leah's determined, brown eyes and sighed. "Let me help you pack."

Chapter 20

Leah stood on the damp sand, oblivious to the mist of rain as she stared out into the horizon.

"We were right to come here," she spoke to the infant cradled within her womb. Six weeks had passed since Capt. Jakes had dropped her off on her island, and she found the peace she sought. It was a melancholy peace to be sure, but peace nonetheless.

Benjamin was gone from her life and would not return. Once she had fully accepted that reality, she was able to think with a clearer head.

She was far better off than her beloved captain. She had their baby. He had no one. She would always mourn his loss, but her grief no longer overwhelmed her. She would go on. She would be happy.

Leah absently stroked her round belly. After their baby was born, she would return to Victoria. There would be those she had considered her friends who would shun her. She accepted that just as she accepted Benjamin's loss. However, her true friends would remain by her side. They would not condemn her for a

340

love she could not deny.

She smiled sadly. The gay balls and afternoon teas were delightful, but they were not what she truly missed when she thought of all she had left behind in Victoria. She missed Cory, Mr. Barnes, and most especially she missed Louisa.

Despite her longing to see her friends again, she had no desire to leave her island just yet. Its solitude was strengthening, calming. Here she could free her mind of cluttering thoughts. Here she could abandon the frantic bustle of city life for the rhythm of nature.

Her eyes scanned the water for some sign of Jonathan. He had given her an enthusiastic greeting when she first returned, but it was soon apparent his mind was on other matters. He had found the mate she had wished for him.

She loved to listen to the soft cooing of their love play, even though she missed his companionship. Leah strained her ears, hoping to catch their song on the wind, but no sound rose above the crash of the waves.

Turning from the sea, she retraced her footsteps to the house.

As her figure became more cumbersome with each passing day, Leah began to feel restless. Whenever the weather allowed, she spent her time walking the beaches of her island, but this particular afternoon the clouds were pouring water from the sky by the bucket.

She tried to sketch, but quickly lost interest. A book lay on the table unopened, and the piano keys remained silent. Nothing she thought to do to occupy herself appealed to her. Finally, in exasperation, she decided to go upstairs to take a nap.

As she ascended the stairs, her gaze fell upon the door leading to her mother's room. Lately she had been thinking more and more about the woman who had borne her. Though she loved her mother, she had never understood her, and she had always been a little frightened of her strange moods. She had not been in her room since her death.

Perhaps, now that she was going to be a mother herself, it was time she make peace with this part of her past.

Slowly opening the door, she wrinkled her nose at the thick layer of dust. It clung to the mauve-colored curtains and counterpane like a blanket of gloom. Leah hesitated. Was it wrong to invade her mother's private place? In life, her mother often retreated to this haven where no one else was welcome, and Leah was unsure if she would approve of her daughter's intrusion.

She stood at the threshold several minutes, debating with herself, before stepping into the room. Her mother was dead. She no longer occupied this room.

Walking to the dresser, Leah lifted a bottle of perfume, but before she could test its scent, the dust caused her to retreat in a fit of sneezing.

When she had recovered herself, she unstopped the bottle and drew in a whiff of the rose-scented liquid. The odor conjured vivid memories of her mama.

Adrienne Daniels was a beautiful woman, with hair the color of gold and eyes the color of emeralds. Even after her shoulders had become bent from the weight of her private torment, she had moved about the house with natural grace.

Leah recalled the stories Emma had told her of her

mother's youth—the balls, afternoon teas, elegant dinners. She now had the color of experience to add to the images she had formerly only been able to paint with her imagination. Her own love of people helped her sympathize with her mother's loneliness when she came to live on the island.

With reverent care she opened each drawer, lifting the contents one at a time for her perusal. She closed her eyes as she stroked the fabrics, allowing only the memories of the loving to fill her mind.

Next, she moved to the armoire. It was filled to overflowing with gowns fashionable over a thirty-year span. As she neatly returned each item back to its place, her eyes fell on a small cedar trunk, wedged between the wall and the far side of the bed.

Dragging the trunk to a more accessible location, Leah tried to raise the lid, but found it locked. She had earlier spied a key while going through the dresser, and she quickly retrieved it. It slid comfortably into the lock. Pushing up the lid, she found the chest filled with baby clothes.

Leah knelt on the floor. Her eyes misted as she held up a tiny white dress. How she longed to hold her own baby in her arms. The waiting was the most difficult part of her pregnancy. She needed to have someone she could care for. Someone to smile upon.

As she lifted each item, she sorted the garments into two piles. One would be returned to the trunk. The other she would carry downstairs and wash in preparation for her own baby.

Leah was almost to the bottom of the chest when her hand brushed against something hard. Pushing back the remaining clothes, she discovered a book. Upon

343

opening it, she found the pages written by hand, and she began to read.

March 22, 1850

I am doomed. Today I have been imprisoned on an island in the middle of nowhere, with no one but my infant daughter, Emma, and my cruel husband.

I have begged his forgiveness a thousand times, but he will not forgive me for what I have done. I admit I am a weak woman. I should have been able to bear the loneliness, but what has been done is done.

At least he has accepted the child as his. In truth I think the only reason he has is because he cannot bear to give the credit to my sweet Roger. Poor Roger. I cannot think of him in his cold grave without my heart being pierced with pain. I wish I could join him there . . .

Leah snapped the book closed and set it aside with trembling fingers. She had found her mother's diary. Within her grasp lay the answers to questions that had plagued her for years, but she had read enough to make her afraid to keep reading.

She touched the book gingerly. Did she really want to know? It took several minutes of contemplation before she arrived at an answer. Rising from the floor, she carried the diary from the room, leaving everything else where it lay.

Leah placed the diary on a table in the parlor while

she retreated to the kitchen to boil water for a pot of tea. She brought in more wood for the fire, stirred the coals, puttering about, stalling for time, but her thoughts never left the yellowing pages.

At length curiosity conquered trepidation, and she returned to the parlor and picked up the diary. Settling herself on a chair before the fire, she opened the book to the first page.

This is an account of the married life of Adrienne Adams Daniels, set forth by my own hand . . .

Leah did not set the diary down until she had read it cover to cover. What it told her left her feeling empty and cold.

The first years of her parents' marriage had been relatively happy ones, though her mother wrote often of her loneliness when her husband was away at sea. Then, the year before she had been born, her mother had had a love affair with a man named Roger Harris, while Capt. Daniels was gone on a voyage. Upon discovering his wife's indiscretion, Jacob Daniels had flown into a rage. Roger was found in an alley the next day, a bullet through his heart. Though she admitted she had no proof, it was clear her mother believed her husband guilty of the murder.

Shortly after, her father had left. When he returned nearly a year later, she had already been born, and he moved the family to the island.

Her mother spoke of her great love for Emma, and the sacrifice she made when she agreed to come with the family. In the beginning neither of the women had known their stay would last a lifetime.

The diary was fairly coherent and complete before Adrienne Daniels came to the island, but at that point it became increasingly garbled and sketchy. Sometimes several years passed between entries.

Emma was constantly mentioned in concert with terms of pity, though her mother's dependence on her was clear. When she mentioned her daughter, she often expressed her love and concern for her future.

Leah's eyes misted with tears. She had always sensed her mother's love for her, but she now realized she had never been fully confident of it. Emma had sustained her with her love and strength, creating a world of serenity and stability to protect her from unhappy secrets in this house. Until this moment, she hadn't fully appreciated the depths of the housekeeper's love and loyalty to her family, and especially to herself.

Some of what she learned was good, strengthening her understanding of Emma and her mother; however, the overriding tone of the diary was one of fear, and Jacob Daniels was the author of that fear. It was clear her mother felt herself abused both physically and mentally.

Her accusations were particularly shrill during the days before the accident that ended her life.

Leah searched her mind for some recollection of her father's violence against her mother, but could find nothing to support her mother's claim. Had her mother's forced residency on the island caused her to imagine harsh treatment when there was none? It seemed likely.

Leah sighed. The diary answered old questions, but replaced them with new ones. She would never know the whole truth about her parents.

Having loved both her father and her mother, she found herself being torn between opposing loyalties.

Her father often spoke of his great love for his wife. Whenever he came home from a voyage, he showered her mother with gifts. Such were not the actions of a man who abused his wife.

Yet, for her father to have imprisoned her on the island—when he knew she was truly repentant—did seem cruel. In her heart, she felt he should have given her mother a second chance to prove her fidelity.

As Leah sat rubbing at the ache in her head, the rumbling of her stomach reminded her she had yet to eat her evening meal. The thought of food held little appeal, but for the sake of her child, she retired to the kitchen to fix herself something to eat.

After the day Leah read her mother's diary, she started to be plagued by doubts. The more she thought on her mother's torment, the more the island began to feel less a haven than a prison. Presently she came to regret her decision not to have a boat return for her until well after her baby's birth.

The serenity she had gained when she first returned to the island was slowly evaporating, and she came to a decision. That decision was to leave.

Carrying her child made her slow and cumbersome, but she felt as strong and healthy as ever. She would conserve energy by rowing only when the current was in her favor, and be careful not to push herself to the point of exhaustion. She was not absloutely sure she could reach Victoria, but she was confident she could make it as far as the Indian Village. If she had miscalculated her strength, she would stay there. If not, she would go on.

Her baby's welfare must come first, and Leah knew there was the possibility that she had waited too long, and she might be forced to stay on the island as originally planned. But whatever the outcome, working toward a goal would make the time pass faster. The remaining half of the log Benjamin had felled so many months ago lay ready and waiting. Tools in hand, she set to work.

Capt. Benjamin Keaton stood on the deck of his newly purchased clipper ship, letting the sea breeze caress his face. It was a strong, solid ship, and he had struck a good bargain. He felt confident she had many years of life left in her, and could compete profitably against the more expensive and modern steamers.

He had plotted a northerly course, and though his hold was full with merchandise to be sold in Victoria, his cargo had little to do with why he was headed there.

He had stayed away as long as he could, but he had to see Leah again. The business of buying a ship had not exorcised her from his mind. Neither had the string of brothels he had forced himself to visit. She was everywhere. If a boy rode by on a bicycle, he thought of Leah. The tinkle of piano keys as he passed a saloon conjured her face. Gas lamps, raindrops, a cup of tea, stray dogs, there was not a waking moment he did not think of her with longing.

He had abandoned his half-hearted effort to convince himself that his duty as her self-appointed guardian demanded he return to check on her welfare before his ship had left its slip. He knew he was returning for himself.

Whether he was by her side, or hundreds of miles away, Leah Daniels would not let him forget her. He smiled as he thought of the way she looked up at him with wide-eyed innocence, and he laughed out loud as he recalled a series of her outrageously honest statements. He was caught. He wasn't sure what love was, but he knew he was willing to give Leah anything she asked, including his name.

The instant the hull of his ship was in jumping distance to the dock, he shinned down the rope ladder and leapt the remaining distance. Having earlier given instructions to his first mate to see to the cargo and crew, he completely dismissed them from his mind.

An excess of energy coursing through his veins caused him to choose to travel by foot, rather than wait for a coach to take him to Leah's doorstep. He covered the distance with rapid strides. As his gaze fell upon the house, his footsteps slowed.

The yard, though tended, boasted no bright-colored flowers, and the little bed set aside for vegetables lay uncultivated. The windows were shuttered. He forced himself to take the remaining few steps to the porch and knock, but he knew there would be no answer.

In all the time he was gone, it had never occurred to him that she might not be here for him when he returned.

Where had she gone? Several possibilities came immediately to mind. She might have moved to another house. She might have moved to another town. Or . . . she might have moved into the home of a new husband.

His last thought caused his heart to constrict with pain. Surely she wouldn't have forgotten him so soon.

The old bitterness seeped into his mind, taunting him with visions of Leah abandoning her love for him, just as he was admitting his for her. He clenched his jaw.

Rather than waste time speculating, he started off in the direction of the real estate offices of Mr. Shawn Sullivan.

"Mr. Sullivan, I am not sure you will remember me," he began as he stepped over the threshold. "I helped a friend, Miss Daniels, lease some property from you some months ago."

"Your face is familiar." Mr. Sullivan studied him carefully as he searched his memory; then, his eyes lightened with recognition. "Capt. Keaton, isn't it?"

"Yes, I was wondering if you could tell me anything about Miss Daniels's whereabouts?" he asked, careful to keep any note of desperation from creeping into his voice. "I have just returned from an extended business trip and found her house closed."

"I'm sorry, but I can't help you. Her bank continues to pay the monthly rent. I didn't even know she was gone." As he glanced at Benjamin's worried mien, he added, "Perhaps she is visiting relatives."

"Miss Daniels has no known kin," Benjamin spoke softly as he tried to decide where to go next. "Thank you for your time."

His next stop was the bank. There he learned that Leah had not only arranged for payments on the house to continue but for its upkeep as well. He was given the address of Cory Jones, but upon questioning him, he quickly discovered the boy knew nothing of her whereabouts, or when she might be expected to return.

Deep lines scored Benjamin's brow as he strode towards Beacon Hill Park and the last place he could think to go. He mounted the steps leading to the raised porch two at a time and knocked on the ornately carved door.

"I would like a word with Miss Hastings," he informed the doorman.

"You may wait here in the hall, Capt. Keaton. I'll see if the mistress is receiving callers today."

"Tell her it's urgent."

"Yes, sir."

A few moments later the doorman returned. "Miss Hastings bids you wait for her in the east parlor." He directed him to the aforementioned room and left him there.

Benjamin clasped his hands behind his back, shifting his weight from one foot to another. He hated dealing with Louisa Hastings, but if anyone knew Leah's whereabouts, it would be her.

Five minutes passed, then another. He began to pace impatiently.

A full thirty minutes expired before Louisa Hastings made her entrance into the room. "I can read your lips. Stop swearing at me under your breath," she admonished.

"You drive a man to swear. Do you have any idea how long you have kept me waiting?"

"Yes." She glanced at the watch she wore on a chain around her neck. "Thirty-three minutes, give or take a second or two. I wasn't sure I was coming down at all."

With effort, Benjamin held back a biting response. "Well, you are here now, and I didn't come to argue with you—"

"What does bring the great and gregarious Capt.

Keaton back to the shores of Victoria?" Louisa interrupted.

"You know very well why I am here. I'm trying to find Leah."

"Why?"

"I don't see how that's any business of yours," he stated, beginning to lose his struggle to remain polite. "Do you know where she is?"

"No," Louisa lied straight-faced.

"Do you know anything at all?"

"I might."

"What's that suppose to mean?" he demanded.

"It means that I think you are the lowest of men. Deserting her when she needed you so much. You knew she loved you, though for the life of me I still can't understand why a woman as intelligent as Leah would give you a second glance. You should have stayed."

"I couldn't," he replied softly.

Louisa's eyes flashed with anger. "Why not?"

"I can't explain it . . . even to myself. Just tell me this much: is she all right?"

The fire in Louisa's eyes abruptly died. "I don't know. I pray so, but I don't know."

"Doesn't she write?"

"No."

"Surely, if Leah was in some kind of trouble, Mrs. Findley would let you know," Benjamin spoke his thoughts out loud.

"Mrs. Findley is dead."

He paled. "What?"

"A few weeks after you deserted Leah, Mrs. Findley was killed by a runaway horse. Leah was devastated, but I'm sure you couldn't give a whit."

"I was very fond of Mrs. Findley," Benjamin protested, as he tried to assimilate this tragic piece of information. All along he had assumed wherever Leah had gone, she had taken her housekeeper with her. He cleared his throat. "As for Leah, I wouldn't be here if I didn't care."

"You have a funny way of showing your regard."

Benjamin ignored her remark. "When did Leah leave Victoria?"

"March."

He frowned. "But why did she go? She loved it here."

Louisa turned her back on him. "She thought she had to leave."

"Why?"

"Because of you."

"That doesn't make sense," he argued. "I know she didn't want me to go. I know I hurt her. But neither of those reasons should have compelled her to leave her friends, just the opposite. If anything has happened to her because of me . . ."

Despite her desire to hate Capt. Keaton for the misery he had caused her friend, Louisa could not dismiss the captain with a wave of her hand. There was something in his voice that pricked her conscience. Slowly turning to face him, she said, "Now, I am going to ask you a question, and I suggest you think very carefully before answering. Do you love Leah?"

Benjamin stared at her. Did he love Leah? Of course he did . . . as a friend . . . as a guardian . . . as a companion . . . as a lover. Why else would he be here? Why else would he be so desperate to find her? This feeling must be love.

"Yes, I love her, and I would give my life to find her."

Louisa pursed her lips. Leah wanted the captain, and the captain wanted Leah. She really had no right to keep them apart. However, she wasn't going to tell him everything. The baby was Leah's secret to tell.

Raising her gaze to meet his, she spoke in measured tones. "I know where Leah is."

"Where?" Benjamin demanded, reining in his rage at her deceit. His fists balled at his sides with the effort.

"She went back to her island."

"Why would she go there?"

"She said she needed time alone to think."

Benjamin glared at her, trying to determine if she was telling him the truth, or endeavoring to send him on a wild-goose chase. He read nothing but concern for Leah in her eyes, but he had to be certain. "I want you to swear on your father's good name that this time you are speaking the truth," he commanded.

"I swear," Louisa vowed without hesitation.

With a swish of her silken skirts, she left him standing alone in the parlor.

Chapter 21

Leah rubbed at the ache in her back and sighed loudly as she stood staring out the upstairs window at the sea. Her plans to carve a canoe had gone awry from the start. The blade of the adze broke, the weather had been relentlessly foul, and her burgeoning belly kept getting in the way. She had had to give up the project almost before she started.

She had never felt so restless in all her life. The house was spotless. The garden tilled. Try as she might, she could not stretch the routine tasks of caring for herself beyond midday. She was ready. She wanted to hold her baby in her arms. She would pour all the love she had out to her child, and the two of them would make their way in the world. They would be happy. She was determined to see to that.

Thoughts of the baby invariably brought Benjamin to mind, and she was forced to blink back tears. She had done everything in her power to stop needing him, but she found she still did. She could not help worrying over him. She desperately wanted him to be happy, even if that happiness could not include her. He looked so handsome when he smiled.

A speck of white on the horizon caught her attention, and she studied it intently a few moments before determining it was not a gull. Perhaps it was the sail of a boat. *His boat!* Despite her assurance to herself that it would not be him, her heart leapt with joy. She quickly retrieved a spyglass and focused it on the object.

It was a ship! And it was heading directly towards her island! She could hardly contain her impatience as she waited for it to come close enough to identify.

As the vessel came clearly into view, her heart slowed, then sunk. This ship was more familiar to her than any other. It belonged to her long-absent father.

She told herself she should feel joyful to discover that he was still alive, but the closest she could come was wary anticipation.

The words of her mother's diary were still fresh in her mind, and she could not repress a wave of resentment on her own account. If he was alive, why hadn't he come back to the island long before now? Why had he left her and Emma to fend for themselves?

After the initial shock had passed, Leah scolded herself for her uncharitable feelings. She loved her father. He had never been anything but kind to her, and he might have a very good reason for being gone so long.

She should not judge him until she confronted him with her mother's words and heard the reason for his lengthy absence. He deserved a chance to speak in his own behalf.

The ship anchored a distance from the island, and

she watched her father row a dinghy to shore, leaving his men on board, as he had always done. Leah watched him pull the dinghy up onto the beach. Her eyes followed him as he strode the trail to the house.

His stout figure was a little fuller, and the gray that had once streaked his hair and beard was now the dominant color. Otherwise, he appeared little changed.

She turned from the window and descended the stairs.

"Where is my little angel?" Jacob Daniels called as he entered the hall. "I have lots of presents for her!" He stopped short, his jaw dropping as his eyes fell upon Leah standing at the base of the stairs.

"Papa, welcome home." She opened her arms to him.

Closing the distance between them, he made a sharp jab at her belly. "Who did this to you?" he bellowed as she backed away from him.

"No one," she replied, too startled to think clearly. Her arms wrapped protectively about her midsection.

"Come now, girl. You didn't get this way by yourself. Tell me his name."

The bannister pressed into her back halting further retreat. "Capt. Benjamin Keaton," Leah offered meekly.

"Where is the bastard?" he demanded.

"He's gone. Papa, it's not what you think. I love him. I want this baby."

Jacob Daniels stared at her with ice cold eyes, as if he was seeing her for the fisrt time. "I should have known you would turn out to be a slut like your mother! I

357

should not have been deceived by your innocent looks."

"Papa, please. Let me explain."

"You have already said more than enough. You're all the same. Nothing a man does can stop it. Not his love, not his money . . ."

"I found Mama's diary," she volunteered the information, in hopes of penetrating the dark cloud that seemed to have enshrouded his mind.

"What did she say about me?" he asked warily.

"She was afraid of you."

"Evil always fears good. I can see fear in your eyes now."

Leah tried to swallow the fear that constricted her throat, but found she could not. "What are you saying?"

"I should have killed you when I did her." He stretched out his hand for her, but she sidled out of his reach. "I tired of her mewling to be off the island. She never loved me. Never! I brought her here to save her from temptation, but she didn't want to be saved. Finally, I had had enough."

Her eyes and ears told her this was happening, but her mind rebelled. A numbness settled into her heart.

"Emma said Mama fell and hit her head," Leah protested as she inched towards the door. "It was an accident."

"Emma?" Jacob's crazed eyes darted about. "Emma would say anything to protect you. She suspected the truth. I could see it in her eyes when she looked at me. That's why I had to go, you see."

"But you came back."

"I couldn't stay away any longer. I wanted to see my

358

little girl." His eyes darted about the hall. "Emma, Emma," he called. When the old housekeeper did not appear, he demanded, "Where is the old fool?"

"She died more than two years ago."

"Good. It will save me the trouble of disposing of her."

"Papa, please don't talk this way," Leah whimpered.

"I will talk any way I goddamn please, you harlot. Now come here! I promise I'll be quick about it." His eyes clouded as he continued to stare at her. "I did love you, you know. I thought you were the only good thing to come from my marriage. But now all that is changed. Still, I am a charitable man. I don't want you to suffer."

"No!" Leah screamed.

"I have to do it. I'll have no peace till I do. Now, be a good girl," he cajoled.

As he reached his pudgy hands to encircle her neck, Leah dashed through the door. She did not pause when she reached the cover of forest, but continued as fast as her legs could carry her awkward body.

"Leah!"

She could hear her father crashing through the underbrush in pursuit. Even in her present state, she had the advantage of speed over his bulky figure, and she put as much distance between them as possible. When she was forced to pause to gasp for breath, she could hear him calling her.

"Come to Papa, angel. You haven't opened your presents yet," he mewed.

Sheer terror drove her on, when the agony of what was happening threatened to sap her strength. She had never seen bloodlust in a man's eyes before this day, but the primitive part of her instinctively recognized it. She was running for her own life and that of her baby.

She tried not to remember that the man chasing her was the father she had always loved. Even after reading her mother's diary, she had had as much sympathy for him as her. How could he want to kill her?

A spasm ripped through her belly, and she was forced to clutch the nearest tree for support. Her ears pricked. She couldn't hear him now. Had he stopped following her, or was the sound of her own blood pounding in her ears drowning out the sound of his pursuit? As she was seized with another spasm, she could spare no thought for anything but her immediate survival.

"Not now, baby. Please not now," she begged. "Let me get us someplace safe before you come."

"There you are." Jacob Daniels smiled evilly as he stepped into the clearing.

A scream tore from Leah's throat, and she took to heel once more.

"Now, Leah," her father called after her. "Dashing about the forest isn't good for that brat you carry. Don't be afraid of your Papa. He'll be gentle with you."

Leah tried to close her ears to the cajoling sound of his voice. It sickened her to her soul.

Her knowledge of the island was superior to that of her father, and she was able to keep ahead of him, but she knew her strength would not outlast his. The cramping of her stomach was getting stronger. She had to find a place to hide.

There was a cave on the nothern side of the island. It was her secret place. Not even Emma had known of it. It could only be reached by wading through the surf, and at high tide was totally inaccessible. If she could reach it, she would be safe.

Circling around, she made her way toward the northern tip of the island by a serpentine route, strewing her path with branches, and following rock beds to obscure her footprints. Every time she thought it safe to stop to catch her breath, the sound of her name being called, or a branch snapping underfoot, spurred her on.

She paused near the edge of a cliff and tore off a piece of her skirt. Dropping it over the edge, she watched it flutter to rest on an overhanging branch. She tore another piece of fabric and left it on a bush near the edge.

Carefully backing from the cliff so her footprints would appear to end at the precipice, she smiled grimly. Perhaps the ruse would fool her father; at the very least, it should buy her some time. She hurried onward, holding her sides as she fled in the opposite direction.

Upon attaining the northern beach, Leah grabbed a bough, brushing the sand behind her to erase her tracks. She further disguised her trail by heaping seaweed in her wake.

Lifting her skirt above her knees, she waded into the surf and turned toward the black wall rising from the sea.

Leah felt on the verge of collapse when she finally reached the cliff. She glanced over her shoulder. There was still no sign of her father. Using her last ounce of strength, she crawled up the slippery rocks leading to the mouth of the cave.

Tears stung her eyes as she curled herself into a ball on the hard rock floor. Jacob Daniels desperately wanted her dead. Whether she had been sired by him or by her mother's lover, it mattered not. He was the only father she had ever known. Her heart felt as if it were withering within her breast. Realizing her tortured thoughts were sapping her strength as much as her frantic flight had, Leah tried to push them from her mind.

It was a long time before she mustered the will to move herself deeper into the cave. Fear and pain wracked her frame, and it took all her energy to endure each passing moment. If her father was still calling her, she could not hear his voice above the thunder of the waves, and for that she was grateful. She was safe here, shielded not only from view, but insulated from the sounds of his search.

As she rested and began to breathe more naturally, the cramping of her belly subsided, allowing her to begin to think how she might ensure her survival.

Leah had no idea how long she could live in this cave. There was a small freshwater spring bubbling in the back, so she needn't worry about dehydration. If she stayed dry, she would manage to stay warm enough. Food would be her biggest problem.

How long would her father stay before he gave up searching for her? A day? A week? A month? From the mouth of the cave, she could see the mast of his ship on the horizon. Until it was gone, she dare not venture forth.

Leah sat on the floor of the cavern, her arms wrapped about her, rocking herself in an effort to maintain her hard-won calm. As the sun set, the blackness of the cave enveloped her, but she did not poke her head out until she was sure it was as dark outside as it was within.

Carefully kneeling at the mouth of the cave, she

reached for a mussel clinging to a rock below. Try as she might, she couldn't budge it. Crawling on her hands and knees, she searched the bottom of the cave with her hands until she found a loose rock.

An hour's cautious labor netted her a handful of the shellfish. She carried her catch to the back of the chamber, where she broke the shells by crushing them with another larger rock.

In the pitch-black of the inner cave, picking the fragments of shell from the flesh was as tedious as chewing the raw, rubbery flesh, but Leah knew if she did not keep up her strength, all would be lost.

Leah had just fallen into exhausted slumber when she was awakened by a new tightness in her belly. She tried to ignore it, hoping it would go away as it had before, but as the night progressed, instead of abating, her contractions became more regular. By morning she knew her baby would come whether she wanted it or not, and she gave up hoping it would wait, and concentrated all her energy on delivering a healthy child.

Removing her garments, she made a bed of one petticoat and her skirt to sit upon, reserving a second petticoat for a blanket. Bracing her back against the rock wall, she gritted her teeth against the pain.

Leah felt as if she would be torn asunder by the pressure on the floor of her pelvis, but she dare not scream, lest her father was nearby and the sound rise above the waves and be carried to his ears. Perspiration poured down her face.

The contractions became stronger and stronger;

then, instinct took over and she was pushing her child into the world. As the babe slid from her, tears of joy mixed with the sweat of her labor at the sound of his lusty cry.

Cradling her son to her breast to muffle his cries, she rained adoring kisses upon his wet, wrinkled skin.

When the afterbirth was delivered, Leah rested while she waited for the cord to stop pulsating. She drew in long deep breaths, preparing herself for what must be done next. Grasping the cord firmly in each hand, she severed it with her teeth and tied it securely.

That done, she wrapped her baby in the clean petticoat and put him to her breast again. Then she slept.

Chapter 22

Capt. Benjamin Keaton lowered his sextant and checked his chart once again. They should sight Leah's island within the hour. The thought of finally seeing her again filled his heart with joy.

In his mind's eye, he pictured her standing barefoot on the beach, the wind wafting wisps of pale hair about her fair face. What should he say to her? Should he start with an apology for leaving, or a declaration of love?

He still believed Leah to be too good for him; yet, he wanted her and she wanted him. He didn't understand this feeling between them, but he was through denying it. He had exiled himself from his emotions for too many years. Benjamin ran his fingers through his thick, dark hair. He was scared, more scared then he cared to admit. He was like a ship sailing uncharted waters.

When at last the island came into view, he was startled to see another vessel at anchor. Who could possibly be on the island? Perhaps in his absence, Leah had found someone else to love.

To contemplate the possibility for more than a moment caused him such anguish, he felt physically ill. Gritting his teeth, he ordered his crew to drop anchor on the opposite side of the island.

If his return was an intrusion, he wanted to have the option of slipping on and off the island, his presence unnoted. He didn't know if he had the strength to exercise that option, but he was determined to put Leah's happiness above his own, if it came to a choice between the two.

With that in mind, he lowered a dinghy and rowed to shore alone.

The moment Benjamin set foot on the beach, a wave of foreboding washed over him. He told himself it was caused by nothing more than his fear that while he was off trying to determine if he was man enough to love Leah, she had replaced him, but he still couldn't shake the feeling of physical danger. The hair on the back of his neck stood stiff.

He crossed the sand. As he reached the trees, a man of short stature and immense girth stepped out of the forest. Leaves clung to his gray-streaked beard, and his eyes held a wild look.

'Who are you?" the two men demanded simultaneously.

"Jacob Daniels, the owner of this island," the older man announced. "And you?"

Surprise registered on his face before Benjamin replied, "Capt. Benjamin Keaton."

"You're trespassing."

"I've come to see your daughter, Leah. I was told she was here," Benjamin explained. Despite an instinctive distaste for the man, he held out his hand in a gesture of friendship. It was ignored.

"How do you know her?" Daniels demanded.

"We're friends."

He shook his head knowingly. "So you've been here before."

"Yes. My ship was wrecked about a year ago, and I washed ashore this island. Leah saved my life."

Daniels smiled malignantly. "I knew all along you were the one she was with."

"She told you about me?" Benjamin's words were half question, half statement.

"Yes! Say your prayers. You're about to face your maker." Pulling a pistol from his belt, he brandished it wildly before pointing the bore at Benjamin's chest.

The bullet whizzed passed his shoulders as he dove for the cover of trees. Scampering to a safer distance, he braced his back against the opposite side of a wide tree trunk.

Obviously, Leah had told her father *all* about their relationship. Convinced he was dealing with an outraged father, Benjamin tried to soothe the man. "I've come to marry your daughter. I know I've taken advantage of her in the past, but I intend to do right by her."

"Marriage, hah!" Daniels sneered. "I'll not be sending you to the altar. I'll be sending you to your graves. You can lie in each other's arms there."

The impact of what he was saying hit Benjamin like the ball of a fist. "Where is Leah?" he demanded.

"Dead. I haven't seen her for three days."

"No!"

"Yep," Daniels chortled. "Fell off a cliff and was tore apart by the rocks below. Nothing left of her but a few scraps that got ripped from her skirt when she took the plunge."

"She can't be dead," Benjamin's voice convulsed with pain.

"Don't feel too bad. If she hadn't done herself in, I'd have had to do it for her. She's not fit to live."

"You're insane." As his indictment echoed through the forest, Benjamin clung to the hope that Jacob Daniels's mental state caused him to believe his daughter dead. Leah *had* to be alive. He refused to believe she was gone. A long silence prevailed before Daniels answered his charge.

"Insane? Could be. That's what being in love does to a man. A woman takes your heart and slowly poisons it with her lies. Doesn't matter how you try to protect them. Their natures always win out. Jezebels, every one of them."

"Whatever went on between you and your wife, Leah is innocent of it," Benjamin argued.

Jacob Daniels spat. "Like mother, like daughter. I'm tired of listening to you. You're no better than them. No respect for a man's property. Come on out, Roger. I had to kill you quick the first time, but this time I think I'll do it real slow."

"Who's Roger?"

"You are."

"I told you, my name is Capt. *Benjamin* Keaton."

"Don't play games with me, Roger. It'll only make me want to hurt you more."

The sound of advancing footsteps warned Benjamin that his position was no longer safe. Cursing himself for his habit of not wearing a gun, he dashed for cover of the next tree. A bullet nicked his ear.

368

He dabbed at the blood with his sleeve. If Leah was dead, he didn't really care what happened to him, but as long as there was a chance she might be alive, he wasn't going to surrender his own life. If she was alive, she needed him. He would not fail her this time.

Now the years of living with dead emotions could serve him well. He pushed his fears and grief from his conscious mind.

If he planned to live out the hour, Benjamin knew he had to move fast. Sprinting from one tree to another, in an erratic path designed to make him a difficult target, he set the house as his goal. It was the only place likely to hold hope of a weapon. If luck was with him, he would find another gun. If not, he would settle for a kitchen knife.

He knew he was gaining distance, but it was far easier to outrun Jacob Daniels than his gun. He barely attained entry into the front door of the house before the wood was splintered by another bullet.

Any weapon was better than none, and he opted for a kitchen knife as his first defense. Choosing the largest he could find, he bounded up the stairs. If there was a gun in the house, Jacob Daniels's bedroom seemed the most likely place to find it.

While he rummaged through his would-be murderer's belongings, he heard the front door open and close.

His search had netted him nothing. Now his only hope was the element of surprise. He needed a place to hide.

The armoire in Leah's room seemed his best option, but as he stepped into the hall, he knew he would never make it that far undetected. Slipping into her mother's room, he used her wardrobe instead, wedging himself behind the gowns.

Knife at the ready, Benjamin waited tensely, mentally visualizing the exact location of every heavy footfall, so he would not misjudge his attack. He had no illusions about the possibility of a second chance.

He listened as Leah's father searched first her room, then the maid's.

Benjamin held his breath as he heard Daniels's footsteps hesitate before the door to his wife's room. The hinges moaned ever so softly as he pushed the door open.

"Adrienne, is your lover hiding in here?" Daniels called as he stepped over the threshold. He stared about the empty room. A single tear ran down his ruddy, weather-ravaged cheek. "Why couldn't you love me like you loved him? I gave you everything I could afford to give. I adored your beauty.

"I really didn't mean to kill you, you know. I just couldn't stand to see the hate in your eyes any more. You should have loved me. Then I wouldn't have had to do it." His tone became cajoling. "Do you know where he is? Please tell me. Then we can get this dirty business over and done with."

As Benjamin listened to Daniels's eerie monologue, he continued to hold his breath. Leah's father was a tortured man, and he pitied him, but his pity stopped short of excusing the cold-blooded murder of his wife. If he had caused his daughter's death also . . . He refused to finish the thought.

Daniels had been moving around the room, lifting the counterpane, pushing back curtains, while he was speaking, "Dear, sweet Adrienne. I know he is in this house somewhere. I'll find him with or without your help. Be a good wife. Tell me where he is." He stopped before the doors of the armoire.

Benjamin knew now was the time to make his move.

Mustering every ounce of force he possessed, he sprang through the doors, knocking his adversary to the ground. The gun went off, shattering the mirror above the dresser.

Daniels fastened his meaty fist around the fingers holding the knife, crushing them to the breaking point. Benjamin clamped his hand around the wrist of the hand holding the gun.

The two men rolled about the floor, gripped in a battle of wills. They dare not release their holds and were forced to rely on their feet and knees to assail their opponent. Groans of pain punctured their struggle. Neither could dislodge the other's weapon or obtain a clear advantage, and at length, their eyes locked.

"Give it up, man," Benjamin advised. "I'll turn you over to the authorities and let them decide your fate."

"Never!" Daniel's spit in his face. Rage supplying him a surge of unnatural strength, he threw Benjamin's weight from him. Both the knife and the gun clattered to the floor.

Daniels grabbed the gun. Sitting up, he aimed it at Benjamin's heart.

Benjamin dove for the open doorway. The bullet whistled over his head.

Scrambling to his feet, he ran for the stairs. He was only a quarter of the way down, when he felt a presence on the landing. Slowly, he turned to face his executioner.

"Die, you bastard!" Daniels cocked the gun and pulled the trigger.

Chapter 23

A hollow click reverberated off the walls.

Benjamin couldn't believe his ears. The gun chamber was empty. But before he could celebrate his good fortune, Daniels lunged for him.

Sidestepping the assault, Benjamin pressed himself to the wall.

Jacob Daniels rolled down the stairs, end over end, landing at the bottom with a dull thud.

Benjamin ran to his side to make sure he did not rise again, but there was no need. Jacob Daniels lay dead of a broken neck.

Pulling the body to the study, Benjamin retrieved a quilt from the linen closet and covered it. As he closed the door behind him, the front door slammed open. In burst a party of his own men.

"We thought we heard shots. Is everything all right?" the first mate explained their presence.

Benjamin looked through him while trying to rein in his emotions and gather his thoughts. Nothing would be all right until he found Leah. His need to hold her in his arms overrode all else, even the whisper of doubt that she was still alive. She must be alive. If she was dead, surely he would feel a hollowness in his heart.

Straightening his shoulders, he assumed an attitude of authority. "There's a dead man in the study. One of you post guard at the door. I don't want Miss Daniels discovering it inadvertently. You," he signaled to another man, "go back to the ship and bring every available man. We are going to search every inch of this island."

"What are we looking for?"

"Miss Daniels. There is no other woman on the island, so you'll have no trouble recognizing her. When we find her, I'm sure she'll be terrified, so be gentle with her. Tell her that her father can't hurt her now, but don't tell her he's dead. Leave that for me to handle in my own way."

"You killed him?" one of his men asked.

"No, he fell down the stairs. Once Miss Daniels is found, I'll take the time to explain in more detail, but not now. You have your orders."

"What about the other ship?" another man asked.

"Trevane, go over and feel things out. If they seem friendly, ask them to join the search. If not, make up some excuse to stall for time. I don't want hostile men on the island getting in the way of finding Miss Daniels."

The island was shortly filled with sailors from both ships. Captain Daniels's men required more of an explanation, but upon learning the facts, they were willing to cooperate.

Benjamin drew a hasty map of the island, assigning sections to groups of two to four men. A signal of a single gunshot was arranged for when she was found.

He and the men searched until well after dark, but there was no sign of Leah. The next morning they were up at dawn. A detail of Daniels's men were assigned to see to his burial.

"Where do you want us to put him?"

"Lay him to rest beside his wife," Benjamin instructed grimly.

All day long, Benjamin strained his ears for the sound of a gunshot as he joined the search in section after section. He fought a constant battle with despair. Each hour they did not find Leah, it became increasingly difficult to ignore his fears that she was no longer alive.

When darkness again forced them to abandon their efforts, Benjamin called a meeting of the ships' officers in the dining room.

Dispirited, he asked, "Any ideas?"

"The island just isn't that big, and we've searched every square inch of ground two, three, sometimes four times. Are you sure she's here, Captain?"

"Yes!" Benjamin snapped.

"I hate to be the one to say it, but maybe he killed her," Trevane, his first mate, spoke up.

"No. He said he hadn't seen her for three days. She has to be here somewhere." Benjamin could not bring himself to admit the rest of what Leah's father had told him, for fear that in the saying he might make it true. He had to believe she was alive. He loved her. He didn't want to face a future without her by his side.

"I don't know exactly what this woman is to you, Captain, but I can tell you she's not on this island."

Benjamin stared at him. He wanted to shake him

until he took the words back, but in fairness he could not. If Leah was alive, she should have answered their calls. There was no place else to search. Still, he couldn't make himself give up.

Facing the men squarely, he stated, "Those of you who belong to Daniels's ship can do what you want. My men stay here. We search again tomorrow. If we can't find her," he swallowed the hard lump in his throat, "I'll deal with that decision tomorrow."

The next day he and the remaining men combed the same territory without finding a trace. That evening Benjamin sent his men back to the ship with a promise to come himself . . . soon.

He spent a sleepless night in the bed he had so often shared with Leah. She couldn't be gone. She was so full of life, the thought of her dead was incomprehensible. Over and over, his mind told him that he must accept facts, but his heart refused to listen.

Leah was life itself. She was his life. He realized that now, now that it was too late. He shouldn't have fought his feelings for her. The fear he had felt at the thought of loving her was nothing compared to the agony of never seeing her again. She had loved him when he was thoroughly unlovable, and he had pretended he didn't care. Now, when he wanted to tell her all he truly felt for her, he couldn't.

The next morning Benjamin was up at dawn. Numbly he walked the beaches, trying to find some reason why he should stay, why he should hope. When he could find none, he sat down on a log and wept.

Leah sat cross-legged on the floor of the cave,

rocking her baby as she nursed him. Deep hollows ringed her eyes, and her hair hung limply about her shoulders, but as she gazed at her son, her weary eyes held the light of love. She kissed his brow.

Her father's ship was still at anchor, and that meant he was still on the island. She blinked back tears of fatigue.

The supply of mussels that had kept her alive thus far was exhausted, and she had not the physical strength to risk a fast in hopes he would be gone in a day or two. She would have to venture out in search of food.

The thought of leaving the safety of the cavern terrified her. She knew she was too weak to survive a confrontation if her father found her. If she died, her baby would also. A fierce wave of maternal instinct rose up in her, and her eyes narrowed. No one would harm her baby! No one! She hugged him close to her body.

If only Benjamin were here. He could tell her what to do. He was always so good at being logical. She thought with her heart, not with her head, and her heart had taken a brutal beating of late. First Benjamin deserted her, and now her father wanted to kill her. The only two men she had ever loved had turned from her. She felt utterly betrayed by fate. Benjamin had once said she had a guardian angel. Where was her angel now?

Her dejected musing brought her full circle, and she accepted that she had no one to depend upon except herself.

When her baby was fed and sleeping soundly, Leah lay him, bundled in her petticoat, in a protected alcove. She kissed the palm of one tiny hand, whispering softly, "Be safe my child."

Rising to her feet, she stretched the ache in her muscles. There was a berry patch that grew not far from here. The fruit would not be ripe, but it would sustain her. Wild greens were plentiful, as were camas bulbs. If she dare take the time, she would gather more mollusks for her dinner. Fortifying herself with these thoughts, she moved toward the mouth of the cave.

The tide demanded she go out in the light of day. She prayed it was still too early for her father to be up and about.

Poking her head out of the cave, Leah leaned out as far as she dare, scanning the landscape with frightened eyes. Her angle was odd, and there was much of the beach she could not see. Taking a deep breath, she carefully climbed down the rocks into the shallow sea.

Wading around the edge of the cliff, Leah stopped cold. A man sat on the beach, his head in his hands.

The instinct to flee was quelled by the recognition that he was not her father. Cautiously, she eased forward for a clearer view.

Benjamin? Her lips formed his name, but no sound escaped her lips. She squeezed her eyes closed, opening them slowly. He was still there. Leah reached the shore and began to run.

Looking up, Benjamin bolted to his feet. "Leah," he called in joyous disbelief as he too began to run.

They met in a crash of embrace. Leah would have lost her balance if Benjamin had not picked her up off her feet. He swung her around and around as he showered her face with kisses.

"Where have you been? We looked everywhere. I had given up hope. My God, I love you. I

377

promise you, I'll never leave you again." He continued to rain kisses upon her as he set her back on her feet.

Leah's gaze rose to meet his. She felt dazed. He had said he loved her. He had made a promise, but she was afraid to trust her own senses. "You love me?"

"Yes, and I want to be your husband, if you'll have me."

As she continued to stare at him, Benjamin took in her bloodstained clothes and ashen face with a sweeping gaze. Immediately, he had no thought but to get her someplace warm and dry and see to her injuries. Scooping her in his arms, he started to carry her down the beach.

"Benjamin. No! I have to go back to the cave."

He did not slow his pace. "Don't worry. You're safe now. No one can hurt you."

"No! I have to go back. You don't understand." She pounded furiously on his chest.

"I know more than you think. Your father has put you through hell. He's at peace now. We buried him next to your mother."

Leah's arms went limp. "He's dead?" she voiced her disbelief with trembling lips. A mixture of emotions filled her breast, but the reigning one was one of relief.

Benjamin nodded as he continued to carry her towards the house. "I'll explain everything to you, after we get back to the house, and I get you to bed."

Once she had recovered from the initial shock, Leah renewed her efforts to gain her release. "Stop! Please, listen to me. I—"

"Sh . . ." he tried to soothe her. "I'm here to take care of you now. You needn't worry about anything."

"Put me down!" Leah demanded frantically. "I have

to get our baby!"

Benjamin stopped in mid-stride. At first he thought she was incoherent—what woman wouldn't be after what she had been through these past days—but when his gaze met hers, her eyes were clear. "What baby?" he croaked.

"Our baby. I gave birth to our son six days ago."

"Son?" He shook his head numbly.

"Come. Let me show you." Leah urged him to set her on her own feet. Taking him by the hand, she led him back the way they had come. "Wait here," she commanded when they reached the end of the beach. Lifting her skirt, she waded into the water.

Benjamin stood riveted to the spot, trying to assimilate what she was trying to tell him. There couldn't be a baby. She would have had to become pregnant before they arrived in Victoria. She would have known her condition before he left. She would have told him.

As he stood arguing with himself against the existence of a child, Leah rounded the corner of the cliff, a baby cradled in her arms. "See," she admonished as she lay the baby in his arms, "we have a son. Isn't he beautiful?"

Benjamin gazed down at the tiny, pink-tinged face of his son. His lips curved into a winsome smile as pride swelled his heart. "He's very beautiful," he assured her. "What have you named him?"

"Benjamin," Leah replied softly. "I thought he should have his father's name."

His gaze raised to meet hers. "Why didn't you tell me about him? You had to know before I left Victoria."

"Because you said you didn't love me. I didn't want

you to feel trapped."

"What about your feelings?"

"You knew them."

"Are they still the same?" he asked, realizing she had yet to say if she was willing to accept him for a husband.

"Yes, I will always love you," she answered without hesitation.

He grinned as he stroked her cheek. "I'm glad, because I intend to be by your side a very long time."

"You really meant what you said earlier?"

He pulled her into his embrace. "I love you, Leah. It has taken me far too long to accept it, but I think it has been true for a very long time. I want to be your husband."

"Because of the baby?" she forced herself to ask.

"Because of you," he assured her. "I didn't even know we *had* a baby when I decided I must have you. I love you. I need you. You're good for me. I can't make the same claim for myself, but I will do my damndest to make you happy."

Leah closed her eyes and sagged against him, as she was awash by a wave of boundless joy. "I think you just have," she murmured.

"Does that mean your answer is yes?"

She opened her eyes and rose on tiptoe, caressing his lips with hers. "Yes."

As he held Leah and his son to his breast, whispering words of love, Benjamin's vision blurred. Just beyond Leah he saw another woman standing in a cloud of mist. She was frail with raven black hair, and he immediately recognized the image as that of his long-forgotten mother. A child's memory of a different kind of love, shared long ago, stirred within his heart, and he tightened his embrace. Once, many years ago, he had loved and been loved. He was ready to love again.

Smiling in approval, Emily Keaton raised her fingers to her lips and blew her son a kiss as she disappeared into the heavens.

Epilogue

Benjamin and Leah Keaton lay locked in impassioned embrace on the bunk in the captain's quarters. Their son slept soundly in a wooden cradle, rocked by the rhythmic rise and fall of the sea.

Leah's lips played love songs upon her husband's flesh, as he stroked her silken skin. Kiss followed kiss as they caressed each other in ways they knew would please, revelling in the intimacy of their lovemaking.

When they came together, their union was slow, smoldering, gentling them to the peak of fulfillment, then wrapping them in a cocoon of carnal contentment.

Sighing happily, Leah petted the damp hair covering Benjamin's chest as she pillowed her head on his shoulder. He kissed the top of her head.

They lay in companionable silence a long while, before Benjamin voiced the question that had been bothering him since they had left Vancouver Island.

"Are you sure you don't want me to sell the ship?"
 ...ed. "I could build you a house, start a business

in Victoria."

"I will miss my friends," Leah admitted. "Did you notice the way Louisa fussed over the baby? I really think she should get married and have some children of her own."

"So you are having second thoughts."

"No," she assured him. "There is much I love in Victoria, and someday I should like to put down roots, but I am happy with our decision. I want to see the world. All of it."

Benjamin rolled his eyes heavenward in mock dismay. "I remember the first day I took you out to explore Victoria, my curious little wife. We are likely to be sailing the seven seas till we all grow old. It's lucky our little Ben is such a good sailor."

Leah rested her hand on his inner thigh, teasing the sensitive flesh with her fingers. "I expect our family will outgrow the captain's quarters long before then." She grinned. "And the children will have to go to school when they get older. I couldn't bear to be separated from them."

"And how many children are you planning on having?" he queried, as his blood warmed under her feathery touch.

"Oh, half dozen at least, if it's agreeable to you."

He smiled. "Anything you want is agreeable to me. You have bewitched me, Mrs. Keaton. I am your servant."

She nestled closer within the circle of his embrace, looping her arms around his neck. "Be careful you don't serve me too well, or I shall grow spoiled. Besides, I think I would miss it if you never scowled at me."

He made a fierce face before succumbing to a peal of riant laughter. Leah giggled.

"I love you, Capt. Keaton."

His expression sobered as he brushed her lips with his. "And I love you. You can depend on that love . . . forever."